Picture Me and You

A Devil's Kettle Romance
Book One

Susan Sey

OTHER TITLES BY SUSAN SEY

Author's Note:

A FEW THINGS you should know before you dig in:

1. Devil's Kettle is not a real town.

2. It is, however, a real thing located in a real state park right here in my beloved Minnesota.

3. Writers are shameless thieves, and the name was too good not to steal. So was the disappearing river, which is why I grabbed them both, made up a town to go with them and set a trilogy there.

4. If you're curious about the real Devil's Kettle, you should visit my website (www.susansey.com) where I've posted photos of some intrepid friends and me (shout out to the Women Scouts of Grand Marais!) checking it out. I've also posted a list of all the books I've ever written along with some large-ish photos of my face. You're welcome.

5. Speaking of gratitude:
Inara gets props because she loved the turkeys from day one and never wavered.
Bryan gets props because he reads my first drafts and has never once asked for a divorce.
Claudia and Greta get props because they tell everybody their mom's a writer, and not just when I go to the grocery store in my pajamas.

Okay, that should do it. Happy reading, readers!

Preface

MARRIAGE HAD TAUGHT Addison Davis three things, all of them surprising.

Number one? Her husband hadn't liked her very much. Not by the end, anyway, and this was a shock because everybody liked Addy. Certainly nobody disliked her. They couldn't. She was just too darn likable, and that was no accident. That was a superpower. Normally it took a chemical spill or some alien DNA to produce a bona fide superpower but Addy had come by hers the old fashioned way — she'd sweated and bled for it. So when it came to people-pleasing, Addy wasn't just good. She was a ninja. Marriage should've been a snap.

It wasn't.

It had been a horrible mistake, actually. She knew that now. She'd said as much to Diego once, and he'd agreed. In fact, he'd seen her *horrible mistake* and raised her a *terrible wife* and a *lifelong disappointment*. She couldn't disagree.

That said? Lifelong wasn't always the same thing as forever. Sometimes it wasn't even quite two years. Diego had turned out to be the *live fast, die a legend* type. That had been surprise number two.

And surprise number three? Addy was one heck of a widow. Maybe Diego hadn't cared for her, but his family adored her. And she adored them right back. They were her family now. Her second chance. Her permanent address. They were simply *hers*, and she intended to keep them. To make them as happy as they'd made her. As happy as she'd tried to make Diego.

This time, however, she was succeeding. And why? Celibacy. The whole family worked better, she'd discovered, now that she wasn't having sex with anybody *in* the family.

She really should have remembered that.

Chapter 1

Devil's Kettle, Minnesota
Lake Superior's North Shore
Late May

ADDISON DAVIS SURVEYED the empty dessert plates littered across the Wooden Spoon Diner's retro-chrome bakery counter and felt faintly ill. She was, she acknowledged sadly, a slut for pie. A shameless sugar whore. And her jeans — nasty, judgy things even on Addy's better days — weren't going to let this lunch go unremarked.

That said? She didn't regret a bite. Why would she? When your guilt-o-meter was scaled for real mistakes (like, say, an impulsive elopement, a predictably disastrous marriage, or a shamefully happy widowhood), dessert for lunch barely nudged the needle.

Gerte Torsen, the pink-cheeked pie pusher who owned the Wooden Spoon, whipped a napkin from the dispenser on the counter between them and handed it over. "Well? What did you think?"

"I think you've ruined me for all other pie, that's what." A little dollop of cream clung to the edge of one of the plates, and Addy looked firmly away from it. *Forget about it*, she told her stomach. *We're done here.* She took the napkin and patted her lips.

"But which one should I offer for Devil Days?"

"Good heavens, Gerte. Ask a mother to choose a favorite child, why don't you?"

Gerte dropped her chin and gave Addy a look that sliced her sugar buzz bloodlessly in two. Addy sat up hastily, surprised at herself. Addy's own sainted mother-in-law might be Devil's Kettle's undisputed alpha female but Gerte was easily the first runner up, and woe to the pie-drunk fool who forgot it.

She cleared her throat cautiously. "But if I had to choose?"

"You do." That was steel glimmering in Gerte's grandma-sweet voice.

"The North Shore triple berry, then. No question."

Gerte smiled smugly. "I knew you'd like that one."

"What's not to like?" Addy widened her eyes appreciatively. "Raspberries, gooseberries and wild blueberries, all harvested within five miles of Devil's Kettle? I'd be over the moon with the local angle alone. But that crust?" She shook her head in wonder. "Gerte, the *crust*. It's like angels kissed it."

"That's the butter." Pleasure pinked those round cheeks, and a reluctant fondness pooled in Addy's chest. Gerte might be a little touchy about her social status, but it was hard to judge her for it when she was standing there in a frilly apron, genuinely blushing over a compliment to her pie crust. "Lainey wanted me to switch to shortening last year when dairy prices went so high but I said why don't you just take me out back and put a bullet in my brain?"

Addy blinked at the bloodthirsty turn of phrase, then took in the wicked amusement dancing in Gerte's eyes. She suppressed a sigh. Suckered again. Darn that frilly apron.

"She actually said that," Lainey called from the kitchen. "*Put a bullet in my brain, why don't you?*" The Wooden Spoon featured an open floor plan — tourists loved to watch the bakers work — and Addy could see Gerte's daughter rolling out traditional Norwegian lefse as she spoke. A few years older than Addy's own twenty-five, Lainey was one of those cleanly-engineered Scandinavian beauties Minnesota was famous for, as angular as her mother was round. She worked the potato-based dough into tissue-thin sheets with the same rolling pin her grandmother — and her grandmother's grandmother before her, probably — had used. The tendons in her forearms flexed and released with an intensity that Addy had always found mildly terrifying. Then again, at least Lainey didn't hide it behind a frilly apron. That was a point in her favor as far as Addy was concerned.

"I said, what if we just replace *part* of the butter with shortening?" Lainey went on. "You'd have thought I suggested murdering orphans." She rolled her eyes, and Addy knew without question that Lainey didn't struggle with pie sluttery. Not if she could dismiss real butter so easily.

"Taste costs," Gerte said, her round little chin going ominously stubborn.

"Everything costs." Lainey lifted a sheet of dough with a long, thin paddle and transferred it to a traditional round lefse griddle with a casual flick of the wrist that suggested any fool could do it. Addy knew from disastrous experience that this was not so. "We're running a business here, Ma. You want to make art? Diego's gallery is right down the street." She jerked her sleek blonde head toward the diner's plate glass window, indicating, of course, the shrine to Addy's late husband that took up the entire next block. "Go for it."

"I doubt the gallery has any more customers than we do at the moment," Gerte said airily but her baby-fine brows drew together as she gazed out the front window. "Not with this weather. Land sakes, I think those are snowflakes."

Addy followed Gerte's frown to the empty, wind-blasted curve of Main Street. In the harbor beyond, a brave handful of boats bobbed at anchor, dodging what Addy would've easily agreed were snowflakes had it not been almost June.

"Summer comes hard this far north," she said encouragingly. "But it always comes eventually, right?"

Lainey went back to her lefse in grim silence.

"Sure, honey," Gerte murmured, her eyes on the snowflakes. "Sure." The *bless your heart* was silent but Addy heard it nonetheless. She was new, not naive. Everybody in town had a granny who'd tell you about the year the ice was hardly out of the harbor before it was September again. Back when Devil's Kettle had been rolling in fish, iron ore and virgin timber, this wasn't a huge problem. These days tourists were the only natural resource left, so skipping vacation season wasn't an option. And Addy, as the CEO of the town's annual tourist bash, knew it better than anybody.

"People will come even if summer doesn't," Addy said firmly. "I promise."

Gerte shook off the uneasy moment and sent Addy that deceptively sweet smile again. "Devil Days isn't until August anyway. The seasons will've changed eighteen times by then."

"And so will our menu if you don't make up your mind about the pie, Ma," Lainey said darkly. "We only have three months until Devil Days, you know, and the ad deadlines are sooner. If we're late getting our menu to the Dispatch again, I'm going to let you explain it to Nan."

"Ouch." Addy gave Lainey a wince that wasn't entirely theatrical. Nan Davis — Addy's sainted granny-in-law — owned the local newspaper, and occupied the number three spot on Addy's list of Women Not To Be Trifled With, right behind Gerte.

Gerte sighed and began clearing Addy's pie plates. The whole lot of them. And that little dollop of cream was still there, calling her name. Oh, mercy.

Gerte said, "When do you need everything, honey?"

"As soon as possible," Addy told her apologetically and looked away from temptation. Again. "I'm having a Devil Days app built this year, and de-bugging that kind of thing takes forever. I think it'll be worth it, though. People like having all the info in their pockets these days. Plus an app will free us up from print deadlines."

Gerte smiled sleekly. "From Nan, you mean."

"That, too. Though, Nan being Nan, I'd stay on her good side if I could. Speaking of whom—" She glanced at her watch and winced. "Cripes. I was supposed to be in her office twenty minutes ago, negotiating ad space. She's going to kill me." She jumped to her feet, reached for her bag and muffled a delicate belch. "Pie for lunch, though." She grinned. "Worth it. Bury me with a slice of that North Shore triple berry in my sticky hand, will you?"

"You got it." Gerte laughed. "Meantime, you'll want your strength if you're going to beard your granny in that lair of hers." She grabbed a to-go cup, filled it with coffee and pressed it into Addy's hand. Oh, help. Addy hated coffee but what kind of ingrate refused a mug full of graciousness and generosity? Her manners were rewarded when Gerte also handed over one of her signature sugar cookies — a spoon-shaped affair with a thick dollop of frosting in the bowl end. "There you go. Come home with your shield or on it, Spartan."

Addy laughed helplessly. "Pie for lunch, now a cookie with my coffee? I think I'm in heaven." She paused, struck. "Wait, *is* this heaven? Did Nan get me already? Am I dead?"

"Oh, go on." Gerte chuckled and flapped a dishtowel at her. "A little pie for lunch never hurt anybody."

"Yeah, yeah. Tell it to my jeans."

"Pish." Gerte dismissed this with a jerk of her soft chin. "Men like women with a little meat on them."

"Great," Lainey muttered from the kitchen, looking conspicuously skinny.

"But I don't want a man," Addy told Gerte. She meant it, too. In the kitchen, Lainey went after another ball of lefse dough with her ferocious rolling pin and something that sounded like *lucky you*. Addy wisely ignored this. "After Diego? Who would I want?"

Gerte didn't have an answer for that — nor did Lainey — and silence fell. It happened a lot whenever Addy invoked her late husband's name, that moment or two of reverent silence. She assumed people used the time to say a short prayer of thanksgiving to whatever deity had blessed womankind with a man like Diego, however briefly. And if people assumed her steadfast rejection of romance since his death was the result of having been utterly ruined for mortal men by his astonishing beauty and electric talent, well, she was hardly going to disabuse them of the notion. Cheerful widowhood worked for her. Why trade it in for keeping tabs on her butt?

Finally Gerte cleared her throat. "You're a pretty enough

girl, Addy," she said kindly. "And young yet. There'll be somebody else for you one day."

"Could be." Addy shrugged doubtfully. "I'm not going out of my way to find him, though."

"Maybe he'll find you."

She laughed. "He'll have to."

Then the door jingled open and Jax walked in.

Chapter 2

A BITTER WIND came in with him. It blasted the hair off the back of Addy's neck and shot her crumpled napkin off the counter. She made a dive for it.

She heard Jax say, "Hey, Gerte."

"Hey, Chief," Gerte sang and Addy — now on her hands and knees between the stools — could all but hear the older woman's cheeks going pink again. Jax flirted with Gerte shamelessly, and as a result she loved him with the same happy, helpless devotion Addy reserved for pie.

"Hey, Jax," Lainey called from the kitchen. "How's the fire fighting business?"

"Slow," he said. "Just the way I like it."

"You must be the only person in this town who can get away with an attitude like that." She sighed. "The rest of us have to pray for tourists."

Addy straightened in time to catch the look Lainey sent her, like the eternal winter and ensuing tourist drought were her fault. She sent back a reassuring smile and turned to her brother-in-law, now striding toward the diner counter. She grinned in spite of herself. Good old Jax. He didn't look a thing like Diego, thank God. At not quite six feet tall, he was only a comfortable handful of inches taller than Addy's own five-five, and was as ordinary as his brother had been extraordinary. With a messy thatch of chestnut-brown hair that sneered in the face of combs everywhere, a proud beak of a nose and warm hazel eyes that all but disappeared when he laughed, Jax was the anti-Diego. And Addy loved him for it.

"Hey, Jax," she said cheerfully. She waited for him to grin at her the way he'd grinned at Gerte and Lainey. The way he grinned at everybody, actually, all warm and friendly and charming. Because maybe Jax wasn't beautiful like Diego — like any of his siblings, honestly — but he *was* charming. Evidently, when people weren't struck stupid by the very sight of you, you developed other skills. Conversation. Compassion. Charm.

He didn't smile at her, charmingly or otherwise.

She sighed. Jax's refusal to like her was the one burr under the comfortable saddle of Addy's life. Oh, he didn't *dis*like her. He just didn't *like* her. He never had. Which baffled her, because he liked everybody, even his family who viewed him more as a curious aberration of the gene pool than a beloved son.

"For heaven's sake, Addy," he said instead. "What are you doing here?"

"Having pie for lunch." Her own smile didn't budge. She was no quitter. "It was work related so don't judge."

"I'm not judging." He lifted easy hands. "Your dirty little sugar habit's no concern of mine."

"Amen, brother."

Something flashed across his face, something bleak and so brief she almost didn't catch it before it disappeared into his customary equanimity. Oh for crying out loud, had she really just called him brother? Not only did he seem to resent the relationship, but her only slim claim to him as her brother had died nearly four years ago with *his* brother. And maybe she didn't miss Diego but she didn't usually toss him willy-nilly into conversations with people who were still obviously grieving him.

"Being well aware of your sugar habit, however," he said, recovering smoothly, "I can't imagine why I didn't start here." He sent Gerte a twinkling look. "Guess Addy can't resist you any more than I can."

Gerte snickered and flapped her dishcloth at him. "Oh, go on with you."

"Start here?" Addy asked. She retrieved her abandoned coffee and spoon cookie from the counter, suspicion uncurling in her stomach. "Start what here?"

"The search." Jax folded his arms and gave her that same fake-warm not-smile he'd been giving her since she'd met him. "I've been looking all over for you."

"You have?" She blinked, astonished. Even running across her accidentally seemed to put him out. Why on earth would he go looking for her?

"Your online calendar said you were supposed to be meeting with Granny Nan at the newspaper office nearly half an hour ago. She's pissed at you, by the way."

"Nan's always pissed at somebody." She waved that away and narrowed her eyes at him. "Wait, you looked at the family calendar?"

"That's what it's for, isn't it?"

She shook her head slowly. "Gerte said I wasn't dead yet."

He frowned at her. "Of course you're not. Why would you be?"

She glanced across the counter at Gerte. "You're absolutely, positively certain I'm not dead?"

Gerte studied her with pursed lips. "Pretty sure, hon." She snapped open a white paper bag and turned her attention to Jax. "The usual, Chief?"

"Only if you want me to pledge my eternal love in front of all these people," he said. Gerte snorted and busied herself at the bakery case.

Addy turned back to him. "Well somebody's got to be dead if you tracked me down via the family calendar. Because if memory serves, you swore you'd sign up for that thing over my dead body. Or was it yours?"

"It was Mom's." He grinned at her suddenly and she stepped back, startled. Jax wasn't a handsome man but when he smiled and meant it? A girl felt it in the backs of her knees. "And I believe my exact words were that I'd wear Mom's electronic leash over her dead body. But if you wanted to wear it, that was your business."

"I see." She gazed at him, so off balance that she accidentally took a sip of coffee. Oh, ick. All the cream and sugar in the world couldn't hide the fact that it was still coffee. "And do you check on my whereabouts often? Or only when Nan wants to kill me?"

"Believe me, it wasn't my idea. But Mom's having a fit, and if I don't deliver you to Hill Top House within the next fifteen minutes, my life won't be worth living. Or so she tells me."

"Oh boy," Lainey muttered from the kitchen. "Bianca could make good on that."

"Tell me about it," Jax said with a goodnatured eye roll. Addy stayed carefully silent. Lainey wasn't wrong — Jax's mom had what you might call an artistic temperament and she'd put some miles on it — but with Gerte head-down in the bakery case, listening avidly, Addy wasn't about to agree. Anything Addy said now could and would be used against her in the court of public opinion, and she knew it. She smiled noncommittally and abstained from comment. Jax had put this ball in play; he could finish it off.

"And since I like my life just the way it is," Jax went on easily, "I'll be fetching Addy home now." He turned back to her and swung an arm toward the door. "Hup hup, sis."

She stared at him, incredulous. *Sis?* Since when did Jax call her sis?

"I'm sorry." She tipped her head and studied him. "Did you just hup hup me?"

"Well, you're dawdling. And milady awaits."

"Oh for heaven's sake." But she started toward the door.

"Hang on, kids." Gerte straightened from the bakery case and held the white paper bag out to Jax. It looked deliciously heavy and suddenly the pie seemed like a while ago. Addy pressed a quelling hand to her hopeful stomach. She was truly a lost cause. "Your usual, Chief. Let us know how it goes up on the hill."

Jax bee-lined back to the counter, dropped a few bucks on it and scooped up the bag. He opened it and stuck his nose in for a deep, enthusiastic inhale. Pleasure spread across his face like a sunrise.

"Gerte," he said, pressing the bag reverently to his chest. "Marry me. Make me the happiest man alive."

"Oh, land. Such a Romeo today!" She colored up prettily. "Go pick on somebody your own age, why don't you?"

He dropped the bag and snatched up her hand. "But I only have eyes," he warbled in a surprisingly rich baritone, "fooooor yooooooou!"

"Uff dah," Gerte said, laughing. "No wonder you're still single." She pressed her free hand to her cheek and rolled her eyes to the ceiling. "Addy, he's singing."

Addy gazed at him, bemused. "Yes, I see that."

She stepped forward, hooked a finger into the bakery bag and peered inside, curious as to what could make the stoic Jackson Davis burst into song. It was a morning glory muffin, studded with nuts and carrots, spangled with sugar, and so dense with butter it was already staining the bag.

Mercy. She felt a show tune coming on herself.

"Well?" Gerte laughed. "Do something!"

"I'm trying," Addy murmured, still a little dazzled.

Lainey poked her head over the counter separating the dining room from the kitchen. "Pull it together, kids. Jax's life is about to be not worth living." She smirked. "Yours might already be shot, Addy, if there's not an excellent reason Bianca couldn't get a hold of you herself."

It was a point. She shook off the muffin spell and said, "I have a cell phone issue. It's been refusing incoming calls." Everybody gave that a moment of skeptical silence. "It is," she said. "It's like the Greta Garbo of cell phones. It wants to be alone."

"Mmm," Gerte said kindly.

Jax, still clutching the older woman's hand, just laughed. Addy sighed.

"Oh, fine." She handed him his muffin and helped herself to a handful of his long sleeved t-shirt. "Come on then." She'd intended to tug him away from Gerte and get him moving toward the door. But his shirt was soft from hundreds of washings and warm from his body, and the urge to put her nose between his solid shoulder blades and inhale caught her off-guard. She stalled there for a moment, frowning and fingering his sleeve. She wondered what laundry detergent he used. Evidently, she liked the smell. A lot. "Hey, where's your jacket? It's freezing outside."

"I'm fine." Jax dropped Gerte's hand and stepped carefully away from Addy's touch, exactly as he always did. The smile he gave her was utterly correct in size and shape, and completely devoid of any true warmth.

"Right. Of course." She shrugged off the sting of his rejection. It never got easier but she'd gotten better at it. He stood there, gazing at her with unreadable eyes until she finally said, "Well? Are we going, or do you want to sweep Gerte off her feet some more?"

"Oh, I'd definitely rather stay here and sweep some more," he said, sliding Gerte that lady-killer grin that a guy who looked like Jax should *not* be so good at. He shifted his attention back to Addy, and the charm fell away, leaving him stone-faced and faintly resigned. "But we should probably go do the other thing." He gestured her toward the door ahead of him, leaving a good two feet of space between his hand and her person. "I'm parked out front of the bait shop."

"Oh, I'll drive myself." Addy shrugged into her jacket and headed for the door. "I'll meet you up there."

She could feel him on her heels, even across that careful margin of empty air between them. "Mom's really in a state, Addy," he said. "I don't think it would be a good idea to screw with her today."

"Like I screw with her ever?" She shot him a look as she pushed through the door and into the wind knifing down the empty street. It whipped her hair into a crazy crow's nest of curls and she clamped it down with her free hand. "I just have a jam-packed day, that's all. Who knows where I'll need to be once Bianca's done with us?" She gave him big, guileless eyes. "I'm sure you're busy, too. No need to be joined at the hip all afternoon, right? Let me just grab my car and we'll be independently mobile."

He frowned down at her a moment, clearly caught between the need to present her at Hill Top House as soon as possible and his omnipresent desire to avoid her. She waited him out, confident. No way he was subjecting himself to the misery of her company when there was a half-reasonable excuse to avoid it.

"Fine," he said eventually and she suppressed a celebratory boogie. She so rarely won when it came to Jax. "But go straight there, Addy. No detours. Mom's really in the boughs."

"Straight up the hill," she said. "Promise."

A few yards down the street, a shop door jingled open and a single tourist ambled out of the Gilded Fish gift shop. Weird, airy flute music drifted out with her, and the pitiless wind snatched at the pretty pouf of tissue paper topping the gift bag over her arm. The woman hesitated, looking right then left, and Jax stepped casually to the side, putting his big shoulders between Addy and the tourist.

"No detours," he said again. "Not even to play Diego's Angel."

She lifted her chin. "I wasn't planning to sprint over there and ask if she recognized me, Jackson."

"But if she did? If she happened to look over here and say *oh, hey! It's Diego Davis' muse and tragic widow! Can I have a picture and twenty minutes of your time to ramble on about how vital your husband's work has been to my development as an artist and a person?*"

Addy's lips twitched in spite of herself. She didn't love her cult status with Diego's still-rabid fans, but she wasn't about to write off a subset of tourists who weren't weather-dependent, either. She peeked around Jax's shoulder. "At ease, soldier. She's heading for the gallery."

"Awesome." Jax pinned her with those hazel eyes. "So you're going straight up the hill now?"

"I just said so, didn't I?"

He only gazed silently at her until she sighed and shoved her coffee cup at him. "Here, take this. To go with your muffin." He took it automatically. Tried to take her spoon cookie, too, but she snatched it back. "Oh no you don't. I'll leave the gun but I'm taking the cannoli."

He blinked at her. She blinked back.

"For goodness' sake, Jax. You've never seen *The Godfather*?"

"Of course I have."

"*Leave the gun.*" She pointed at the coffee. "*Take the cannoli.*" She held up her cookie. He continued to study her in grave silence. She sighed, defeated. "I'll just see you at Hill Top House, okay?"

"You bet."

She turned her back on him — petty but satisfying — and walked away. She didn't know how long he stood there watching her but if eyes were knives, she suspected she'd have a back full of stab wounds by the time she turned the corner. She tucked her bag more firmly into her side, aimed her shoulder into the wind and wondered — not for the first time — what the heck she'd ever done to piss that guy off.

Even driving the department-issued mini-pumper, Jax was pretty sure he was going to beat Addy up the hill. All that big-eyed, crazy-curled innocence she'd hit him with on Main Street? A sham. Oh, she'd probably meant it when she'd said it. *Straight up the hill, Jax. Promise!* But Jax knew his sister-in-law and, worse, he'd seen her calendar. Addy's afternoon was a labyrinth of tiny commitments wedged together like the gears of a pocket watch. If even one failed to turn at the appointed hour, there went the whole operation.

And Addy — lord help him — wasn't a quitter. He devoutly wished she were but no. The girl just didn't give up no matter how lost the cause, and Jax ought to know, as he'd made himself as lost as causes came. If she hadn't given up on him after all these years — and she hadn't — there was no way on God's green earth she could possibly drive past Buck's Bait and Tackle, not when her calendar had her picking up the city council meeting minutes from Soren Buck forty-five minutes ago. (Which wouldn't be necessary if Soren would either learn to type, learn to email or resign his position as secretary of the town council, but that was a different battle.)

It would take two minutes, she'd think. Of course she'd stop! And of course she'd swing by the newspaper office afterwards to drop them off, also as indicated by her calendar. That would be another two minutes but still, less than five total, right? How could Jax be mad about less than five minutes? Plus, she would reason, he was driving the mini-pumper, so she'd catch him on the hill. No problem.

Except, whoops, she wouldn't because she hadn't accounted for the extra twenty minutes she'd lose at the newspaper office apologizing to Nan for blowing off their meeting while Nan chain-smoked and ignored her. Jax nearly smiled at that. Nobody held a grudge like his granny. She'd make Addy dance to her tune for weeks over this.

There was some comfort in that, he supposed, and

downshifted the wheezing mini-pumper. It surged gamely, climbing the winding path to the very top of Devil's Kettle with determination if not speed. Jax eyed the odometer. He'd probably roll over 300,000 miles within the year but budgets being what they were, there was no retirement in sight for the old girl. He eased off the accelerator a bit. When the mini-pumper went, she'd go the way a faithful public servant should — rolling hot into a three-alarm fire with her lights blazing. She'd die with her boots on, by God, not racing to yet another of his mother's manufactured emergencies.

When he finally crested the hill, it was at a gentle thirty miles per hour, and Jax let the pumper catch her breath. He cruised along the ridge line nice and easy, an army of massive pines to his left, a rock-strewn meadow to his right with Lake Superior brooding darkly away in the distance beyond it. The road dead-ended after a mile or two at a massive boulder. Two private drives split off the turn-around, both owned by his family. The one on the right was a well-kept gravel thoroughfare aimed toward the million dollar view at the cliff's edge. The one on the left was a stingy, overgrown two-track snaking yet farther uphill to a more expensive — if more difficult — view. Jax turned right toward his childhood home.

Hill Top House was two-and-a-half sprawling stories of glass and pine overlooking the harbor far below, presiding over the view like a queen over her subjects. The lake stretched away into a bleak haze today, gray and unsettlingly vague about the existence of a horizon. It was gorgeous even as it lifted the hair on the back of his neck. All the same, it felt like home to Jax.

At least it used to.

Chapter 3

HE FOLLOWED THE drive to the rear of the house where it spread into a prettily landscaped circle between a gracious veranda and a four-car garage. (The *carriage house*, according to his mother. Looked like a garage to Jax.) He pulled around the circle, aimed his hood toward a quick get away and killed the engine. The beleaguered truck farted with relief, shook like a wet dog, and went silent. Jax did smile this time. Nothing like announcing your arrival with style. He hopped out, slammed the door nice and loud, and headed for the back porch.

Everybody used the back door in this neck of the woods. The front of the house always faced the view when there was a view to be had, and Hill Top House had one. Hell, Hill Top House *was* one. The front of the house was just one huge stretch of glittering glass, all doors and windows, rising up into a cathedral-worthy arch that had boats down on the water stopping to take pictures. Our Lady of the Lake. Of the lake view, anyway.

But the Davises didn't do anything by halves, so the back of the house was no slouch, either. A veranda ran the entire length of the rear of the house, and a set of half-moon steps curved graciously out into the circular turn-around. Jax took the steps at an easy jog and landed in front of a set of double doors. They were glossy black, about twelve feet tall, and came complete with massive wrought iron knobs dead in the center of each, right where they'd look amazing and be completely impractical in terms of actually pulling the damn door open. Every time Jax used them, he half expected to be stopped by a little person demanding to know why he wanted to see the wizard.

He let himself into the foyer and was suddenly immersed in a world of snowy white. Pale pine floors, soft white walls, creamy white woodwork, white flowers in white vases on shiny white tables. It would've been a bit much except that his mother, with her unfailing radar for the razor-thin line between art and parody, had crowned the whole thing with a blown glass chandelier in every color Crayola had to offer. It splattered the floor with sunsets, dripped sunrises down the walls, shot rainbows off every shiny surface. It was, he had to admit, impressive. Lord knew it was supposed to be. Bianca Davis was an artist, and in her hands Hill Top House wasn't a house so much as a canvas.

Still, home was home.

The museum quality hush his mother fostered always made him sound like a fully-shod Clydesdale, and Jax clomped happily through the echoing foyer and into the great room. It soared even higher than the foyer, but this room wasn't about the height or the white (although it was still extremely white). It was about the view. It was all about the dizzying cliff-drop to the water, the gut-clutching sweep of Superior, and the wall of windows that framed it all like a priceless masterpiece.

"Hey, Jax," his sister called from an enormous U-shaped couch in (what else?) white suede that anchored the vast space.

"Hey, Georgie."

She was draped across one corner of the couch like a sleek blonde cat, and he dropped a noisy smooch on the sharp blade of her upturned cheek. She wiped it off with a lazy swipe of her sleeve.

"So nice of you to finally join us," she said dryly.

"Us?" He eyed the yards of empty suede, then plopped down onto the couch right beside her with a cheerful bounce. She sighed and sat up marginally straighter to make more room. Judging from the side-eye she gave him, even his clean jeans weren't up to Hill Top House standards. He suppressed a grin and made a show of glancing around the airy room, empty but for the two of them. "Us who?"

Light streamed through those giant windows, but even the epic view they offered paled next to the slashing, vibrant paintings hanging on the narrow walls between the panes. His late brother's paintings. Diego. He rubbed a palm over his heart, the pang predictable and brief. He'd forgotten. How had he forgotten? It was never just him or Georgie or anybody else in this room. It was Diego, too. Always.

"I've decided to start using the royal we," Georgie informed him. She slid one elbow along the back of an over-stuffed cushion and pillowed her cheek on her forearm. She regarded him with sleepy eyes of the Davis blue, the same blue their dad's had been, and their grandpa's too. "I think it enhances my consequence."

"Yeah?" He smiled, diverted. You just never knew what Georgie was going to say. "Your consequence, huh?"

She shrugged and curled her long legs underneath her until she looked like a lazy *S*. "Either that or I was expecting you to bring Addy with you." She arched a significant brow. "As instructed."

"What was I supposed to do? Knock her unconscious and drag her up the hill by her hair?" Jax lifted helpless shoulders. "You know Addy."

"I do." She studied him idly. "She's the cooperative type. Nobody else seems to have any problem getting her to behave. I wonder why you do?"

"Because I don't want anything from her." Or anything to do with her. "It throws her off."

"She's task-oriented, no question. Lives to serve, that girl." Georgie smiled smugly. Addy made her life extremely comfortable. "Which is why she should've hauled her cookies up the hill the instant you asked. You finally needed something from her. She must've been over the moon."

"Not quite."

"Oh. Maybe she just doesn't like you, then."

Wouldn't that be nice?

"Maybe so. Be a welcome change of pace, considering the way you people worship me up here at Hill Top House. It's embarrassing." Jax tossed a boot over the opposite knee and stretched his arms along the back of the couch. Georgie gave an elegant snort which he magnanimously ignored. "And speaking of the universally adored, where's Matty?"

"Disappointing our mother in the upstairs studio." Georgie closed her eyes in preparation for one of the hundreds of micro-naps she enjoyed on a daily basis, often in the middle of on-going conversations. "Again."

"Christ's sake." Jax winced on his baby brother's behalf. For a long time their mother had barely been able to even look at Matty, which was understandable given that the kid was wearing Diego's face almost exactly. Matty's very presence was a constant reminder to her of a loss she couldn't accept. Of a wound that wouldn't heal. But time had a way of moving on, and kids had a way of growing up, and lately Matty didn't look so much like Diego the toddler anymore, or even Diego the kid. No, he was starting to look more like Diego the man. Diego the artist. And Bianca had started looking at the kid with hungry eyes, because if Matty looked like Diego, maybe he could paint like Diego, too. And that changed the game.

Guilt nibbled at the edges of his heart and Jax forced himself to face the reality he'd been avoiding for the past couple years. He was a bad brother.

Well, not *bad* precisely. He hadn't abandoned the kid, after all. He'd left him to Addy, and she'd loved the hell out of him. But the kid was thirteen now, and Bianca had finally decided to engage him. If there really was genius in Matty, Bianca was definitely the right one to pull it out. But if there wasn't? If Matty was just a normal kid born with an extraordinary face? He needed more than Addy protecting him from the steam-roller of his mother's ambitions. He needed somebody who'd been there and come out the other side. Somebody who could prove that failing to live up to Bianca's artistic expectations — and possibly those of an entire town — was tough luck but ultimately survivable.

He needed Jax.

The back door clicked open and a finger of cool air drifted into the great room. It curled around his nape, tickled his jaw and brought the lake air to his nose, along with a dash of sunshine and a hint of mint. But there was no sun today and his mother eschewed mint as too common for her landscaping.

Addy had arrived.

And suddenly Jax remembered why he didn't come up here all that often. Because even the scent of Addy had his gut clenching while a twinge of longing uncurled inside him like a dandelion, all green and persistent. He pinched it off before it could bloom into anything more substantial. His soul bled a little, even though he'd been uprooting this particular hope several times a week since the day Diego had presented his fresh-faced bride to the family as a done deal over four years ago. You'd think he'd be used to it by now. Or that he wouldn't have to do it at all. But Bianca wasn't the only one nursing unreasonable ideas, or wounds that wouldn't heal. Jax knew his way down that particular street better than most.

But where Bianca embraced her delusion, Jax preferred to do what any reasonable person did when presented with an unsolvable problem. He avoided it. Or tried to. But sometimes he ended up trying to drag it up the hill at his mother's request.

"Hey, guys." Addy jogged into the room, her ugly old bag banging off her hip, an apologetic smile barely flashing her dimples. God, those dimples. They just killed him. He looked away.

She flung herself onto the couch a few feet from Jax — of course she did — leaving the end nearest Georgie open so Bianca could use it for a throne. His mom did enjoy a good grand entrance, and they'd all learned the hard way not to mess with her stage. Still, Addy's caramel-colored curls couldn't be more than a yard from his cheek, and her bag was practically in his lap. She smelled like sunshine and mint shampoo, and he reminded himself that he was grateful for her presence. For the way she'd watched over Matty in his absence.

"You're late," he said to her.

"Later than you. But I beat Matty, so points to me." She

grinned unrepentantly. "And as long as I beat Bianca, I'm good."

"You promised," he reminded her. "Straight up the hill."

She tipped her head, lips pursed, eyes still dancing. "Since when have you been such a stickler for the rules?"

He suppressed a sigh. She had no idea how many rules he followed where she was concerned. "I'm not. I just thought you were a person of your word."

"I am. I always keep my word. I just keep it in the order in which it was given." Her dimples peeked out again. "And since I gave my word to Soren Buck and Granny Nan before I gave it to you—"

"—I lose?"

"No, you just have to wait."

"You might've mentioned—"

"Children, children," Georgie murmured, her eyes still closed, and Jax snapped his mouth shut mid-sentence. How did Addy always *do* that to him? How did she make him forget who he was and where he was and what he'd promised himself? How did she get him all tangled up in trying to win? Winning wasn't an option where Addy was concerned. It was all about survival. Self-preservation. Both of which meant keeping a solid football field between his heart and those cookie-soft dimples of hers.

"I'm sorry, Jax," she said. She lifted a hand and let it drop. "I really meant to come straight up the hill, if it counts for anything. I was driving out of town to do just that when I passed Buck's and remembered..." She trailed off and gave him a mournful moue with that curvy mouth, her eyes huge and forest-green.

"Forget it."

She scooted forward, probably to apologize more

27

earnestly, maybe even — God help him — to touch his knee, then salvation arrived. Steps rang out on the stairs behind them and Jax turned to find his baby brother clumping down from the studio upstairs, all oversized boots and sagging jeans, a gym bag with a lacrosse stick poking out the back slung over his shoulder. Sullen resentment clung to him like a dark cloud but all the scowling in the world couldn't mask the purity of that bone structure. The eerie beauty that had been Diego's was blooming all over the kid's face, as undeniable as the man-sized shoulders and feet he'd recently sprouted.

Matty paused for a moment at the bottom of the stairs, surveying his assorted siblings as if they were his own personal guillotine. Then he sighed and ambled over. Jax feared Addy was about to scoot closer to him to make room for the kid so he mashed himself up against Georgie instead.

"Goodness, Jax." Georgie, wedged between Jax and the corner of the couch, cracked an eye open. "There's about six miles of couch here. Do you have to sit on top of me?"

"Matty's here. Sit up, lazy bones."

She grumbled but hauled herself upright. Addy, meanwhile, leapt to her feet and went to Matty. She dropped her hands on his shoulders — well, reached up to his shoulders, now that he had her by a good five inches — and looked him over with a gimlet eye. She frowned.

"What? What happened?" She sniffed him like a mother dog and said, "You've been painting?"

"Not according to Mom." Matty shook off her hands, dumped his bag and ambled over to the couch. Addy sheepdogged him into the spot Jax had carved out for him and plunked herself down on the kid's other side. Give thanks for small miracles. She snatched his hand and hit him with the giant, irresistible eyes.

"And according to your mom?" she prompted. "What were you doing if not painting?"

He tipped his head back against the couch and stared holes into the ceiling. "Apparently, I hacked several canvases to death with my haphazard abuse of light, while my wanton disregard for form convinced one to actually commit suicide. She offed the rest with a canvas knife. Said she couldn't stand to see them suffering." He jerked one skinny shoulder and closed his eyes. "I wish she'd just let me go to school on Fridays."

"Oh, honey," Addy murmured and patted his knee. "Me, too."

"This Friday Art Academy thing is killing me."

"Cheer up." Jax gave the kid a bracing shot to the shoulder. "Canvases used to leap to their deaths by the dozen on my watch. Mom doesn't even like me to visit the gallery. Says it demoralizes the existing art."

Matty huffed out an almost-laugh and Jax carefully avoided the look of gratitude Addy sent him.

Then his mom appeared at the top of the stairs. "Jackson, you're here."

Bianca Davis swept down into the great room on bare feet, her blonde-and-silver-streaked hair swinging below her shoulders. She crossed the gleaming pine floor and held out long, elegant hands to him. He rose dutifully to peck her smooth cheek. She smelled the way she always did — of soft perfume undercut with faint notes of paint and turpentine. "I didn't keep you waiting, I hope?"

"Not all of us." He shot Addy a significant look that Bianca didn't catch and that Addy serenely ignored. Bianca drew back, wrinkled her nose. "I know I said it was an emergency but really, Jax." She cast a critical eye over his jeans and t-shirt. "You could have showered."

"I did." He riffled a hand through his nearly dry hair. It flopped back into his eyes, brown as dead leaves and about as interested in staying combed.

"You still smell like smoke. Please tell me Walt didn't try to burn down the Sugar Rush again with that deep fat fryer of his." She paused. "Not that that would be all bad, considering."

"Nope." Jax shrugged. "Must be the truck."

She dropped lightly onto the vacant end of the sectional, crossed her legs and sent him a look of delicate disapproval. "You drove up here in that city-issued jalopy?"

"Yep." He folded himself back onto the couch between Georgie and Matty. "I'm on call. Rules are rules."

"No, darling. Rules are for people who require employment. You do not."

Jax spread his hands. Big, square hands just like his dad's, if you didn't count the lack of art in them. "Sure I do."

"As a fireman? Really?"

"Fire chief," he said easily.

She ignored this, as she always did. She tipped her head to the side and peered at him with eyes as dark and bright as a bird's. "If you want to play with fire, you could always try metal working. Or you could blow glass. Or—"

"Or I could keep people's iffy deep fat fryers from burning down the town."

She sighed, undistracted. "You parked it right out back, too, didn't you? The truck."

He smiled again. "Yep. The mini-pumper." He loved that truck. Converted from a Ford F350 diesel, capable of putting out 100,000 gallons per minute, it was generally the widest, tallest thing on any given road. Driving it was fun, but parking it between his mom's cherished veranda and the *carriage house* was pure entertainment.

"Oh, Jax."

"Oh, Mom. It's a jacked-out pickup truck not a scarlet letter."

"Surely a visit with your family doesn't require several hundred gallons of water?"

"Foam."

"What?"

"It pumps flame retardant foam, not water."

"Whatever." She lifted a brow. "Surely a visit with your family doesn't require it."

He grinned. "You said it was an emergency."

"For heaven's sake, Jax, I didn't mean—" She broke off and pressed her lips together. "I don't think you can solve this particular problem with several hundred gallons of...whatever you said that thing out back dispenses," she said. "You're sweet to come prepared, though."

Jax frowned, off balance. "I am?"

She drew in a deep breath. "Children," she said, "I have some bad news."

Chapter 4

ADDY WATCHED BIANCA reach for Georgie's hand and lace her fingers through her daughter's without even looking. As if it had never occurred to her that she might not find a hand where and when she needed it. It sang to Addy, that confidence. That rock-solid faith in another person. In *family*.

"Bad news?" On the other side of Matty, Jax leaned forward, elbows on knees, frown in place.

Bianca inclined her head. "Of a financial nature."

"Financial?" Now Addy leaned forward, too. "Have you spoken to Jason?"

Jason Bloom was the Davis family's long-time financial advisor, the latest in an unbroken string of money-minded Blooms stretching all the way back to Prohibition. Evidently some clever lake-faring Davis had discovered that his boat was just as handy for smuggling Canadian whiskey across the border as it was for fishing. That piratical Davis had hooked up somehow with the original Bloom — a shifty numbers guy from St. Paul where the gangsters ran tame — and a fortune was born. At least that was how the legend went. The Davises had never confirmed or denied the origins of their money, but they'd never moved that money away from the accounting firm that helped them make it, either.

"Well I certainly tried." Bianca's smile was sharp and blindingly bright. "But as he's currently enjoying Bimini with a hair model and most of our ready cash, he's a difficult man to reach. Or so the police tell me."

Jax cursed under his breath and Addy's head went light. Oh dear lord. This was a disaster. The Davises were generations removed from the entrepreneurial spirit that had made their fortune. They were artists now, rich ones, and as such were desperately ill-equipped for poverty. None of them had even held a real job as far as Addy knew, except Jax, of course, who'd made a point of carving out a living independent of the family fortune.

"How bad?" he asked tersely.

"Bad enough," Bianca replied, equally tersely.

"Wait, we're…" Georgie blinked twice. Slowly. "We're poor?"

"Oh, heavens no." Bianca squeezed Georgie's hand with a reassuring smile. "We simply have no cash."

Matty narrowed his eyes. "How is that not the same as poor?"

"It *is* the same," Georgie said. She dropped her mother's hand and let her head roll back on the sofa cushion. She gazed blankly at the ceiling. "Oh my God."

"It's not the same, actually." Jax spoke to Georgie but didn't look away from his mother. "Why don't you let Mom explain?"

Georgie closed her eyes and waved weakly for Bianca to continue.

Bianca folded her hands neatly on her lap. "According to Jason's assistant, only our cash accounts were emptied. Evidently, he left the rest untouched."

"The rest?" Georgie's voice had dropped to a sleepy

murmur. Addy blinked. Good heavens, was she taking a nap? Now? "What rest?"

Bianca hesitated and looked helplessly to Addy.

"I imagine that would be all your investment accounts," Addy said. "Your mutual funds, savings bonds, IRAs, shares in individual companies, that kind of thing. You're heavily invested locally, if I remember correctly." She hadn't met with Jason in a professional capacity since shortly after Diego's death but she remembered the meeting in detail. For a guy four generations deep in money management, he'd been shockingly mediocre at the job. She'd immediately relieved him of her business and had tried — gently, diplomatically — to persuade Bianca to do the same. But Bianca was steadfast: their money stayed with the Blooms, where it had always been. And Addy didn't persist because Jason wasn't doing anything *wrong* precisely. He just wasn't doing anything particularly right. He didn't love numbers, that was all. And people who weren't in it for the love of the game shouldn't have access to other people's money, in Addy's opinion. It was just too tempting. Clearly it had been too tempting for Jason, the thieving weasel. She pressed her lips together and went on, her tone carefully neutral. "You likely retained all your properties as well, both personal like Hill Top House and commercial like the rentals."

"What's available for immediate liquidation?" Jax asked his mother. "I assume Carly had the numbers?"

Addy shot Jax a startled look, but he hadn't moved his gaze from Bianca since she'd said the word *financial*. But, honestly, since when was Jax on a first-name basis with Bianca's money manager's assistant?

"I'm sure she did," Bianca murmured, and touched the worried line between her brows as if it were something new and unfamiliar. Which it was. "I *was* paying attention, Jackson, I swear I was. I wrote things down." She dropped her hand, and her eyes were bleak and lost. "I don't remember what, though." She shifted that wrecked gaze to Addy. "I'm sorry, I just can't seem to remember."

Addy was off the couch and on her knees in front of her mother-in-law in a heartbeat. She caught one of Bianca's slim hands between both of her own. "I'll call her," she said softly. "I'll get Carly on the phone and we'll figure this out, I promise. Everything's going to be fine."

Bianca blinked back a rush of tears. "Oh, Addy."

"It will, I swear it. I won't let it be anything else." She gave Bianca's hand a reassuring squeeze, then sat back on her heels, scanning the spreadsheets her brain had automatically ordered up. Maybe she'd broken up with the Wharton School of Business for Diego, but she'd never managed to kick her budget habit. It had disgusted her old-money husband, of course, to discover his new bride had such a parsimonious streak but Addy couldn't help it. She couldn't in good conscience indulge in fancy bras and handbags without being absolutely, positively sure she wasn't dipping into the grocery money. Even when the grocery money was, for all practical purposes, unlimited. "It'll take a few months at least for you to restructure your portfolio, but I can help out." She'd have to significantly rearrange her own assets to free up that kind of ready cash, but Addy lived to rearrange her assets. Other people had hobbies; Addy had spreadsheets. "I'm sure I can cover at least a month or two of living expenses while you're getting back on your feet."

"Oh, my dear. You're such a treasure." Bianca cupped Addy's cheek in a soft palm that carried the most delicate whiff of turpentine. "I don't know what we'd do without you."

Addy put her hand over Bianca's and smiled. "Let's not find out."

Bianca's lips trembled into a watery smile. "Oh, heavens. Let's not."

Jax said, "Yeah, what would we do without Saint Addy?" But there was a hard edge on his voice that had wariness coiling inside her.

"I'm hardly a saint," she said with a careful smile for him. "Just family." She turned back to Bianca. "And this is what family does, right?"

"No, this is what *you* do." Jax aimed a finger at her. "You raid your savings without a second thought to bail the family out of a disaster they could have headed off years ago if they'd just listened when you told them their money manager was an incompetent ass. Which you did, repeatedly." He shifted that accusing finger to Bianca. "What the *family* does, however, is blow you off like you don't have an MBA from Wharton."

"Almost." Addy's response was automatic, and she heard her own voice through a thin film of shock. Because evidently Jax was as conversant with her transcripts as with his family's finances. What on earth? "I dropped out."

"With, what, your capstone project to go?" He waved that off as inconsequential. "For all practical purposes, you have an advanced degree in managing a giant corporation, the validity of which I'd have seriously questioned if you hadn't brushed the likes of Jason Bloom off your portfolio as soon as humanly possible."

"The likes of Jason Bloom?" Bianca drew back, her nostrils flaring with a flash of her old spirit. "And what, precisely, does that mean? Jason's family has been managing our finances for generations, and with great success! How on earth were we supposed to foresee that—"

"He's been running you into the ground for years." Jax interrupted without heat, just implacable logic. "From what Carly's let slip, Jason's already liquified as much of your portfolio as possible over the past few years, and with your consent."

"Well, yes, but—" Bianca frowned. "He said it had been a lean period, economically speaking. Perfectly normal. But we'd been through thin times before. It was nothing to worry about." She blinked, suddenly uncertain. Addy's heart ached. Bianca didn't falter, not ever. She almost hated Jax for making her do it now. "Should I have worried?"

"Yes." Jax was relentless. Addy glared at him but, as usual, he ignored her. "You should always worry."

Bianca sighed and sat back. "I paid Jason so I wouldn't have to."

"And look how well that's worked out for you."

Bianca simply closed her eyes and Addy stood up from her crouch, hands on hips. She stepped between Jax and his mother.

"Enough," she said softly. "Jax, enough."

He scowled but jerked those bulky shoulders and looked away. Addy took this as capitulation. She sat down next to Bianca and took her hand.

"This isn't your fault," she murmured. "This is Jason's fault." She sent Jax a significant look. "This is *his* failing, not yours."

Jax rolled his eyes, but when he spoke again it was more gently. "Okay, look. Fault doesn't matter, not at this point. What matters is figuring out where things stand now and where to go from here. I'm sure Addy will get all the details when she talks to Carly but I think it's probably safe to say that — setting aside your retirement funds and anything else that you can't liquify without prohibitive tax penalties — all that's left of your investments is what you hold in Devil's Kettle proper. And you can't liquify any of that without significant local impact."

Bianca blinked at the ceiling, then rolled her head to the side to blink at Addy. "Was that English? Is my son speaking English to me?"

Jax's mouth tightened but his tone remained gentle. Almost kind, in fact. "In plain English, then. Liquifying your local investments would mean selling whatever you own in town. Some of it's property, but a lot of it is stock in local businesses. Selling that stock would mean demanding a cash buy-out from Gerte and Lainey down at the Wooden Spoon, for example. Same goes for Soren Buck at the Bait and Tackle, and for Walt at the Sugar Rush, and so on and so forth." He sent Addy a sideways look. "It would mean pulling out of the Devil Days festival, too. The Davises own forty percent of that corporate entity, you know."

"Of course I know." Addy squeezed Bianca's hand. "Devil Days would survive."

Matty blinked. "Wait, we own a festival?"

"You do," Jax informed his brother. *You*, Addy noticed. Not *we*. It was never *we* when it came to Jax and the family. Not that you'd know it from this conversation. "About the only person you wouldn't have to put the squeeze on is Peter Zinc."

"Peter," Georgie murmured, her perfect lips curving up into a cat-like smile. She didn't even open her eyes, just purred her boyfriend's name like he was a really good dream, or a bar of the richest chocolate. A spark of envy took Addy by surprise. Even when she'd been in love with Diego, she didn't think she'd ever said his name quite the way Georgie said Peter's.

"We are not pulling out of Devil's Kettle." Bianca's spine snapped straight and her tone went flinty. Relief was a warm rush in Addy's chest. Bianca was back. "This town is our home. Our heritage. We'd sooner sell Hill Top House than pull out of our investments here. These people are our family, Jax! How could you even suggest such a thing?"

"I'm not, necessarily." Jax met his mother, flint to flint. "But you need to understand the extent of the trouble you're in here. This isn't a simple cash-flow crisis, Mom. Your entire financial structure has just crumbled." He gripped his knees and leaned in. "You're not broke — not yet — but if you want to keep it that way, you're going to need to make some serious lifestyle changes."

Addy swallowed but didn't argue. Jax was so rarely wrong. He wasn't wrong now, much as she wished he were.

"What about my trust fund?" Georgie asked suddenly. "I know nobody can touch Matty's till he's twenty-five but I'm twenty-seven. Can't I, I don't know, sign it over to Mom or something?"

"I doubt you're in any better shape than Mom is," Jax told her. "Jason likely screwed you, too."

"He did." Bianca told her, then sent a glance to Matty. "He couldn't touch Matty, obviously, but Georgie is over twenty-five, so..." She dwindled off delicately. Georgie only closed her eyes and deflated into the couch cushions again.

"All right, now, it's not so grim as all that," Bianca said, rallying with a visible effort. "We aren't without options."

"We aren't?" Matty asked, alarm making his face sharper

than his years should allow.

"Of course not." Bianca's smile spread, sleek and satisfied. It warmed Addy's heart even as foreboding twitched inside her. She exchanged a guarded look with Jax. Bianca with a plan was sometimes a dangerous thing. "We're Davises, aren't we? We may not have cash but we still have talent."

"Not me." Matty's tone went from alarmed to grimly resigned. "I'm completely talent-free. You said so earlier."

"Having talent and taking the trouble to hone it are two separate things," Bianca said serenely. "However, in this instance, I'm not talking about your talent. I'm talking about mine. UMD's Art Department has offered me several positions over the years. I'm considering taking one."

"At UMD?" Matty stared. "As in the University of Minnesota? In *Duluth*?"

"Unless the D stands for dumbass." Georgie said without opening her eyes.

"Georgie," Addy murmured reprovingly. Georgie only snuggled deeper into the couch.

Matty said, "Duluth is, like, four hours away. You said we wouldn't sell Hill Top House. You said we weren't moving."

"We're not." Bianca reached across Georgie and Jax to touch Matty's knee. "Darling, we're not. We're a family. We stay together. But—" She drew in a deep breath. "—it may be prudent to take an apartment in Duluth for the school year." She held up a hand to forestall any protest. "We would be home on the weekends, of course."

Matty recoiled. "You want to live there?"

"Of course I don't," Bianca snapped. "But—"

"Neither do I!" Matty's mouth trembled, then firmed into

a black scowl. Addy's heart twisted inside her. Matty was thirteen, for pity's sake. He was in middle school, and those places were shark tanks. Addy was something of an expert on the subject, having survived six of them. Being the new kid in middle school qualified as cruel and unusual punishment. No kid should experience it, let alone her beloved Matty.

"But it looks like I don't get a choice, do I?" Matty said. "Mom screws up, so *I* have to move." He dropped forward, elbows on knees, to scowl at the plush white rug between his feet. "What the crap am I supposed to do in Duluth?"

"You could consider focusing on your art." Bianca glared at him. "On developing your gift."

"I don't have a gift," Matty muttered.

"Of course you do." She turned away from him, uninterested in further discussion on the subject. "Not that reading piles of silly comic books—"

"Graphic novels," Matty snapped.

"—is going to help you discover it."

"Geez, Mom! When are you going to get it?" Matty leaped to his feet, eyes alight with a pain-laced fury that made Addy's heart constrict inside her chest. "I'm not hiding my talent under a pile of graphic novels. You're not finding it because it's *not there*."

Bianca pressed her fingertips to her eyes. "Matty, please. I'm having a difficult enough day without you throwing tantrums."

"I'm not throwing tantrums, I'm telling you the truth."

"You're thirteen." She laughed wearily. "What do you know about the truth?"

"Enough to know that I'm not Diego."

Addy stopped breathing and Bianca's face went the cold,

hard white of marble. "Excuse me?"

"I'm not Diego, Mom. Okay? *I'm not him.* I look like him but I can't paint like him and the sooner you—"

"*Enough.*" Bianca's voice cracked like a whip and Addy had the insane impulse to fling herself in front of Matty to protect him from it. "That's enough."

Matty flinched back, a little boy cowed by the icy fury in his mother's voice. Then the little boy disappeared under a wash of answering rage, and Addy's stomach leapt into her throat. "No, it's not enough," he snapped. "It's not nearly enough. Because I'm sick of this crap. I'm sick of paying for everybody else's mistakes." He shot a finger at his mother with teenaged fury, but that was a man-sized fist trembling at his side. "You effed up our money, Mom, not me. If somebody has to move to Duluth, it should be you. I'll stay right here."

Bianca rolled her eyes. "Oh, *that's* a workable plan."

But Matty wasn't finished. "And as for Diego, he's dead." Bianca's gasp was sharp and shocked, and Addy's heart thudded once — hard — then froze in her chest. "He went on a bender in New York City and he died, okay?"

Addy's mouth was so dry she didn't know if she could speak. They'd kept the uglier details of Diego's death from Matty. He'd only been nine; they'd tried to protect him. "Matty," she managed weakly, "how do you—"

"Kids talk, Addy." He laughed, and it was Diego's laugh. Harsh. Bitter. "I know more than you think." He glared at his mother again. "So I'm sorry he's dead, Mom, but it wasn't my fault. It was his. And I'm sick of paying for his mistakes. I'm even sicker of trying to replace him."

"Matty, no." Addy jumped to her feet, her stomach twisting violently. "You're wrong. It's not like that."

"It's exactly like that." He gave his mother one last glare, one last chance to deny it. Bianca sat silently, an exquisitely rendered portrait of abused love and bottomless grief. Matty gave a disgusted snort and turned from her. Snatched up his lacrosse bag and swung it over his shoulder with an athlete's fluid grace. The shock of seeing him in such easy command of his rangy new body went off in Addy's stomach like a little bomb. He even *moved* like Diego these days. "I have to go."

She shook off the weight of memory, dragged herself back to the present. "Matty, come on—" But her lips were numb, clumsy.

"I have practice, Addy. Josh is picking me up." He shot one last bitter look toward his mother. "I'm going to wait outside." He loped toward the door.

"You *should* practice," Bianca called after him. Evidently getting the last word trumped silent guilt trips in her hierarchy of argument winners. "Only instead of hitting your friends with sticks, you should practice something that matters! Like your painting!"

The door slammed in answer and Bianca pressed her fingers to her closed eyes, her lips white, the tendons standing out in the backs of her slender hands. Addy jammed her fists into her hips and stood there, torn between Bianca's grief and Matty's pain. Jax frowned thoughtfully at his mother while Georgie, to all appearances, continued to snooze comfortably in the corner of the couch.

"Well," Bianca said finally. She dropped her hands and released a long breath through her nose. "I think that went well, don't you?"

Chapter 5

ADDY HESITATED, CAUGHT between reassuring her mother-in-law and going after Matty.

"Oh, yeah," Jax said, nodding slowly. "Smooth sailing, Mom."

Bianca dropped her hand and glared at him. "Heaven's sakes, Jax. Can't you just be supportive for once? We're in crisis here. Doesn't family mean anything to you?"

Addy drifted a few steps toward the back door, toward Matty, toward his pain.

"Of course it does," Jax said, and snagged Addy's elbow. Suddenly her butt was planted on the sofa beside his and she stared at him, shocked. She didn't know what startled her more, his interference or the fact that he'd voluntarily touched her.

"No," he said to her quietly. "Let him hit his friends with sticks for a few hours first."

She opened her mouth to argue but the look he sent her shut it again.

Bianca said, "And yet Addy's the only one to offer anything but criticism."

"I offered you my trust fund," Georgie put in. She didn't even lift her head to speak.

"Which no longer exists," Jax reminded her.

"Not my fault." Georgie snuggled deeper into her corner of the couch.

Jax turned back to Bianca. "Look, I'm not criticizing, okay? I'm trying to help."

"You could pony up your trust fund," Georgie pointed out. "That would be helpful." She actually sat up and there was a suppressed glee in her voice that lifted Addy's eyebrows. "I'll bet it's fat and healthy, too. You being so...you."

"It probably is," Jax said evenly. "The folks who run the Burn Survivors Foundation have crack accountants."

Addy blinked at him. Jax had given away his trust fund? Her shock melted as quickly as it had come. He didn't use the money; of course he wouldn't keep it. She should've known that. Georgie certainly had.

Bianca, however, had not. She stared at him. "You gave away your trust fund?"

"Not all of it." Jax rolled his eyes. "I'm not an idiot. First I bought myself a house and a very nice long-term disability policy. It seemed prudent, given my line of work. But the rest?" He smiled. "Yeah. I gave it away."

Bianca continued to gape. "You gave it *away*?"

"Mom, come on. I didn't exactly leave myself destitute."

"That money was your legacy!"

"That money was a straitjacket. Plus I think we're all clear on the fact that I'm never living up to that particular legacy. I don't need money that comes with expectations; I can make my own."

Make his own what, Addy wondered? Money? Expectations? Both?

Jax paused, as if he'd caught himself on some old path he knew better than to wander down. He said, "You can make

45

your own living, too, you know. But if you didn't want to try it out, maybe you should have kept better tabs on your money manager."

Bianca smiled thinly. "Unfortunately, prevention is no longer an option here. But I do agree with you about one thing."

"You do?" Jax's brows rose. "What's that?"

"It's time to focus on the now." Bianca pulled in a deep breath, let it out slowly. "We need to understand where we are, what our options are and how to select one." She shifted her gaze to encompass Addy and Georgie, too. "Which is why I've called you all here. Not to fight. To think." She reached for Addy's hand this time. "Addison, I'm so grateful for your offer to tide us over. You can't know what it means to me."

"It's my pleasure," Addy said, squeezing her hand. "I wish I could do more."

"It's too much already." Bianca's smile trembled. "But even as generous as it is, Jax would be the first to point out that it's a temporary solution. And as I don't particularly want to begin my tenure as an art professor—"

There was a beat of silence, thick with the effort it cost Jax not to comment. In spite of everything, a smile tugged at Addy's mouth. He was practically sweating.

"—I'm hoping that between us we can develop an alternative solution," Bianca finished. "So let's brainstorm." She tilted Jax a look. "That's *brainstorm*, darling. It's a term creative people use. It means to think freely, broadly and without judgment."

"Ah." Jax nodded wisely. "I'd wondered."

Addy shook her head. These two were like Gerte and Lainey, only with the gloves off. She'd be more worried about it if they both didn't seem to enjoy the brawl so much.

She looked at Georgie — mostly asleep again in the corner of the couch — then at Jax, who was simply gazing at his mother with undisguised impatience and equally undisguised affection. Nobody offered a suggestion, so Addy finally blurted out the words that had been wedged in her throat since Bianca's first mention of money trouble.

"I could sell the art."

The silence that dropped over the room was as thick as Gerte's coffee and Addy tried not to fidget under the weight of three startled stares. She waved weakly at the canvases that all but pulsed with power and energy between windows. The brutal beauty of Lake Superior radiated from those paintings just as strongly as it did from the lake itself. Addison had her arguments with Diego the man, and held grudges she would probably never let go of, but Diego the artist? Nobody could argue with the man's talent. It was incandescent.

"What?" This from Bianca, faintly.

"Diego's art," Addy said again, more firmly this time. "We could sell it."

Disbelief started to surface through the shock on her mother-in-law's face, and Addy's stomach rolled. She'd made a career out of being Diego's dedicatedly grieving widow, and here she was offering to sell all she had left of him? But drastic times and all that.

"Not the whole collection," she said quickly. "We wouldn't touch anything in the gallery in town, of course. But there's the triptych in this room, the large panel upstairs, the smaller works in the bedrooms. I haven't looked at the inventory in storage in ages but surely we could come up with a few pieces we're willing to part with. And if we went to auction with them—"

"No." Bianca cut her off. "Absolutely not. I won't allow you to even consider such a thing." She leaned forward, took Addy's hands in hers and gave her a stern look. "This?" She raked her dark gaze across the paintings. "This is all we have left of Diego. All you have left of your husband, Addison. It's yours, as he was yours." Bianca touched the diamond ring still sparkling on Addy's finger, a smile ghosting over her lips. "As you were his. And ours. Your heart is so generous, dear. You've been a blessing to us since the moment Diego brought you home. Fate's been unkind to you but I never will be. You're my child as much as he was, and I won't allow you to lose anything more. Not on my behalf."

"Oh," Addy said, her throat going hot and tight with emotion. "Oh, Bianca. But—"

There was a sudden yelp from the back yard. A squawk? Certainly a noise of distress. And it was accompanied by a strange yodeling call that Addy instinctively associated with...

Turkeys?

"Holy crap!" Matty shouted from outside, his voice thin and high with panic. "Addy! Help!"

Addy ran.

She raced through the rainbow splattered foyer, jerked open the door and hit the back veranda. Matty was down in the yard, knee-deep in the shrubbery, his back pressed to the porch spindles while a dozen or more wild turkeys milled with vague menace between him and the little Acura that had come to pick him up. His buddy — Josh, she thought — had evidently decided that discretion was the better part of valor and had taken refuge in the car.

"What on earth?" she said, staring at the yard full of

birds.

Jax hit the porch behind her, his boots skidding for purchase on the wood. He grabbed the veranda railing beside her and said, "What the hell?"

"Beats me," Matty said grimly, and renewed his grip on the lacrosse stick he held in front of his body like a sword. "They busted out of the woods from over there." He jerked his chin at the stand of pines at the far edge of the meadow. "At first it looked like they were pissed at the car. That one is still giving the headlights the hairy eyeball."

Addy looked, and sure enough one turkey still was standing eye to eye with the Acura's driver's-side headlight, its feathers fluffed out, its turkey chin thrust pugnaciously forward.

"The rest of them are more interested in—" Matty swallowed audibly. "—me."

Bianca made it to the porch. "Good heavens. Are those wild turkeys?"

"Looks like it," Addy said.

Jax frowned. "We don't have wild turkeys this far north."

"Tell it to the turkeys," Addy said.

Georgie finally drifted onto the veranda. Her laugh chimed out like silvery bells. "Those are some big birds," she observed. "What did you do to them, Matty?"

"Nothing," Matty snapped.

"Clearly you did something," she said. "Those guys are pissed." She tipped her head and considered them. "And big. Those are some big, angry birds. Seriously, Matty, what did you do?"

"*Nothing.*" He shot her a black look then refocused on the turkeys. "This is not my fault."

"Yeah," Georgie murmured. "Sure."

He hissed with fury — actually hissed — and the flock surged forward a few feinting steps. He fell silent, his attention back on the turkeys, his knuckles very white on the grip of his lacrosse stick.

"Don't move," Jax said, his voice low and calm. "Just stay still, Matty."

It was good advice. Definitely the prudent course of action. Jax's specialty. But something hot and foreign filled Addy, something that felt disturbingly like rage. Because Matty was right. This wasn't his fault. Nothing was his fault, but life just kept slapping the kid into the ropes. First there were Bianca's unfounded expectations, then bankruptcy, then a potential move to Duluth, and now feral *turkeys*? Enough was enough.

"Screw that," she muttered and marched down the steps.

"Addy, what are you—" Jax began but she ignored him.

"Go on," she shouted, slapping her hands at the turkeys. "Get out of here. Shoo."

"Oh boy," Jax said. Because the turkeys didn't shoo. They simply swiveled their heads on undulating necks and fixed her with a flat-eyed stare. "Okay, now you stay still, too, Addy."

She did. Not because Jax had told her to, but because she was simply frozen in place. The turkeys angled their bodies toward her as one and her mouth went dry. She wasn't afraid, she assured herself. Not precisely. It was just kind of eerie, the way they did that. No single turkey emerged as the leader. No single turkey took the first step. It was as if they were operating with a pod-brain or something, and moved in perfect lock-step. All except that one still giving Josh's car the stink eye.

Addy's heart kicked and she remembered suddenly why

people didn't stand up to bullies. Why *she* didn't stand up to bullies. It had a lot to do with the very real chance that instead of seeing justice served, you'd just get your butt handed to you. For pity's sake, hadn't middle school — any of the six she'd attended — taught her anything?

She scrambled back up the porch steps and Jax slid her a sideways look.

"Shoo? Really?"

She shrugged. "I had to do something."

"Gosh, why didn't I think of that?" Matty rolled his eyes. "Get my air rifle, Jax."

"Absolutely not." Jax tucked his fingers into his pockets and rocked back on his heels, considering the turkeys. "Shooting turkeys — even with a pellet gun — is illegal outside of the proper season. Plus, you're unlicensed."

"Then you do it!"

"I try not to shoot things just because they scare me."

"But it's the American way," Matty snarled, and she heard Diego. Saw him in the flat mouth, the gorgeous bones, the angry eyes. Recognized that sneer, the way he aimed it right at the object of his fury. Her stomach pitched. Oh, mercy, she was losing him. Matty. She was losing the boy she loved to the ghost of the man she didn't and her heart cracked under the weight of it.

"Jax has to set a good example when it comes to firearms," Georgie said solemnly. "As an officer of the law."

"He's a firefighter," Matty pointed out.

"Fire chief," Jax said absently, still watching the turkeys.

Bianca simply blinked at her serene meadow, overrun with belligerent poultry.

"Well, we have to do something." A flush crawled up Matty's neck even as he glared at the turkeys. "Any other bright ideas?"

"You know what?" Addy said. "I have one."

"It better not involve the air rifle," Jax said as Addy stalked away from the veranda railing and disappeared through the open back door.

"It doesn't." She crossed the foyer and helped herself to the coat closet. Weapon selected, she marched out onto the porch again.

Jax stared at her then sighed. "Seriously, Addison?"

She ignored him.

"Hey, turkeys!" She came down the steps, this time with one hand concealed behind her back. "Hey!" The flock did that bizarre head-swivel-as-one thing again, consulted their communal brain and oozed toward her. "That's right, come on over. I've got a treat for you. You'll like it, promise."

She eased toward Matty until he was safely behind her back, and let the turkeys advance on her. Weird rubbery wattles covered their beaks and hung down from their chins. Weak chins, she thought. These were weak-chinned, mean-spirited, child-hating bullies. It was a bolstering thought. And when a girl found herself within arm's length of a dozen or so three-foot-tall wild animals with questionable intentions, a little bolstering never went amiss.

"Um, Addy?" Georgie didn't sound at all concerned, merely amused. "What are you doing?"

"Letting them get closer," she said. "Just a little closer."

"Good heavens." Bianca sounded appalled. "Why?"

"So I can give them something to remember me by."

"Oh hell." Jax pinched the bridge of his nose.

"Hey, Addy?" Matty said from behind her.

She didn't take her eyes off the turkeys. "What?"

"That's not the pellet gun."

"No."

"That's Mom's golf umbrella."

"Yep." Her enormous *purple* golf umbrella. Addy adjusted her grip. Her slippery, shaky grip. "Come on, you stupid turkeys. Another foot..."

"You should have gotten the gun."

She shot him a narrow look over her shoulder. "We are not shooting—"

Then Jax shouted, "Addy!"

She spun to find the turkeys surging forward with unsettling speed and grace. On a spurt of panicked adrenaline, she whipped the umbrella out from behind her back and hit the spring-loaded release button. The umbrella snapped open to its full six-foot diameter with the majestic crack of unfurling sails. Addy unleashed a war cry full of righteous fury and charged.

She sprinted across the gravel drive behind her make-shift shield. She caught a brief glimpse of Matty's friend behind the windshield of his car, eyes huge, mouth open. She hit the carriage house at the far side of the circle and spun, heart thudding, to survey the field of battle. Half the turkeys had gone wattle over drumsticks, and were rolling around the yard like rogue bowling balls, taking out their blinking companions with satisfying efficiency. The few lucky enough to have remained upright began hefting themselves into the air on vast, ungainly wings. Even sheltered by the umbrella, Addy's curls danced madly on the chaotic breeze those wings created.

She wrestled with the umbrella for a few seconds, then finally collapsed it in time to see the birds who'd gone claws-up after her bright purple assault come back to their feet like an army of those sand-bottomed punching bag clowns. They flung themselves into the air and hurtled toward their colleagues in the boughs of the giant pines.

She dredged up a cocky grin for Matty, still standing in the shrubs, his lacrosse stick hanging loosely in his slack hands. She shot her umbrella into an imaginary holster. "Looks like there's a new sheriff in town."

He didn't say a word. He just bent, snatched up his bag and stalked toward the Acura.

"Some officer of the law you are." Georgie gave Jax a poke in the arm. "You should be ashamed of yourself, letting Addy do your job for you."

He shrugged. "She does everybody's job for them. Why not mine?"

But his eyes stayed pinned to Addy, and there was something speculative and assessing in that steady gaze that had her stomach lifting inside her. She pressed a hand to it and swallowed.

Matty jerked the passenger door open and tossed his bag into the back. He folded his endless legs into the car and slammed the door. Addy sighed and crossed to the Acura on shaky knees. She tapped on the driver's side window with her umbrella. It slid down.

"Hey, Mrs. Davis," Josh said. He was a good-looking kid — sandy haired, square-jawed, with an aura of laid-back surfer-cool that probably had the girls lining up for days. He was one of the Martin kids, she realized now. He played for the high school lacrosse team. Must be doing assistant coach duty for the middle schoolers or something. "That was—" A lazy grin spread across his face. "That was *awesome*."

"No, that was offense, Josh. We play offense up here." She paused meaningfully. "Especially when somebody younger and smaller is taking it on the chin. No solider left behind, right?"

He dropped his gaze in chagrin. "Yes, ma'am."

Matty stared out the windshield as if she were invisible, mouth tight, eyes blank. Addy sighed and slid the umbrella to him through Josh's open window.

"In case you have trouble after practice."

He tossed it into the back without a word. She stepped away and Josh pulled off, but she followed the car with her eyes until it disappeared into the pines. Then she turned to face her family on the porch. Georgie was leaning up against one of the pillars like she was contemplating another nap. Bianca stood beside her, frowning at the trees to which the turkeys had retreated. Jax, however, was still looking at her.

He spoke to his mother. "You need to get Willa Zinc up here."

"Willa." Georgie said the name like it smelled bad. "Do we have to?"

"Unless you want to go *mano a mano* with the turkeys whenever you need to visit the garage," Jax said.

"Carriage house," Bianca murmured, gazing thoughtfully into the trees.

Georgie just shrugged and sat down on the railing. Addy walked slowly to the porch and settled herself on the railing beside Georgie. She hooked a companionable elbow through Georgie's, just in case she fell asleep for real and took a header into the shrubs. Georgie sighed and snuggled into Addy's shoulder. "Don't make us, Addy," she murmured. "We don't want Willa up here."

"We don't like Willa Zinc?" Addy asked. "Why not? She's very good at what she does. Plus she's Peter's sister. She could be your sister-in-law one day."

"Don't remind me." Georgie shuddered. "I can't believe

I'm dating a man whose sister traps rats for a living."

"I like Willa," Jax said easily. "She does way more than rats, too. Remember last spring when that bear wandered into the liquor store?"

Addy laughed. "I'm still sad I missed that. Did it really climb the tower of beer cases?"

"Yep. Camped right out on top of the Leinie's Summer Shandy," Jax said. "Willa didn't even blink."

"Why would she? She probably recognized it as one of her own." Georgie wrinkled her nose. "Lord, that girl smells."

"She does not." Addy jostled Georgie gently. "Willa smells just fine."

"Maybe now. But in high school? Yikes."

Jax shook his head. "Her mom took off when she was, what, twelve? And you know her dad was a hopeless drunk. That girl raised herself."

"So did Peter." Georgie shrugged elegantly. "But Willa smelled like it. He didn't."

"Georgie," Addy said.

"Well she did," Georgie said serenely. "Happily for me, Peter has the very good taste not to be particularly close to his family. I doubt he'll insist on my inviting Willa the Skunk Girl to Sunday dinner or anything."

"You'll have to invite her to the wedding, though," Jax pointed out. "Which will be way worse than inviting her up here to chase off the turkeys."

"I'll burn that bridge when I get a ring on my finger." Georgie yawned, as if a proposal were a foregone conclusion. "And when I see how many carats of rising-above Peter springs for."

Jax gave up on Georgie and turned to Bianca. "Seriously,

Mom. Call Willa."

Bianca's lip curled, exactly as her daughter's had.

Addy sighed. "I'll do it," she said.

Bianca smiled. "Thank you, dear."

Chapter 6

ADDY PUT MORE hours into her Save The Davises campaign over the weekend than she would ever publicly admit to. But she was onto something. By mid-morning on Monday, she really thought she was onto something.

She pushed off her desk and went zinging across the teeny faux-wood-paneled office on her wheeled chair. She grabbed a few sheets off the printer and inspected them. Smiled. She needed a closer look — an in-person walk through — to see if her gut said the same as her spreadsheets, but maybe, just maybe this could work.

And if it did — when it did — Bianca could kiss UMD goodbye. Better yet, Matty could graduate from the same school district he'd started kindergarten in. But best of all? By saving the Davises, Addy was going to save the whole darn town.

Because there was no denying it — the Davises *were* Devil's Kettle. They owned a chunk of nearly every business in town, of course, but it went deeper than that. That rich strain of artistic ability in the Davis DNA — Diego being the most recent example — had kept Devil's Kettle awash in tourist dollars while other equally pretty towns up and down the North Shore died off with alarming speed. It was a quirky little ecosystem but not hard to grasp: the town's continued existence depended almost completely on both the Davis money and the Davis talent.

Keeping the talent at home was no problem, of course. Addy was the sole heir to Diego's entire body of work, and while she'd lent out carefully chosen pieces to top-flight museums from time to time, she'd kept the majority of his oeuvre — including his masterwork — right here in Devil's Kettle.

The money was trickier.

The Davises needed a dependable cash flow if they were going to maintain their local investments, the more immediate the better. Unfortunately, their most obvious path to ready cash would be selling the art. Some of it, at least. Without the Diego Davis collection, however, the tourist traffic would unquestionably wither, and the town along with it. Which left Addy darn few options.

There was one, though. It was an option Addy had kept tucked away in an ugly old folio between some discarded closet doors in the carriage house these past four years. Kind of a rainy day option. A break-glass-in-case-of-emergency option. Putting it into play now would generate all the tourist traffic Devil's Kettle needed, no problem. It would also create a flood of gossip-mongers and gawkers, and blow Addy's self-respect into the next universe but, hey, nothing in life was free. All good things came at a price, and Addy had no problem paying when she had to.

But she might not have to. Not this time. Not if this big idea of hers actually worked. Which it would, because it was brilliant.

Optimism bubbled up inside her and she grinned. About the only thing that could make this morning better was a big old plate of Lainey's famous sweet lefse.

Addy's stomach gave an agreeable rumble. She pressed a hand to it, and checked her watch. Smiled again. It was time for Monday Brunch. Oh glory hallelujah.

There were drawbacks to living in a tourist town, one of which was working through each and every evening, weekend and holiday. But the upside? The biggest upside as far as Addy was concerned? Monday Brunch. In Devil's Kettle, every single tourist operation shut down on Mondays — much like museums in New York City — and everybody gathered at the Wooden Spoon for brunch. It wasn't an official thing, there was no set time or price. But every Monday around eleven or so, every shopkeeper in Devil's Kettle walked past the CLOSED sign on the door and sat down for brunch. It was sort of like the family meal some restaurants put on for the waitstaff before they opened for the evening. Nobody ordered; they just ate whatever Gerte and Lainey brought them, and left a few bucks to cover expenses.

Devil's Kettle, Addy thought fondly, operated more like a family than the family she'd grown up in. The sweet weight of gratitude settled in her chest and she rubbed at it with the heel of her hand. Diego's legacy was a complicated one, certainly, and Addy didn't always carry it comfortably. But this town and her place within it? She would always be grateful for that, no matter what it cost.

She shoved the papers from the printer into her bag along with her laptop. She tossed the bag over her shoulder and locked up the office. It was for form more than security, of course. Who would rob her when everybody in town was at brunch?

Still, it was a good habit so Addy locked up, jogged downstairs and hit Main Street at a brisk walk. Devil's

Kettle's downtown was about three colorful blocks of quirky charm cupping one of Lake Superior's smaller natural harbors, and Main Street ran parallel to the shore, from the southwest to the northeast. The first block was entirely taken up by the dignified red brick City Building Addy had just left, which housed the library and town hall on the main floor. Addy's office, Nan's newspaper office, the town's single lawyer and a realtor were upstairs.

The next block was occupied by a long, low cinderblock building with a faux wooden front that created the illusion of both a second story and four separate establishments. The Wooden Spoon was the second of the four businesses. It was sandwiched between the Devil's Tap Room (a tourist favorite for obvious reasons) and the Gilded Fish, where a person could buy anything from a singing refrigerator magnet to a hand-painted, four-hundred-dollar scarf.

The last retail space on the far end of the block was Buck's Bait and Tackle, which sold exactly what the name implied. A separate-seeming facade wasn't enough for Soren Buck, however, so he'd set himself apart by commissioning an enormous papier mache walleye to leap through the northeastern corner of his false second story. Good advertising, Soren claimed, and he was probably right. The thing had to measure forty feet from the jauntily flipping tail in the sky to the gaping mouth and bulging eyes that stuck out over the sidewalk like a bizarre awning. Addy's mother-in-law had been understandably horrified when it had gone up, given that the Davis gallery had front row seats to the spectacle. To this day, Bianca made the sign of the cross every time she had to walk underneath it. Tourists loved it, though, which meant that Addy did too.

The Davis Gallery occupied most of the third block, of

course. A gorgeous two-story building of glass and native pine, the gallery was ground zero for the art-minded tourist. The gallery itself seemed to expand with the force of Diego's talent, all but pushing a little doughnut shop — its only neighbor — off the north end of the block. It hung on, though, a tiny fishing shack that Walt Kovacz had painted shocking pink last year and transformed into the Sugar Rush, a deep-fried, yeast-raised nirvana so small that it handled only foot traffic or drive-throughs. Bianca hated it, of course. (The giant walleye to her south wasn't enough? She had to have a garish pink fishing shack to her north?) But Addy wasn't complaining. Sweet mercy, the smell of that place. She looked forward to her shifts at the gallery just so she could breathe and dream.

And she liked sweet lefse even better than doughnuts.

She crossed Second Street and broke into an actual trot as she closed in on the Wooden Spoon. Soren Buck stepped out of the bait shop at the far end of the block. "Hey, Addy," he called from the shadow of his giant fish, and shambled her way. Soren was a big man who walked with the habitual stoop of a guy who'd conked his head on enough doorways for one lifetime, thanks. Between that, his lumberjack beard, and his prodigious gut, he'd always reminded Addy of a circus bear, the kind that wore silly hats and rode tricycles but with an injured dignity.

"Hey, Soren." She stopped to wait for him next to the pansies joyfully overflowing the Wooden Spoon's window box. She pulled in a bracing lungful of sharp air and grinned. It was sunny today, if cool, and the lake was flirting and winking like mad at the handful of art-minded tourists who'd set up easels on the beach. "Pretty day."

"Eh." Soren squinted doubtfully at the clear blue sky.

"Won't hold."

"Well, it's not summer or anything but—" Addy waved a hand toward the beach. "Look at that. We've got painters."

Soren sniffed at the air like a giant shaggy dog and shook his head. "They've got until mid-afternoon." He paused, considered. "At best."

"You think?" She aligned herself to his view of the sky and followed his squint. Bucks had been hunting, fishing and trapping on the North Shore for generations, and Addy had to respect that but this sky was a perfect dome of sunny blue. "There aren't even clouds."

Soren tucked meaty hands into his pockets, rocked back on his heels and squinted some more. "Yet."

She gave the sky one last doubtful look. "Huh."

"Huh," he agreed. Then his deep-set bear eyes skated past her shoulder and he nodded. "There's your men."

"My men?" Addy turned and found Jax and Matty ambling up the block toward her. Probably coming from the fire station and the middle school, which were both just off Main Street and up Second a few blocks. Devil's Kettle Middle School didn't have an open campus lunch policy normally but exceptions were made for Monday Brunch. Which meant more family time for Matty. Addy sighed. Just what the kid wanted, surely.

Soren ducked into the Wooden Spoon and left Addy to watch her menfolk coming up the sidewalk toward her. They were almost of a height now, she noticed, and the proof of Matty's rapidly disappearing childhood put a pang of increasingly familiar regret in her stomach. But where Matty trudged along as if he resented sidewalk itself, Jax strode toward her like he owned it, a black t-shirt hugging his broad chest and strong arms while the sun pulled russet sparks out of the unruly mess of his hair. She reached up and tried to flatten her own curls which were, of course, bouncing madly in the breeze.

"Hey, Addy," Jax said, smile-free as usual. "Waiting for us?" He made it sound like an accusation. She suppressed a sigh.

"No, I was about to go in. Then Soren showed up and started predicting the weather."

"Yeah?" He arched a brow. Matty stood beside him in sullen silence, completely incurious. "What's the word?"

"We're in for a nasty turn," Addy told him. "Mid-afternoonish."

"Ah." Jax nodded. "Well, he's usually right."

"I know." She peered at the sky again. She couldn't help it. "But there aren't even clouds."

"I think he can smell it," Jax offered.

"Maybe that's it."

They fell into their usual awkward silence, like strangers thrown together at a party with nothing left to chat about. As if they weren't family, for heaven's sake.

"Well," she said, brightly enough to cover the frustration and hurt this particular silence always put in her throat, "should we go in?"

Jax reached past her for the door with obvious relief — she ignored the extra little dollop of hurt that brought on — but then Matty said, "Heads up." He jerked his chin toward the beach. "Art lover, three o'clock."

Addy turned and found a college-aged guy in a worn sweatshirt locked in on them like a heat-seeking missile. He jaywalked Main Street with fevered determination, a sketch pad clamped in paint-stained fingers. Apprehension snaked through her belly and she stepped in front of Matty. He looked so much like Diego these days, and Diego's fans weren't big on boundaries, as Addy had excellent reason to know. She could handle herself but she'd tried to shelter Matty. With that face of his...

The art lover jumped up the curb and hurdled a big glazed urn of pansies. He landed on the sidewalk in front of them, staring, and Jax hooked a hand through Addy's elbow. Her heart thudded twice, hard, then just stalled. Because Jax was touching her again. And not just touching her, either, but *holding* her. His wide, warm hand was clamped around her elbow like it meant business, and he stood close enough that his big shoulders actually blocked the lake wind. It pushed that delicious fresh-laundry-and-smoke scent her way and enveloped her in the heat from his body. No wonder he never wore a coat, she thought through her shock. He must run incredibly hot for her to feel him from nearly a foot away.

"You're her," the art lover announced, his eyes locked on Addy, panting a little from his exertions. Relief washed over her, cool and welcome. He was after her, not Matty. Thank goodness. A goofy smile spread across the stranger's face. "I can't believe it," he said. "You're Diego's Angel."

"In the flesh." Addy smiled back and arranged herself a bit more completely in front of Matty. She nodded toward the sketch pad. "You're an artist?"

He flushed and shook his head. "Not really. Aspiring, I guess. But I'm no Diego Davis."

"Yeah," Matty mumbled behind her. "Me, neither." Addy stepped on his toes.

"But you're her." The guy grinned at her again. "You're Diego's Angel. You're his masterwork. I was in the gallery yesterday and I saw it. Her. You. And now here you are, and

you're all *her*." He wiggled all over like a happy puppy.
"I'm sorry, this is ridiculously forward but—" He broke off,
looked at his shoes, and the trickle of nerves in her stomach
exploded into a bright flash of fight-or-flight. She threw both
hands up but he'd already grabbed her shoulders and planted
an enthusiastic kiss right on her mouth.

"Hey!" Jax jerked her into his chest but the guy — just a
kid, really — had already let her go. Addy forced a startled
laugh and put her fingers to her mouth. There had been a lot
more energy than skill behind that kiss, and not one whiff of
true desire. But it had still been pushed on her, and not even
on *her*, which was sort of worse. She wasn't a real person to
this guy. She was Diego's Angel.

The guy sighed. "I'm totally in love with you."

Addy squashed the urge to sneer, and smiled kindly
instead. Nothing in life was free, after all. "With Diego's
Angel, maybe. I'm just Addison." She glanced at her watch.
"And I'm sort of late, so—"

"Oh, hey, sure." He gave her a cheeky grin and picked up
the sketch pad that had fallen at their feet. "You ever want an
instant replay, I'll be right over there all week." He hooked a
thumb toward the stretch of beach framing the harbor where
the aspiring artists liked to set up their easels.

"I'll keep it in mind," she told him and he loped off
across Main Street.

"What the crap," Matty muttered and disappeared into the
Wooden Spoon.

Addy looked up and found Jax scowling after the art
lover. "That guy just kissed you."

"Yeah, I caught that." She pressed a hand to her jumping
stomach and let out a shaky laugh. "He was like a hugger
times ten. If I had to choose, though, I'd take the huggers

over the critics any day. They're sweeter, I guess. Even the critics are more fun than the weepers, though. Those people are exhausting."

"That wasn't a hug." Jax turned that scowl on her, and she blinked. Jax scowled at her about as often as he smiled, which was approximately never. He was Mr. Carefully Neutral where she was concerned, always. Except now he was glaring at her like *she'd* done something wrong. And interestingly, she could feel it in the backs of her knees, just like his unexpected smiles. "It was a kiss," he snapped. "A total stranger just kissed you. On the mouth."

"I know." She shrugged, and realized that Jax still had his hand wrapped around her arm. And her knees — already beleaguered — went watery. What on earth? "Just like I know he'll probably buy a bunch of art supplies at the gallery, do breakfast at the Sugar Rush, lunch at the Wooden Spoon and dinner at the Devil's Tap Room every day until he leaves."

"And that makes it okay that he kissed you?"

"Mercy sakes, Jax, calm down. It was just a kiss, and not even a very good one, frankly."

He stared. "You rank them?"

"Of course I don't. It's rare, that's all. The kissing. Which makes it memorable." She sighed. "Look, they mostly just hug my neck or cry on my shoulder, all right?" *Or slap my face.* She didn't mention that one. It had only happened once or twice. "Usually they just want to take my picture. My point is, they're harmless."

He gazed at her in open disbelief. "Harmless."

"Mostly, yes. That guy in particular was about as dangerous as a mosquito. He got carried away, that's all." She met his eyes carefully, and the anger burning in them had her breath hitching in her throat. "He wanted to kiss Diego's Angel, Jax." She needed him to understand that for some reason. Nobody had wanted to kiss *her*. Not in years. "It didn't cost me all that much to let him."

"You're not Diego's Angel, Addison." His grip on her arm tightened, and she found herself on her toes suddenly, face to face with his odd, unprecedented anger. Shock licked at her skin, cracked at her nerves. "You don't have to be, anyway."

"Oh, Jax." She laughed, and it surprised her, the black, bitter sound of it. "Of course I do. I'll always be Diego's Angel. I don't have a choice."

"Bullshit." He dropped her arm and stepped back, and his anger disappeared behind that awful neutral composure she was more used to. It stung far more than his fury. "You always have a choice. But apparently you'd rather sell your self-respect to tourists than look for it." He held up both hands in a gesture of surrender and backed away. "Sorry I stepped in. I shouldn't have." His eyes dropped to her hand, which was spread stupidly in the air between them. Was she reaching for him? Goodness. His gaze touched deliberately on the enormous diamond on her ring finger, sparkling gaudily in the thin sunlight. "In the future, I won't bother."

Then he turned on the heel of one steel-toed boot and disappeared into the Wooden Spoon. She stood there on the sidewalk, baffled and hurt, and watched him go.

Well how about that? Soren had been right. The day had taken a nasty turn after all.

Chapter 7

A FEW MINUTES later, Addy stepped into the jingle and hum of Monday Brunch in full swing. She pulled the door firmly shut behind her. Maybe it was gorgeous out — for now, anyway — but when it wasn't, the lake wind could belt a full cup of coffee clean off the counter. Tourists didn't think about it, and locals didn't have to think. They just shut the doors. Transplants like Addy had to be careful.

You always had to be careful when you didn't belong.

Jax's parting shot still stung, so she pasted on her brightest smile and excused herself through the crowd. Counter seating faced the open kitchen on the right side of the room, a small forest of tables grew up on her left, and decades of foot traffic had worn the cement floor in between into a shallow groove. She followed it to the prime booth in the back corner that the Davises had claimed as their due for as long as anybody could remember. She caught a glimpse of Jax's unruly hair through the crowd, and her gut tightened. He'd judged her pretty harshly, and it bugged her, though she couldn't imagine why. It wasn't like she'd lost his good opinion of her, she reminded herself. He'd obviously never *had* a good opinion of her. Still, she slowed her pace until she was sure her smile was good and bullet-proof.

She arrived at the table. "Hey, all," she said with breezy

good cheer.

"There you are!" Bianca's smile was the real thing, all warm and welcoming. "We were starting to think you were going to stand us up."

"When there was a chance of sweet lefse?" Addy forced a laugh. "I'm not sure you grasp my deep and abiding respect for dessert as breakfast." Matty was sitting beside Georgie on one bench seat while Jax sat with Bianca on the other. Both men were on the outside and Addy made the wise choice. She poked Matty's shoulder. "Budge over, buddy. I'm hungry."

Matty elbowed Georgie, who only blinked at him like a beautiful owl. Matty looked back at Addy and shrugged. Jax rolled his eyes and rose to his feet. "I'm on call," he said shortly. "You'll have to sit in the middle."

Addy maintained her plastic smile. "Sure, no problem."

She scooted in and Jax slid onto the cracked vinyl booth beside her, his jeans warm and sturdy against her thigh. And once again, Addy's system went on high alert. She snatched up a menu and studied it like her life depended on her order, overcome by an unexpected nostalgia for the days when Jax hardly looked at her, let alone sat practically on top of her.

Matty smirked across the table at her. "You know we don't get to order Monday Brunch, right, Addy?"

"Of course I know that."

"Then why are you staring at the menu?"

Because Jax's thigh was pressed up against hers, and she could still feel judgment radiating off him like smog. Plus his scathing dismissal of her hurt for some inexplicable reason, and she was suddenly and uncharacteristically pissed off about it. So she could either burn him to cinders with her laser eyes or she could pretend to read the menu.

She didn't think she should say as much out loud, however.

"Oh, you know me. Always checking out the marketing."

"Whatever," Matty said, and Gerte appeared at the edge of the table, a pot of coffee in one hand, an oversized mug in the other.

"Well now," she said, cheeks pink, apron frilly. "Look who the wind blew in."

"Blew in is right," Bianca said. She gave one of Addy's curls an affectionate boing. "Brisk out there today, hmm, Addy?"

"Hush, now, Bianca," Gerte said stoutly. "Don't you listen to a word of that nonsense, Addison. Your mother-in-law's always been more interested in what's on a person's head rather than what's in it, that's all." She gave Bianca a sugary smile and awaited return fire. Bianca only gazed back at her with the bemused curiosity a queen might extend an uppity peasant. Finally Gerte turned back to Addy. "We love you just the way you are, dear," she said warmly. "Don't you change a thing."

"I doubt I could." Addy smothered a grin. Gerte could bait all she wanted but Bianca wasn't the queen of Devil's Kettle for nothing. "It's the curse of the naturally curly. My head is a weather vane."

Georgie gave her a languid once-over. "Your head is a crow's nest."

"Because it's windy," Addy reminded her.

Georgie arched a skeptical brow. "It's not that windy."

"Like you'd know?" Addy turned up her nose. "Your hair is like Teflon. You don't even have to try. You just wake up like—" She fluttered her fingers Georgie's way. "—that. All perfect and stuff."

"Mmm," Georgie murmured and fingered a silky-straight lock with smug satisfaction. "And yet I own a comb and use it regularly."

"I comb." Addy reached a furtive hand to her hair and winced. It really *was* windy.

"Like Jax combs, I'm sure." Georgie gave her brother a once-over of his own. "It's a good thing you didn't fall for him instead of Diego. Your children would look like troll dolls."

"Good thing," Jax muttered.

A strange stab of something sweet and piercing went clean through her soul. Grief, maybe, for the children she'd never have. Possibly just another pulse of high-octane rage, this time at Jax's disgusted response to the idea of their imaginary kids.

Addy said, "It's *windy*."

"Sure is sunny, though," Gerte said. She set the mug down in front of Matty and every confusing emotion grappling around inside Addy was replaced by pure envy. Because there was hot chocolate in that mug, topped with a minor mountain of whipped cream and sprinkled with shaved curls of the extra dark chocolate Gerte special-ordered from Sweden. She watched with resignation as her own mug was filled with coffee.

And she knew with soul-deep bitterness that Jax was wrong. Not everything was a choice. Sure, she could reject the coffee Gerte had just poured her. She could explain that she hated coffee, hated every burnt, slippery, oily drop. She could ask for a hot chocolate or a tea or a blessed, blessed Diet Coke. But everybody knew that coffee wasn't about coffee. Coffee was a ritual, an offer of hospitality and friendship. When somebody poured you a cup of coffee, you didn't push it aside and ask for something else. You said *thank you*, and you drank it. Period.

"Gerte," Jax murmured as he lifted his own coffee cup and buried his nose in the rising steam. "Love of my life, light of my eyes. When are you going to marry me?"

"Oh, never." She laughed. "You'd only leave me for Lainey whenever sweet lefse day rolled around."

"Has it?" Addy asked with naked hope, her cold hands wrapped around her warm cup. "Has sweet lefse day rolled around, Gerte?"

Gerte grinned. "It has."

"Jax is all yours," Addy said promptly. "For sweet lefse? I'm marrying Lainey myself."

"You probably would," Jax murmured, barely loud enough for her to hear. She scowled at him but he never even looked her way. He was too busy smiling at Gerte. "You're the lady with the coffee pot," he said and held out his now half-empty cup. "I'm yours forever."

She grinned into her collar and topped off his mug.

Addy waited until Gerte had swished away on her sturdy shoes, then said, "So, I spent some time this weekend brainstorming solutions to our...problem."

"So did I," Bianca said unexpectedly.

Addy blinked at her. "You did?"

"Yes, of course." She gave Addy a beatific smile. "You didn't expect me to drop the whole problem in your lap, did you?"

"I did," Jax said. Bianca leaned around Addy to deliver an icy glare to her eldest son who grinned back unrepentantly. "What? You asked."

"I asked," Bianca said pointedly, "for everybody to give the situation some thought. And as I have no desire to move

73

to Duluth — even temporarily — I included myself in everybody." Her lips curled into a cat-like smile and Addy's heart rate clicked up a few beats per minute. "As it happens, I came up with something."

"You did?" Jax put a hand to Addy's shoulder and nudged her back into the bench seat so he could see his mother more clearly. Addy swallowed. Why was he *touching* her so darn much suddenly? And why couldn't she get used to it?

"I did," Bianca said and turned in her seat to face them all more fully. Georgie emptied a packet of fake sugar into her coffee cup and picked up her spoon. She didn't stir, however. She paused with the spoon suspended over her coffee, and drifted into another mental vacation.

Addy frowned and wondered, not for the first time, if Georgie was mildly epileptic. She'd read about stuff like this, where some unmotivated dreamer finally gets a CAT scan and his parents are shocked to discover that all those daydreams were actually violent electrical storms hijacking the poor kid's brain.

Then Georgie grinned, tipping her spoon this way and that, playing with the tiny needle of sunlight that had somehow shot all the way to the back of the diner and into the bowl of her spoon.

Addy sighed. Nope, Georgie was fine. She just wasn't paying attention. As usual.

Jax's phone beeped and Addy jumped. He checked the screen. "Ah, crap," he said. "Paul's out. His grandson gave him pinkeye. I've got to go cover the shift." He rose and dropped a twenty on the table. Pointed at his mother. "I want to hear about this idea later."

"Of course, Jackson," she murmured. "Go."

He went. Addy sighed with abject relief and scooted over into the luxury of all the space Jax's departure had provided. Space that smelled like coffee and clean laundry, and still burned with his astonishing body heat. She couldn't help herself; she snuggled into it. She was chilled all the way to her bones, and he ran hot. And he smelled so good. She really needed to find out what detergent he used.

"So, Bianca," she said. "Let's hear about this big idea of yours."

"Well Georgie and I were talking this weekend about how we'd like to freshen up the gallery for the season," she said, her dark eyes sparkling. "Not just put a fresh spin on the paintings we're already displaying but do something new. Something novel. Something people have never seen before that'll really drive tourist traffic."

"You came up with something?" Georgie asked, finally stirring. "Who are you thinking of spotlighting? Tessa MacAdams has been doing some really interesting stuff with wood cutting lately, and David Belvin's blown glass work is—"

"I was thinking of Diego."

"Diego?" Addy's mind went the pure blue blank of the sky outside, empty, bright and cold. "But you said you wanted something never seen before."

"I did. I do." Bianca's lips curved into that cat-like smile again. "And I found it."

Addy's heart stumbled to a halt. Oh mercy. The grenade in the garage. Bianca had found it.

"You did?" she managed weakly.

"I did. And it's been right in front of me all along!" Bianca laughed, a delighted bubble of sound that froze the blood in Addy's veins. "Well, not in front of me, precisely."

Her eyes danced merrily, and she lifted her coffee cup for a delicate sip. "More like in the gallery's storage room." She chuckled again. "To think I've been sitting on this display for nearly fifteen years!"

Addy's heart began, tentatively, to beat again. Her doomsday option was in the carriage house, not the gallery. But if Bianca hadn't found Diego's little…legacy, what had she found?

Georgie stared at her mother. "You wouldn't."

Bianca smiled. "I would."

Matty frowned. "Would what?"

Gerte arrived, her arms lined with large china plates of sweet lefse, and began dealing them out onto the table. She paused. "Where's Jax?"

"He's on call," Addy murmured, her heart still decelerating from panic mode. "Paul got pinkeye."

"Oh, dear." Gerte shook her head and slid the extra lefse toward Matty. "Can you do double duty, young man?"

"No problem." Matty drew the additional plate his way. It was piled high with paper-thin lefse, stuffed with what looked miraculously like Gerte's North Shore triple berry pie filling and mounded with whipped cream and — glory be — a generous helping of those dark chocolate shavings Addy had envied so cravenly on his hot cocoa. He barely looked at it, his eyes still pinned to his mother, and Addy sighed. Oh, for the metabolism of a thirteen-year-old. "You would *what*, Mom?"

Georgie laughed, a merry peal of wicked amusement, and shook her head in admiration. "Show *those* paintings. Of course she would."

Bianca smiled like a cat in cream. Gerte's baby-fine brows shot nearly to her hairline, but all she said was, "More coffee?"

"No, thanks." Georgie waved her off with an elegant hand. "We're good."

"What does that mean?" Addy asked cautiously when Gerte had moved reluctantly to another table. "*Those* paintings?"

"Diego's early stuff. From when he was, what?" Georgie glanced the question at her mother. "Thirteen? Fourteen?"

"About Matty's age, yes," Bianca said, her eyes resting on her son with a thoughtfulness that had Matty ducking his head and scowling. "When all he thought about was sex."

"And all he painted was boobs and asses," Georgie added cheerfully. She plucked a strawberry from the edge of her plate and nibbled at it, still smiling. "Boobs and asses, asses and boobs."

"It was a youthful obsession," Bianca admitted with an indulgent shrug for Matty. "Like your thing with the comic books."

"Graphic novels," he muttered.

She ignored him with easy serenity. "Only Diego got over it."

Addy choked back a burst of wholly inappropriate laughter. *Not really.* "So," she said with careful composure, "you want to fill up the gallery with Diego's early nudes?"

"The Boob and Ass Period," Georgie said helpfully.

"Georgie, please." Bianca lifted patient brows. "I raised you better than that. There is a world of difference between erotic art and cheap porn."

"True enough." Georgie's eyes danced. "Diego was a lot of things, but he wasn't cheap."

"Amen," Addy murmured, and sipped her bitter coffee. Diego had been the most expensive gamble of her life. She was still paying him off. "I wouldn't mind seeing these paintings. Maybe tonight?"

"Of course, dear," Bianca murmured and picked up her fork. Addy did the same.

In what seemed like moments, her plate was clean. Not quite licked clean but she'd been shamefully tempted. She leaned back, riding the mother of all sugar rushes, happy enough to think about tackling the last swallow of her lukewarm coffee. She was just about to reach for it when a man she'd never seen before appeared at the edge of their table and took her plate.

He wasn't tall but he wasn't short either, and had one of those bones-and-tendons builds that suggested either hard times or an ultra-marathon habit. He was probably around thirty, and wore a black t-shirt, an apron, and a pair of those indestructible canvas pants that had clearly been on the business end of a construction site or two. His hair was buzzed down to a mere shadow across his scalp, leaving the bones of his face brutally exposed.

She immediately wanted to see it better, that face. There was a story behind it. She didn't know how she knew that, but she did. Besides, since when did strangers bus tables at the Wooden Spoon? That was probably a story in and of itself.

"Thanks," she said automatically. "You must be new in town. I'm Addy."

"I know," he murmured and wedged the dish tub between his hip and the table, and began gathering their empty plates.

Bianca lifted a brow at this, and even Georgie sat up. Matty continued to plow his way through his second plate of sweet lefse with single-minded devotion.

"You do?" Addy tipped her head and studied him.

"How?"

He glanced up at her and his eyes were shockingly, brilliantly blue, set wide over the hard angles of his cheekbones. She blinked, startled. He wasn't handsome, not by any stretch of the imagination, but those eyes were downright beautiful. They'd show every bruise, though, eyes like that. Or they once had, probably. Now they were a gorgeous blank. Her throat tightened in sympathy. Not a good story, then.

He said simply, "I've been in town five minutes. And you're Davises." He cleared the table like it was a military operation — no hesitation, no waste. He simply eyed the situation, formulated his strategy and implemented it.

"So you must also know my mother-in-law Bianca?" Addy gestured to her left while the stranger deposited the plates and silverware in his tub, and scooped up the napkins. "My sister-in-law Georgie? My brother-in-law—"

"—Matty, yes."

They were down to coffee cups now, and curiosity was roaring through her like wildfire.

"And you are?" Addy asked.

"Busing your table."

And he was, too. He left Bianca and Georgie with their coffee cups, but swept Jax's abandoned mug and Addy's last lukewarm swallow into his tub.

"Eli!" Gerte appeared with the coffee pot and gave the stranger an exasperated look. "You're not supposed to clear the mugs until I've done one last round of refills!"

Eli — it fit, Addy decided — turned those unreadable eyes on Gerte and nodded toward Bianca and Georgie. "Go ahead," he said.

"You took Addy's mug," Gerte pointed out.

He shifted those eyes to Addy and the urge to squirm took her by surprise. It was a tough gaze to hold. "She was done," he said. He hefted his tub and moved off.

Gerte shook her head and followed him with her eyes. "That one's an odd duck," she said, and began topping off the remaining mugs. "Lucky for us he turned up, though."

"How so?" Addy leaned in on her elbows. Gerte's gossip habit could be a dangerous thing but sometimes it came in handy.

"Oh, didn't you hear?" Gerte set her coffee pot on the table and settled in for a chat. "Josh Martin got a stress fracture in his foot. Took a bad step at lacrosse practice on Friday or something?" She glanced at Matty, who grunted a confirmation while shoveling one last enormous bite of lefse into his mouth. "We thought we'd be out a bus boy for at least a month." She glanced across the thinning crowd at Eli and his dish tub. "Then Eli walked in off the Superior Hiking Trail looking for just enough work to resupply and move on." She lifted her shoulders. "He passed the standard background check, and lord knows he's efficient."

"Not big on conversation, though." Addy grinned.

"Tell me about it." Gerte sighed. "Aside from *yes, ma'am* and *no, ma'am,* I doubt I've heard him speak a dozen words altogether."

"There's a story there," Addy murmured, and watched the stranger move through the tables with that machine-like precision.

"I think so, too," Gerte said, her mouth a dissatisfied pout. "I just wish he'd tell me what it is."

Addy laughed. "I have no doubt he will." She patted Gerte's arm. "You're irresistible."

Gerte grinned. "Oh, you. You're getting to be as bad as

Jax, flattering old ladies."

Bianca — Gerte's exact age, give or take a few months — serenely declined comment once again. Her eyes fell briefly to Gerte's very practical shoes, however.

"Flattery?" Addy snorted. "Truth. You're ruthless, Gerte. When it comes to getting the dirt? Bloodhounds only wish they were you."

Gerte patted her hair modestly. "I do enjoy staying current." She nodded across the room to a raised hand at another table and scooped up her coffee pot. "Got to run, dear. I'll let you know if I ever do get that story."

"You're the best, Gerte." Addy watched her fondly as she trotted across the diner on her thick white runners.

"Speaking of the best." Bianca lifted her freshened coffee and eyed Addy over the rim. "Didn't you have an idea you wanted to share with us? A weekend brainstorm?"

Addy smiled. "I did, actually."

"An idea that doesn't involve lowering myself to teaching?" Bianca asked, her eyes bright with sudden hope.

"Mmm," Addy said carefully.

"Well?" Bianca said. "We're all ears, dear."

Addy reached for her bag, for the numbers and her beloved spreadsheets. Then she stopped. "You know what? I think I should show you."

Chapter 8

AN HOUR LATER, Addy was parked at the summit of Devil's Kettle, higher even than Hill Top house, the wind tugging at her little Honda. The weather had gone steadily downhill in the last half-hour, just as Soren had predicted, and was now bordering on hostile. Addy didn't care. She was too excited. She shoved open her door and leapt onto the weed-choked gravel drive of Davis Place.

Where Hill Top House stood peacefully in a grassy meadow overlooking a pretty slice of water, Davis Place clung to a craggy peak above the snarling lake like some massive wooden ship run afoul of the tides. A sharp-toothed pine forest pressed in on the house from behind, ready to nudge it over the edge the instant nobody was looking. Addy couldn't hear the Devil River over the wind but she knew it was there in the trees to the northeast, hiding. Sneaking and snaking and whispering pretty little promises like the soul stealer it was named for. And just before the cliff's edge, the river revealed itself. It burst from the treeline, mad with the need to fling itself — and anybody it had seduced along the way — over that suicidal drop.

But just before that triumphant leap, just before it surrendered itself to the madness, the river disappeared. It simply dropped into the earth, leaving nothing behind but a sheet of suspended mist, an outraged roar and a gaping black maw.

This kind of thing happened sometimes, Addy had learned. Evidently the Devil River's underbelly was so ragged and relentless that it had literally drilled a hole through its own stream bed. Geologists called it a kettle, or sometimes a pothole. And this one? Devil's Kettle? It was huge. Big enough to swallow the Devil River whole, anyway, and get a town named after it.

As fate would have it, however, the devil himself wasn't so easily digested. At least that was how the locals liked to tell it. Because maybe a hundred vertical feet down from the cliff's edge — but still several hundred feet straight up from the lake — the river burst violently out of a fissure in the basalt. It shot out over Lake Superior under high pressure, shattered and needle-sharp, wretched and magnificent and thrilling.

And Davis Place had front row seats to the show.

Addy hugged herself and danced in place with pure, undiluted joy.

"Addison?" Georgie unfolded herself from the passenger seat of Addy's Accord, draped an elbow over the open door and squinted at the monstrous old house perched sullenly on the cliff's edge. "What are we doing at Granny Nan's old place?"

"Dreaming."

Georgie hooked her other elbow over the car roof and rested the point of her chin on her forearm. Addy grinned. Georgie never stood when she could lean, never sat when she could recline. It was her particular gift, making everybody around her seem ridiculously tense. And not very good looking, too, though Addy had a feeling she didn't even try at that one.

Georgie studied the house idly. "Looks like a nightmare to me."

"It is." Bianca stepped out of the Honda as well, stood next to Georgie and glared at Davis Place's back porch. One sagging pillar let loose a nonchalant flake of paint and it spiraled away on the wind. "I haven't set foot in this place since—" She paused. "Since I was pregnant with Matty."

Georgie rubbed her mother's arm. "Since Dad died, you mean."

"That, too."

Addy stopped dancing in place. "This is where it happened?" she asked, though she knew very well it was. She'd simply hoped enough years had passed to make it a painful fact rather than an outright deal-breaker. "This is where Joe died?"

"Yes." Bianca gazed at the porch, her mouth drawn, her eyes tight. "In the basement."

"He had a little kiln down there," Georgie said. "Built it himself when he was a teenager."

"I told him it was a death trap," Bianca murmured, and touched the line that seemed to live between her brows these days. "Dangerous. Stupid. Everybody knew it."

"You know Dad," Georgie said and smiled fondly. "Couldn't tell him anything he didn't want to hear."

"Just like his mother." Bianca pressed her lips together. "Who absolutely should've known better than to let her stubborn son build something so ramshackle in the first place, let alone use it. And to keep it after we built Hill Top House, with a brand-new, up to code kiln?" Bianca broke off and cleared her throat. "Well. That's neither here nor there now, is it?"

Georgie rubbed her mother's arm again and sent a look over the car at Addy. "Granny Nan hasn't been back since Dad died, either." She shrugged. "Put a massive padlock on that kiln and moved to town. Never looked back."

"Guilty conscience, I expect." Bianca scowled.

"Mom." Georgie looked at her mother again. "It was an accident. You know that."

Bianca shrugged and smiled wanly at Addy. "The ventilation failed. The official report cited carbon monoxide poisoning, but it was really just stubbornness. Sheer, stupid stubbornness." She didn't say whether it was her late husband's or her mother-in-law's. Addy didn't ask. Didn't figure it mattered.

"I'm sorry." She circled the car, put her arms around Bianca. "I'm so very sorry."

Her mother-in-law squeezed her back, the scent of sorrow and perfume mixing with the bitter lake wind. "It was a long time ago." She drew back and swiped a delicate finger under each eye. "Goodness, fourteen years now!" She turned to peer at the house. "Has nobody really set foot in this place for fourteen years?"

"Well, no. Look at it." Georgie snorted. "Why would they?"

"Give me ten minutes and I'll show you," Addy told her. She turned to Bianca, took her hand. "Do you feel up to coming inside? You don't have to."

"Do you mind?" The edges of Bianca's smile trembled. "I really do want to hear about this idea of yours but I don't know that I'm up for a tour. Not just yet."

"Of course." Addy squeezed her hand. "Georgie and I can do this."

She gently ushered her mother-in-law into the passenger

seat and clicked the door shut on Bianca's pale gratitude. She turned to Georgie, who was standing hip-shot on the gravel drive, her arms crossed over her model-thin torso, her perfect face wide awake for once and full of suspicion.

"We can do *what*, Addy?"

Addy ignored her. She ignored the sagging back porch, too, and marched through the knee-high prairie occupying the side yard, Georgie dogging her heels. She popped out into a stingy front yard ringed by a low stone wall, the wind tearing at her hair. She walked to the front porch steps, her back to that incredible view, and fished in her pocket for the key. Anticipation bubbled in her veins and she grinned at Georgie like a lunatic. She held up the key and said, "Ready?"

"What, to go in there?" Georgie laughed. "Hell, no."

"Don't be such a baby." She swept her gaze from the peaked roof to the stone foundation, took in the stark, no-nonsense lines and angles that had stood for generations without bending and looked likely to stand for several more, paint and porches be damned. There weren't even any obviously broken windows. "This house is indestructible."

"This house is a zombie," Georgie said darkly.

"A what?" Addy blinked at her, surprised. You just never knew what Georgie was going to say.

"A zombie," she said again and stabbed a finger toward it. "We abandoned this place, Addison. It should have fallen into the lake by now. We *wanted* it to fall into the lake but did it? Hell, no. We come up here fourteen years later, and it's still standing right where we left it, staring at us with its one weird zombie eye." She glanced up at the circular attic window, which gazed out over the lake with what Addy had to admit was a decidedly malevolent air. Georgie shuddered and folded her arms. "I'm not going in there."

Addy gave her a patient look. "You're stalling."

"Of course I am! Why would I risk even my outfit let alone my life going into this—" She broke off, circled a manicured nail in the air taking in the whole situation in front of her "—place?"

Addy hesitated. *Delicately*, she reminded herself. *Ease them into it.* Plus, until she saw the interior for herself, she couldn't be sure her idea was even workable. She smiled innocently. "How else are we going to know how much we can sell it for?"

"You want to sell it? Oh, thank Christ. That's the first sensible thing you've said all day." She pulled out her cell phone. "I'll get Marcia Mays up here right now. She can do the walk through, then figure out how to list it. Which is what realtors are for, I might remind you."

"Or we could just tell Gerte that Jason Bloom took all our money and a hair model to Bimini and we're this close to demanding cash buy outs from every last one of them."

"Except Peter," Georgie said, but stopped dialing.

"Except Peter," Addy allowed. "All things considered, I really think it would be better if we did this part ourselves. Quietly. Don't you?"

"Hell." Georgie put her phone away and gave the house a baleful look. "I'll bet there are bats in there."

"It's a good possibility."

"Mice?"

"I wouldn't bet against raccoons, Georgie."

"Oh God." Her head rolled around on the stem of her neck like a wilted flower and her arms dropped to her sides. But she put a cautious foot on the steps. "If I die in here, make sure I'm buried in that vintage Diane von Furstenberg wrap dress I just got."

Victory. "It looks great on you."

"I know." She tippy-toed up the steps and stood fingering a silky lock of pale golden hair while Addy fitted her key into the rusty lock. A small wrestling match ensued but Addy eventually prevailed, wrenching the door open. Georgie's perfect face registered a sour disbelief.

"You'll make a beautiful corpse," Addy assured her. She grabbed Georgie's elbow and dragged her inside.

Willa Zinc parked her rusty Ford pickup next to Addy's neat little Honda in the overgrown driveway of Davis Place. She had one boot on the gravel before she noticed Addy's mother-in-law inside the car beside her, pointedly looking the other way and pretending — as usual — that Willa didn't exist. Fine by her. That street went both ways.

She heaved the truck door shut. Had to put some muscle into it as the truck was as old as she was, but that was fine. She had plenty of muscle. Didn't look like it, she knew, not when she barely hit five-two in her work boots. But she knew how to use what she had, and a little muscle was plenty when nobody expected you to have any. The surprise was as useful as the strength.

She squinted into the wind at the monstrous old house squatting on the basalt bluff like a melting candle. It wasn't as bad as it could be, she admitted. Not nearly. The windows looked intact, and there were no obvious cracks in the foundation, but the shingles were a mess. The siding was shot clean to hell and unless Willa missed her guess, the back porch was thinking about seceding from the union and getting itself an apartment in town. Looked like those wild turkeys stalking Hill Top House had been making themselves right at home up here, too.

She shook her head. Rich people. They'd throw money at any old thing. As a rule, Willa was only too happy to catch it. But Davis money? Her lip curled involuntarily. It had been years since she'd been desperate enough to take money from a Davis.

This, however, wouldn't be taking. This was *earning*, and that was a different thing altogether. Besides, did she really care who was signing the checks so long as she made the mortgage and paid the lawyers?

Her lip curled again. Well, yes. Yes, she did. But refusing the Davises their heart's desire was a petty pleasure she simply couldn't afford. Not then and not now. At least she'd earn it this time. Cold comfort, true, but comfort nonetheless.

She grabbed a metal clipboard box from her backpack, dragged a pen from the ponytail sticking out of her ball cap and steeled herself to do business with the Widow Davis.

Not, she told herself with a shameful little twinge of relief, the one in the car to her left. No, she'd be doing business with the one who presumably valued her life little enough to be inside this ugly old tumble-down house. The one who valued her reputation little enough to have called Willa twice now in a single week.

She pulled the brim of her cap nice and low, and started with the foundation.

Addy stood in the doorjamb and studied what had been the foyer once upon a time. A layer of dust — okay, dirt —

coated the floor, and the sidelight was grimed by years and years of weather. An enormous granite-faced fireplace squatted directly ahead of them, the heart of the house from back in the days when it had supplied heat to the entire place and doubled as the oven. The kitchen, she knew from the blueprints she'd studied, was through a swinging door beside the fireplace and took up the back half of the entire first floor. She turned left and walked down a short, useless hallway that connected the foyer to an equally cramped parlor. Large piles of God only knew what — hopefully just furniture — were draped with moldy sheets.

It should have felt a lot bigger, Addy mused as she returned to the foyer and followed another five-foot-long hallway the other direction into a somewhat larger dining room. Yet more sheet-draped piles filled up the stingy space, and Addy rolled her shoulders under a twinge of claustrophobia. She shook her head. Six thousand square feet, and she was feeling cramped.

"I think the original Davises might've accidentally hired a maze maker instead of an architect," Addy called back to Georgie, who had refused to move beyond the front door.

"Drop breadcrumbs or something then," Georgie said. "Because I'm not coming after you if you get lost."

"Right, thanks."

She skirted a pile of furniture and found the lake-facing window. Even handicapped by years of dirt and a miserly eight-pane, the view grabbed Addy's heart like a fist and wouldn't let go. She turned away from the window with an effort and squinted back toward the foyer. She mentally knocked out the hallway between them — and the one leading to the parlor, too. In her mind's eye, she replaced those ridiculous eight-panes with a couple of generous bay windows, and surrounded them with window seats and some built-in book shelves. She'd save that fireplace for sure, she thought as she walked slowly back to the foyer. Give it a good polish and make sure it was functional. It would provide a visual anchor opposite the view and give people a reason to gather outside their rooms when they couldn't paint. As for the kitchen...

"Uh oh," Georgie said, and Addy snapped back to the present. "I know that look."

"What look?" She stopped at the staircase which gave out — ridiculously — into the teeny hallway between the dining room and the foyer. Intricate woodwork, she thought. Match or replace?

"That look. The one you're doing right now."

"I'm doing a look?" Addy pressed a thumbnail into the bannister at her elbow and satisfaction licked through her. Hardwood. No pine here.

"Yes. Right now. And that look usually means—" Georgie broke off. Addy hardly noticed. She was too busy buffing the balustrade with her shirt sleeve. A dull glow emerged that had satisfaction deepening into something more like anticipation.

"What," Georgie asked in venomous tones, "is *that*?"

Willa Zinc appeared in the open door behind Georgie. She followed Georgie's offended stare to a pile of what was surely dried raccoon droppings on the hearth.

Willa said, "Scat."

"Gladly." Georgie turned on the heel of her delicate sandal but Addy sprang into action and caught her arm before she could hit the porch.

"She means the noun, Georgie, not the verb," she said, laughing. "Hey, Willa. Thanks for coming up on such short notice."

Willa gave her a neutral nod while Georgie glared at her. "Noun?"

"Person, place or thing," Willa offered helpfully, her small face perfectly blank. Addy thought it was blank anyway. Hard to tell with that Saints cap pulled down so low.

"I know what a noun is," Georgie said as she tugged her elbow from Addy's grip. "But scat is a verb." She lifted an expertly shaped brow at Willa and gave her a saccharine smile. "An action word."

"It's also a noun," Willa told her.

"It is," Addy said. "It means animal dung."

Georgie gave an involuntary little skip. "Shit?"

"Yep," Willa said, a whiff of amusement in her dry voice. "Good thing you wore sandals."

Chapter 9

GEORGIE FROZE ON the spot, though Addy couldn't tell if she was terrified of the poop or outraged at Willa's little poke. "Yes, well." Georgie treated Willa to the tight-lipped smile that ordinarily turned offenders into pillars of salt. "Not everybody is willing to do trucker chic with such enthusiasm." She dragged a scornful eye over Willa's jeans, down vest, long sleeved t-shirt and dark ponytail. "Or so long beyond when it was actually in fashion."

"Well, ouch, Miss Davis." Willa rubbed the heel of her hand over her breastbone. "Just ouch. I can't tell you how your condemnation of my sartorial choices wounds me." Willa arched a brow. "That's *sartorial*. I can spell it if you like. It means—"

"As if my day weren't already crap," Georgie cut Willa off and spoke directly to Addy. "As if it weren't enough to drag me up to Granny Nan's moldy old death trap and make me stand around in shit. You just had to invite Willa the Skunk Whisperer, too? God, Addy. What did I ever do to you?"

Willa pushed herself off the doorframe and stuck her pen into her ponytail. "Well. That's my cue. I'll just leave you ladies alone with—" She eyed the pile of scat significantly. "—well, with whatever poops like that."

"Willa, wait!" Addy spread staying hands Willa's way then glared at her sister-in-law. "Georgie, be nice." She turned back to Willa. "I'm sorry, Willa. Georgie's having a difficult day."

"Aren't we all?" Willa murmured.

Addy glanced from her fuming sister-in-law to Willa's utterly blank composure. "Evidently we are. Somebody will have to explain that to me one day but right now I have to focus, so can everybody just put it on pause for a minute? One minute?"

Georgie rolled her eyes dramatically but stayed silent.

"One minute," Willa said finally. "One."

"Thank you." Addy jogged across the room to poke her head through the swinging door near the fireplace. And there was the kitchen, in all its badly laid-out glory, just as the blue prints had promised. "Awful design but plenty of space," she called back. "Good bones."

"Fabulous," Georgie muttered. "I'm so glad."

Addy all but danced back to the foyer and paused in front of the stairs with naked longing. She sent a pleading glance Willa's way. "One more minute? Because if there are even four bedrooms—"

"Six," Georgie said, carefully ignoring the dark little woman beside her.

"Six?"

"If you include the master suite."

"Six!" Addy bounded toward the stairs, delighted.

"Addison! Do *not* leave me alone down here!"

"Willa's right beside you!"

Georgie sniffed. "That's worse than alone."

Willa rolled her eyes. Addy sympathized. Georgie was way too lazy to be this bitchy on a regular basis. Something must really be buried between those two.

Later, she promised herself. For now, she wanted to see the upstairs like she wanted her next breath. "Come *on* then, Georgie. And quit being so mean to Willa. We need her."

"Yeah, I can see that," Georgie muttered as she minced around another crusty pile of crap on the floor. The old-growth hardwood floor, Addy noted. The buzz in her blood was rapidly escalating to a gleeful roar. This could work. It really could.

The instant Georgie was within arm's reach, Addy latched onto her elbow. "Willa, you come, too. Please? I need your opinion." Willa gave a long-suffering sigh but ambled forward. As soon as her boots hit the steps, Addy bounded upward.

She hit the upper landing and darted down the narrow hallway with — yes! — six doors lining it. Six! She flung open the first one, sprinted across the floor and ripped down a pair of ridiculous puce drapes.

The Devil River's kamikaze leap into the lake below was even more dramatic from up here. Rocks speared up out of the swirling water in the bay, went under and fought their way clear again with implacable determination. Dark clouds slid by overhead, completely unconcerned by the life-and-death drama playing out below.

Everything inside Addy sang. A straight-up hallelujah chorus went off in her head. Because this endless tug of war between beauty and danger, peace and violence, beginnings and endings? This astonishing, impossible force of nature throwing itself endlessly off the edge of the world?

This was beauty, albeit a terrible one.

Addy had known her share of disappointments in life but one of the greatest was the fact that she'd been born with an artist's soul but not an artist's hands. Beauty rang inside her like a bell but she had absolutely no talent. At least not for art. Her gene pool was full of accountants and nurses. Comptrollers and lawyers. (Corporate lawyers, though. Never even a semi-flashy trial attorney.)

But here? Now? In the new reality Jason Bloom (that thieving weasel) had unleashed on the family? It was Addy's gifts that mattered. It was her unique combination of talents — her eye for beauty combined with that ruthless pragmatism that had so disgusted her husband — that was going to save the family he'd left her. And the plan that was forming inside her head? If it wasn't art, she didn't know what was.

"Ladies," Addy said, "this is a house worth saving." She squeezed Georgie's elbow and flung her free arm around Willa, who stiffened in surprise. "And you're going to help me do it."

Jax stepped back from an impressive array of spanking clean fire hoses. It was past five o'clock but he took a minute to savor the sight of those hoses drying on the wind-whipped pavement outside the fire station, and the satisfaction of having put them there with his own two hands. Well, mostly his own two. He'd used Matty's as well. Liberally. Physical labor cleared the mind and provided perspective, which was something he figured his brother was short on just now. And he couldn't do much about their mom jumping all over the kid's crap but he *could* provide some perspective on the situation. And if he could get his hoses cleaned at the same time? Win/win, as far as he was concerned.

"Now that's a decent day's work." He wiped his hands clean — sort of — on the butt of his cargo shorts and slapped Matty's skinny shoulder. "Feels good, doesn't it?"

"It feels like I lost a cage match with a python." Matty swiped his cheek on the hem of his sopping t-shirt. "In a swamp."

"I know, right?" Jax threw a companionable arm around his brother. "Good times." He gave the kid a hearty squeeze, then nudged him toward the fire station door. "We deserve a treat."

"Yeah?" Matty pushed through the heavy metal door, and glanced back at Jax with a comic mix of hope and wariness. "What kind of treat?"

"How should I know?" He nodded Matty into the kitchen/break room down the hall to their left. "We're men. We forage."

The space was small but sported all the essentials — a two-burner stove, a microwave that made everything smell like burnt popcorn and an industrial-strength coffee maker. A warped linoleum counter separated the cooking area from an eating area. The evening's on-duty volunteers — two gut-heavy guys with an easy couple of decades on Jax — sat at the ancient dinette set, frowning over a hand of cards. Jax nodded to them on his way to the dorm-sized fridge under the counter.

"Matty, say hello to Frank Wilson and Mason Kennebec." He helped himself to a bottle of water. "The unsung heroes of every other Monday night."

"Hey, Jax," Frank said. "Hey, kid."

Jax handed a second bottle to his brother with a glance that reminded him of his manners. "Hey, Mr. Wilson," Matty said obediently. "Mr. Kennebec."

Mason only grunted and stared at his cards. Matty polished off his bottle with one long swallow and reached for a second one.

"Got the Monday chores done," Jax told the men.

"Hoses and all?" Frank surveyed his cards absently. "That's good."

"Matty was a big help."

Mason discarded a jack like it was a weight off his shoulders, and finally looked up. "Glad to hear it." He smoothed an impressive mustache. "Dirty job, that one."

"Tell me about it," Matty muttered and muffled a belch in his sopping sleeve.

Jax grinned. "Told him he'd earned himself a treat."

Frank tipped his head toward a hot pink pastry box on the table beside the discard pile. "Have at it, kid." Then he smiled and picked up the jack. Mason's walrus 'stache twitched.

Matty's eyes lit up. "Doughnuts?"

"Stopped by the Sugar Rush on my way in." Frank laid down a winning hand with leisurely triumph. "Gin."

Mason scowled and tossed down his cards. "Damn it."

Frank leaned back, rubbed his belly and grinned. "Not my fault you suck at cards."

"Not cards, *gin*. And that's because it's a stupid game." Mason leaned in to thump a knuckle on the discard pile. "Now, cribbage. *There's* a two man card game."

"Always with the cribbage." Frank sighed and pulled the cards in for a shuffle. He riffled them between his big fingers like a magician and started to deal a fresh hand.

Mason picked up his cards. "Eat fast, kid," he said to Matty. "Your sister's here for you, and you know how women feel about spoiling dinner."

"His sister's here?" Jax said, his gut tightening. He hardly needed to ask but he did anyway. "Which one?"

"Addy." Mason ran a thoughtful finger over his mustache and considered his cards. "Put her in your office while you were finishing up the hoses. Said she wanted to talk to you before she left."

Oh, hell. Of course she did. Addy hated being at odds with anybody, let alone family. He should've known she wouldn't be able to let the sun go down on that little incident outside the Wooden Spoon this morning. She was here to make peace, and there would be no peace for him unless he let her.

He eyed the pastry box Matty was face-down in. There were at least eight doughnuts left. Given the rate at which Matty was shoving them into his face, there was probably just enough time for Addy to smooth things over without putting Jax's self-control into the red. He hoped.

"I'll go see what she needs," he said to Matty. "Come on back when you're done."

The kid grunted around a mouthful of custard-filled bismarck, and went to work on a chocolate long john.

Jax walked down the short hall to his office and, sure enough, there was Addy sitting in his desk chair. Graham Graves, another of his volunteers, sat on top of the desk in front of her, arms folded to better display his biceps while he chatted her up. Union carpenter for the paycheck, volunteer firefighter for the glory, Graham was as sweet-faced as a daisy and as horny as every other twenty-two-year-old guy on the planet. And he was looking at Addy like Matty had looked at the doughnuts.

Jax fought a scowl. Every damn time he turned around today, somebody was putting the moves on this girl. He

leaned a deliberately casual shoulder into the doorjamb.
"Hey, Graham."

"Hey, Jax," Graham said, his gaze never veering from
Addy. She leaned around the guy to send Jax that high-
octane smile of hers, though. The one that made perfect
strangers lay fat wet ones on her in the middle of Main
Street. Not that he could blame them. It was those damn
dimples. Who could resist?

He scowled at her. He didn't mean to. He never meant to,
but a guy could only expect so much of himself. The polite
disinterest was only a veneer, after all, and a damn thin one
at that. It had served him well these past four years but
occasionally it slipped and he just flat-out scowled at her. It
was either that or kiss her, and while random tourists
apparently got away with that shit all the time, he doubted he
would.

Even as he scowled at her, though, he knew it was a
mistake. Addy would only take it as a challenge, and turn on
the charm.

"Hey, Jax."

And, oh holy hell, did she ever. That smile didn't just
amp up; it went fucking supernova. Suddenly, he wasn't just
looking at those dimples, he was *feeling* them — in the soles
of his feet, in the palms of his hands, and in other more
alarming places he wasn't going to think about. He was
literally sweating with the effort it cost him not to reach out
and just touch one. Because, Christ, he wanted to know what
they felt like. They *looked* as soft as fresh-baked bread, but
he couldn't know for sure. Not until he touched one.

Which he'd never do, so he should probably quit being
such a scowly bastard so she could stop smiling so goddamn
hard.

He shoved his fists into his elbows, blanked his face and glanced at Graham, who had no problem at all with Addy's blinding smile or with her fresh-baked dimples. No, he was just sitting there, happily and openly admiring the view.

Jealousy caught Jax on the raw. He himself was shaking — literally *shaking* — with the effort of resisting her. But nobody else was even trying. Not Graham, and certainly not the handsy tourist who'd kissed her on the sidewalk. Bitterness filled him and it took every ounce of his considerable self-control to keep it off his face.

"Addison," he murmured politely but without even a smidgen of warmth. Her smile flickered. A casual observer would never even have noticed but Jax was hardly casual, and he knew he'd hurt her. And he was desperately sorry for that but he simply couldn't afford the kindness. This shit was just too hard. "To what do I owe the pleasure?"

"I thought I'd grab Matty before I headed up the hill. But I also wanted to talk to you about something." She paused. "About a few somethings, actually."

"Ah." He looked at Graham. "This explains why she's behind my desk. What remains unexplained, however, is why your ass is *on* my desk."

Graham popped to his feet, caution finally seeping through the hormones. "Sorry, Chief."

Jax pushed off the doorframe and strolled into the office. "I know you're not on duty today, Graves. Weren't you on a job site down in Hornby Harbor?"

"I got off early." He edged toward the door. Smart kid. "Thought I'd catch a workout in the station's weight room before dinner."

Addy pursed her mouth into a flirty little question mark. Jax was glad his shirt was already soaked from the hose washing, because he was truly sweating now. God, that *mouth*. It was killing him. She said, "What, swinging a hammer all day doesn't count as exercise?"

"Not if I want to slay the ladies at the slip and slide again this year." Graham paused in the doorjamb to flex. Jax sighed. Last year for Devil Days, he and his staff had covered the sledding hill behind the middle school with plastic sheeting, then charged people a buck a pop to be squirted down it with fire hoses by shirtless firefighters. It was — predictably — one of Devil Days' more popular attractions, and the highlight of Graham's young life so far. "I have a reputation to maintain."

She laid a hand over her heart. "We're only women, Graham. Have mercy."

The guy inflated his chest until Jax feared for his shirt.

"Okay, go lift weights," Jax said, nudging him the rest of the way out the door. "Addy wants a word. With me."

"Sure thing, Chief." Graham aimed his puffed up pecs at Addy one last time. "So long, Addy. Call me sometime?"

She grinned. "As it happens, I might have some work for a decent carpenter."

"Awesome." He sent her a good-natured leer over Jax's shoulder. "I do like to hammer stuff."

Addy turned a laugh into a sneeze and Jax shut the door in Graham's face.

Chapter 10

JAX PUT HIS back against the closed door and murmured, "Bless you."

"Thanks." She grinned again, dimples flashing mercilessly.

"Having fun?" That was pure acid in his voice but he couldn't help it. He really couldn't.

Addy didn't even notice, or if she did, she didn't respond. She leaned back in his chair, crossed her legs and sighed happily. "Oh, yeah." She wore a black fleece zip-up over a plain white tee, a threadbare pair of jeans and some bright red clogs. Her curls didn't even clear the top of his big leather chair but the clean, sunny scent of her filled the air. "That kid is *adorable*."

"Adorable?" He could feel the scowl building again. "Try horny."

"Well, sure. He's, what, twenty?"

"Twenty-two."

"Give him a break, Jax. Horny is the only gear they've got at that age. That and hungry." She smiled fondly. "He was just being friendly."

"Friendly?" The scowl broke free. "He offered to *hammer* you."

She waved that off. "Oh, for pete's sake. He did not."

"Yeah, he did. In those exact words." Jax stalked across the office and thrust a finger into her face. "And that guy outside the Wooden Spoon this morning? He *kissed* you."

"He did not."

"Yeah, he did." He stared. "He goddamn frenched you on Main Street."

"No," she said with insulting patience, "he frenched Diego's Angel."

Jax had to close his eyes to absorb that one. He'd suspected tongue action but hadn't been one hundred percent certain. Now he was. His scowl tried to give way to outright rage so he pinched the bridge of his nose. Hard.

"Jax, come on—"

He cut her off with a raised hand. "No, stop. Just stop talking, okay? I need a minute."

She didn't argue or ask why, thankfully. She just fell silent and gave him his damn minute. He took a brisk walk around his tiny office, searching for the flapping reins of his self-control. When he made it back to the desk, he thought he had it. He really thought he had himself in hand. She was still sitting in his office chair, composed and calm, though her cheeks were bright and pink. He wondered if he'd embarrassed her, then decided he couldn't worry about it. He was too busy hanging onto those reins. He just had to focus here. He had to let her smooth things over between them and go the hell away so he could get a hold of himself. Because he was close — perilously close — to scooping her out of that damn chair and showing her exactly how dangerous horny and hungry could be.

He doubted she'd give him the same pass she'd given Graham.

He leaned back against the front edge of his desk and

folded his arms tightly over his chest and said, "Okay, go ahead."

"Go ahead?"

"Apologize. You can't stand it when anybody's mad at you, especially family. You're not going to sleep at night unless we kiss and make up, so let's just get it over with."

Her cheeks flushed deeper and Jax could have bitten his own tongue off. *Kiss and make up? Jesus, Jackson. Freudian doesn't begin to cover it.*

She stood up, slowly, and for one heart-stopping moment, Jax thought maybe she'd taken that kiss-and-make-up bit literally. Hope and terror slammed into one another, shattered into confusion and left him frozen on the spot. But she didn't make a move to narrow the gap between them. She simply rose to her full five feet five inches, slapped her hands onto her hips and lifted long-suffering eyes to the ceiling.

"You know what?" she said conversationally. "I've about had it with you."

"Excuse me?"

"I've had it, Jackson. With you." She brought her gaze down to his and he felt the impact all the way to his steel-toed boots. Holy hell, Addy was angry. She was seriously pissed. He didn't know if he'd ever seen such a thing. "I have been as nice to you as I know how to be. I've excused you and explained you and forgiven you, but I've taken as much from you as I'm going to take." Her cheeks blazed now, blood-red roses in bloom, and she stamped across the two feet separating them to drive a finger into his deltoid. Oh, God, now she was touching him? "You're such a jerk."

He stared at her, mouth open, system utterly flooded with lust and shock. "I—"

"Oh, no, you just shut up. I'm talking now."

He shut up.

"I don't know what I ever did to make you hate me so much but you can just get over it, do you understand me? Your family is in crisis, Jax. *Our* family is in crisis." She poked him again. Jax sucked in a sharp breath and tried not to moan. Oh, Christ, he'd thought the dimples turned him on. Angry Addy was flat-out destroying him. She was tough and mean and laying into him like some outraged fairy princess and if she didn't stop *poking* him, he wasn't going to be responsible for his behavior.

"Yeah, that's right," she sneered, utterly misreading his blank blink. "I said *ours.* And I know that pisses you off for some unfathomable reason, that your family is somehow mine, too, but it's a fact and you can just swallow it. Because I love those people like they're my own but lord help us all, Jax, they are not quite capable of taking care of themselves. So if this situation is going to come right at all, it's up to you and me here. So I need you to stop fighting me." She jabbed him one last time for good measure. "Whatever it was I did or said or was or am that bugs you so darn much? It's time to *get over it.*"

"I—" He had to stop, clear his throat and hope like hell that she continued to hold that merciless eye contact. Because if she looked anywhere south of his belly button, the cat was out of the bag. "I don't know if I can," he said finally. Because it was true.

"Screw that." She folded her arms and glared at him with magnificent disdain. "Why not?"

He pushed a hand across his mouth, wiping away the completely inappropriate grin trying to blossom there. Because, damn, she was hot, all pissy and mean. Addison

Davis, being unrepentantly rude, right to his face. Who knew she had it in her? "It's…complicated."

"I'm pretty bright." She smiled poisonously and Jax's amusement was instantly buried under a tidal wave of lust. "Go slowly and I'll try to keep up."

Jax paused, groping helplessly for his next move. Because the only explanation that made any sense here was the bald-faced truth, and he knew it. Just like he knew he wasn't going to give it to her. Not here, not now, not like this. Hopefully not ever.

Then Matty opened the door and hesitated there, wearing a powdered sugar mustache and a soaking wet shirt. "Hey, Addy," he said. "Can I catch that ride up the hill with you now? I'm drenched. And dirty. Which reminds me—" He shifted seamlessly from put-out kid to sarcastic semi-adult. "—thanks for the fantastic afternoon, Jax."

Jax gave that a magnanimous wave, his eyes pinned to Addy. She treated him to one more beat of that razor-blade smile — Shirley Temple in a smoking rage — then shifted to Matty and let the dimples bloom for real. Oh, Christ. She was killing him.

"Of course," she said to the kid. "That's why I'm here." She turned back to Jax with ill-concealed malevolence and the dimples died. "Mostly."

"Mostly?" Matty stepped over to the waste basket and began to wring out the hem of his shirt. Jax, grateful for the distraction, opened a desk drawer with his boot heel, pulled out a fresh t-shirt and tossed it Matty's way. Grabbed one for himself while he was at it.

Addy said, "I also came to ask your brother to dinner at Hill Top House."

Jax stopped, the fresh shirt balled in his hands. "You

did?"

She treated him to that furious smile again while Matty wrestled free of his dirty shirt. "I did. I have something I want to discuss with the family and thought it would be easier if everybody heard it at once."

"Oh." Jax didn't look away from Addy when Matty held up his shirt in question, he only hooked a thumb toward the laundry basket he kept in the corner for just such occasions. Matty launched it in for an easy two points. "I thought you wanted to talk about—"

"How rude you were to me this afternoon? No." She lifted her chin, peered regally down her cute little nose. "But if you're really attached to the idea of an apology, you could offer one."

Jax let that go without comment, mostly because he knew she was right. He'd been a jerk. But front row seats to another guy frenching her on Main Street was more than his manners could handle.

Which was not something he was willing to discuss. At all. So he kept his mouth shut and his eyes on Matty's violent struggle to put Jax's dry t-shirt on his wet body instead. It was about the right length on him, Jax noted once the kid finally got it yanked on, but about twice as wide as his skinny self could fill up. He'd have to drag the kid into the weight room with him one of these days. Nothing wrong with skinny but a man wanted to be strong. And he was pretty sure, after the kind of work Matty had shown himself capable of today, that there was a man inside the kid he could work with.

"Well?" Addy said. She had her arms folded over her jacket, that lush mouth pinched tight, one clog actually tapping the linoleum. "Are you coming to dinner or not?"

"If this is about Diego's Boob and Ass show, Matty already told me."

"It's not."

Jax blinked, surprised. "No? What then?"

She smiled, dimples barely flickering. "Come to dinner, Jackson, and find out."

He sighed, defeated. "I have to change my shirt."

"You could change a lot of things." She wrinkled her nose. "Definitely start with your shirt, though."

Three hours and one family dinner later, Addy's hands were still shaking. With fury, with terror, with remorse? She had no idea. All she knew for certain was that she'd finally unloaded on Jax, and with both barrels, too.

Not that he hadn't deserved it. He had. He totally had.

He'd thought she'd gone to the fire station to apologize. *Apologize!* And why? Because a stranger had stuck his tongue down her throat in the middle of the street? Because she'd maintained her temper and risen above? Because she'd also refrained from punching Jax's stupid lights out when he'd berated her for said rising above?

She picked up her wine glass and shot a broody glare to her right where he lounged at the foot of the table like the first born son he was. He gazed back at her with the same watchful equanimity he'd maintained from appetizers straight through dessert and said, "So, Addison. I understand you have something you want to discuss with the family?"

He sounded so indulgent and patient, like she was an overtired toddler instead of a dangerously angry woman. She set her wine down before she tossed it in his sanctimonious face.

"In fact, I do."

"Oh boy," said Georgie from her left and took possession of Addy's wine glass.

On her right, Jax's brows went up. "Would you like more wine, Georgie?"

"I might," she said and knocked back a slug. "Let me finish Addy's first."

"Any reason Addy shouldn't drink her own wine?"

"She doesn't need it as much as I do. Not if this big idea of hers involves Granny Nan's nasty old house and Willa Zinc."

His eyes flew back to Addy. "This is about Davis Place?"

"And Willa Zinc?" Bianca asked sharply from the head of the table.

Addy looked to Jax and sighed. "You should probably just pass them the bottle."

"Gracious," Bianca said and sat back. Jax got up in silence and refilled his mother's glass. Wisely, he left the bottle between her and Georgie.

"Uh oh." Across the table, Matty looked up from the mountain of pie he was plowing through with dedicated devotion. "Okay, so before you all come completely unglued—"

"Nobody's coming unglued," Jax said with a stern look for his mother and returned to his seat.

"They always come unglued about Willa Zinc," Matty pointed out.

"Not this time," Jax said with an implacable serenity that brooked no argument. Addy clamped her molars together and Georgie belted back some more wine.

Matty gave that a beat of doubtful silence. "Okay, then,

so before you all engage in a productive and calm discussion about Willa Zinc like the rational adults you so clearly are, can I have my birth certificate?"

Bianca went still for the space of two heartbeats. She might've been carved from marble. Addy stared, concerned. "Your birth certificate?" Bianca asked, her lips as pale as her cheeks.

"Yeah." Matty scooped up a massive spoonful of apple pie and melty ice cream. It was a testament to the riot going on in Addy's stomach that she wasn't even jealous.

"What on earth for?"

"Coach is taking us to see the Winnipeg Whiteouts this summer."

Bianca blinked. "The Winnipeg what now?"

"Whiteouts." Matty swallowed heroically. "You know, the professional lacrosse team? Coach used to play for them." He shoveled in another enormous bite of pie and spoke around it. "He's putting together a field trip for the team. We get to go into the locker room and meet the players and everything. Even do a practice on their field."

"You need a birth certificate to meet the Winnipeg whatevers?" Bianca asked.

"Whiteouts. And yes, you do, because it's in Winnipeg." Matty tipped his dish and scraped up the last bit of melted ice cream. "Which is in Canada."

"I'm aware."

"So I need a passport."

"But you're under eighteen. And it's Canada. You don't need a passport to get into Canada, for heaven's sake."

Matty shrugged. "Coach says we do."

Jax said, "He might, actually." He met his mother's sharp glance and said simply, "9/11."

"Coach says we have to have them because we're not traveling with our parents. I guess the paperwork takes forever which means the application was due, like, yesterday. So do I have one?"

"A birth certificate? Of course you have one." Bianca waved an irritable hand. "You were born, weren't you?"

"That's the assumption." Matty waited a beat. "So where is it?"

"Around here somewhere." Bianca seemed to shake off whatever had gripped her for a minute there. She lifted her wine glass for a long swallow. "I'll have to look for it."

"But I can go, right?" Matty set down his spoon and leaned in. "On the field trip?"

"This field trip that I've seen no documentation for, and have received no communication whatsoever about from any responsible adult?" Bianca asked, brows rising. "That field trip?"

Matty's mouth went hard, and Addy's stomach pitched. Oh, she hated seeing Diego on her beloved boy's face. "There was an email."

"An email." Bianca rolled her eyes. "Of course there was."

Matty shoved to his feet. "I'll go print it out for you."

"You do that," Bianca murmured into her wine glass. Georgie nudged the bottle a few inches closer to her mother's elbow.

"Addy?" Jax said when Matty had stomped from the room. His eyes were dark on her, and more unreadable than usual. "You might want to hop in here. Before the discussion gets any more adult and rational on us."

"Right." She linked her fingers together on the tablecloth in front of her. "Georgie's right, about Davis Place *and*

Willa Zinc."

"Crap," Georgie breathed and took the wine bottle back.

"I don't see what one has to do with the other," Bianca said.

"I'm getting there." She paused, pulled in a fortifying breath and said, "Okay, so as we've discussed, you need an income stream."

Georgie lifted her replenished glass. "May Jason Bloom rot in hell and his hair model go bald."

"Amen," Bianca murmured.

"Your investments will recover," Addy said, "given time and room to breathe. But this means you'll need to be disciplined about your spending for at least the next five years, if not ten. Or longer. And since you'll want to reinvest your gains until you've built your holdings back up, you need an income stream independent from your investments."

"An independent income stream," Bianca repeated cautiously.

"A job," Jax translated, his eyes on Addy. "She means you need a job."

Georgie drank.

Bianca blinked. "But I thought you were opposed to that teaching position at the university."

"I'm opposed to a move," Addy said. "But I think you should definitely consider teaching."

"What, locally? Where?" She shuddered. "And please don't say the high school."

"I wasn't going to. I think you should teach at Davis Place."

Chapter 11

SILENCE. THICK, CONFUSED silence. Jax watched the color rush into Addy's cheeks, and wondered what the hell she was talking about.

"It has massive potential as a high-end bed and breakfast for artsy amateurs," she said quickly. "Davis Place does. And I think we should renovate it into exactly that." She turned a high-beam smile on Bianca. "Especially if you, the woman who trained Diego Davis, agreed to teach there."

It took Jax a couple seconds to recover his powers of speech.

"That," he said finally, "is the most ridiculous thing I've ever heard."

"That's what I said." Georgie spoke mournfully into her empty glass.

"You want to turn Davis Place into a bed and breakfast?" Bianca asked slowly.

"For aspiring artists, yes," Addy said, and held out staying hands. "Now I know it sounds crazy, but hear me out. I really think this can work. I haven't drawn up a formal proposal or anything yet but—"

Matty stomped back into the room, a piece of paper in his fist. He slapped it down beside his mother's plate. "There you go," he said. "Documentation, right in your inbox."

"My inbox?" Bianca turned slowly, and looked up at him. "Since when do you have access to *my* inbox?"

Matty froze, and Jax thought *Oh, hell, kid. You have no poker face.* And he didn't. He shot Jax a panicked look that only served to underscore the vast canyon between him and their dead brother. Because while Diego's eyes had been a deep, dark brown that concealed everything, Matty's were a gun-metal gray that revealed everything. And the funny thing was, nobody knew where they'd come from. If Jax wanted to see Diego's eyes, all he had to do was look down the table at his mother. Georgie's were the same brilliant blue as their father's had been, and his father's before him. Jax's own were an ordinary hazel, and he could thank Granny Nan for that, but Matty's silvery eyes were a family mystery. It was the only mysterious thing about him, though, because holy hell, the kid could not lie. Not with those eyes.

"I, uh—" He started, but Bianca cut him off with a sharp hand.

"Matisse. You hacked into my email program?"

He collected himself enough to roll those transparent eyes. "Right. First I'm an artistic genius, and now I'm a computer hacker? Make up your mind, Mom. Which superpower are we going with?"

"The one that explains your ability to print out my emails." She smiled without teeth, a close-lipped threat. "I'd like to hear more about that one."

"What the crap, Mom. Your password to everything is *DIEGO.* All caps. It doesn't take a genius." He shoved both hands into his pockets and scowled. "So can I have my birth certificate now?"

Bianca picked up the paper, fished a pair of bright blue cheaters out of her hair and inspected it. "This trip is scheduled for the week before Devil Days."

"So?"

"So you can't leave town the week before the new show! It's going to require an enormous amount of work from all of us, but especially from you."

"From me?" Matty went still.

Bianca ignored him and smiled at Jax. "I've decided to bring out Diego's early work."

"The Boob and Ass period," Georgie said helpfully.

Jax sighed. "Yeah, I heard."

"I'd like to do a chronological layout, like at the Van Gogh museum in Amsterdam," Bianca mused. "When the viewer progresses through the journey alongside the artist, it allows him to truly appreciate each incremental step forward. And it makes those sudden leaps of ability and insight all the more stunning."

He shot a look at Addy, who lifted helpless shoulders and made *what-can-you-do* eyes at him. "Not sure it's the best idea you've ever had."

Bianca only smiled. "It isn't art if it doesn't challenge the viewer, Jax." She shifted her gaze to Matty, who hunched automatically, as if protecting his internal organs. "And it should definitely challenge the artist. Which is why we'll also be displaying your work right next to your brother's."

He folded into his chair slowly, those silvery-gray eyes blank with terror and pinned to his mother.

"I know." Bianca patted his elbow calmly. "I can't believe I didn't think of it earlier either."

Jax stared at his mother, at the manic light in those dark eyes that said she was attached, firmly and irrationally, to this idea.

What the crap, he thought wearily. Just…what the crap.

"Oh, don't look so terrified." Bianca smiled warmly at Matty. "I know you can't support an entire show just now." She leaned forward urgently, laid her hand over his on the tablecloth. "But the potential in your canvases is so enormous, so raw. It would be a crime not to put them, to put *you*, in your rightful place next to your brother."

Jax had no idea if she was right. All he knew was that the kid was practically vibrating in his chair, the rage and helplessness rising off him like smoke from a house fire. He glanced at Addy and found her gazing at his younger brother with a tender sorrow that took his breath away. Addy loved the kid, loved him with everything in her. He knew that, and had never doubted the sincerity of her attachment. But that sorrow, that aching grief he sometimes caught in her eyes when she looked at him? That was for Diego.

And that was Jax's sorrow to bear, wasn't it?

Bianca gazed at Matty and said, "If we can come up with even three or four canvases to hang alongside the work Diego was doing at your age, I think it'll be an enormous draw. And, not coincidentally, it'll be exactly the money maker Addy says we need right now." Addy watched, horror-struck and mute, as Bianca reached out a single reverent finger, and drew it down the edge of Matty's cheek bone. "Nobody will be able to deny the likeness."

"Nobody's even trying," Jax pointed out, and if Addy had been capable of speech, she'd have cheered. She herself had been an utterly unnecessary accessory to her own parents, one more bit of baggage they dragged from one job site to the next, and dutifully made arrangements for. Like an elderly cat, or a hideous heirloom. She'd always thought being unnecessary to her own family the worst thing that could happen to a kid. Now she wondered if the opposite weren't just as bad. If not worse.

"But I'm sorry to say that it'll make this—" Bianca moved that finger to the paper on the tablecloth between them, to Matty's hopes for a summer field trip with his team. "—very difficult."

He lifted his eyes to hers, and they were full of grim realization. "You're saying no."

"I'm not saying no." Bianca arched a brow. "But you know our position just now. If we're going to keep our lifestyle—" She paused, cast a significant glance around the bright, airy space that was Hill Top House's formal dining room. "—intact, we'll all need to make some sacrifices, you included. I know it isn't fair, but that's simply life right now, and this is something only you can do for us. You'll need to focus, darling. Perhaps apply yourself a bit more?"

"I could apply myself," Georgie murmured. Addy frowned and turned to her, wondering what on earth *that* meant but Matty shoved his chair back with an abrupt jerk.

"Like I haven't been *trying?*" He dropped those bony elbows to his knees and sneered at his boots. "Like I've been withholding a masterpiece just to piss you off?"

"I'll admit, I've started to consider the possibility." Bianca leaned back and inspected her youngest son with narrowed eyes. "If you put even half the effort into your oils, for example, as you do into those ridiculous superheroes of yours—"

"Maybe it's time," Georgie said to nobody. Addy didn't even look at her this time. The smile Matty sent his mother was too fierce, and the pain and anger simmering underneath caught in her throat like tears.

"Yeah but there's the thing," Matty said. "I like superheroes. I don't like *art*." He gave the word exactly his mother's customary undertone of reverence but with a layer of disdain smeared over the top.

"Don't you dare!" Bianca shot to her feet. "Don't you dare *smirk*. You have the kind of world-class talent most artists will work their entire lives just to glimpse. And why? Because you were born with it. Because you're a Davis, and it came with your blood. Because you're lucky, almost impossibly so, and I'll be damned if I'll allow you to toss it over because it doesn't interest you." She spun away, as if she couldn't bear to look at him. "Don't be a child, Matisse."

"Maybe, maybe," Georgie said, apparently still engrossed in the conversation she was having with herself. "Hmm." Addy ignored her and watched Matty.

Matty said nothing. Nobody did. Bianca's temper was fast and furious but never long-lived and she'd already been raging longer than usual. A weepy collapse and a remorseful return to reason was due any second now. Or so Addy devoutly hoped.

"It's just…" Bianca broke off and pressed trembling fingers to her closed eyes. "I know talent when I see it, that's all." She released a long breath and her shoulders wilted. "And when it slaps me in the face, I have a hard time not taking it seriously. I saw it in Diego, and I see it now in my baby. My Matisse." She came back to the table, drew her chair to face Matty's and sat. She was close enough to touch him, though she didn't. "I've been seeing it since you drew your first caped crusader."

"I'm not Diego, Mom." He muttered it, refused to look up and Addy wanted to fling her arms around him. "I look like him but I'm not—"

"—him. Oh, darling, you're not. I know that." She came out of her chair, went to her knees and took Matty's clenched fists in her hands. "Matty, you're better."

"I'm *what*?" His head shot up, his eyes wild and terrified.

"Better." Bianca gave a delighted laugh and squeezed his hands. "I know I'm hard on you but it's only because what you're producing now is miles ahead of where Diego was at your age." She rocked back, a breathless joy lighting her face, making her beauty incandescent. Addy stared, concern giving way to outright dismay. Grief was making her delusional. Matty was a child. He wasn't *Diego*, for heaven's sake.

"What he had?" Bianca went on. "What was in him? It's in you, too. But *more*."

No. Addy's heart flat-out rejected it. But she knew better than to contradict her mother-in-law when she was like this. She just had to hope Matty had the strength to endure this little scene and trust that she and Jax would never let this happen to him.

"Mom, no. I'm not—" He stopped, his breath whistling like he was having an asthma attack though he'd never had an asthmatic moment in his life, so far as Addy knew.

"You *are*. I can see it there, just under the surface. It's so close, but you're blocking it. You're afraid." She put her forehead against his, closed her eyes and breathed him in. "You're a good boy, Matty. You're just afraid."

"Mom, no," he said again. He reared back, shot huge petrified eyes toward Addy, then Jax. "I'm not him. You want me to be him but I'm not. I'm just—"

"A child." Bianca pushed up to sit on the edge of her chair again, her eyes shining. "A frightened child. But we can work through fear, Matisse. With proper motivation, we can turn that fear into something spectacular. Something that'll rock the art world on its axis." She beamed. "And a showing is just the motivation you need."

Chapter 12

MATTY GAZED AT his mother for a long, taut moment. Addy didn't breathe, didn't blink. Finally he said, "Mom, are you insane? You can't do this!"

"Why not?"

He leaned in urgently, elbows on his frantically bouncing knees. "Because *I can't paint*."

"Of course you can, darling." Bianca waved this away, her remorse shifting to confidence in a blink. Addy, dizzy from the speed of it, gave her head a little shake. "He *can*," Bianca told her, obviously mistaking her bafflement for resistance. "And he will." She shifted back to Matty. "We have nearly three months until Devil Days. Three properly motivated months. We'll have to work like hell, of course. All of us. But we can do it."

Lord help them all, she looked happy about it. Eyes shining, hands clasped, she looked positively delighted.

"Wait, do what?" Georgie asked, checking into the conversation for the first time in minutes.

"Feed Matty to the tourists," Jax said grimly.

"Introduce Matty's work to Diego's fans," Bianca correctly easily. "To the people who loved him." She beamed at Matty. "Just like they're going to love you."

Matty gazed back, evidently beyond words. It was, Addy

figured, the best opening she was going to get.

"Bianca." She cleared her throat. "I completely agree that Matty's extraordinary." She tried for a smile, because it was the truth. She loved that kid. "He's amazing. But he's thirteen. Talent aside, it's a squirrelly age. Hormones, lacrosse sticks, comic books—"

"Graphic novels," Matty growled.

"—and whatnot." She shrugged vaguely to fill in the teenager blanks. "He's supposed to be difficult just now. And on the off chance that, because of that, we have to postpone his triumphant debut for a year or two—"

"We won't," Bianca said firmly.

"Understood." Addy amped up her smile and twisted slippery fingers together in her lap. "But just in case, don't you think we should develop some alternative solutions to this cash flow crisis?"

"Like your Davis Place idea?"

"Exactly," Addy said, relieved.

"It's a lovely idea, darling. And I have every confidence you can make it work." Bianca's smile was diamond-hard. "But if I'm understanding you correctly, we need an influx of cash now, not next year or whenever Davis Place will be open for business."

"Well, a lot depends on the contractors but—"

"—but Matty's debut will bring us the influx we need much, much sooner. And even if it didn't, I would still be absolutely committed to it. If you want to pursue the Davis Place project, I have no objection. We can discuss my teaching duties once the showing is behind us."

"But—"

"But nothing. This showing is going forward. I have an obligation, Addy. This is my son, and he has a rare gift.

What kind of mother would I be if I allowed him to squander it on comic books and lacrosse? He's uniquely positioned to both preserve the family tradition and further the legend. I agree he's young. I wish it could be otherwise but fate has chosen to offer him his chance sooner rather than later." She shifted those dark eyes to her son. "Which means that play time is over, Matisse. You need to get your head around this, and quickly."

"Actually, I don't." Matty shook his head on a half-laugh that sounded more like a suppressed sob to Addy, and stood up. "I really don't. You're the grown ups." He jerked a shoulder that encompassed the dining room table and everybody at it. "You figure it out. I'm out of here."

He spun on one heel and stalked savagely out of the dining room. He disappeared through the arched entrance to the great room, and moments later, the back door crashed shut. Addy's lungs inflated suddenly and she realized she'd been holding her breath.

She shot to her feet but for the second time in a week, Jax snagged her elbow, and suddenly her butt was planted on the arm of his chair.

"Let him go, Addy."

"Are you kidding me?" She stared at him, stunned, her throat aching. "Thirteen-year-olds don't make dramatic exits to be left alone, Jax. They do it for the attention. And not the kind of attention you get from an art show, for heaven's sake!"

"Are you questioning my parenting, Addison?" Bianca's voice was icy and cracked like a whip in the stillness.

"Somebody has to," Jax said pleasantly. "Because, yikes, you are *deep* in crazy town on this. If Addy doesn't want to question your parenting, I will."

"Great," Addy said. "You do that. I'm going after Matty." She tried to push to her feet but found — to her astonishment — Jax's hand on her thigh, keeping her firmly planted. He caught her furious gaze and lowered his voice. "I've got this, Addy. Trust me?"

She gazed at him for a long moment, then realized she did trust him. No matter how much she resented him, no matter how much he pissed her off, Jax fixed stuff. He took care. And he loved his brother, no question. She gave him a reluctant nod, and he took his hand back.

"Okay, so let's assume for the moment that Matty's out back, punching trees and otherwise reconciling himself to his fate in a very manly fashion." Something about the way he said it suggested to Addy that Jax wasn't reconciled to anything where Matty was concerned, and the burn of her anger toward him abated a few degrees more. "Why don't we amuse ourselves while he's doing that listening to Addy's grand plan for Davis Place?"

"I wouldn't mind hearing more about this myself," Bianca allowed, magnanimous in her triumph. Georgie simply lounged across her chair and blinked lazily into the archway through which Matty had disappeared.

"Addy?" Jax prompted.

"Right." She blew out a breath and reeled her aching heart in from the backyard where Matty was presumably punching those trees. "Okay, sure. I have the numbers if you want to see them but the basic idea is to make Davis Place over into a bed and breakfast for amateur artists."

Bianca shuddered. "It's such a mausoleum."

"Hell of a view, though," Jax said, and leaned back in his chair.

"Exactly." Addy grinned down at him, and realized —

with a thrill of alarm — that she was still sitting on the arm of his chair for heaven's sake. She rose hastily and went back to her own chair. "I stood there in that ugly old house today, looking through those ridiculous little windows while the Devil River did its kamikaze thing into the lake and I thought to myself *only here*, you know? Only here, in this place, in this town, in this house, could you get a view like that." She made a frame of her hands. "A view that makes even people like me want to paint."

The back door banged open abruptly and Addy heard Matty stomp back into the house. She shot forward in her seat but then he stomped back out and the door banged shut again. She glanced at Jax, who shook his head at her. *Not yet.* She sighed.

"The view up there is quite something," Bianca said as if nothing had happened. "Diego used to paint up there for hours when he was Matty's age. For days. I have dozens upon dozens of those canvases in storage somewhere. I thought about hanging a few of them here but I—" She broke off, pulled in a breath and smiled crookedly. "Well, I haven't looked at them in years."

"But the fact that he found so much to paint there just goes to my point," Addy said. "That place, that particular view, has a unique power. A transcendence that speaks to everybody from your artistic geniuses to your drop-out mathletes. It also has an enormous, empty house standing on it, unkempt but solid. We're talking six rooms on the upper story — all with natural light and killer views — and the space to accommodate a commercial kitchen below. So I asked myself, what would people pay for the chance to spend a weekend with the view that inspired Diego Davis? What would they pay, I further asked myself, for the chance to paint that view under the tutelage of Bianca Davis herself?"

Jax said, "Serious art students aren't going to train at a bed and breakfast, Addison. Doesn't matter who's running it."

"I'm not talking about serious art students," Addy returned. "There are schools and programs for them. I'm thinking of an older demographic, middle-aged to retirement. People at the stage of life where you start to regret missed opportunities, and to wonder about the road not taken. People who've been sensible their whole lives but are hungry for a taste of transcendence, and can finally afford to buy themselves a little."

"A little transcendence?" He gazed at her, his eyes dark and shuttered. "Or a little Diego? What exactly are you proposing to sell here?"

"Opportunity." Addy held that gaze and didn't flinch. Why would she? She'd been enduring Jax's disapproval for years. "The chance to stand where Diego stood, to paint what he painted and be critiqued by his teacher. He was a great artist, Jax. Probably the greatest of his generation. It comes with a mystique, and it's an asset we haven't done nearly enough to monetize."

Jax's face went hard. "I know the family's hard up for cash, Addy, but I draw the line at selling artsy fairy dust to unfulfilled senior citizens with more money than sense."

"Heaven's sakes, Jax, listen to yourself." Bianca laughed. "She's not proposing we sell junk bonds to the vulnerable elderly. She's talking about offering well-to-do art lovers the chance to paint. And what's wrong with that? Just because a talent isn't world-class doesn't make it worthless. Beauty enriches us all. If people feel a call to create — or even just try to create — why shouldn't they?"

"Thank you!" Addy punched a finger toward Bianca, then turned back to Jax. "*That's* what we're selling. Not a guaranteed masterpiece, just permission to try for one. So many people never even *try*, Jax. They're sensible and prudent and they save and invest and send their kids to college but that thing inside them that responds to beauty, that goes breathless at a stunning view? The part that loves, unreasonably and without caution? It goes hungry their whole lives. All I'm offering them is the chance to finally feed it, to pursue the dream. To dream at all." She caught herself and paused. A little too passionate for a business proposal, she realized, and dialed herself back. "People are just so afraid," she said, more lightly. "When they're finally ready to take a chance, to dream for real? To admit what they've always wanted and finally, finally reach for it? We can be there for them. We can help, and that's not just a money-grab. That's a worthy endeavor, and I'd be proud to be part of it. The question is, will you?" She looked around the table. "Will any of you?"

"Of course," Bianca said warmly. "Goodness, that you even have to ask!"

"I'll do my bit," Georgie said cryptically and Addy wondered what exactly *her bit* might be, but was distracted by the evil grin that slid across her perfect face as she turned toward her brother. "But what about you, Jax?"

"What about me?"

That grin grew. "Are you finally ready to take the chance? To reach for the dream?"

He didn't answer, only shifted his gaze to Addy and let several beats of considering silence pile up.

"Well?" Addy asked finally. "Are you in or not?"

Her heart beat uncomfortably and she realized suddenly that she wanted him to believe in this. To believe in her. She wanted him on her side, and desperately. But why? Why was his approval so excruciatingly important? He opened his mouth and her heart crawled into her throat in anticipation of rejection.

Then the back yard exploded. Or something did. Something huge enough and close enough that the floor literally rumbled underneath her.

"What the hell?" Georgie yelped, clawing herself upright. "What was *that*?"

There weren't a lot of answers to that particular question, Addy knew. Hill Top House was the sole occupant of an exclusive and very expensive chunk of bluff-top real estate overlooking the lake. If something enormous had just exploded nearby there were only a few possibilities: The carriage house. Joe's old kiln. A vehicle.

But that wasn't what turned her heart to stone in her chest.

"Oh good lord," she breathed, panic shoving her to her feet. "*Matty*."

Chapter 13

JAX WAS ON his feet before the floor stopped trembling. Addy was faster, though. Figure that. The rest of the family sat stunned, blinking at each other in the hollow silence the blast left behind, but Addy had already shot out of the dining room like an Olympic sprinter.

He snatched up his cell phone and dialed dispatch even as he raced after her. He ran through the foyer and out the open back door, skidded to a halt at the porch railing. He stared in horror at the carriage house, at the flames roaring from its roof, streaking high into the dark sky. His gut screamed for him to get to Matty and Addison — wherever the hell they were — but training was stronger than panic. He bolted instead for the mini-pumper which he'd parked nose-out at the far edge of the circle, poised as always for a quick get away.

Even as adrenaline stole his thoughts and lit up his brain, he yanked open the side compartment to retrieve a drop kit and an oxygen canister. He suited up with steady, automatic hands even as he and the dispatcher went back and forth in the staccato shorthand that had become his second language.

Trucks en route, paramedics responding. Thank Christ. But the truck from Hornby Harbor was eighteen miles out and his own staff was all volunteer. Which meant a scramble out of a day job and into firefighter mode. Which meant he could be on his own for the next two minutes or for the next fifteen.

Fifteen minutes was an eternity when it came to fire.

He'd do what he could. And he wouldn't think, wouldn't feel, wouldn't panic until it was over.

He glanced at his mother and Georgie behind him on the veranda, staring at the flames, eyes huge, mouths open. Bianca ran down the steps to him as he fastened his helmet. He took — wasted? — a precious moment to snap, "Stay here. Both of you." But he looked only at his mother. She was the one he had to convince. He stabbed a finger toward the house. "Get on that porch and stay there until I or a uniform tells you otherwise." He leaned in, pinned her with a hard stare. "Don't screw with me on this, Mom. Understand?"

She snapped her mouth shut, nodded once and went back to the porch.

Jax turned his back on her, threw an axe over his shoulder and ran toward the fire.

Addy stood frozen in the line of giant pines behind the blazing carriage house. Oily black smoke poured into the sky, clogging her throat and burning her nose. She panted through her mouth — lord, the *smell* — and squinted at the flames sprouting from the shingles. A white metal sphere squatted right in the heart of the blaze, ripped open and vomiting up a geyser of flames like some kind of hellish egg. Good heavens, was that a *propane tank*? How on earth had a propane tank ended up on top of the carriage house?

There were a limited number of answers to that question, too, but if pressed, she'd say it probably had something to do with Matty, his air rifle and the row of old propane tanks that had been peacefully rusting behind the garage for as long as she'd been in Devil's Kettle. Especially given the way the kid was sprawled at the base of a massive pine tree, the gun still cradled in his arms.

She ran to him as he wobbled to his feet, blessedly whole and healthy if dirty and shocked.

"Matty!" She snatched him into her arms and hugged him fiercely. His collar bone was a sharp ridge under her cheek and the stock of the gun poked into her stomach. She drew back to look into his dear, dirty face. "Are you all right? What happened?"

He stared blankly past her to the fire that waved and undulated on the roof like prairie grass on a windy day. "The turkeys came back. I got my—" He broke off. Jiggled the air rifle in his hands. "And then—" He shook his head. "Oh my God, Addy. The *garage*."

She followed his gaze over her shoulder to the carriage house. "It's just stuff, Matty," she said. "You're safe, and that's all that—"

Matters. She was going to say *you're all that matters* but horrified realization stopped the words in her throat. He *was* all that mattered, she told herself. Keeping him safe, keeping him happy, giving him the chance to grow up like a normal kid and not Diego 2.0? That was the most important thing here, and she'd go to war for it if she had to. But love didn't win wars; ammunition did. And hers was burning down with the carriage house.

"Okay, I want you to stay here." She gave him a little shake and waited until his eyes drifted to hers. "*Matty*. Stay here. Got it?"

His Adam's apple bobbed and he said, "Stay here. Got it." His knees folded and he planted his butt on the ground, skinny arms draped over his knees, chin on his forearms, gun on his lap as he stared at the rapidly disappearing roof.

She eyed the flaming shingles herself, then squinted at the carriage house's back door now hanging drunkenly on its hinges. She had no idea what the ramifications were, structurally speaking, of a flaming propane tank being catapulted onto a garage roof. The shingles were disappearing at an alarming rate, but so far the interior looked relatively flame-free.

Good thing, too, because she was going in there.

She said a brief prayer — she didn't know to whom — then bolted inside before she could think better of it.

It was dark and oppressively hot but she could still see the cars under a greasy blanket of smoke at the far end of the space, nearest the rolling doors. The fourth stall — Joe's once upon a time — had been allowed to catch all the household junk for the better part of fourteen years, and that was where Addy raced. Fire clawed at the ceiling above her. She could hear it even if she couldn't see it yet, gnawing and smacking its lips on the roof like some ravenous beast trying to eat its way inside. Panic made her hands fast and slippery as she shoved some old lumber aside and hurdled a tool box. Or tried to. It caught the toe of her clog and dropped her to one knee. Pain radiated all the way up to her hip, bright and hot as the fire above. It was noticeably cooler there on the floor, though, so she didn't bother getting up.

She scrabbled ahead on her hands and knees, toward the stack of old doors leaning tip-tilted against the far wall. She reached them and leapt to her feet, tore at them with shaking hands. She threw them to the ground one by one until finally she found it sandwiched between a couple of old closet doors — the plain brown folio that held her own personal hell. The ugliest thing she'd ever encountered, experienced or — God help her — owned. Diego's version of an insurance policy. His last little joke on her.

The beast on the roof tore through the ceiling with a roar and she cried out as flames raced hungrily along the beams above her. Sparks showered down, melted holes in her fleece jacket and stung her arms and shoulders. Smoke poured in like a flood, shoved the breath from her body and stole her sense of direction. Panic replaced the oxygen in her aching lungs but she clutched the oversized folio to her chest, guessed for the door and ran.

She crashed headlong into something solid and unyielding. Her knees tried to fold in blind terror and then she recognized Jax. She'd run straight into the brick wall of his chest. Gratitude rushed through her in a wave so intense she went the rest of the way to her knees. Jax dropped the muscular axe over his shoulder and caught her by the upper arms. He yanked her upright, his eyes wild and furious behind a light plastic mask. He didn't bother speaking, just snatched the folio from her hands and ripped open his coat. He spread the fire-proof jacket like a great sheltering wing and shoved her under it. Then she was cool and safe, her nose filled with hot plastic and that delicious Jax-smell she'd only recently discovered but already equated with safety.

She stumbled but it didn't matter. She knew he wouldn't let her fall, and he didn't.

Jax hauled ass away from the burning garage, Addy nestled against his side like something newborn and fragile. He doubted her feet hit the ground more than once or twice as he dragged her toward the mini-pumper at a forced march, but he didn't care. The sight of those brave shoulders and that curly head disappearing into a burning building had unleashed within him a terror the likes of which he'd never even imagined. And he was pretty familiar with terror, given that he did burning buildings for a living.

But he'd found her. Thank God, he'd found her. And the instant she was in his arms — warm, sweet, alive — he'd discovered a gratitude as astounding as his terror. The kind of gratitude that tried to close his throat, unstring his knees, open his heart. He wanted to laugh, to shout, to roar. Because holy hell, she was everything that mattered, and she was *alive*.

And now that he knew it, he was going to kill her.

He nodded tersely to his crew, to the men he'd known most of his life who'd dropped everything and raced up the hill to save his family's garage.

"Anybody else in there?" Mason asked. They'd brought the big rig, and he and Frank were wrestling a hose into place while Graham clambered to the top of the engine to position the floodlights.

He didn't trust himself to speak yet so he just waved a flat hand in front of his face shield, giving them the all-clear. He glanced at the veranda where his mother and Georgie were clucking over Matty. The boy sat on the porch swing between them, his eyes blank and a little shocky. He shot to his feet when he saw Jax, scattering the women like autumn leaves, a question urgent on his face. Jax gave him a brief thumbs up and relief hit the kid in a visible wave. He sagged back down onto the swing in a boneless heap. Bianca flew to his side, put her arm around him and murmured into his hair. Georgie headed for the porch steps, though, murder in her wide-awake eyes.

Oh, hell, no. Nobody was going to yell at Addy right now but him.

Jax stabbed a furious finger at the porch. *Stay.*

Georgie froze, startled, but she stayed.

Jax marched Addy to the far edge of the circle and stopped by the mini-pumper. They weren't as far from the fire as he'd like but Mason and Frank already had the first stream of foam arcing onto the roof with a sizzling howl. He could see the porch from here, too, so he could keep an eye on the rest of the family if they decided to get into yet more trouble. A fresh wave of fury tried to overtake him but he shoved it down. He'd deal with Matty later. With his mom. With all of them. Right now, though, he had to shout Addy out of her goddamn death wish.

He peeled open his coat and she blinked up at him like a baby bird, all giant eyes, loopy curls, and shaking hands. His own hands were none too steady, he realized grimly.

"Can you stand on your own?" he asked gruffly.

She didn't answer but she didn't buckle to the gravel when he stepped away, either. He propped the over-sized folio he'd taken from her against the mini-pumper, then pulled off his gloves, jacket and face shield. Procedure, he reminded himself. Protocol. Rules. They existed for a reason. So he piled his gear neatly on the ground, then took her by the shoulders and dipped his head to check her pupils.

Equal and reactive, thank God, but he was shocked at how fragile the bones of her shoulders felt under his cupped palms. He'd spent years noticing everything about her whether he wanted to or not. How had he missed the fact that the girl was built like a damn china doll?

Fury drained away, leaving him hollowed out and weary. Worried.

"Addy, hey. Right here. Look at me. Are you all right?"

"Jax?" She blinked one more time then her mossy green eyes finally focused. "Oh, hey, Jax. Matty blew up the carriage house."

"Yeah. I saw."

"I had to go in."

Fresh terror swirled through him, anger right behind it. "Not sure I agree with you on that one."

"You saved me."

"Well, I couldn't let you die. I'm planning to kill you later."

Her dimples flickered. "For being stupid?"

"For giving me a goddamn heart attack."

"A heart attack?" That seemed to confuse her, and he blinked at her, startled. He'd kept her at arm's length, sure, but did she really think he wouldn't care if she *died*? "I'm sorry, Jax. I didn't mean to—"

"Shut up, Addison."

"Oh, but I—"

He hauled her into his arms. Just yanked her right into his chest and nestled his chin into the wild chop of her hair. It took all his concentration to breathe through the vicious ache of gratitude in his throat and the mortifying sting of tears in his eyes. Because, God, he could have lost her today. She could have died but here she was in his arms instead, whole, healthy, and beautifully, gorgeously alive. Smoke and sunshine filled his nostrils and the soft, warm weight of her filled his arms and all he could think was *finally*. Oh, God, finally.

He'd never before regretted fighting what he felt for Addy. It was pretty clear she was happy playing Diego's Angel, and he had better things to do than tilt at windmills. Or so he'd told himself. But in that throat-closing moment of pure terror when he'd watched her disappear into the gaping black mouth of their burning garage, he regretted with every cell in his body that he had no idea whether her dimples were as soft as they looked. He'd kept his hands to himself for four long years, and why? Loyalty to his brother at first, then later respect for Addy's grief. Okay, fine. But lately? Habit. And maybe to keep the peace with a mother who didn't know the meaning of the word. But screw it. Life was too goddamn short.

"Jax?" She squirmed in his arms. "A little air?"

"Oh. Sorry." He forced himself to open his arms and she stepped away. He fought the urge to snatch her up again. "Are you okay?"

"Yeah. I think." She held her arms out to the sides and inspected them, as if her eyes could tell her something her nervous system couldn't. A vision of her running *toward* the fire chased itself through his mind again and when left-over terror burst into fury he let it. Fury he knew what to do with. Fear? Not so much.

"Damn it, Addison," he snapped. "What were you *thinking*?"

She looked away, her face dirty, her eyes as green as the pine forest. "I—"

"You know what? Don't bother. I know what you were thinking."

"You do?" Her eyes snapped back to his, wide and wary. "What?"

"*Nothing.* Because thinking people don't run into *burning buildings.*" He rubbed the center of his chest, as if he could settle the panicked thud of his heart with his bare hands. "What the hell was so important that you'd risk your life for it?"

She held out her hands in mute appeal, in apology, and his rage faltered. Damn, she looked fragile. All huge bruised eyes and soft pale skin. Throw in the dirty face and the loopy curls and, God, who could stay mad at Addy?

He stepped forward to take her outstretched hands but her eyes flickered just past his shoulder and he realized she wasn't reaching for him. She didn't want forgiveness. She didn't want a hug. She wasn't sorry. She was reaching for whatever she'd risked her life to pull out of the flaming garage.

"That?" Fury spiked higher inside him as he followed her gaze toward the folio. "A painting? You risked your life for a *painting*?"

Chapter 14

"PAINTINGS," ADDY SAID warily. "Plural."

"Oh, that definitely makes it better," Jax snapped. "So long as it's more than one. Dying for just one would be silly. But paintings, *plural*. Well, that's different."

Jax wasn't tall and lanky like the rest of his family. He wasn't beautiful like the rest of his family. But what he lacked in elegance he more than made up for in raw, blunt strength. In width and power and force. Addy didn't notice it that often because he was so friendly and *nice*. To other people, anyway. But she noticed it now. How could she miss it with him looming over her like an enraged angel, all hard jaw and fierce eyes? Fighting fires clearly brought out Jax's inner alpha male. Big time. Wow.

"Well, then. Let's see it, shall we?" He snatched up the folio he'd propped against the truck and went to work on the tangle of string that held it closed. "Let's see what you risked your goddamn life for, Addison."

"Don't." Her hands knotted into fists at her sides.

"Don't what?" He gave up on unwinding the string and just snapped it off. "This?"

He jerked open the flap and shoved a hand into the thin cardboard packet and Addy said, "Yes, that. Don't."

He hesitated for the first time since he'd snatched her off

her feet in the flaming garage. "Why not?"

"Because they're mine," she said desperately. "They're private."

"They're *private*?" He laughed, a sharp, startling bark. "You're going to have to do better than that, Addy. You shredded my *private* all to hell when you ran into a burning building. Why should your private get special treatment?"

"I don't want special treatment," she snapped. "I just don't want—" She broke off. "Wait, your private? How did I shred your private?"

"Because I thought you were going to die!"

She stared, open-mouthed, transfixed by the raw fury in his face. Fury and something else she had no name for but that nailed her clogs to the gravel drive and had her heart knocking inside her chest. "I didn't die," she managed. "I'm fine. Jax, I'm—"

"And it occurred to me," he interrupted grimly, "that if you died, I'd never get the chance to do this."

"Do what?"

"This."

He seized her upper arms, dragged her into that hard, hot body and kissed her.

Mercy, did he kiss her.

One big hand speared up into her hair and his hot, seeking mouth caught hers, sending her brain into a vicious tailspin. A bolt of white-hot shock ripped through her, knocking whatever was left of her reality right off its foundation.

He wound her curls around his fist and lifted her straight into the raw demand of that kiss. Shock disappeared in a mushroom cloud of nuclear heat, leaving behind the bare, bleached bones of something sharp and painful. Need?

Hunger? She hadn't felt either in so long, she wasn't sure she recognized them, or could even tell the difference. It hardly mattered, though, because her brain had barely registered need when he shifted gears.

Suddenly, that fist in her hair eased. His mouth gentled on hers. Then his tongue was tracing the inner edge of her lower lip with a deliberate relish that had goosebumps breaking out on her thighs.

An invitation, she realized on a bright flash of want. A question. For all that his hands were tangled in her hair with an unequivocal *mine*, his mouth said *please*. His mouth coaxed. Waited. Invited.

She dragged in a breath, desperate to clear her head but all she could smell was him. Soap and smoke. Coffee and wine. The scents reached out and curled sneaky, fragile tendrils around her better judgment. But where coffee smelled divine and tasted awful, Jax on her tongue was all golden shimmer and glorious promise, the kind that had appetites dead and buried lo these many years roaring back to life and demanding more.

She was still reeling under the languid assault of his mouth when he lifted his head and set her away from him. Beyond speech, she lifted a hand — a shaky hand — to her lips and blinked at him.

"I waited four years to do that," he told her darkly. "I'd have probably waited forty more. But then you tried to kill yourself and you know what I thought?"

"What?" she asked faintly.

"I thought *fuck that*." One corner of his mouth quirked up and her heart gave a funny little bump. "I decided to kiss the hell out of you while we were both still breathing and apologize later if I needed to." He lifted a brow. "Do I need to?"

"Heck if I know." She touched her lips again and tried to think but her brain just pulled a bunch of gleeful doughnuts in the outfield. "I honestly have no idea. It's been a very disorienting couple of days."

"Tell me about it." He sighed and threw a glance over his shoulder at the battle his colleagues were waging against the burning carriage house. "Listen, I should get over there." He put the folio in her hands and she clutched it to her chest with equal parts relief and astonishment.

"You're not going to look at it?"

"Not right now. Not without your permission."

"Jax—"

"Hey, you know my secret now." He gave her that bent smile again, and it sent her heart knocking against her rib cage just like the first time. "So do they." He waved a casual hand toward the veranda, where Bianca and Georgie stood on either side of Matty, staring at them with large, shocked eyes. Mason and Graham were dealing with hoses but Frank gave them a cheerful wave. Oh, boy. "When you're ready to tell me yours, you know where to find me."

She surprised herself with a laugh. "Jax, please. I've kept this secret for nearly four years, but now that your mom knows it exists?"

"You won't keep it for even four more hours, I know." He shook his head ruefully. "Well, that's family for you." He bent to retrieve his gear, flapped the gravel off his bright yellow fire-proof jacket. "Speaking of whom, get them inside, will you? And tell Mom I'll be in to kill Matty later."

"Sure," she murmured, distracted by the sight of him shrugging those big shoulders into that jacket. Disturbed, actually. Because she'd seen Jax's shoulders about a million times over the years, both with and without a shirt, let alone a jacket. They'd never before sent this hot shock of awareness skating across her nerves. Had they? She didn't think so, but then again, she'd never imagined he'd been suppressing the urge to kiss her into next week, either.

Apparently, she'd missed a few things over the years.

She hadn't missed that kiss, though. Lord, no. When Jax kissed a girl, he really *kissed* her. Good for him. She hoped he'd gotten it out of his system. *Her* system, however, was going to need a moment to catch its breath.

Which was fine. Completely understandable. But she really hoped it didn't take too much longer because a steady diet of high-octane sexual awareness between her and Jax would be…complicated. And given what she was about to do, what she was about to reveal, her life was plenty complicated already.

But she didn't look away — couldn't look away — until he disappeared behind the fire truck to join his crew.

Addy didn't know how much longer she could hold Bianca off. It had been hours since she'd led the family into the great room as instructed and laid the folio on the coffee table. Hours since she'd announced that nobody would so much as touch it until Jax joined them.

Georgie had simply shrugged and curled herself into the corner of the couch for a nice nap. Matty had thrown himself down to Georgie's right and descended into broody silence, legs stretched out, boots twitching restlessly. Bianca had taken her place on Georgie's left with queenly patience, ankles crossed, hands resting gently in her lap. But she hadn't moved her burning eyes from the folio, not for an instant.

Probably wise. If a good artist challenged the viewer, a great artist changed the viewer. And Diego had been unquestionably great. Beyond great. Which meant that this soot-smeared folio was nothing but a leash for what was inside it, and a pitiably inadequate one at that. The instant she opened it, lives were going to change irrevocably.

You didn't turn your back on such a thing, not ever.

The back door finally opened and Jax's bootfalls shattered the silence.

"Thank God," Bianca muttered and shot to her feet. "Jackson—"

He didn't even pause. He simply walked past his mother, one hand lifted like a stop sign.

"Shower," he said. "Then questions." He hit the stairs at a weary jog, but aimed a finger at Matty as he went. "As for you—" He bared his teeth in what might've passed for a smile. On a mountain lion. "—you're first on my list."

"Jackson, for heaven's sake." Bianca glared at his back. "It was an accident, and he's very sorry. The turkeys attacked him, and he made a bad decision."

"He fired a gun at a propane tank," Jax called back.

"At the turkeys! And it was a pellet gun!" Bianca lifted her voice to follow Jax up the stairs. "There's no way he could've foreseen the consequences, so there's no point traumatizing the child further with—" A bedroom door shut and moments later, the hot water heater rumbled to life. "—threats." She gave a bad-tempered sniff and dropped to the couch again to glare at Addy.

"I'm sorry, Bianca." She gave an apologetic shrug. "But I need the whole family together for this. I won't explain it more than once. I just...can't."

In less time than Addy would've believed possible — Jax must've set land-speed records in the shower — the Davises were all present, and Addy was out of excuses. She reached for the folio, then hesitated. She knew what was waiting for her inside it, and she knew she had to face it. But she also had to face the family, along with whatever judgment they rendered. Even if that judgment wasn't in her favor.

She took the folio in her hands and waited for her heart to stop throwing itself against her ribs like a panicked bird. She lifted her eyes to the family. She wanted to look at them once more while they were still unquestionably hers, to fix them in her mind before they...knew. Bianca's gaze was glued to the folio again, Georgie was back to snoozing, and Matty was still communing with the ceiling. But Jax was looking at her, his eyes warm and dark and strangely inscrutable. Her heart took an odd tumble in her chest and she dropped her eyes hastily, began fumbling with the cardboard flap. Suddenly the folio seemed like the least dangerous of two ominous options.

"So I kissed Addison tonight," Jax announced abruptly and Addy's fingers froze.

"Yes, we saw." Bianca's voice was impatient. "The folio, Addison?"

"Everybody saw," Georgie said, and slitted one eye at her brother. "I'll give you this much, Jax — when you make a move, you make a *move*."

He smiled. "I'm not a subtle guy."

"No," Bianca said. "You're not. You're very like your father that way." She turned back to Addison. "Now the folio?"

"Would anybody like to discuss said move?" Jax asked.

"The timing, the motivations, my future intentions?" Addy's heart felt too big for her chest. It was interfering with her breathing, and the lack of oxygen must be hampering her brain function because she could *not* figure out what on earth was happening. "Understand, people, that this is a once-in-a-lifetime offer that will not be made again. I'm giving you a free shot, so if you want it, you'd better take it."

There was a beat of taut silence, and Bianca made a noise, almost a growl. Addy understood it as her mother-in-law's internal gears grinding, competing desires crashing up against one another like speeding cars.

Georgie laughed. "I have one."

He spread easy hands. "Shoot."

"Not for you, dumbass." She sat up, went from half-asleep to wickedly, sparklingly awake between one heartbeat and the next. "For Addy."

Addy looked automatically to the folio in her hands and Georgie made an impatient noise. "Not about that. Put that thing down. It's filthy."

Addy set it carefully on the table at her knees. Bianca reached out a finger and stroked the edge, exactly — disturbingly — as she'd stroked Matty's cheekbone earlier at the dining room table.

"Mom." Jax's voice was a warning, a whip.

"I'm not opening it. I just wanted to touch it."

"It's not yours."

"I know that. It's Addison's." But her eyes were hungry. Addy's chest constricted cruelly and she tried to swallow but her throat refused to cooperate.

Georgie said, "Did you really not know?"

Addy blinked at her. "Not know?"

"About Jackson's desperate plight." She pressed her

147

hands to her heart and tossed all that shiny hair. "About the secret torture of coveting his own brother's wife. About the scandalous torch he's been carrying for said brother's widow all these years." She tsked at Jax. "Your own sister-in-law, Jackson! For shame!"

He said mildly, "Shut it, Georgie."

Georgie grinned and turned back to Addy. "Well?"

"Don't be ridiculous." Addy couldn't think. Her brain had gone dark, all synapses severed, all switches disconnected. "You're reading way too much into a simple stress response."

Georgie wriggled like a happy puppy. "So you didn't know?"

"There was nothing to know." She avoided Jax's eyes carefully. "We had a near-death experience tonight, that's all. People do crazy things under that kind of pressure. It wasn't personal."

Georgie laughed. "So Jax would've kissed me like that had I been stupid enough to run into a burning building?"

"Well, no." Addy frowned. "Probably not."

"So you really didn't know that he was in love with you?"

Addy gaped at her. When had they gone from an impulsive kiss to love?

Georgie laughed. "Oh lord. I guess not." She curled her legs under her again and reached across Matty to pat Jax's knee. "I really don't think she knew, buddy."

"Of course she didn't," Bianca snapped. "Why would she even think such a thing? And about Jackson, of all people?"

Jax smiled and murmured, "Gosh, thanks, Mom."

Bianca turned those sharp eyes on her son. "I didn't raise a fool, dear. If you didn't want her to know, she wouldn't know. Since you clearly didn't, she…doesn't." Bianca shifted that gaze to Addy. "Didn't."

Addy blinked at her. "Bianca, no, he's not…this isn't—" She turned helplessly to Jax. "This is ridiculous. You're not—" But she couldn't force the words out of her mouth. They were too impossible.

Jax smiled. "What, in love with you? I'm not, no."

"Thank you." She deflated into the couch cushions, both relieved and strangely hollow. She stared at the ceiling and waved weakly his way. "See?"

"How could I possibly know?" he added. "I only just finally kissed you."

"So prudent." Bianca rolled her eyes. "Children today know nothing of romance."

"We grew up with the internet," Georgie pointed out. "We don't splash out for grand gestures we'll never live down."

Addy said, "I'm so confused."

"I know." Jax reached over, patted her knee with a big, warm hand. "You must have questions."

"One or two."

"I'll answer them."

Georgie sat up eagerly.

"In private," he said, and she subsided with palpable disappointment.

"Oh, good." Addy scrubbed both hands over her face and raked her fingers through her hair. "That'll be…fun."

"That's the idea." His voice was rich and certain, and so full of promise that Addy's hands froze in her curls, and something shocking and needful rolled through her belly.

She said, "Oh."

Georgie said, "Ew."

"Mom?" Jax said, turning to Bianca. "Questions? Last chance."

"Like you'd tell me anything I don't already know?" Bianca flicked the idea away with one elegant hand. "Please. You're my child, Jax. My first born. Do you really think you have any secrets from me?"

"Yes."

"You don't." She smiled smugly. "Addison, however, is a different story." She shifted her gaze and Addy felt it like a hammer strike. "I love her like she's my own, of course, but as I didn't raise her, I don't know quite as well where to look for the truth. Which means that my questions, when I have them, will be for her." Those burning eyes dropped to the folio at Addy's knees again. "And I do have questions."

"I know you do," Addy murmured. She pushed aside the chaos filling her head and pulled in a breath. "I have answers. You won't like them, but I'll give them to you." She paused to gather her courage. "What you do with them — with me — will be up to you."

"Addy." Jax spoke again, his voice soft, his eyes warm. "You don't have to do this, you know. Whatever's in that folio? It's yours, legally and morally. You're under no obligation to—"

"Of course she is!" Bianca surged to her feet, her elbows cupped in tense hands. "And she knows it." She turned to Addy. "Don't you, dear?"

"Yes," she said softly. "I've kept this from you — from the world — far longer than I should've. I just…" Tears crawled up her throat and she swallowed them back. "I was just afraid."

"Of what?" Jax frowned at her.

She shook her head. "You'll see."

She placed the folio in Bianca's waiting hands, and let her mother-in-law bear it into the dining room like a high priestess or something. Was Addy the faithful follower, she wondered as she fell in behind, or the sacrifice?

She guessed she'd know soon enough.

Chapter 15

JAX STOPPED AT the edge of their massive dining room table. Bianca stood at the head — her rightful place as the matriarch — clutching the dingy folio Addy had risked her life to retrieve from the carriage house. He wanted to snatch it from his mother's hands and fling it into the Kettle. His fists ached with frustrated violence but he knew he had to let this happen.

They had to look, to see. All of them. Whatever was in that folio was a sickness that had been festering for too long. It was time to excise it once and for all, pain be damned. Addy couldn't be free any other way, and God help him, he wanted her free. Free to be whomever she wanted to be, to live whatever life she chose. Free from the goddamn angel Diego had made of her. Free to choose him if she wanted to.

Maybe she didn't want to. Maybe she never would. Maybe he'd blown his chances to kingdom come with that stupid, impulsive kiss earlier. Not that he regretted it. Holy hell. That kiss had changed his life. He'd never be the same. But one thing hadn't changed and never would — he wouldn't waste his life chasing somebody who didn't want him. And until Addy dealt with whatever Diego was still holding over her, she couldn't know what she wanted.

So he had to let this happen.

He stuffed his fists into his pockets and let his mother lift the folio's flap. Let her slide in a slim, white hand and withdraw a canvas.

"The chairs, please?" she murmured.

He poked Matty and together they pulled the chairs away from the table, giving Bianca a clear field to spread out whatever Addy had deemed too shameful, too hurtful, to share with the world. Then he was crowding in to look just like everybody else, driven by a morbid curiosity he hated but couldn't control.

It was a woman's nape, Jax saw after a moment. Just her nape, filling the entire canvas. Beautifully pale, so very white. A lock of black hair trailed across it, as if the woman who owned that nape had just flung her head to the side in shocked pleasure. A deep shadow ran down the center, the indent of her spinal column, and it was so powerfully inviting that Jax felt Diego's intention to run his tongue down it in his own gut. Lust punched out of the canvas, raw, hungry, and all the more potent for the cutting edge of despair it carried.

He cleared his throat. "Who is this?"

"Not me," Addy said. He looked up, found her gazing at his mother with pale determination. "But it was after me."

She pointed to the corner of the canvas where Diego had scrawled his signature and a date. A date hard on the heels of their wedding. Anger started a familiar churn inside Jax, and Bianca reached into the folio again. She drew out another canvas, then another, and another. One held the ripe undercurve of a woman's breast, another the dark cleft of a woman's sex. On and on it went, until the dining room table was a hideous buffet of infidelity, Diego's dark appetites and his self-hatred mounting in unbearable tandem. And then one final canvas.

Addison.

Addison crumpled across her bed, face down. Anguish in every line of her precious body. A body still adorned with something a porn star might call lingerie but that anybody who loved her would burn to ashes. Something a selfish dick might demand of his wife once he got bored with angels. This was love defeated, the fairy tale debunked. This was the bitter dregs of a failed marriage as experienced, signed and dated by his own brother.

Titled, too.

Broken.

Apt. This canvas was a masterpiece, no question, but it was also a confession. Penance. Diego had broken his pretty little wife, just like he broke all his toys. But he hadn't walked away whistling this time. No, breaking Addy had broken something inside Diego, too. Something vital, something necessary. It must have, because exactly one week after the date scribbled under that title, Diego had flown halfway across the country, pumped himself full of heroin and drifted out of this life.

Jax's throat closed. He stepped away from the table. Away from the sight of Addison's shattered heart smeared across the canvas by his brother's unflinching hand. He simply couldn't bear to look.

Addy stood beside the table she'd shared so many times with these beloved people, and gazed at the ruin of her marriage spread across it. The urge to scream or laugh built in her throat with every beat of her heart but she pressed it ruthlessly down.

"You didn't know?" she asked Bianca. "You really didn't know about—" She tossed a hand toward the canvases all but smoking there, and everything they implied. Diego's infidelity. His underground masterworks. Her smiling denial of it all. "—this?"

Bianca huffed lightly. "Do you really think I'd have let you sit on unshown works of this caliber if I'd known about them?"

She didn't say anything, Addy noticed, about the infidelity. Addy closed her eyes on a punishing sweep of hurt. It wasn't a new pain — she'd spent her childhood learning that her well-being mattered somewhat less than other people's ambition. That was why she was so exquisitely sensitive to Matty's situation. She knew better than anybody that familiarity with the knife didn't dull the slice.

"Right," she said around the bitterness in her throat. "What was I thinking?"

"Good question," Georgie said slowly. "What *were* you thinking, Addy? Because if you knew this was going on—" She tapped the table full of canvases with one sharp nail. "—why the hell did you stay? Why didn't you put your pointy high heel right in my brother's cheating crotch, then serve him up some hot, fresh divorce papers? Sue his ass off then spend the rest of your life living off the alimony? Because it would've been a very nice alimony."

Addy stared at her, her brain blank with shock. Nobody circled the wagons like the Davises, but Georgie was coming down on her side on this?

"Seriously, Addy." Jax took a jerky step toward the canvases, violence in those big hands of his. "You were twenty-two years old and smart as hell. You could have gone anywhere, done anything. You should have left."

"Easy for you to say." She laughed but it was as bitter as black coffee. "You grew up in the same house you were born in, just like your dad, his dad, and his dad before him. But it took me fourteen years and seventeen change of address forms just to convince my capital-A-ambitious parents that boarding school wasn't a dirty word."

She widened her focus, took them all in. "You Davises." She sighed with reluctant fondness. "With your history and your roots and your place in the world? You can't have any idea what belonging here meant to a girl like me."

Or what she'd do to stay.

"So tell us," Jax said, and shoved those hard fists into his pockets. "Make us understand."

She lifted helpless shoulders. "It's just...I didn't think places like Devil's Kettle even existed before Diego. And families like his? Like you? Forget about it. Only in the movies, you know?" She shook her head. "Then Diego did that sweep-you-off-your-feet thing he did so well—"

"His signature move," Georgie said.

"Tell me about it." She rubbed her hands up and down her chilly arms. "By the time I could tell up from down I was already married into roots sunk so deep that I couldn't tell the family from the town. Which was a huge mistake, obviously. Diego was over me in, like, five minutes."

"Which was four minutes longer than he'd given anybody else." Georgie rubbed a hand up and down Addy's arm too and she leaned gratefully into the warmth. "Ever. So don't be too hard on yourself."

"Trust me, I'm not." She smiled and forced herself to step away from Georgie's touch. From her sympathy. "By the time I understood exactly how big a mistake I'd made, it was already too late. I was in too deep, ready to do whatever it took, pay whatever it cost, to stay."

"You were that in love with him?" Georgie asked. She eyed the canvases spread across the table. "Even after this?"

"Oh, I wasn't in love with *him*. Not by then. I was in love with the rest of you."

Uncomprehending silence. From everybody. Which she should've expected. This part didn't reflect well on her. She knew it. Had always known it. The trick was going to be making them understand.

"*Diego's Angel* was a moment," she said softly, "not a marriage. That canvas isn't love; it's *falling*. It's the drop. It's the realization that another person, a stranger, somebody you didn't even know last week, last month, two hours ago, whatever, has somehow become your sun. That your galaxy spins for her, for him. And Diego caught it. He caught that specific moment, that—" She rubbed a fist over her heart. "—fall. And being Diego, he made other people feel it too." She shook her head. "He didn't love me for very long, but he loved me brilliantly while he did."

"And publicly," Jax said darkly. "Very, very publicly."

"That was the thing about Diego." Addy smiled wryly. "He didn't understand his own heart until he saw it splattered across a canvas. Until he saw what other people saw in what he'd painted. It was the only way he knew to live, to be. It was the only way he could breathe." Her smile faded. "Which was a wonderful gift to the world, but no way to do a marriage."

"No." Georgie frowned. "Probably not."

"He probably didn't even know he was in love until he saw *Diego's Angel*," Addy said. "Just like he didn't know he

157

wasn't in love with me anymore until he saw these." She waved a trembling hand at the dining room table. Nausea churned in her stomach and she forced herself to go on. To say the rest. "But he still cared enough about me to keep it — these — private. To let everybody believe that he'd simply peaked with *Diego's Angel* and stopped painting. He was prepared to let that be his legacy." She threaded her fingers together, and squeezed until they went numb. "He didn't love me anymore, but he protected me. And God forgive me, I let him." She bowed her head under a crashing wave of grief and guilt. "I convinced myself that maintaining appearances was for the best. People loved *Diego's Angel*."

"The painting?" Bianca asked suddenly, those black eyes shrewd and sharp. "Or you?"

"Either." Addy lifted helpless shoulders. "Both. People love fairy tales, and Diego painted one. A great one. He convinced people that we were living it, for goodness' sake. Convinced them that our living, breathing fairy tale was on display along with *Diego's Angel* right here in Devil's Kettle. So they came. They came by the busload — bought out the gallery, booked every hotel room. They ate in our restaurants, shopped in our bookstores and geared up at the bait and tackle. *Diego's Angel* made him a legend, and she was good for everybody. But, yes, she was especially good for me. Because she let me matter to you."

Bianca drew back sharply. "I beg your pardon?"

She forced herself to lift her eyes, to meet the outrage burning in Bianca's gaze. "You were so broken after Diego died," she said softly. "Losing him just sliced you open. And even as I hated that, *hated* the way you hurt, I envied him. Envied how deeply he'd been loved." She gave a jagged, bitter laugh. "Which is horrible, I know. Believe me, I know.

But my parents didn't — don't — love me like you love Diego. Like you love any of your kids. I don't think they know how. I'd spent my whole life not mattering to anybody. Until you." Her smile fell apart and she let it go. "Being Diego's Angel made me matter to *you*. She allowed me to be a comfort and a solace to you. She allowed you to believe that Diego had been…happy. That he'd been not only a great artist but a good man. A good husband, loving and beloved. She was the fairy tale to you, and to me? She was what I accepted in lieu of alimony, I guess. She was what I got instead of a divorce — the chance to be necessary to the people I loved." She stopped, cleared her aching throat. "But I should've told you the truth as soon as Diego died. I know that now. I should've let you choose how you wanted the fairy tale to end, but I was selfish. Being yours — being a Davis — was the most important thing I'd ever been, and I didn't know how to give it up." She spread trembling hands. "I only hope you can try to understand. To someday forgive me."

Georgie gazed at her in blank wonder. Matty remained slouched against the table's edge. Jax stood silently beside him, frowning down at the paintings. Bianca clasped her hands in front of her waist and drew in a long breath.

"How dare you?" She fired the words like bullets, and Addy absorbed the deadly impact of each one.

Jax started. "Mom?"

Bianca knifed her hand through the air, sliced off the protest with cold precision. She leaned in, her face a stony mask of rage. "How dare you stand there and ask my forgiveness? You killed my boy."

Addy flinched but refused to look away. She deserved this.

"Jesus, Mom." Jax stepped up to Addy's side, put a hand on her arm. It nearly sizzled, it was so warm against her frozen skin. "She did not. You're being—"

"Oh I don't deny that Diego was a terrible husband." Bianca flicked it away, an inconsequential detail, and her eyes burned into Addy like a brand. "I doubt you were a perfect wife, for that matter. You married ridiculously young, and young people are prone to stupidity. But my son needed to paint — needed to *show* his painting — like he needed to breathe. You said so yourself. You *knew*."

"I did." Addy let the weight of that truth settle onto her. "I knew."

"And you took that from him." Bianca's chin came up, and she stepped closer, close enough to strike Addy if she wanted to. Addy wondered if she would. She wouldn't stop her. "You let him pay for a handful of indiscretions with his *life*. So how dare you stand there and ask for my forgiveness? You as good as killed my son." She stepped back, her face cold, her lips white. "Get out of my house."

Chapter 16

SHE DIDN'T ARGUE. She went upstairs to the suite of rooms she and Diego had shared during their short marriage — the rooms she'd never left — and pulled her suitcase from the closet. Expensive, durable, and black, it had been a gift from her parents for her college graduation. They'd expected her to occupy the same world they had, of course. That she'd divide her time between airports and hotels, board rooms and conference centers, criss-crossing the globe and living up to her education.

She hadn't taken it out of the closet once in four years. Not since the day she'd set foot in Devil's Kettle with a massive diamond on her ring finger and a lump of terror in her heart.

Georgie drifted through the door and sank to the bed. "Mom's pissed," she announced.

Addy laughed, but it came out more like a sob. She plunked the suitcase onto the bedspread beside Georgie. "What tipped you off?"

"She's pissed," Georgie said again, "but she never stays that way. You know Mom. She's all shock and awe, but give it five minutes and she'll blow herself out."

Addy moved to the dresser. She grabbed a few tops, a few sweaters, and eyed the closet. Winter coat? Surely she could get by without it for a few—

She shook her head against the hope trying to take root. This wasn't a weekend holiday, she reminded herself ruthlessly. This was exile. She went to the closet, took out her winter coat and tossed it onto the bed. She snatched up some wool socks from the dresser and shoved them into the suitcase with shaking hands and a throat that ached like fire. Tears, she understood belatedly. She was fighting a desperate battle against sobbing like a child. Cripes.

"Addy, for heaven's sake, you're taking this way too seriously."

"She thinks I killed Diego."

"Don't be stupid." Georgie scooted back to lean against the headboard and curled her legs comfortably underneath her. "First off, you didn't kill anybody. Diego was an addict." Addy flinched. Nobody had ever said it out loud before, or so baldly. "Drugs, sex, trouble. He had a problem with limits." She shrugged. "So believe me, you didn't kill anybody." She traced the elaborate seam stitching on her skinny jeans with an idle finger. "Plus, you're family."

"I just got thrown out of the family."

"No, you got thrown out of the house."

"What's the difference?"

Georgie made an impatient noise. "I can't believe I'm supposed to be the dumb one in this partnership."

"Pretty," Addy said and went back to the dresser for her own jeans, none of them skinny, thanks be. She had kind of a pie habit. "You're the pretty one."

"Which makes you the smart one, so start acting like it, will you?"

"I'm trying." She stuffed the jeans into her suitcase and turned toward the bathroom to gather up her toiletries.

"Try harder." Georgie caught her elbow and tugged. She was surprisingly strong for a woman who spent her entire life lying down, and Addy found her butt planted on the quilt next to Georgie's knees. "Just think for a minute, will you? Even if Mom's mad as hell right now — which she is — she's not stupid. Those paintings she's all heated up about belong to you. You think she's going to let you walk out of our lives with them?" She snorted. "Fat chance. And then, of course, there's the Jax situation."

Addy's heart crashed painfully into her sternum. She rubbed her palm over it. "There is no Jax situation. He thought I was going to die, and he overreacted."

"You keep telling yourself that." Georgie patted her knee genially. "Mom's on another page."

"Which page is that?"

"The one where you trade out this ugly thing—" She tapped the admittedly gaudy diamond on Addy's ring finger. "—for something that suits you much better." Her lips curved in a sly smile. "Something a firefighter can afford."

"Fire chief," she said automatically, her brain a blank, white sheet. "And, Georgie, that's ridiculous. We're not...Jax doesn't—"

Georgie lifted innocent hands. "I'm just telling you what Mom's going to think. What she thinks Jax is thinking."

"Which makes no sense!"

"Since when has that been a requirement for what Mom thinks?" She shrugged. "She already lost one son. She's hardly going to risk losing Jax by playing the old her-or-me card against his One True Love."

"His One True—" Addy broke off. "Georgie, come on." She wished her heart would just settle down into some kind of predictable rhythm. She was going to have a stroke soon.

"It was one impulsive kiss. It's over."

Georgie sighed deeply. "I can't believe I have to be the dumb one in this partnership. But, hey, listen. I've got your back. When Mom implies that he's only marrying you for your money—"

"Oh, lord."

"—tell her it's a non-issue." Her smile grew into something sleek and satisfied. "I've got the family fortune covered."

"You do?" Addy's brows shot up. "How?"

Georgie wiggled her own ring finger, which was markedly free of diamonds. "I'm in expectation of an interesting event."

Addy gaped. "You're pregnant?"

"Bite your tongue. I may not be a mathlete of your caliber but I do know how birth control works." She smoothed a lock of hair behind her ear. "I'm getting engaged."

"You are?" Addy hesitated. "Does Peter know?"

"He will." Georgie waved airily.

She frowned. "I know you want to do your bit for the family, Georgie, but I don't think you need to sell your hand in marriage to the highest bidder just yet."

"I'm not selling anything, Addison. Goodness." She rolled her eyes. "That said, marrying money is a time-honored tradition for girls like me."

"What, impoverished?"

"And gorgeous." Georgie shrugged lightly. "I guess I'm just a traditional kind of girl."

Addy maintained a skeptical silence.

Georgie laughed. "Okay, so maybe I'm more a life-of-leisure kind of girl."

Even Addy couldn't argue with that one. "Are you sure

Peter's going to ask you?"

She inspected her manicure. "As sure as a woman can be about these things."

"And you're going to say yes?"

"I like my silver spoon, Addison. I have no intention of giving it up now." She slanted Addy a look from beneath her lashes. "Plus I'm going to make a spectacular bride."

"No argument," Addy said automatically. "But...Georgie, are you sure?" She leaned forward, touched her knee. "I mean, Peter is..." She broke off while a picture of Peter Zinc floated into her mind. Tall, handsome, dangerously bright and unapologetically ambitious, Peter was nobody to screw with. "Do you love him?"

"Hmmm, let me think." Georgie pursed up her perfect lips and squinted into the distance. "He's gorgeous, rich, has an Ivy League education and wants to keep me in pampered splendor for the rest of my life. Do I love him?" She patted Addy's hand. "I'd be stupid not to, wouldn't I?"

"That's not exactly a declaration of true love, Georgie."

She smiled. "Define true love."

Addy turned her hand up under Georgie's, laced their fingers together and said, "Please tell me you're not doing this just for the money."

"I'm not doing this just for the money," Georgie said obediently.

"Because I'm on top of the money situation." She looked hard into her sister-in-law's giant blue eyes, into all that studied innocence. "The family is going to be fine. You don't have to do this if you don't want to."

"Do what?" she asked lightly. "Marry the man I love? The man who loves me? Who enjoys keeping me happy and can afford to do it with style?" She rolled her eyes. "Yeah, that's really taking one for the team, Addy."

"It is if you don't really love him."

"Well I do, so stop worrying." She slipped her hand from Addy's and rose.

"I can't help it." Addy stood, too, and wrapped her arms around Georgie's rail-thin torso in a fierce hug. "You're the little sister I never had."

Georgie patted her hair with fond exasperation. "You're, like, two years younger than I am, Addison."

"I know but you were Diego's little sister. It translated. I can't undo it now."

"Oh, fine."

Addy drew back but kept Georgie's elbows in her hands. Kept her close. "I know things are weird right now but you Davises are the family I never had. I'm always going to take care of you."

Georgie leaned forward and put a smacking kiss right in the middle of Addy's forehead. "Honey. You can't even take care of your hair."

Addy touched her head and winced. "Oh. Yeah. That's been a problem today."

Georgie laughed. "Try every day."

"I'm serious about this marriage thing, Georgie."

"I am, too. Which is why I'm going to call Peter right now." She smiled again, the sleek smile of a woman confident of her man. "He's left me about twelve messages. Heard about the fire, probably. He's sweet to worry, isn't he?" She drifted toward the door, then paused with one hand on the jamb to eye Addy's suitcase. "Where are you going to stay tonight?"

Addy's lungs went dry and dusty. For the first time in four years, she didn't know where she was sleeping. She didn't know where home was. She forced her lips into a breezy curve. "I'll figure something out."

Georgie only laughed. "I doubt you'll need to."

Ten minutes later, Addy was in her little Honda following Jax's tail lights down the bluffs. The mini-pumper had a backdraft like a planet had gravitational pull. She barely had to steer, let alone touch the gas. And if there were other parallels there — like the way Jax had taken uncontested custody of both Addy and her suitcase — she wasn't going to think about it too much right now. She was too desperately relieved not to be spending the night in a hotel.

Because Addy hated hotels. Hated every impersonal, generic bit of them, from the bland art to the weird smell to the polyester comforters that were an insult to their very name. Those comforters weren't even remotely comforting, and Addy ought to know. When her mom had launched her own consulting agency, none of the assignments that first year had been long enough to justify even a rental house. In Addy's memory, third grade was still nothing but a queasy blur of new schools, hostile strangers and stiff hotel blankets.

So when Jax had taken the suitcase out of her hands and informed her that his guest room was hers until further notice, she hadn't argued. First, she was too pathetically grateful. But second, she'd been too darn shocked. He'd spent four long years politely but firmly rejecting her efforts to be *his* family, but all of a sudden he was hers? Had he just been waiting for her to need him? She'd have to ask him sometime. She would, too. Just as soon as she regained the powers of speech she'd lost when Jax had turned to his mother and delivered this parting shot: "When you're ready to apologize, give us a call."

Bianca had pointed her nose to the ceiling and sailed grandly up the stairs. Georgie had rolled her eyes and seen them to the door where she'd given Jax a quick hug and sent Addy a knowing smirk over his shoulder.

The bluffs eventually gave way to coastal flats and Addy followed the mini-pumper through the sparse few blocks of town. Jax turned right on Second, angling away from the lake toward the fire station. A couple of blocks later, he pulled the mini-pumper into the station garage. Addy pulled into his driveway across the street.

A blast of icy wind shoved the clouds aside, revealing a brilliantly full moon just as Addy's feet hit the pavement. In spite of the cold, she paused, shivering, to study Jax's house in the moonlight. It was a neat white two-story, the yard tiny but well kept. Of course it was. Because this was Jax, and yards didn't go untended in his universe any more than banished sisters-in-law went unclaimed. She'd bet her laptop that the cute blue screen door on that jewel-box of a sun porch didn't squeak either.

She retrieved her suitcase from the trunk and headed for the front steps. Jax hadn't crossed the street yet but she doubted the house was locked. Nobody locked up in Devil's Kettle. Nobody but Addy, and it was just one more thing that marked her as an outsider.

She let herself into Jax's porch through the screen door (which didn't squeak) and headed for the main door. She tried the knob and frowned. Locked? Then the screen door opened behind her and suddenly the porch was full of Jax. Smoke and soap, safety and warmth. She stood there, blinking at him stupidly. He held up his keys and nudged her away from the knob.

"You locked your door," she said.

"Of course I did." He threw her a quizzical glance over his shoulder while he dealt with the locks. "Don't you?"

"Well, yes, but—"

The door swung open. He picked up her suitcase, took her elbow and drew her inside. He hit the light switch and she found herself surrounded by old, lovingly polished wood and leaded glass sidelights. A thick, beautifully carved newel post anchored the staircase. The foyer was small by Hill Top House standards — well, by modern standards, probably — but it didn't feel small to Addy. It felt...snug. The kind of snug that made her want to sit down right there on the stairs and soak up all the cozy.

"But what?" he asked, and deposited her suitcase on the landing.

"But I'm not from here." She studied him carefully. "You are."

"Which is exactly why I lock up. An unlocked door is an invitation around here, especially to the family. If I didn't lock up, Matty would adopt my fridge as his own and I'd have a Georgie-shaped divot in my couch." He paused to frown. "If I even kept a couch long enough for her to make a divot, which is unlikely given how often Mom would buy me new ones. And I actually like my couch. So, yeah, I lock up." He took her arm again, drew her through an arched entry way into the living room. "Come on. I'll give you the tour."

Chapter 17

HE FLIPPED THE wall switch in the living room and banished the moonlight. It was too romantic and Jax was aware that now wasn't exactly the time to press his suit. Not when Addy was still blinking those big Bambi eyes like a bomb had gone off in her face. Which it sort of had, actually. A bomb they both loved. A bomb he called Mom.

The anger in his gut grumbled ominously but he ignored it. Not as easily as usual, but he ignored it. If self-control was an art, Jax had mastered it years ago. He'd never been an honor-roll student but he was bright enough when it mattered. And since his mom mattered and always would, he'd figured her out. Bianca had a hair-trigger temper, but if you kept your cool, she blew out as fast as she blew up. But if you blew up when she did, holy hell, there went the neighborhood. The situation blazed inevitably out of control and shit burned down that should've been sacred. So the key to familial harmony — the key to familial survival — was to keep your damn temper. Even when the adults were losing theirs.

So he had. He did. No matter what crazy-ass stunt Bianca pulled, he never shouted. He never engaged. He never fought fire with fire. He put fires out, for God's sake. It was his job. But then his mother had kicked Addy out of the house — out of her *home* — knowing full well what home meant to her. Bianca had been absolutely aware that it was the cruelest, most lethal blow she could deliver. And she'd enjoyed delivering it. Jax had seen that in her face. She'd *enjoyed* watching Addy's hollow shock melt into staggering pain. Such was the power of that temper of hers. She wasn't a cruel woman, not generally, but her better angels were no match for her rage. She knew this about herself as well as Jax did.

What she'd never understood, however, was that the wounds she inflicted while lost to fury didn't disappear along with the fury. They stayed. They scarred. She knew exactly how deeply she'd wounded Addy tonight, and in the moment, she'd been glad. Tomorrow morning, she'd regret those words with everything in her. But she'd expect Addy to forgive her.

Addy probably would, too.

The rage in his gut grumbled again, and he breathed until it subsided. He focused instead on the sight of Addy, here in his house. He'd imagined her here so many times. The fact of her here now, even under these circumstances, was grounding. Gratifying. He sank down on the arm of his big leather couch, tossed a boot onto the banged up steamer trunk that served as his coffee table and leaned back against the windowsill to watch her. She circled the room slowly, stopping at the far end to inspect the built-in bookshelves that hugged the doorway to the kitchen. She bent to read a few of the titles, her manners so ingrained that — even reeling with pain — she could exhibit polite curiosity about his collection of worn paperbacks and grease-spotted repair manuals.

"Well?" he asked. "What do you think?"

171

"Of your house?"

"Yeah."

Her gaze drifted around the room, touched on the couch, the man-sized TV on the wall opposite, the trunk under his boots. "I like it."

"Yeah? Why?"

She ran her finger down a row of second-hand thrillers, stopped at the framed photo serving as a bookend. It was of him and Diego goofing around at Granny Nan's old place — a twelve-year-old Diego pretending to get dramatically sucked into the Kettle while a thirteen-year-old Jax fought heroically to pull him back out. Georgie had taken it during her *maybe I'm a photographer* phase, playing with perspective to make it look like they'd been right on top of the Kettle while they'd actually been half a football field away. Addy smiled, a wispy ghost of her usual high-wattage charmer. "It's very you."

"Ah." He suppressed a wince. What had he expected? "Thanks."

She finally turned her back on the bookshelves and pointed at the steamer trunk. "Did you haul that out of a fire?"

"Yeah. House fire. Two Harbors." He glanced at the singe marks and missing corners he hadn't noticed in years. He leaned forward for a good sniff. "It doesn't still smell like smoke, does it?"

She smiled again, managed it a little better this time. "No. I like it. In fact—" She wandered over, sank onto the other arm of the couch to give the trunk a better study. "I like it a lot. It looks like one of those old guys you find in dark little bars. That kind that'll tell you stories all night if you keep the beer coming."

"Exactly." He nodded with satisfaction and his self-consciousness evaporated. He loved that damn trunk. Loved the way fire had nibbled at the thing, put miles and mystery on it. His own roots were deep and certain but he liked that little piece of the exotic in his living room. And Addy got that. Which meant that she got him, too. At least on some level.

And that was encouraging enough for one night.

"Kitchen's through there," he said and nodded toward the door snuggled inside his wall of bookshelves. "You can see it in the morning." He rose to his feet. "Come on. It's bedtime."

"Oh." She blinked and looked down. "Ah, Jax—"

"Easy, Addison. You get your own bed."

"For goodness' sake." She flushed and smoothed down a particularly boingy curl. "I didn't mean—"

"—that I'm the kind of guy who'd rescue you from a shitty situation then expect sex as repayment?" He gave that a beat of damning silence. "Of course you didn't." He circled the trunk and slid a hand into the crook of her elbow. That mint-and-sunshine smell of hers drifted to his nose, along with the crisp scent of cold lake air. He wanted to pull her into his arms and just hold her. Keep her until she wasn't afraid any more. Until nothing hurt, and never would again. He settled for pulling her to her feet and stepping carefully back, hands up and open. "I'm a grown man, Addy. A kiss is nothing but a kiss. I know it doesn't give me license to take whatever else I might or might not want. Plus you've had one hell of a night. I'm not going to jump you."

"Pete's sake." She closed her eyes and let out a breath so long and weary that Jax had to wonder exactly how long she'd been holding it. "I didn't think you were going to jump me."

"Well, of course I'm not." He nudged her toward the foyer. "Not right now, anyway."

There was a startled little hitch in her step. "Not right—" She shot him a wary glance. "What about later?"

"Well, gosh, Addy, I just don't know." They hit the landing and he scooped up her bag. "I mean, I like you and all but when it comes to jumping folks, I expect a good, lively tussle."

"Lively." She eyed him skeptically.

"Yep." He started up the stairs, smiled when he heard her follow. "Energetic." He hit the top of the stairs and pushed open the door on the left. "Creative, even."

"Creative?"

He hit the switch and golden light spilled from the bedside lamp. It rolled softly across the hand-stitched, locally-made quilt he'd bought at the Gilded Fish a few years back in a fit of home town pride. He'd eventually thrown it on his guest bed because his goose-down duvet was a good sight warmer than even his love for Devil's Kettle.

"Oh, yeah." He set her suitcase inside the door and straightened to pat her shoulder sympathetically. "Frankly, I don't think you've got it in you at the moment."

"Hmm." But he liked the way she eyed him, half wary, half amused.

"Not for what I have in mind."

"You have something—" She stopped, startled. He didn't know if he liked that, or if it pissed him off. Because a woman like Addy should be used to being wanted. She should understand what those dimples of hers did to a man, should be able to deploy them like the weapons-grade asset they were. She should *not* be shocked into sentence fragments by a little flirty innuendo.

"In mind? Oh, yeah." She had no idea what he had in mind. Neither did he. Not exactly. He'd definitely be giving it some thought, though. "Just not for tonight."

"I see," she said faintly.

"Good." He leaned against the doorjamb, hooked a thumb over his shoulder. "Bathroom's at the end of the hall. I'm right across, in case you need anything." He gave her a purposefully wicked smile. "Anything at all."

She blinked, startled again, then suddenly, she laughed. Just gave an exasperated crack of laughter that showed him those dimples he couldn't resist. It struck him like lightning, the urge to touch her. To inhale the heat and sweetness of her. Need flashed up inside him — fast, startling, and impossible to resist.

So he didn't.

He cupped a hand around her nape and lifted her into his mouth. Just pulled her right in without so much as a do-you-mind. Shock ripped through the want — kissing Addy was still a vicious jolt to his system. It threaded brightly through the dark need, rippled over every inch of his skin while the scent of her wrapped around him. Clean, sunny woman with a little mint and smoke thrown in for good measure.

Smoke. The carriage house fire still clung to her hair and a wisp of remembered terror floated through his gut. It tangled with the heat curling there, and pushed it higher. Because she could've died tonight. He could've lost her. It was a gift, then — this moment, this kiss, this permission. He wouldn't waste a second of it.

Her mouth was open and startled under his and he took deliberate advantage, stroking his tongue lightly over the plump inner curve of her bottom lip. God, he liked that little bit of her. So secret and warm and delicious. She gave a funny sigh, and holy hell, did her *knees* just give out a little? It was a subtle thing — her skull sinking just a little deeper into the cradle of his palm, her spine melting just a smidge inside the circle of his arm. But he stopped wondering because suddenly he realized that her lips had softened under his, they clung and answered and asked. Addy had joined the game.

A fierce satisfaction rose up inside him, crashed into the raging want and sent it roaring into the sky like a house fire. He clamped down on it with every ounce of his considerable self-control. He slid a slow palm up the lovely long line of her back, threaded his fingers into the riot of her curls and gave himself three more heartbeats to sink into the wonder of her kiss. Into the wonder of *her* kissing *him*. Three more seconds to live inside that happy little miracle.

Then he pulled back. Everything in him howled in protest but he set her away from him. Were his hands shaking? He didn't know. He kept them clamped around her upper arms, just in case they were. Or in case he lost his mind and put them somewhere more interesting. She blinked up at him, her eyes huge and green and gratifyingly vague.

He said, "Goodnight."

"What?"

"Goodnight, Addison." He managed to let her go and even put a few feet between their bodies. Every inch hurt him, but it was the right move. She was in no shape to deal with whatever the hell had just caught fire between them. He didn't know if he was. Jesus.

Her pretty mouth dropped open. "Goodnight?"

He paused in his own doorjamb to give her a respectful

nod. "Sleep tight now."

"Sleep *tight*?"

He clicked the door shut on her disbelief, then put his back against it and breathed. Just breathed, because his heart was trying to jackhammer its way out of his chest. Each beat sent punishing waves of lust crashing through his system, along with a trembling, almost frightening knowledge.

First kisses were fine. He liked them a lot, actually. The shock and surprise, the risk and the rush? Nothing better. But if first kisses were fireworks, second kisses were verdicts. Strip away the adrenaline and the novelty, and all you had left was chemistry. A second kiss told you if you should pursue a third. So, yeah, Jax liked a first kiss just fine, but he paid attention to the second one. It was probably why he hadn't been able to resist kissing Addy goodnight. Their first kiss had all but leveled him. His nervous system had still been billowing smoke and yelping out alarms hours later. How much of that had been first kiss stuff, though? How much of it would carry over to the second? The third? How much had been surprise, and how much had been reliably reproducible chemistry?

All of it. Plus more, evidently.

He sucked in a shaky breath, released it slowly. Something happened when he kissed Addy. When she kissed him back. Something blindingly bright and dangerously combustible. Something he'd never experienced before and wasn't quite sure what to do with. Especially not if it got bigger, brighter and more dangerous with every kiss.

"Jackson!"

On the other side of the door, she was shouting at him. In spite of the foreboding snaking through his lust-addled system, he smiled. She'd been doing that kind of a lot lately, the shouting. He liked it.

"What?" He sounded so ordinary, he thought smugly. Polite, curious, conversational.

"You can't just *do* that!"

"Do what?"

"You can't just, just—"

There was a sputtering pause, during which he pictured her batting at the air with clawed hands in a furious search for words. A laugh welled up inside him which he carefully squelched. "Can't just what?"

"Just *french me goodnight.*" A thud drifted through the door. Had she actually stamped her foot? Kicked the door? "You're not allowed to french me goodnight, Jackson!"

Joy welled up inside him, golden and thick and astonishing. "Sorry."

"You are not!"

"Neither are you."

Startled silence. He nodded with satisfaction. That was probably as far as he could push her for one night.

"Goodnight, Addy."

Her goodnight was a heartily slammed door.

Chapter 18

THE KEY TO hiding, Addy knew, was staying right
where people could see you. See you, stop you, maybe even
chat with you a bit. The trick was looking busy. Actually
being busy was better, of course. *Oh, gosh, there's a
customer, I'm late for a meeting, I need just a minute with
that person over there, can I get right back to you?*

It wasn't an easy trick to pull off in a town the size of
Devil's Kettle, but Addy was a pro. She hadn't slid
unscathed through all those middle schools by accident, after
all. She had skills. And by using every last one, she'd
successfully avoided in-depth human conversation for four
whole days now. It was a hot streak, even for her.

It ended on Saturday afternoon.

She was sitting at the shiny white desk in the middle of
the Davis Gallery, halfway through her usual Saturday shift.
The slim curve of white plastic that passed for a chair in an
art gallery bit into her butt and Addy wondered — not for
the first time — how a woman as bony as Georgie could
possibly sit on it for any length of time. She thought
longingly of the comfy, butt-sprung chair in her own office,
of her big scarred desk. Of her latest Davis Place cost
projections spread across the top of it.

Her heart yearned toward those spreadsheets. Good old

reliable math. So soothingly unambiguous, so completely clear. So utterly unlike the rest of her hosed up life. So completely useless when it came to fixing said life.

She sighed wearily. Her avoidance skills were ninja-level, but even she couldn't keep this up forever. She was going to have to confront Bianca eventually. And when she did, she should have a plan. A proposal. You never went into negotiations without knowing what you wanted, so what did Addy want? What were her options here?

She supposed she could accept Bianca's banishment as permanent.

Pain roared through her and she rejected the idea hastily. Even if she was prepared to accept being kicked out of the family on a personal level, how could she abandon Matty to Bianca's grief-addled parenting? She couldn't. She wouldn't. Maybe there was no shaking her mother-in-law's faith in Matty's talent, but Diego's new paintings were one heck of a trump card. If showing them would buy Matty even a few years of breathing room, Addy was prepared to do it.

She'd have a lot more leverage, however, if negotiations were friendly. Which brought her to option number two: repairing her and Bianca's relationship, and fast. For Matty's sake, yes, but also for her own. Because, lord help her, she wanted her family back. They were crazy and impulsive, spoiled and dramatic, but they were loyal and loving and they were *hers*. In spite of everything, she loved them. She wanted them back. She wanted her cherished normal back.

Unfortunately, keeping Diego's paintings from Bianca — from the world — for all those years might've damaged her precious normal beyond repair. She had to acknowledge that. But where love existed, so did hope. And Addy loved her family desperately so maybe a third option existed: maybe they could rebuild rather than repair. Maybe the old normal was shot but they could create a new one, couldn't they? They could make a new normal, something healthy and honest this time. Something with no secrets or shadows. Something with room for—

Well, with room for the french-me-goodnight situation that had cropped up between her and Jax. Addy sighed. It was getting out of hand, really, the way Jax simply grabbed her up at random, unpredictable moments and kissed the daylights out of her. Even worse was the way he then walked off like nothing unusual had even happened, leaving her sputtering and spinning, her heart on pause, her libido on fast-forward.

Nothing normal about that, except for the fact that it happened all the time. Which made it...normal? Well, no. Nothing that knocked her nervous system clear into orbit like that could be plausibly termed *normal*, but it could definitely become a habit. Maybe it already was one. Which would be a problem because Addy could hardly talk let alone think when Jax was done kissing her. And obviously thinking was a top priority right now. Unless Jax was nearby and had that look in his eye. Then kissing Jax was her top priority. Her only priority. Her only coherent thought, in fact.

Crap.

No wonder she was binging on spreadsheets.

Suddenly the door jingled and Bianca and Georgie sailed in. At least Bianca sailed. Georgie moved more carefully, her eyes hidden behind a pair of enormous sunglasses.

Addy's cheeks went up in flames and she rose slowly. "Bianca," she said, her blood throbbing sickly in her wrists, her ears. "Georgie."

Bianca crossed the room and patted Addy's cheek as if she hadn't booted her out of the family home a few days earlier. As if she hadn't accused her of murder, for heaven's sake, then maintained a hostile silence ever since. "Hello, dear."

Georgie didn't speak. She only elbowed Addy away from that deeply uncomfortable chair and lowered herself into it with a small moan. Then she folded her arms on the desk and gently placed her forehead on them.

Addy blinked at Georgie's shiny head. "Everything okay there, champ?"

"I got engaged last night," she announced from the cradle of her arms. She wiggled her ring finger and Addy's stomach did a little swoop and dive. It was one thing to talk about an on-demand engagement but it was another thing entirely to be presented with five blinding carats of reality.

"Wow. Congratulations." She paused, sent Bianca an uncertain look. "You celebrated a little, I take it?"

Bianca held up a thumb and forefinger about an inch apart and shrugged lightly.

Georgie said, "Mom and I drank mojitos all night and looked at wedding dresses online." She started to sit up, then stopped. She touched careful fingers to her temple and gingerly lowered her head to the desk again. "You know how I feel about a good mojito."

"I do."

"And that was on top of the wine at dinner."

"Oh dear."

"It's possible there was a bottle of champagne in there somewhere, too."

"Ouch."

"I think Mom and I called Chou in Paris."

"We did," Bianca confirmed.

Addy winced. "At least the time change worked in your favor."

"She says she can fit Georgie in for a custom dress if we send her the measurements immediately and she doesn't gain an ounce." Bianca stroked all that silky hair. "No more mojitos for you, darling girl."

Georgie moaned.

The gallery door jingled again and this time Jax strode in on a blast of lake-tinged air. Something lifted inside Addy's chest at the sight of him, something odd and breathless and unmistakably joyful. She saw Matty hunching in behind him like a reluctant shadow, but her brain registered that as a non-essential detail. Her body shot to attention for Jax. She could be thoroughly frenched at any moment.

Oh boy. She might really be in trouble here.

"Hey, great," he said. "You're here."

"It's Saturday," she managed. "I'm always here on Saturdays."

"I know." He gave her curls a fond pat. "I wasn't looking for you, though it's nice to see you. You've been scarce lately." She suppressed a guilty wince. She'd been avoiding him, of course. She'd been avoiding everybody. But she had skills such that nobody should've noticed. Trust Jax to notice anyway. He turned to his mom. "I was looking for you, actually." He glanced at Georgie's head on the desk. "Her, too." He poked his sister's shoulder. "What's wrong with you?"

"I got engaged last night."

"Congratulations. To Peter?"

Georgie rolled her head to the side to glare up at him. "Who else?"

Jax shrugged cheerfully. "Always good to be sure." He turned to Bianca. "So, you're finally ready to apologize?"

Bianca fixed him with an icy gaze. "For what?"

"Not ready yet. Okay." He sighed. "What are you doing here then?"

"Trying to have a private conversation," Bianca said sweetly. "I'd have thought it would be easier, given Addison's unexpected talent for keeping secrets."

"Mom." Georgie sat up. She closed her eyes for a moment, held out a hand for silence though nobody had said anything. She regained her equilibrium and fixed her mother with a hard blue stare. "We went over this. I know you were hurt by the way Addy handled the paintings Diego left her—"

"The very personal, private, revealing paintings of which she has sole ownership?" Jax said, a small smile on his lips. "Those paintings?"

"Yes," Georgie said, rubbing circles into one temple. "Those ones. Now I know she didn't handle them the way you'd have liked, but she had a right to grieve her own way just like you've been allowed to grieve your own way."

"God help us all," Matty muttered.

"And now I'm getting married." Georgie held out her ring finger for Jax's inspection.

"Yikes." He glanced at the massive diamond. "Either Peter's doing better than I thought, or he loves the crap out of you."

"Why choose?" She turned back to her mother. "I won't choose between you and Addy either, you know. You're the mother of the bride." Bianca pressed her lips together and looked away, her eyes suddenly soft and shiny. "That, however—" She shot a finger Addy's way. "—is my only sister, and therefore my maid of honor."

Addy blinked. She didn't know what shocked her more, being somebody's maid of honor, or Georgie so casually claiming her as a sister. As if their relationship were more than the fragile paper her marriage certificate was printed on. Her throat went tight and she swallowed down four days' worth of tears.

"So it's time to work this shit out," Georgie went on, "because *I am the bride here*." She folded her arms on top of the desk and lowered her forehead to them once more.

Matty rocked back on his heels, fists in his pockets, eyes narrow on Georgie's shiny head. "Is she hungover?"

"Well," Addy said carefully. "She might've had a toast too many."

Jax frowned at his sister, too. "Of what?"

"Everything," Bianca said. "Mojitos, champagne, wine—"

"Either stop talking about it," Georgie said darkly, "or bring me the trash can."

Matty laughed. It had been a while since Addy had heard him laugh that sincerely, or really at all. She found herself smiling at him. Everybody was smiling at him, actually. He must've felt all the fond eyes on him because he immediately broke off to glare at the floor.

The door jingled again and a pair of middle-aged women wandered in. One was small and wren-like, with a cap of shocking red hair and ambitious earrings. The other was long and slim, draped in a deep, quiet blue. Actual customers? Sing hallelujah.

"I'm telling you, Carol," the smaller one said, "if you don't go back to the Gilded Fish to get that scarf, you're dead to me. I'd kill to wear that color and I'll probably have to kill you if you don't.'"

Carol laughed and patted at the smooth twist of her pale hair. "Down, girl. It's just a scarf."

"A *great* scarf." The smaller woman adjusted the pretty shopping bags that dangled from her arm like bangles. "Which you would be criminally insane not to own." She angled her chin for a sideways glance. "Buy me a cup of coffee, though, and I'll consider not institutionalizing you."

"Oh, Amy." Carol's lips twitched. "You say the sweetest things."

"If it's coffee you're after, you can't do better than the Sugar Rush." Jax hitched a hip onto the desk and gave them a warm smile. He also blocked the women's view of Georgie snoozing on the desk. "Right next door. You can get a to-go cup and a doughnut the size of a dinner plate."

"Lovely." Carol grinned at him. "My ticket out of the institution."

"Welcome to the Davis Gallery, ladies," Addy said, planting herself at Jax's side. Close enough to complete the human shield. Close enough to feel the burn of his body heat. Lord, he ran hot. "The Sugar Rush is definitely a favorite but I'd be remiss if I didn't at least mention the Wooden Spoon as a sit-down alternative. That'll be out the door and a block to the right." She leaned in confidentially. "You haven't lived until you've tasted Gerte's North Shore triple berry pie."

"Pie?" The smaller woman — Amy, she thought — ran a speculative gaze over Addy. "Pie plus caffeine, and all in the direction of the miraculous scarf?" She nodded decisively. "I like you. You might be my new best friend. I was in the market for one, you know." She gave Carol a dismissive wave. "That one has no taste."

Carol laughed. "Says the woman who didn't know who Diego Davis even was until her former best friend—" She broke off and stared. "Good God. You're her."

The smaller woman blinked at Addy, then at Carol. Frowned. "Her? Her who?"

"*Her*." Carol pointed at Addison. "She's the angel."

Jax stiffened beside her, and Addy fixed her smile more firmly in place.

Amy lifted a plucked brow and considered Addy more closely. "I do sometimes hear angels singing when somebody suggests pie but—"

"Amy, you cultureless cretin." Carol sighed, took the colorful little woman by the shoulders and pointed her toward the central wall of the gallery where *Diego's Angel* hung in all her golden glory.

The Addison on the canvas glowed with good humor and innocent sexuality, her curves filled in with a round generosity, while an aura shone around her ringlets like she was the virgin madonna. It was compelling, Addy knew, that contrast. The ripe sexuality and the pure innocence. The fresh beauty and the naughty laughter. It just wasn't real. Wasn't *her*.

"That, my girl, is *Diego's Angel*." Carol turned Amy gently back to face Addison. "And so is that."

"Oh. Oh my."

Addy watched with a twinge of regret as the warmth in the women's eyes melted into something else. As Addison became something both more and less than a fellow human being to them. As the facts of her life that most people kept private — her body, her sexuality, and her late husband's opinion of them both — fell into the public domain. Addison the friendly shopkeeper disappeared, and Diego's Angel took her place.

Then the door jingled and Nan Davis marched in, a sour frown on her tiny face. Addy was almost grateful.

"Hey, Nan," she said brightly. "These ladies were just trying to decide between a doughnut at the Sugar Rush and a slice of the North Shore triple berry at the Wooden Spoon. What do you think?"

At seventy-five, Nan was a tiny, wizened thing with a bullet-proof mushroom cap of dyed black hair, a three-pack-a-day smoking habit and a newspaper at her disposal. She stretched her thin, bright lips into a rictus of a smile for the tourists. "Either one is good," she said. "Can't go wrong."

"I'd go with the Wooden Spoon, myself. Oooh, they could try the sweet lefse!" Addy turned back to the tourists. "It's worth every calorie, I swear."

But Carol was communing with the painting. "God, she's gorgeous," she murmured, devouring it with avid eyes. "She's so clearly you, and yet—" She threw Addy a glance over her shoulder. "—so clearly not."

No kidding, Addy thought.

"Bianca," Nan growled at her daughter-in-law. "I need to talk to you."

Bianca serenely ignored her, and watched the tourists worship at the shrine of *Diego's Angel*.

"He idealized you," Carol mused. "Made you beautiful."

"Made her beautiful?" Amy gawked at her friend in near-comic dismay. "For God's sake, Carol. You have manners, I know you do. How about you use them?" She turned stricken eyes on Addy. "I'm so sorry. She didn't mean that the way it sounded. You're a very pretty girl."

"Pretty as a painting," Jax said. "Prettier." Addy put her elbow in his ribs.

"Don't worry about it," Addy assured her. "Besides, she's right. That's not really me up there. Diego painted with his heart, not his eyes."

"That's it exactly," Carol breathed, and she gazed in wonder at the canvas. "God, it just drips devotion. Pure adoration. I can feel it, right here, like gravity." She pressed both hands to her chest and stepped reverently toward the canvas. "I have to..." She broke off, shook her head. She turned back to Addy and fished her phone out of her purse. "I have to have a picture of the contrast. Of how love elevates the ordinary. Do you mind posing?"

As the ordinary? Addy put on her company smile. "Of course not."

"Let me." Bianca stepped forward, all gracious benevolence, and held out a hand for the camera. She nudged Matty into the spot Addy had just vacated in the Georgie shield. "I'm Bianca Davis, by the way. Diego's mother. I love to meet such well-informed fans of his work."

So Addy stood to have her inadequate picture taken next to Diego's dream of her. The dream that — as Carol had so astutely observed — wasn't based in any kind of reality, and had survived about twenty minutes of real-life marriage. But the women left with two hand-thrown vases, a framed woodcut print, and a snapshot of Addy with *Diego's Angel* that would fuel a dozen dinner party debates on the nature of love. They'd spend the rest of the afternoon sprinkling their tourist dollars all over Main Street like fairy dust, too. Which was exactly why Addy had nurtured the illusion of *Diego's Angel* all these years. It had been for her own benefit, of course, but it had been for everybody else's too. Unquestionably.

Was there room for this in her new normal? Did she want

there to be?

The door hadn't even swung fully shut behind the women when Nan hissed, "When were you going to tell me, Bianca?"

"Tell you what?" Bianca asked while Addy walked back to the desk and leaned on the edge, suddenly exhausted.

"About Devil Days." Nan hitched up her enormous purse and stalked over to shove a finger in her daughter-in-law's face. "About putting porn on Main Street, for God's sake."

Chapter 19

BIANCA SAID, "OH, calm down, Nan. There's not going to be any porn on Main Street." She turned her back on Nan and strolled to the desk as well.

"Like hell there's not." Nan dogged her across the room. "Everybody knows Addy pulled a set of paintings out of that garage fire, Bianca. Paintings that were obviously important enough to risk her life for, but that nobody's ever seen. Which means — knowing our Diego — that they were probably too dirty to show widely."

Bianca chuckled and fluttered her fingers at Matty, who dutifully stood up. She took his place on the edge of the desk beside Addy and gazed coolly up at Nan. "Is that what people are saying? That Diego left behind a series of erotic post-*Angel* works featuring Addison?"

"It's what you're saying," Nan growled. "Implying, anyway, judging from the national press release you sent out." Addy stared at Bianca. *Press release?* Bianca didn't look her way. Nor did Nan. "I have Julia goddamn Gates of the *New York Art Report* leaving me voice mails fishing for the particulars, Bianca. Would you care to share them?"

The air left Addy's lungs on a punch of shock. Julia Gates. Diego's favorite reporter. A powerful journalist whose unfailing devotion had made him the darling of the art world before he could legally buy a drink. And the woman — the first of many — with whom he'd broken his vows to Addy.

Bianca's lips curved with smug satisfaction. "Julia's interested in our little showing, is she?"

"Very." Nan stared down at Bianca, a shrewd speculation in those hazel eyes. "Why is that, do you suppose?"

Probably because she had long black hair, Addy thought bitterly, and a nape of the neck that Diego couldn't resist. Because she might be wondering exactly how prominently Diego's newly discovered body of work displayed *her* body. Because people tended to question a reporter's ethics when she'd gotten so thoroughly naked with a subject.

"Diego was a particular favorite of hers, if you remember." Bianca shrugged lightly. "As well he should've been. He made her career as much as she made his."

"She wanted to make more than his career," Nan said darkly. A crack of laughter wedged itself in Addy's throat and she made a strangled noise. Bianca gripped her knee with merciless fingers. "That's what I remember. Fifteen years older than he was, too. Maybe twenty."

"So what?" Bianca returned. "Older women fight irrelevance every single day of their lives but Diego didn't equate beauty with youth the way so many do. He saw the beauty in every woman. Found it and showed it to her. I promise you, Julia Gates wasn't the only reporter half in love with an artist half her age." She rolled a nonchalant shoulder. "Besides, she introduced Diego to the world. It's only natural that she'd want to introduce Matty, too."

Addy stared. Bianca was still planning to show Matty's work?

"Matty?" Nan's sharp eyes swung his way, caught the

flinch he tried to suppress. He drove his hands deeper into his pockets and scowled darkly at the floor. "Why the hell would you introduce a thirteen-year-old smart ass to the world?"

Matty jerked a shrug. "Beats the hell out of me."

Nan reached up and flicked his ear. "Language, young man."

"Ow." He scowled and rubbed his ear.

"Because he's producing work that has potential for miles," Bianca said, serenely ignoring the byplay. "It's not mature work yet, of course, but when you hang his canvases beside what Diego was producing at the same age—"

"Oh hell." Nan stared. "Oh shit. You wouldn't."

"Language," Bianca said primly.

"Fuck that," Nan snapped, and Matty choked back a laugh. "I know exactly what Diego was producing at Matty's age. He was painting it on my goddamned front porch, wasn't he?"

"What, the Kettle studies?" Bianca blinked innocently.

"The naked women." Nan fixed her daughter-in-law with a gaze that should've burned her to cinders. "The extreme close-ups of their genitalia, Bianca. Otherwise known as pornography."

"Only if you consider Georgia O'Keefe a pornographer, too." Bianca smiled coolly. "Which the world decidedly does not."

"Because she had the good grace to disguise the sex parts she painted as flowers, for God's sake. Diego's early stuff is nearly photographic, and you know it." Nan shook a furious finger. "Don't play semantics on this, girl. Devil's Kettle is a small town, and that right there—" She stabbed that finger at *Diego's Angel* which was serenely exuding adoration, rainbows and soft-focus lust. "—is about as racy as the citizenry is prepared to tolerate. They're proud of Diego. He put this town on the map, and they know it. We all know it. God knows you never let us forget it. But if you think they're going to let you frame up a bunch of pussy paintings and hang them on Main Street during Devil Days, you don't know this town at all."

"You're right about one thing — Diego did put this town on the map." Bianca rose slowly from the desk and gazed icily down at her mother-in-law. "In fact, my son is the only thing *keeping* this town on the map. That painting right there, that *racy* painting that's evidently pushed you and your delicate-minded neighbors to the edges of your moral endurance? It's the only thing standing between this town and an epidemic of bankruptcy. The Davis family's decision to keep it here, to keep the entire collection here instead of placing it in a world-class museum where it belongs is pure generosity. This whole town's continued well-being depends upon that generosity, and you know it. I know it. Everybody knows it. So please understand this: I will display whatever I please, whenever I please, wherever I damn well please." Her smile was chilled malevolence, slow and deadly. "You might want to use your little newspaper to make sure everybody else understands it, too."

The smile alone would've put Addy on her knees, never mind the speech. But Nan just gazed at Bianca like a chess master assessing a worthy opponent. "You're going to play it that way, huh?"

Bianca's smile spread. "When it comes to art, I don't play. You know that, Nan."

"You should." Nan sighed. "You damn well should play. Just shows how little you understand." She turned to Matty.

"I almost wish you'd managed it."

He blinked. "Managed what?"

"To burn down that damn garage and every painting in it."

"It was an accident," Matty muttered. "I wasn't *trying* to burn anything. And besides, the paintings in the garage weren't even the ones you're so—"

"Carriage house," Bianca cut in smoothly. She put a hand on Matty's arm. "We have a carriage house, darling."

Addy's brows shot up. Okay, so Bianca didn't want Nan to know exactly what had been in that folio. But why? To build anticipation for the eventual show? Because she intended to use those paintings as a weapon and didn't want to give up the element of surprise? Because she was plotting something else altogether? Foreboding gripped Addy's stomach. This was Bianca, she reminded herself grimly. It was probably all of the above.

"Fine." Matty rolled his eyes. "Carriage house. And I didn't burn it down, okay? I just burned the roof off it. Accidentally."

Nan studied him for a long moment, then shifted that gaze back to Bianca. "We're not done with this."

"Of course we are."

"Then you're dumber than I thought, and I always thought you were dumb."

"So you've always said." Bianca didn't bother to smile this time. Nan hitched up her bag, spun on one heel and headed for the door. Bells jingled violently and they all watched until she disappeared up the sidewalk, her dark helmet of hair utterly unruffled by the snatching wind.

Bianca tipped her head to study Jax. "I assume this is why you tracked us down today? To warn me about the apocalypse of public disapproval bearing down on us?"

Jax laughed. "Of course not. Why would I chase you all over town to tell you something you already know? Something you manufactured yourself, and entirely on purpose?"

Her lips curved reluctantly. "Just when I think you're a complete disappointment."

"I rolled as far from the tree as I could."

"I know, darling." She leaned down to peck his cheek. "I know." She tipped her head to study him. "So why are you here?"

"I wanted to see if you'd take Addy's shift at the gallery today."

Addy blinked. "What? Why?"

He rose and slipped a hand through her elbow. Everything in her leapt to life and she managed only through the most desperate of efforts to keep from hissing a breath in through her teeth. Oh, help. She was like water on a skillet around Jax lately, dancing and steaming and evaporating into a whole new form of herself. "I have something to show you."

"You do?"

"Yep." He looked to his mom. "So can you? Take the shift?"

Bianca eyed Georgie snoring softly into the surface of the desk and sighed. "We're not going anywhere."

"Super." He scooped up Addy's bag and handed it to her, jerked his chin at Matty. "You, too, buddy."

"Super," Matty echoed sourly. "A field trip."

"Don't be long," Bianca called after them as they headed for the door. "We're celebrating the engagement tonight over dinner. Hill Top House, seven o'clock."

"Super," Matty muttered again. Jax pulled open the door and shoved him onto the sidewalk.

Addy went to follow, then hesitated, one hand on the doorjamb. She glanced a question back at her mother-in-law, one she was half afraid to ask out loud.

"Don't be foolish," Bianca said almost kindly. "Of course you're invited. You're family." She folded her hands and fixed Addy with a penetrating gaze. "And we have a lot to discuss."

Jax smiled. "There it is."

"There what is?" Addy asked, her eyes on Bianca while relief and foreboding fought a bloody battle in her gut.

"The opening volley. Finally." And he shoved her onto the sidewalk, too.

Out on Main Street, Jax pointed Matty and Addison toward the little red Nissan pickup he was driving today. It was almost twenty years old and had nearly as many miles on it as the mini-pumper but he kept it for special occasions. Like now.

"Oh crap," Matty said. "We're driving that?"

"Yep. I'm off duty today." He nodded the kid toward the cab and headed for the driver's side. "It's unlocked. Get in."

"Fine. But I'm not riding in the middle." He frowned at the compact pickup. "I don't think I even can. This thing is snack-sized."

Addison pulled open the passenger door and crawled in. "I'm short. I'll do it."

Jax helped himself to the driver's seat, and tried hard not to grin. Victory. He'd been hoping he'd get to shift gears between Addy's pretty knees all the way up the hill.

He wasn't ashamed of it. He was only a man, after all, and he'd pushed his endurance to superhuman limits lately. If first kisses were adventures and second kisses were verdicts, every single kiss after that was a promise. And the promises he'd been making Addy lately were the sort a guy wanted to follow through on. Soon.

But he'd be damned if he'd make his move — his real move — before he was sure he'd cleared the field. Because you didn't get involved with a woman — like set-the-bed-on-fire involved — unless you were damn sure there was nobody else in that bed. Even a ghost. The way she was starting to kiss him back suggested he was making progress, but Jax wasn't a risk taker. People always seemed to be surprised by that — how could you fight fires for a living and not be a risk taker? The truth was that only shitty firefighters were risk takers. The good ones were methodical guys, analytical thinkers who liked to work with their hands and the occasional axe. They weren't afraid of pain but they didn't go looking for it, either.

So, yeah, Jax was waiting for his moment with Addy. It hadn't come yet but it was getting closer. *She* was getting closer. Every time he kissed her, he could feel her mouth ripening under his like a warm berry, getting softer and sweeter with each desperate ounce of patience he carved off his soul. The harvest was going to be so worth the wait but Jesus, you could only kiss a woman that thoroughly and that well so often before you were looking for excuses to shift gears between her damn knees.

Jax fired up the Nissan, released the parking brake and reached for the gear shift. Addy sucked in a sharp breath and Jax clamped down on a smug grin.

"Sorry," he murmured. "It's a little tight."

"No problem." She squirmed, trying to give him more room but only succeeded in sliding the inside seam of her jeans along his thumb. Lust roared to life inside him, and Jax had to squirm a bit, too, looking for a little more room himself. Not much to be had at this point, at least not inside his jeans. "So where are we going?"

"Davis Place."

"Really?" She turned those big green eyes his way as he swung into a U-turn and headed north out of town. "Why?"

"As it happens, I'm not the only guy with a little free time today." He shifted again, turned inland and gained speed for the climb up the bluffs. "Your plan for Davis Place came up the other day at work. Turns out Frank, Mason and Graham are all pretty interested in the business."

She frowned at him. "They are?"

They hit the hill and he downshifted. Her eyes went glassy, and she blinked. He sent her an innocent sideways glance. "Problem?"

Those eyes narrowed. "With what?"

"With taking Mason, Frank and Graham on a walk-through today? They're planning to meet us there in about—" He consulted his internal alarm clock. "—I'd say about twenty minutes. That's a plumber, an electrician and a carpenter, by the way, all in one fell swoop. And they're prepared to give estimates. Which will be a hell of a lot more accurate if you tell them exactly what it is you want them to do."

"Oh, but I don't know if I'm quite ready to—"

"Addy, please. If you revise your spreadsheets even one more time, you'll have it fined down to clean room specifications. Don't even pretend you don't know exactly what you want."

"Well of course I know what I want." She paused and Jax seized the opportunity to downshift again. He knew what he wanted, too. She shivered and opened her knees around the shifter in an effort to accommodate him. Oh, Jesus. He hoped he made it up the bluffs without disgracing himself. "I just don't know what Bianca wants."

"So what?"

"So it's not just my project is it?" She frowned out the windshield. "It's my idea but her property. I checked. Nan signed it over to her when she moved out. I wondered why she'd just get rid of it that way, just sign it over to a daughter-in-law who already has a place and a huge one at that. Then I heard about your dad." She touched his elbow, and he looked over to find her watching him, her face soft and sad. "I'm really sorry, by the way. I didn't know. Diego never talked about him."

"Nobody talks about him." He smiled at her. "They should though. It was a long time ago, and my dad was awesome." He glanced at Matty, whose face was turned to the window. "*Our* dad. I wish you'd known him, Matty. He'd have loved you."

"Yeah?" The boy didn't turn but something about his slouch was just a little too studied to be natural and Jax tasted guilt, bitter and reproachful. Bianca wasn't great with grief — obviously — so Jax doubted she'd been sharing stories about Joe over the dinner table. Georgie followed their mother's lead in all things, of course, and Addy had never met the man. It had been Jax's job to give the boy his father, and he'd failed.

"Oh, yeah," Jax said around the lump in his throat. "He was always blowing something up. If he'd lived, he'd have burned down the carriage house so many times, nobody would've blinked when you tried."

"I didn't *try*."

"Of course you didn't." Jax reached across Addy to give the kid's knee a deliberately patronizing pat. Brushing his arm across her soft sweater was a nice bonus, as was the black scowl he earned from his brother. He liked it way better than that blank facade Matty liked to affect these days, and was getting damn close to perfecting. "But if you *had*, who would blame you? That kiln he built in the basement of Davis Place—"

"The one that killed him?"

"That's the one," Jax said easily, not that it was an easy memory. His dad's death still hurt. Of course it did. But it had been a long time ago, and Matty's pain was fresh. Raw. He needed to unload some of it, and Jax could take it. He owed his brother that much. More, probably. "It was a death trap. Literally. And the one he built at Hill Top House wasn't much better. Mom knew she couldn't stop him from building it, but she insisted he do it away from the main house. That way when it blew — because everybody knew it was going to blow eventually — at least it would only take out the garage."

"You're saying everybody's been just *waiting* for the garage to blow up?" Matty turned to stare. "It was like a time bomb or something?"

Jax gave him a good, hard stare in return. "You discharged a firearm in the direction of a propane tank, Matisse. Don't even think you're off the hook on that."

Matty fell back into his slump and resumed his stare out the window. "A propane tank I didn't even know was *there*," he muttered.

"It wasn't a secret," Jax said reasonably. "It wasn't even hidden. But if you can admit that you failed to maintain the situational awareness necessary to safely operate a firearm — even a pellet gun — then I can certainly concede that nobody probably ever mentioned Dad's leftover propane tanks to you." He rounded the bend and approached the giant rock marking the end of the road. Even as he turned left, he pointed his chin toward the right fork, the one that led to Hill Top House. "After all, they hardly even say Joe's name over there. Of course they wouldn't mention his deathtrap kiln. It's a shame Mom's so reluctant to talk about him, though. You'd have loved him. And he'd have loved the crap out of you." The Nissan fell into a huge pot hole, and Jax winced and downshifted. He enjoyed that part but holy hell his suspension. "Especially when you tried to burn down Mom's carriage house. He always meant to do that one day himself."

Matty only grunted but Jax thought he might be fighting a smile. He glanced at Addy for confirmation. She was always so attuned to the kid's mental state; she'd know if he was leaving this conversation in a good place. But Addy was staring straight ahead between them, gripping her knees and exuding concentrated silence. It was as if she were trying to erase herself, he realized suddenly. As if she imagined that Jax could reach across the cab to grab hold of the brother he'd somehow lost track of over the years, but only if she willed herself into invisibility first.

Something surged inside him with a violent churn, ripped his heart from the bedrock of his soul, and sent it spinning like an unmoored boat on a vast ocean. Good Christ, he loved this woman. He'd wondered about that over the years. Love was an easy word to toss around, a convenient way to describe — at least to himself — the upheaval Addy wreaked on his mental state, not to mention what she did to his body. He'd been very careful not to imagine himself in love with her for real, though. Real love wasn't something that existed, one-sided, in the confines of a person's head. Or even in their sweaty little dreams. Real love required two people, two hearts, and a hearty dose of real life.

But watching her try so damn hard to get out of the way while he fumbled to reconnect with the only brother he had left? It kicked the shit out of that theory. Fuck it, he loved her. He was in love with her. Desperately, irrevocably, forever and ever, say amen.

Silence reigned for a few minutes, and Jax concentrated on negotiating the private drive's truck-eating pot holes with every shell-shocked ounce of his attention. Finally, he pulled into the weed-choked drive behind his grandma's saggy old back porch.

"Yikes," Matty said, and shoved open his door. "This place is a disaster."

"Don't burn it down," Jax said. "I think Addy wants it."

"Ha ha." Matty threw him a scowl. "So funny, Jackson." He stepped onto the gravel drive and headed for the porch, leaving the door hanging open for Addy. She threw her knee over the gearshift and scooted across the bench seat toward it. She stopped before she got there and turned back to him, her face shining.

"That was a good thing you did just now." She reached out, took his jaw in one soft hand and rubbed her thumb over his cheekbone. "A very good thing, Jax."

"What?" he asked, staring. He *knew* he was staring, could feel himself doing it, but was helpless to stop. A guy didn't come face to face with his own heart all that often. He wasn't firing on all cylinders just yet. "Asking Matty not to burn your house down?"

"Yeah." She leaned in and kissed him. Just put her mouth right on his and kissed him. It was, he realized dimly, the first time *she'd* kissed *him.* She just touched her lips to his — a blessing, a kindness, a reward. A miracle. She drew back and laughed. "For that. I do want to keep it. Thanks." She slid across the bench seat, got out and slammed the door behind her. She trotted toward the porch, calling for Matty, probably to wave him off the back steps — which were surely more dangerous than Joe's old kiln — leaving Jax with both hands still on the wheel, and a stupid smile lighting up his whole damn face.

Chapter 20

AN HOUR LATER, Mason and Frank were squabbling happily about how a smart person might create a fully plumbed and wired island counter in Davis Place's ruined old kitchen, and Jax went looking for Addy. He found her standing in front of a miserly window in what she assured him would soon be a breathtaking great room. He didn't doubt it, not with that view.

Over her shoulder he could see a thin strip of lawn, a low rock wall, and then nothing but empty air and miles of water. The land simply fell away, sheered off into a cruel drop that ended in the lake's snapping jaws while the river jetted out of the facing cliff in rainbow splattered shards.

Beauty wasn't the right word for it, he mused. It was too sharp, too unsettling—

"Holy crap," he said abruptly. He joined Addy at the window and stared. "This is the view!"

Addy cocked a brow. "Uh, yeah. Sort of the reason for this whole project, remember?"

"No, I mean, *this* view. It's the one hanging in Hill Top House, in the great room. Diego's tryptich." He stepped back, squinted at it. "How did I never know that?"

Addy tipped her head and studied the windows. "You're right," she said slowly. "It's that same vibe. Like a thin layer of beauty smeared over—" She broke off, bared her teeth and made claws of her hands.

"Right." Jax shot a finger at her, in perfect harmony. "Over something damn dangerous."

"But compelling, too." She pursed her lips. "You don't want to look but it doesn't feel safe to turn your back on it, either."

Jax slung a friendly arm around her shoulders. "He should have named that series *Mom*."

She gave a weary laugh. "Bianca." She sighed, and was quiet for a long moment. Then she tipped up her face to his, hit him with huge worried eyes. "Jax, what's going on in her head?" she asked. "I know she has a plan. I just have no idea what it is, which means I have no idea what to say when she asks for it."

"And she will ask for it." He watched Graham Graves cross the narrow strip of the front yard, clipboard in hand, his eyes narrowed on the tumble-down porch. Matty trailed after him, lugging a metal tool box. "Probably at dinner tonight."

"Yeah, that's what I figured, too." Matty knelt in the grass and rifled through the box to come up with the tape measure Graham had presumably requested. "But what? She had every opportunity today to tell Nan about the new paintings but she didn't."

"Didn't let Matty tell her, either."

"Yeah." She slid him a sideways glance. "I noticed that as well."

"He didn't know it was a family secret, though. If he had, Nan would have picked it up in an instant." Jax shook his head. "Kid can't lie to save his life."

"I know. Thank God."

Jax didn't imagine her gratitude was all for Nan not finding out about the paintings, or even mostly for that. It was for Matty's inherent bent toward honesty, and Jax was right there with her. Diego had been an incredible liar, with a special talent for deceiving people who believed in him. Who loved him. It was damn hard to separate Matty from Diego when he was wearing that face, but this was an important distinction. The kind of distinction that could — if Bianca was right and the kid did have some freaky talent that would eclipse even Diego's — save his damn soul.

"But why would she show Matty's work when there's such a lucrative alternative?" She frowned. "Or why would she at least pretend to? Why would she want the entire town to go all torches and pitchforks on us?"

He shrugged and tucked his fingers into his pockets. "Guess we'll find out at dinner."

"For pity's sake." Addy watched Matty hand Graham a crowbar out in the yard. "If she's not planning to show Matty's work, why would she put him through this? He's so angry already."

"To be fair, he's thirteen. Thirteen is an angry age."

"I know." She sighed. "You should talk to him."

"I just did."

"I know." She smiled up at him, and something shifted inside his chest. Something tender and vulnerable. "But you have to keep talking to him. Talk to him about this."

He shook his head doubtfully. He was also trying to clear the stars out of his eyes. He didn't think straight when she smiled right at him like that, all dimples and admiration. "Talking only goes so far with guys. I vote for keeping him busy." He put a single finger in one of those dimples — soft as dreams, those things — and gently aimed her face toward the yard where Graham had Matty jogging back to his truck on his third fetch-and-carry of the last five minutes. "Until we have something concrete to talk to him about — like some idea of what Bianca's trying to do here — I say we put him to work. If he's not at the fire station with me, let's keep him here at Davis Place with you. Let him tag after the guys, learn to build, saw, hammer, wire." He trailed his knuckle down the curve of her cheek, followed the pretty line of her neck and let his hand rest on her shoulder. "Let him develop some skills, Addy. Let's give him something to hang his self-esteem on that has nothing to do with art. It'll protect him better than a million heart-to-hearts, I promise."

"I believe you." She watched Matty out in the yard with worried eyes. "I think you should talk to him again anyway."

"You're such a girl." He drifted his hand down her back to her bottom, fit the lovely curve of it into his palm. Yep. Definitely a girl. His blood started humming, heating, but she stepped out of reach.

"For heaven's sake, Jackson. We're standing in front of a window." But her cheeks were pink and interested. "Graham and Matty are right there."

"And Mason and Frank are in the kitchen." He tugged her away from the window, pressed her back into the wall and kissed her. He'd only meant to have a quick taste, a quiet taste, but she smelled so good. Like sunshine, he thought, the strong kind that baked the earth dry in August and left the whole North Shore standing around like a fresh pack of matches, waiting for one good lightning strike. And when she wound her arms around his neck and offered up her soft, sweet mouth, well, God. There went the lightning.

He crushed her to his body, until he could feel every gorgeous curve, every secret hollow. His hands raced over her, taking, claiming. It roared inside him, this need to mark her as his own. Desperate, he thought vaguely. He felt desperate, hungry. He wanted more than he had, more than she'd given him. More, he knew, than he'd actually asked her for just yet.

His fingers, he realized suddenly, were twisted fiercely in her curls, the fragile curve of her skull hard in his palm as he plundered her mouth. Like he was trying to, what, consume her or something? Mark her? Own her? *Easy*, he commanded himself, even as his heart thundered and arousal pounded. *Dial it back, Jackson*.

But when he tried, when he gentled his grip and shoehorned an inch or two of daylight between them, Addy arched back into him with a noise of demand that hit his system like napalm.

Right. He jacked her off her feet, pressed her into the wall and lost himself in the hot rhythm of his need. When she hooked her legs around his waist, he slapped a hand to the wall beside her head and picked up the pace, rubbing himself shamelessly against her, his desire hard and hot against her melting welcome. His knees went wobbly and a climax gathered prickly and devastating at the base of his spine. Her mouth was open next to his ear, and she was gasping, panting. Damn close herself, he thought and a roar of dark-edged satisfaction crawled up his throat.

Jax wasn't entirely sure what he would've done next. He had a feeling it would have involved the floor and a significant rearrangement of their clothing and almost certain scandal when Mason and Frank rolled out of the kitchen to see what the commotion was all about.

But then Graham yelped, "Holy *buckets*!" out on the front lawn and Matty just bellowed. There was an unholy clatter of metal on metal, like somebody'd pitched a silverware drawer down the stairs and Jax and Addy sprang apart, panting.

For one sticky moment, they just stared at one another. Her chest heaved under her pretty purple sweater, and her nipples pressed clearly against the fabric, begging for his touch. His mouth.

And then she grinned at him. One loopy curl dangled in front of her eye, and a smile — a smirk, really — spread across her face, naughty and delighted and *hot*.

And suddenly Jax was done playing. He was flat out of patience. She was *it*, this woman. She was the love of his life, goddamn it, and he didn't want to dry-hump her against the wall in secret anymore. Well, he did want that — it was a nice little appetizer — but that wasn't all he wanted. Not nearly. He wanted the main course, plus dessert. He wanted hours, days. A lifetime. He wanted *her*. All of her — body, heart, soul. And there was only one way to have her.

He had to ask.

"Addison."

"Mmmm?" She patted her chest and blinked, her cheeks flushed, her eyes dazzled, and he thought *fuck it* and almost reached for her again.

He pulled himself back with a superhuman effort. "We can't keep doing this," he said tightly.

"We can't?"

"Hell, no." A damn, dirty lie. He could take her up against the wall all day long. His hands twitched for her so he raked them through his hair instead. "We have to talk."

"Oh." Her hand crept to her throat. "Already?"

He frowned. "Already what?"

"What the hell was *that*?" Mason bulled out of the

kitchen belly-first.

Frank followed more leisurely. "Somebody get struck by lightning out there?"

You have no idea, Jax thought, shoving his hands into his pockets for some emergency rearranging.

Addy snapped into action. She flung herself toward the front door and jerked it open. "Graham!" she shouted. "Matty?"

The stream of cursing Matty cut loose was so creative, so vile, so fascinatingly prolific that Jax was impressed in spite of himself. He shared a lifted eyebrow with Frank and Mason, and they all trotted out to the porch.

Matty lay on the lawn, all cursed out. His eyes were open, his arms out, and he stared blankly into the blue sky. He didn't appear injured but was evidently occupying his own plane of existence for the time being. The tool box had barfed up its entire contents on the grass around him and Graham hopped from foot to foot a few feet away, folded nearly in two with laughter. Addy fell to her knees beside Matty.

"Matty!" she cried, patting frantically at his arms and legs. "Are you hurt?"

Matty blinked, gathered himself, sat up slowly. "I don't think so, no."

"What *happened*?"

He pointed solemnly to the porch. Jax walked down the steps to examine the broken lattice panel somebody had removed from the base of the porch and rested against the railing. He peered into the dark cavity under the porch, then turned to Graham, an eyebrow raised in question.

Graham sucked in a deep breath but couldn't quite wipe the grin from his round, sweet face. "We found Turkey

Ground Zero," he announced. "Pulled off that lattice work, and fifty, sixty birds pelted out of there. It was like the Boston Marathon, and Matty was standing on the starting line, facing the wrong direction." He choked on a laugh, stuffed it down manfully and carried on. "They trampled the poor kid flat. Like he was Wile E. Coyote and they were the Road Runner." He shook his head sympathetically, then ruined the effect with a snorting laugh he couldn't quite suppress.

"You need to get Willa Zinc up here," Frank observed, tucking his fingers into his belabored waistband. "Had raccoons in my attic last winter and she had them out on their furry asses quick, fast and in a hurry."

"It was like he was wearing a shirt that said FREE BIRD SEED, THATAWAY," Graham observed. He gave one last chuckle and wiped his eyes happily.

"Zinc's good," Mason agreed, smoothing his 'stache. Jax suspected there was a smile behind it. "Her daddy was a son of a bitch, but Willa's all right. You want her number?"

"I have it," Addy said.

Matty sighed and lay back down. "I hate my life."

Jax wasn't sure he blamed the kid.

Chapter 21

A FEW HOURS later, Addy dragged herself into Hill Top House for Georgie's engagement dinner. The chandelier in the foyer dripped a whole crayon-box of colors onto the gleaming pine floor, and despite her bone-deep weariness, Addy had to smile. All those blues and reds and oranges, the sunsets and sunrises, the modern edges next to all those antique curves and swirls. It was both a warm welcome and a solid punch to the throat, visually speaking. Bianca had always taken a very brace-yourself approach to hospitality.

She stopped in the middle of all those colors and waited for the sweet comfort of coming home to fill her. She needed it so badly. The past week had left ragged edges all over her soul, the kind of raw patches that home had always healed. But nothing happened.

Anxiety stirred inside her as she walked toward the great room, toward that kick-in-the-teeth view. She waited for her breath to catch, for the relief of sanctuary to wash over her.

Nothing.

Panic fluttered restless wings in her chest and she quickly pictured the shabby old comforter she'd left spread over her bed upstairs. Brought to mind the smell of lake wind and white pines, made herself hear the low rumble of water that had underscored every moment of her life here at the summit of Devil's Kettle. Still nothing. She felt only that same grinding unhappiness that had filled her since the moment Jax had pinned her against a wall, kissed her halfway to madness, then announced that he was done with her. That he'd enjoyed frenching her whenever the mood struck and privacy allowed, but he wasn't going to keep doing it. He was over it. Bored.

He hadn't said it in exactly those words, of course, but Addy wasn't new at this game. She knew what *we have to talk* meant, especially when it was delivered in that particular shade of grim. Her novelty had worn off. She hadn't managed to keep his attention very long, she noted dully. Even Diego had lasted longer. He'd at least slept with her before losing interest.

She gripped the back of the huge white sofa and stared blindly at the sunset. She'd tried for a week to figure out the mess of her life and was no closer than she'd been the night Matty blew the roof off the carriage house and the lid off her secret. The night Bianca had kicked her out and Jax had kissed her madly. Now suddenly Bianca wanted her back, but Jax didn't want her at all, and everything she understood was shattering around her. She had no idea what was going on anymore, let alone how to fix any of it.

People were going to do what they were going to do, she decided, and no amount of preparation was going to protect her heart from this night. So when Jax asked for a private conversation — and he would, probably tonight — she'd give it to him. And she'd survive it. Of course she would. She'd abandoned chunks of her heart all over the stupid country. If heartbreak was saying goodbye, Addy was a pro.

She pulled in a deep breath, hoping for calm and courage, but got instead a lungful of that singular mix of smoke and soap that belonged only to Jax. She turned to find him in the arch between the foyer and the great room, his eyes dark and steady on her. Sunset streamed through the massive windows at her back, touched that unruly chestnut hair and pulled out streaks of amber and copper. She took in the determined line of his mouth, the deliberate quality of his stillness.

This was it, she thought, even as she pushed her lips into a friendly smile. He was letting her go. Right now. And all the goodbyes she'd said over the years weren't going to help her at all. Because this wasn't goodbye. This was neither of them going anywhere. This was her seeing him across the family table at least twice a week. Saying hello in the gallery, crossing paths at the Wooden Spoon. This was her smiling at him over paintings, over pie. Over Matty's head until the day the boy didn't need them anymore. This was her heart breaking a dozen times a day for the next forever.

How on earth was she supposed to live through that?

Oh sweet mercy. Realization crashed through her like a rogue wave, tried to drag her to her knees. She hadn't been kissing Jax all week. She'd been falling in love.

Well, maybe not *love* precisely. Maybe it hadn't gone quite so far as that. She took a careful inventory of her heart and soul. *Not yet.* The knowledge was a bitter relief. *Not quite yet.* She was teetering on a very dangerous ledge, but she hadn't fallen. She'd held back, and he had, too. Both of them waiting for…something. For what, she had no idea. She knew only that Jax, evidently, hadn't found it, not in her. She'd been found lacking. Again.

She cleared the agony from her throat and said, "Hey, Jax."

"Hey, Addy." He kept those fingers tucked into his pockets and rocked back on his heels. Watched her with careful eyes. "You've been avoiding me."

"Yep. All afternoon."

"Try all week."

"You caught me once or twice."

"We didn't talk much."

"Nope."

"We need to."

She smiled a little. "Looks like my luck's run out, then."

He studied her for a long moment, face cool and closed. "Care to explain?"

"Not really." Pain-laced exhaustion lapped at her.

"We really do need to talk, Addison." He moved toward her, a subtle, sideways circling that made her feel like prey. "I know this isn't a conversation you want to have and I'm sorry for that. But you need to hear what I have to say. You owe me that much."

"I know." Her voice was small in the vast room, her words disappearing in the echoing space. She cleared her throat and steadied herself. "I know. Just..." Tears rushed up her throat and she stopped. Swept up the shreds of her composure. "Just not right this minute, okay? Not here. Not now."

"Then when?" It was a tight demand. "Tell me when, Addison, because I'm not going to chase you all over town again, begging for an appointment."

"After dinner." She backed toward the dining room, toward the arch at the side of the great room that led to a long table set for a full house. "Let's just get through dinner, okay? We'll celebrate Georgie, then talk when we get back—"

Home. Home? Oh good heavens, no wonder she hadn't gotten the usual home-and-hearth buzz off Hill Top House.

Not only had she been stupid enough to fall halfway in love with *him*, she'd fallen completely in love with that tiny bucket of charm and built-ins he called a house! She cursed her stupid, needy heart. Now she'd be doubly orphaned when he dumped her, and wasn't that just what she deserved for being an idiot? She closed her mouth, swallowed, and tried again.

"We'll talk when we get back to your place, okay?"

He studied her, and something shifted in those green-brown eyes. "Tonight?"

"Yeah, tonight." No time like the present. "You want to say something, I'm ready to hear it." Just like she was ready for the end times. She gave him what she hoped looked like a smile. "Promise."

He stepped forward yet again, close enough to touch her if he wanted to. And God help her, she swayed toward him, yearning for him to reach for her. "I'll hold you to that, Addison," he murmured.

So anxious to be done with it, Addy thought on a stab of anger. To be done with her. She latched onto that flash of temper and thought, well, fine. Have it your way, you jerk. She'd rebuilt her life before. She would again. If there was one thing she knew how to do, it was start over.

"Fine." She lifted her chin, shook back her hair, and turned toward the dining room. Away from him. Jax could follow or not. Or he could just go to hell. His choice. She didn't look behind her to find out which he'd picked.

Chapter 22

JAX HAD NO idea how he survived the following hour and a half. Peter Zinc arrived — his brother-in-law-to-be — with a bottle of champagne that made Bianca coo like he'd presented her with a human child. An endless round of champagne toasts followed, of course, then dinner came and went in a series of pretty dishes scattered like confetti across the table cloth. As usual when his mother cooked, however, the food was more decorative than edible.

The cold carrot-yogurt soup hadn't been half-bad, though kind of a strange choice while eternal winter was upon them. He'd tried with the salad, he really had, but gave up when he ran across an actual twig. He had to admit, though, the couscous-fig thing with the tiny skewer of lamb sticking straight out of it had been tasty. All two and a half bites of it. Lucky for him, he was too busy trying to get a handle on Addy's mood to pay much attention.

She sat at his left elbow, pale and unhappy, pushing a few twigs around her plate. Was it really that awful, he wondered wistfully? The prospect of hearing him out? Of hearing that he loved her and wanted to build a life together? Or was he pushing her too hard, too fast? His palms felt a bit clammy and he pushed them surreptitiously down his khakis under the table. Maybe he was. Maybe he should—

"Peter, have a little more whipped parsnip," his mother urged from the matriarch's chair at the head of the table. She waved her wine glass at a glazed pottery dish full of white mash sculpted into a perfect curve, as if it had been dispensed from a soft-serve machine.

Peter smiled up the table at her from his place at Jax's right. He was handsome bastard, no question, that bald-by-choice look a winner when a guy had cheekbones as pretty as his fiancée's. Throw the looks in with the money and he figured Peter would make Georgie as happy as anybody possibly could.

"Oh, I couldn't," Peter said, patting his lean stomach with a rueful appreciation. Given that the parsnips had functioned more like cement than a side dish, Jax knew this to be the stone-cold truth. He had to admire the way the guy had made it sound like a compliment, though.

"More roasted sprouts?"

"Ah, no. Thanks." Peter glanced at Georgie beside him, appreciation glowing in his dark eyes. "I can't think of another thing I want right now. This pretty much fills me up." He smiled at Bianca again. "I mean, a table like this, the family around it?" He moved those big shoulders. "It's not something I grew up with. That's no secret." Bianca inclined her head regally, acknowledging if not dismissing Peter's less-than-impressive pedigree. "It's certainly nothing I ever anticipated having myself. But Georgie's brought all kinds of surprises my way." He put a tender hand on hers and she stopped fiddling with her twig salad long enough to smile up at him.

"Good ones, I hope?" she said.

"The best." He smiled back, a couple of ultra-manly slashes appearing in his lean cheeks. Jax shot a quick look at

Addy. Women loved that Clark Gable shit but she was still frowning at her twigs. She must've felt his eyes on her, though, because she lifted her head and met his gaze. And Jax all but reared back from the accusation and anger burning in her face. What the hell? "I don't have anything to offer in return that even comes close," Peter was saying. Jax hastily tuned back in. "But I do want to give you something."

Georgie perked up. "Presents?"

He laughed. "Think of it more like a dowry."

Addy spoke for the first time in minutes. "Doesn't the bride traditionally give the dowry to the groom?" she asked Peter, her own dimples winking out.

"Depends on the culture," Jax said. Addy kept her eyes — and her dimples, damn it — on Peter.

"That's true," his mom said from the head of the table. "In some parts of the world a good wife can run a man several hundred heads of cattle."

Georgie lifted a lock of hair from her shoulder, inspected it idly then flicked it behind her. Her eyes laughed into Peter's. "I'll be worth every moo, I promise."

"Of course you will," Bianca said serenely. "There's no such thing as free milk, not in this life." She sent Peter a wicked smirk. "Boys do like their milk."

"I think we're mixing metaphors now," Addy said, smiling. But there was something off about that smile. Something tight and forced and inherently un-Addy-like. She glanced his way and the smile died.

On Addy's left, Matty froze, a massive forkful of parsnips half-way to his mouth. He said, "I think I lost my appetite."

"Over sexual innuendo at the dinner table?" Jax looked

down the table at Bianca, his own tone deliberately light. Because lord knew letting his family get even a whiff of the discord between him and Addy wouldn't speed things up, and his patience with this dinner was thinning dangerously. "What kind of thirteen-year-old are you raising here, anyway?"

"The kind who tries not to think about that kind of thing when I'm eating." Matty set aside his fork. "With my family."

"Sex among family members is how you got here though," Jax pointed out. "Or did you have a different theory?"

"Adoption?" he said hopefully

Bianca laughed. "With that face? You look exactly like Diego at thirteen."

"Oh, gosh, right. I forgot." Matty's mouth twisted into a tight, ugly smile that Jax liked about as much as the one Addy had given him. "I'm just the off-brand Diego replacement. Thanks for reminding me, Mom."

"We have company, Matisse," Bianca said, her voice suddenly icy and sharp. "Either mind your manners or excuse yourself."

Matty shoved himself away from the table and stalked out of the room without another word. His boot heels pounded up the stairs and Addy's eyes followed the stomping all the way to the upper floor where a door slammed. She half-rose to go after him but a look from Bianca had her subsiding with an inaudible sigh.

"Forgive him," Bianca said to Peter. "Something's gotten into that child."

"Nothing to forgive," he murmured. "Thirteen's a difficult age."

"Diego was exactly the same, you know. Just a wild flame trapped inside a boy's body. But he came around, and Matty will, too." She released a long, slow breath. "I'm afraid we've spoiled him, though. It was hard not to, given the age gap." She sent Peter a half-smile. "He was a bit of a surprise, you know. I was touring Italy with Georgie when he was born."

"I'd heard," Peter said. No surprises there. Everybody in town knew the story of Matty's birth. It was the stuff of legend.

"Georgie — my baby — was fourteen. Can you imagine? We had agreed we were done with babies but—" She shrugged, and her eyes went shiny. "I was just barely pregnant when we lost Joe. I had no idea. Then the grief took me over, and I didn't feel anything — heart, body or soul — for months. So Matty was a shock, yes, but a blessing, too. He brought me back to life." She blinked away the tears and smiled. "He was such a happy baby."

"That's true," Jax said. "Kid was bullet-proof." He made himself grin at Georgie. "Remember how you used to cart him around like a doll?"

"I remember you taking him to student council meetings in a camouflage sling," Georgie returned.

"My soldier phase."

Addy turned to him, evidently surprised into addressing him directly. "You had a soldier phase?"

"Sure. Until I realized that soldiering included, you know, shooting people." He leaned back and sent her a smoky smile. "I'm a lover, not a fighter."

"Ah," Addy said, that inexplicable rage flickering back into her eyes. And that snapped it. Jax was done here. Because a woman didn't look at a man like *that*, not when

222

she'd kissed him halfway to embarrassing himself a few hours earlier. Something had happened between the kissing and the glaring, and Jax was going to find out what it was. He just needed a suitable exit line. For God's sake, when would this dinner *end*?

"Sure you are." Georgie rolled her eyes then turned to Peter. "Can we get back to the part where I get presents, please?"

Peter smiled at her. "Anxious for your cattle, are you?"

One silvery brow lifted and Peter laughed. "How would you feel about a little real estate?"

Avarice lit up her eyes. "Real estate?"

"It *is* the family business." He leaned in. "Are you up to managing a little project of your own?" He grinned at the surprise in her angular face. "I was thinking about the Hideaway. That abandoned resort I picked up last summer, north of town? It sort of fell off my radar when I got busy with the dealership, and now it's just sitting there, waiting for some love. How about I deed it over to you?"

"You want to give me a *resort*?"

"It's just a dilapidated lodge right now. But if you rehab it properly, it could be a very nice little investment for you."

She gazed at him, a small frown ghosting over that perfect face of hers. "You think I have what it takes to rehab it properly?"

"I know you do, Georgie," he said quietly. "You can do anything you set that brain of yours toward."

She launched herself into his lap and Peter rocked back in his chair. Silverware clattered and his surprised *oomph* ended on a surprised chuckle.

"I love you," she said fiercely. "I'm going to be the best wife you can imagine."

He stroked a palm down all that shiny hair. "Of course you are, honey."

Georgie linked her hands behind his neck and leaned back, excitement lighting up her face. "Does it have to be the Hideaway?" she asked. "Or can I pick something else?"

"Whatever you like." He tapped the end of her nose with a crooked smile. "I think the Hideaway's a nice entry point for you, but you can pick anything you like. I'll put together a list of—"

"I already know what I want."

His brows shot up. So did Jax's. "You do?"

"Yep." She glanced across the table at Addy and said, "I want to buy into the Davis Place make over."

"Davis Place?" Peter asked his face blank. "You mean Nan's old house, up on the bluffs?"

"That's the one." Georgie bounced on his lap with excitement. "Addy's turning it into a bed and breakfast for aspiring artists."

"Nobody's set foot in that place for years," Peter said faintly.

"No kidding." Georgie wrinkled her nose. "Addy took us on a walk through last week, and it's a disaster. It's going to take the world and a fortune to bring it up to speed but oh, Peter, the views! People are going to come from all over the country to paint those views, and I want to help."

"You do?" Across the table, Addy shot her a wary look.

"You do?" Peter echoed.

"I do." Georgie's mouth went flat and stubborn. "Don't you think I can do it? You just said I could do anything I set my mind to."

"And I meant it," Peter said helplessly, and Jax almost smiled. Underestimating Georgia Davis was a rookie mistake. Peter ought to know better by now but some guys only learned the expensive way. And Georgie was nothing if not expensive. "It's just...I mean, it's a big project." He hesitated. "It sounds like it's Addy's project, actually. Are you sure she wants a partner?"

"Of course she does."

Peter sent a questioning glance her way and Addy shrugged. "It's not exactly what Peter offered you, Georgie," she pointed out gently.

"What difference does that make?" Georgie asked. She was perilously close to pouting. Jax found himself smothering a grin in his collar. "Either he signs one of his properties over to me or he signs a check for me to buy into Davis Place." She turned her face up to his. "It's all the same in the end, right?"

"Of course it is," he assured her. "But honey—" He gentled his voice, as if speaking privately when really the entire family was listening shamelessly. "What if Addy doesn't want a partner? What if she'd rather work alone? Don't you think this is something the two of you ought to discuss another time? In private?"

Georgie waved this away. "This is a whole family project. We're all in. Mom will be teaching the classes, Jax is helping with the contractors, Matty will be general grunt-and-carry, but so far there's been nothing for me. Not until you. Not until now. Right, Addy?"

Addy gave Peter an apologetic smile. "I *am* in the market for an investor. I don't want to put any pressure on you, but if this is really something you're interested in, I could show you the paperwork."

Georgie turned big, pleading eyes back to Peter. "Please?" she said. "Please? I really want this, Peter. I can make you so proud of me."

Peter smiled but it looked a little forced to Jax. "I already am proud of you, sweet pea. You can have whatever you like."

She searched his eyes. "It's not too much?" she asked hesitantly, as if it had just occurred to her that she was asking for something very different from what he'd offered. "Oh my God, it is," she cried, tears spilling into her huge eyes. "It's too much. I'm sorry, I didn't think." Her hand went to her mouth. "Oh, Peter, I'm so stupid. I ruined everything."

"Hey," he said, wrapping his hands around her wrists and pulling them away from her face. "What are you talking about?" He dipped his head until he caught her eyes and held them. "Georgie, come on. Who do you think you're talking to, huh? It's six of one, half dozen of another to me. And even if it weren't, nothing's too good for my girl. You want a falling apart house on the hill? It's yours."

A tentative smile curved her trembling mouth. "You mean it?"

"You bet. It's no herd of cattle but if it's what you want, it's what you'll have."

"It's what I want."

"Then that's all I need to hear. If anything, I'm worried it's not enough. You want something else, too? Hey, how about that old amusement park out on Route Sixteen? It's got a ferris wheel."

She toyed with his collar. "What do I need with an amusement park? You're all the excitement I'll ever need."

"Same goes." He lifted his voice to Addy though he kept his eyes on Georgie's. "Bring the paperwork by my office tomorrow," he said. "We'll make this thing official. Hey, if I like what I see, maybe I'll buy myself in, too. You *are* really looking for investors?"

"I really am," Addy said and Georgie flung her arms around his neck to kiss him with serious enthusiasm. "Thank you, Peter." She pulled back to rest her forehead against his. "This means everything to me."

"*You* mean everything to me," he said.

Jax hoped to hell he meant that.

Chapter 23

GEORGIE MET ADDY'S eyes across the table and gave her a smug look that said *you're welcome*. Addy sighed. Oh, Georgie. Addy knew she was trying to help but putting Peter on the spot like that, and in front of the entire family? She suppressed a twinge of nostalgia for the days when Georgie had been too lazy to help out.

From the foot of the table, Jax leaned over to pour her some more champagne. "Ease up," he murmured. "You look like you're chewing tacks."

"What?"

He handed her the glass. "To Georgie's ambition," he said, raising his own glass and lifting his voice. "And Peter's generosity. A match made in heaven."

Addy drank and Jax's hand found her thigh under the table. Heat bloomed under his hand and Addy swallowed carefully.

"Better," he said softly. "You were grinding your teeth into dust. It can't be good for your jaw."

"My jaw is fine," she muttered.

"Of course it is." His fingers dipped into the hollow of her inner thigh to toy with the seam of her trousers. Her stomach muscles clenched and a completely inappropriate desire curled through her bloodstream like smoke. "Georgie step on your lines?"

"What lines?" She shifted away from his touch and he shrugged, draping that casual arm across the corner of the table between them.

"I don't know." His big hand dangled inches from her arm and scrambled the air between them into an electric froth. Or something. She didn't know what the heck it was doing over there, only that she could *feel* it. He was a good six inches from her and she could feel that hand as if he were running it up and down her arm. As if he were getting ready to follow it up with his tongue.

She squeezed her knees together, and fury ran together with the desire bubbling in her blood. He had no business toying with her like this. Not when he'd just made a date to break her stupid heart. "That makes two of us, then," she snapped in an undertone. "Because I have no idea what you're talking about."

He shrugged again, and that hand slid closer. Close enough now to brush her elbow. If she slouched.

She felt her spine melting, her usually crisp posture coming undone next to the impossibly radiant heat of his body. She scooted to the far side of her chair. Contemplated switching over to Matty's empty chair on the pretext of joining the conversation that had moved to Bianca's end of the table. She and Jax had become an island of two down here.

"I'm just saying, you look tense." He reached up and danced his fingers across the curls at the nape of her neck. Her entire body erupted in chills and she shivered hard.

"Addy?" She looked up to find Bianca gazing at her with concern. "Are you all right?"

"Yes!" She gulped back a healthy swallow of champagne

and moderated her tone. "Yes, of course. Why?"

"You shivered hard enough to rattle the silverware, dear."

"Oh." She surveyed the table. Georgie and Peter regarded her with mild interest, Jax with suppressed amusement. "Huh. No, just a chill, I guess." She forced a chuckle. "Goose walked on my grave or something."

"Or something," Jax said, a dark laugh in his voice. "Let me have a look at you."

"What? No!" Heat surged through her entire system, loosening her grip on sanity and pulling her toward him even as her brain hit the fire alarm "I'm fine, Jax." She gave him a tight-lipped smile to prove it. "I just—"

He slipped one hand — oh mercy — into the hair behind her ear and reeled her in until her forehead was cradled against the wide palm of his other hand. The words dried up on her tongue. "You're a little warm," he announced.

"You think?" she hissed furiously.

"You *are* a little flushed, dear." Bianca regarded her critically from the end of the table. "Do you think she's feverish, Jax?"

"I'm *fine*," Addy said. She threw Jax a killing look and he lifted his shoulders.

"You're a little warm," he said again.

"Why don't you take her home, Jackson?" Bianca said.

"What? No!" Addy bolted upright in her chair and snatched up her champagne glass. She'd promised to hear whatever he was so determined to say, to face it like an adult but her courage failed her. "Jax is overreacting. I'm not sick—"

"Maybe not but you've been working sixteen hour days all week," Jax said. "Even if you're not sick, you're exhausted. Now wish Georgie and Peter happy, and let me take you home."

Addy opened her mouth to argue, then took in the blooming interest in Georgie's face. The curiosity in Peter's. The slowly lifting brows on Bianca's. She set her glass down with precise fingers and rose. She deposited her napkin on her plate, walked around the table and kissed Georgie's cheek. "Happy engagement," she whispered, then laid her cheek next to Peter's and gave him a little squeeze. "Welcome to the family."

He covered her hand on his shoulder with one of his own and smiled warmly. "Thanks, Addy."

Then she straightened, looked Jax dead in the eye and said, "I'm ready."

Ten minutes later, she parked her Honda in Jax's drive. She sat in the car, windows down, listening to her cooling engine tick a counterpoint to the distant water. Then Jax pulled his beloved mini-pumper into the drive behind her, blocking her escape. Oh, the jerk. At the very least, he could have parked that beast across the street at the station the way he usually did. Now he was going to dump her, then force her to wait to make her escape while he moved his stupid truck.

The anger that had been simmering in her veins for hours burst into a rolling boil and she shouldered open her car door. Slammed it shut with a violent slap that did absolutely nothing to cool her temper. She stalked to the mini-pumper and yanked open its door. Jax blinked at her in surprise and she said, "Out. Now."

He gave her a wary look, but unfastened his seat belt and

slid to the ground. He closed the truck door and leaned back against it, hands tucked into his pockets.

"How dare you?" she snapped. She wanted to slap him. Shake him. Do something, *anything*, to snap him out of this smug, serene calm. Because she couldn't bear it that he was unmoved when she was half undone with pain. "How *dare* you?"

He let an infuriating beat pass. "How dare I what?"

She stepped forward, putting herself dangerously close to arm's reach. "Why don't we start with your ridiculous performance during dinner?"

He lifted a brow. "Performance?"

She folded her arms over her waist as the memory washed over her, half anger, half heat. "I don't have a fever, Jackson."

He grinned suddenly. "And yet you were definitely hot."

She couldn't argue with that, and her shame pulsed as hot as her desire. He took a step forward, and the heat of his body slid out to touch her. Suddenly she could feel her heartbeat in her wrists, in her ears. In other more interesting places. She thought about stepping back but found her shoes nailed to the asphalt.

"You haven't talked to me — really talked to me — for a week," he said softly. "Can you blame me for going above and beyond to get you alone?"

"Well you've got me alone now, you jerk." The bitterness in her voice was thick and startling, and he reared back from it. Good for him. "You have my complete and undivided attention, so why don't you start talking?"

He shook his head. "Not here." He took her shoulders, pointed her toward the house and gave her a little nudge. "Inside."

"For the love of—" She broke off and shoved both hands into her hair. "Why are you being so difficult about this?" He nudged her again and she stomped up his porch steps.

"I'm a difficult guy." He dealt with the locks and held open the door for her. She blew out a breath and sailed into the foyer. *Home*, she thought involuntarily. Oh, *crap*.

"No kidding." She stalked into the living room, stopped by the battered old steamer trunk and spun to face him, arms laced tightly over her middle. She braced for the punch. "Okay, I'm ready. Just say it."

He opened his mouth, then stopped. Tipped his head. Studied her closely. "What exactly do you think I'm going to say?"

She stared at him while pain and disbelief blazed through her lungs like a prairie fire. "You've never been cruel, Jackson," she said. "Don't start now."

"Seriously, Addy." He eased closer to her, hands out like she was a flighty deer. He sank onto the steamer trunk in front of her and made a show of gripping his knees. *See? No touching.* "I don't think we're on the same page here. What do you think I'm trying to tell you?"

Silence spun out between them. Indecision, pain and fear chased themselves pell-mell through her heart, bashing and crashing and breaking. Then her shoulders slumped, the tension deflated and she shrugged. He wanted her to say it? Fine.

"I think you want to tell me it's over. Whatever this thing is we've been doing? You're done with it. With me." She pushed the words through numb lips. "I think you want to tell me you're bored." She wrapped her arms tighter across her middle in case her guts wanted to fall out.

"You think I'm bored with you." He stared at her. She

looked away. She couldn't stand it. "*Bored* with you?"

"What else am I supposed to think? I know what *we need to talk* means, Jax. I'm not stupid."

"Could've fooled me."

"Hey." Her eyes snapped back to his, anger a welcome flame inside her. "You want to walk away from this? Fine. But you don't have to be a jerk about it."

"And you're okay with that?" He studied her.

"With your being a jerk? No. Quit it."

"With my walking away from this. You're fine with that, are you?"

She opened her mouth to lie then stopped. What was the use? "No. But it hardly matters. My feelings are my fault. They're my responsibility and I'll deal with them."

"Your feelings?" His knuckles were white against his khakis. "For me?"

"No, for Matt Damon." She glared at those knuckles. "*Yes*, for you."

"Which are what precisely?"

The question was calm but something about his voice wasn't. She looked up slowly, wariness a sudden clutch in her chest.

"Addy?" His gaze was steady on hers, and he lifted a brow. "Your feelings for me?"

"You know, I think it might be better if I didn't say." She eased back a cautious step, concerned by the grim set of his mouth. "Easier to recover from, maybe."

"Fuck recovery." He rose slowly to his feet.

"Not *your* recovery." She melted back another step, fighting the hot spurt of adrenaline that said *run*. "You're a jerk. You're on your own. I'm talking about my recovery." He followed. She bumped into the wall beside the TV and he

stepped up. Caged her between two strong arms. The move
left a bare inch or two between them, an empty space that
was suddenly as thick as the fog rolling in off the lake.
"Don't—" She broke off, swallowed. Closed her eyes.
"Don't be a jerk, Jackson."

"Stop calling me that."

"Stop making me. A guy with any class would've parked
at the station."

"What? Why?"

"So I could just leave when you broke my stupid heart
without having to wait for you to move your stupid truck."

He froze. "I could break your heart?"

"Not quite." She sucked in a breath, forced herself to
meet his eyes dead on and give him what he was determined
to have. "But it's a very near thing. You could put a decent
crack in it." She knocked away one wrist and stepped out of
the cage of his arms. "Is that what you wanted to hear? Is
that what I needed to say? Will you move your stupid truck
now and let me leave?"

He closed his eyes, one hand on his heart as if pained.

"Oh for pete's sake," she snapped and turned her back to
him. She couldn't bear to watch the shock melt into pity.
"Pull yourself together. It's not permanent. I'm sure I'll
recover. You took me by surprise, that's all. I'd never done
the casual thing before. I didn't understand the rules, but I
get it now. You didn't do anything wrong, Jax. You never
promised me anything. You're absolutely in the clear on this.
Plus I'm *fine*. Ready to—"

She broke off. Her throat simply closed. She couldn't
make herself say what she was ready to do. Maybe because
she wasn't ready to do it, or maybe because she just didn't
know what on earth she was supposed to be ready to do. She

rolled a shoulder to fill in the blank and finally risked a look at him.

"Jesus God," he murmured, gazing at her in wonder. He came to her, caught her cold hand. He brought her palm to his chest and spread his own on top of it. "Christ on a cracker."

"Prayer doesn't actually help, Jackson." She smiled bitterly. "Believe me, if it did—"

He curled a hand around her nape, drew her in and laid his lips against hers. Shock tried to rock her back but he threaded his fingers into her hair, tipped her head back and kissed her with a slow care that unstrung her knees.

"Addison. My God, *Addison*." She felt him shape the words against her mouth, felt the aching tenderness in them. He turned, pressed her back to the wall, set his body against hers and leaned in. Put that gorgeous mouth right next to her ear. "I'm not bored with you. I'm in love with you. I always have been, I always will be, and if you're anywhere remotely close to in love with me, I'll let you recover from it over my dead body."

She froze, stunned rigid, while joy licked to life under her skin. She wedged her fists between their bodies, pressed him back until she could look at his face. What she saw there had a whole choir of angels singing in her head but she pushed a knuckle into her forehead and tried to hear over them. "Say that again," she whispered.

He glared at her. "No recovery."

She fisted a hand in his shirt. "The other part."

"I love you."

"That's the one." She shook her spinning head. Narrowed her eyes to glare at him. "But you said we couldn't do this anymore."

"I meant the sneaking around. Not the being in love with you. Jesus." He shook his head. "I could sooner stop breathing."

"Don't, then," she heard herself say. "Don't stop."

He laughed. "Like I have a choice."

And then he was kissing her. Kissing her like he was a thirsty field and she was the rain. Then it slipped effortlessly into something sweet and greedy, slow and seeking. Something that sang inside her like somebody had struck a tuning fork off her soul. The anger and pain of the last week — of the last lifetime — suddenly drained away and peace spilled cool and clear through her. She twisted her hands into the crisp cotton of his shirt, breathed him in and thought, *home*.

It wasn't the house. It was never the house. It was him.

She let herself tumble.

Chapter 24

JAX SLID HIS arms around her. Just wrapped her up until there wasn't anything between them anymore, not even air. His body went liquid with heat and need, and that hungry place inside him sighed with satisfaction then howled for more.

How could she have thought he was done with her? How could she not have known?

She arched into him then, made some noise, something hot and inviting that he felt against his lips and deep inside all at the same time. She opened her mouth under his and he fell into her on a dizzy rush. Into the warmth and generosity and welcome that he'd always loved in her and absolutely adored in her kiss. He filled his hands with the sweet curve of her bottom and hiked her up. Her legs came around him and he somehow managed to make it to the bedroom without collapsing from the sheer, crushing weight of his desire. For a second there, he'd seriously contemplated the couch. Or the floor.

Love blew through him like a wind, strong and settling. Addy was a gift, and he'd be damned if he'd treat her like anything less. He seized the reins of his desire and laid her on his comforter — an inches-thick, hot chocolate colored indulgence — with all the gentleness he could muster from his big, clumsy hands. She sank into it with a laugh, her curls framing her face like a halo.

"Addy," he said. His heart gave a funny bump as he stretched himself alongside her. The press of her body, the heat and the scent of her, rose to him, surrounded him like a dream. "Addy." He ran his palm down the ladder of her rib cage, treated himself to the indent of her waist, the ripe curve of her hip. Slowly, slowly, he brought his hand down to her thigh, let it rest there, gloried in the intimacy of it. He was *allowed*, he thought. She was giving him this. Giving him herself. She loved him — or she would, he'd see to that — and that was nothing short of a miracle.

"You're so..." He shook his head, unable to find the words.

"What?" she asked, her lips curved just for him. Her eyes warmed with welcome.

"Beautiful," he said finally. He slid his palm up over the bump of her hip bone, across the soft curve of her belly. He nudged his fingers under the hem of that pretty purple sweater, and her skin under it was smooth as rain. "You are so...damn...beautiful."

Her eyes closed as his fingers crept upward, climbed slowly, deliberately. That well of tenderness she always opened inside him overflowed, and for once he simply let it. Because there was no longer any need to disguise it, to dial it back or make it look like simple desire. His heart was in his fingers, and he wanted her to feel it. To know it.

"It's like Christmas morning," he murmured and cupped the softness of her breast. "Touching you. Being allowed. Every single time. It never gets old."

She bowed into his touch, arching off the bed with a soft noise. Pushed the plump curve of her breast into his hand.

Need roared through him, twining with the tenderness and going up in an inferno unlike anything he'd ever experienced before.

It was madness, and he fell into it. Happily.

Addy was lost. Her world had shattered and dissolved, narrowed down to the fact of her breast in Jax's palm, to those clever fingers on the tight bud of her nipple. Liquid fire raced down her thighs, curling her toes, arching her back, lifted her up to him on a wave of brilliant, blinding need. A need that built with every thud of her heart, with every pull of his fingers, every drag of his lips until it was more madness than desire. Until it was a slicing imperative that defined her, created her, consumed her. She glowed with it, like a star or a planet. And Jax was the sun, pulling her in endless ellipses through a black velvet sky.

She threw a leg over his hip, trying to get closer. He growled impatiently in his throat, then there was a dizzying swirl as he unmoored himself from her side. He shifted over her, caged her between his knees, and stripped her sweater away. He loomed above her, gazing down at what he'd uncovered, his eyes hot and avid. Then he lowered his mouth — warm, wet, thrilling — to her skin, and she stopped breathing. She stopped even wanting to. His teeth dragged lightly at one nipple, and want slid straight to her core.

The blast of pleasure was shocking and so sharp that her eyes flew open. She stared uncomprehending at her own hands, saw them lying open and stunned on the comforter at either side of her head. Just lying there, she realized dumbly. Doing nothing. The realization of her selfishness swept over her like a cold lake wind. She was so wrapped up in the staggering pleasure he was giving her that she hadn't thought about his pleasure at all. She wasn't even touching him, for heaven's sake! She was just lying there, limp and passive, exactly the way Diego had always said she did, letting somebody else do all the work.

Her throat went hot and tight and she blinked against a rush of shamed tears.

Well, screw that. Screw *him*. Diego was dead. She, on the other hand, was very much alive, and she wasn't going to make the same mistake twice. No, she was going to make Jax as happy as he was making her.

Her brain was busily charting the wonderland Jax had made of her body, but with some effort she took control of her hands again. She reached up, tunneled her fingers slowly into the thick warmth of his hair. It slid against her skin like raw silk, rough and warm and expensive. How had she lived within arm's length of Jax these four years, she thought wonderingly, and never touched him like this? How had she denied herself the visceral pleasure of his hair? It drifted from her fingers and she followed it into the dark warmth of his collar. His shirt had come untucked at some point. Unbuttoned, too. It hung open on either side of their bodies. Had she done that? Had he? She had no idea. She didn't care. She was just glad for the access to all that skin, to that fascinating play of muscle and bone she'd seen a million times but had never thought to touch.

Remorse tangled with need and she arched into him. She'd touch him now. She'd touch him until they both forgot how long it had taken her to wake up, to see him. To need him. Because she did need him. She needed him now like she'd never needed anything — anybody — in her life. It ate at her like hunger, like thirst. Touching him had become utterly necessary to her very survival.

She tunneled both hands into the invitation of that open shirt, moaned at the hot pleasure of his skin under her palms. She lifted her mouth to his throat, breathed him in and set herself to the delicious task of learning him. Of tasting him. Knowing him. She wanted the size and shape of him burned on her fingertips, the scent of him branded on her brain. She wanted to recognize him in the dark.

She found the fastening of his khakis and desire shuddered through her. It made her fingers fast and clumsy as she tore at the button, worked the zipper. He hissed and jerked himself up suddenly, away from her hands, and the rush of air on her super-heated skin chilled her to the bone.

"Sorry." She squeezed her eyes shut and let her hands fall away from him as a familiar humiliation ripped through her. She should've just stayed still. "I'm...sorry."

"What the hell for?"

She opened her eyes and found him braced a careful foot above her on his hands and knees, his face a mask of agonized...pleasure? "I thought you didn't want me to—" She had to swallow down a half-formed lump of rejection. "Did I do something wrong?"

"Why would you think that?"

"You jumped back like I'd burned you. I thought—"

"You thought what?"

She shrugged miserably and turned her face away. He took her jaw in his hand and turned her face back to his.

"Don't do that, Addy," he said softly. "Don't bring him into bed with us."

"But you wouldn't let me touch you." Her voice was small, unhappy, and a complete surprise to her. She hadn't meant to say that out loud. She trusted Jax in a way she'd never trusted Diego but that didn't mean she would happily hand over a loaded gun and invite him to take aim.

"Christ's sake, Addison. I needed a second." He sat back on his heels and gazed down at her, his mouth a self-deprecating twist. Moonlight spilled across those wide, heavy shoulders, threw the bumps and ridges of his abdomen into fascinating relief. Her eyes fell to the erection jutting up from the vee of his unfastened pants. A ripple of pure lust shot across her skin and she shuddered. His laugh was low and ragged. "Yeah, you see my problem."

He planted his hands on either side of her head and lowered himself slowly, agonizingly, until that erection was pressed right into the madness at her center. "You feel too good, Addison. I've never felt anything as good as your hands on my body."

Desire punched through her, and she lifted herself into him with a mewl of pure need.

His mouth was next to her ear, his voice dark and rich. "You can touch me any time, any place, anywhere."

"Now." She had to close her eyes against the pulsing, radiant want inside her. "I want to touch you *now*."

He laughed, and his teeth found the shell of her ear. "Well, any time *except* now. I've been waiting for this, for you, for too long, Addy. I'm too close. You can touch me next time." His teeth tightened the slightest bit, rode the merciless edge between pleasure and pain. "I promise."

A hot wash of need slid over her, but she dredged up her last ounce of reason. "Jax, please, it's not fair. I want to give you something, too."

"Fine." He laced his fingers through hers, drew his lips down the cord of her neck. "You know what I want?"

She didn't care what it was; she'd give it to him. "What?"

One big hand slid under her bottom and lifted her into him, into the heat and flash and demand that roared between them. "I want to hear that noise you make when I do this." He stroked himself against her, and lust speared through her so viciously that she whimpered. He smiled against her skin.

"Yeah," he murmured, "that's the one. But there's this other one, too. The one you make when I put my mouth right—" He slid his lips, hot and wet and open, to the sensitive skin just under her jaw, pulled hard enough to mark her. She gasped and flung her head to the side, but not to object. Lord, no. Just to give him more room. "—yeah, right there."

He gave her his weight then, his body big and hard and hot against hers, his hips kneading into her with a rhythm that promised and commanded and demanded. "What I want — all I want — is for you to want me." Her bra was bunched beneath her breast, offering it up to him, plump and eager. He plucked the nipple with quick, devastating fingers, then soothed it with his tongue. "Do you, Addy? Do you want me?"

"Yes." She sobbed it out, the breath sawing from her lungs, a sharp need clawing under her skin. She couldn't breathe, couldn't think. There was nothing else, only him. "Jax, *please.*"

Then his hands were dragging at her pants and she was lifting her hips and kicking desperately free of them. His bedspread was slippery under her naked skin, foreign and exciting. She watched, dazed and dizzy, as he tossed off his boots, got rid of his own pants, and dealt with the condom he magically — God bless his practical soul — conjured up.

Then he was between her knees again, his hands both

commanding and gentle as he spread her legs, positioned himself between them and slid into her.

"Oh," she said on a gasp. It was all she could manage. Because this — this was ridiculous. This was stretched and challenged and filled and *Jax*. "Oh my—"

He braced his hands on either side of her head, just outside her own. They were lying there again, her hands, limp and shocked and helpless. He stared down into her eyes, his face hard and fierce, and he said, "*This* is what I want, Addy." He stroked into her and her eyes drifted closed. It was...good lord, it was *delicious*. He moved inside her like a dream, steady and determined and utterly assured. She lifted a foot from where it rested on the mattress. She thought about trying to wrap it around his waist, to hold on, but then he dropped to his elbows, spread his knees and started moving for real.

Oh sweet mercy. Her thighs stretched wide to accommodate him and she hooked her elbows around his biceps just to brace herself. She felt her own hair against her stunned palms and twisted her fingers into the craziness of her curls. That small pain, that small familiarity was such an inadequate anchor against the colors starting to pop behind her eyelids, the shattering beginning to gather and swirl inside her. Her palms tingled and the arches of her feet went twitchy, curling and flexing spasmodically. What was he doing to her?

"Give it to me, Addison." He turned his head into the space between her shoulder and her face, his breath hot and sweet against her cheek. "Give it to me now."

"Jax," she whispered. It was all she could manage. Just his name. Because in that moment, he was all she knew. In that moment, he was everything. Her universe, her reality, her body and soul. He was the pounding of her pulse, he was the gravity that held her to the earth and the sun that pulled her away from it.

Everything inside her went brilliant and breakable and impossibly tight. And then everything shattered and she said it again. Cried it. Wept it. Howled it.

"Jax!"

He made a noise, something she could barely perceive let alone comprehend, but it was ragged, raw, and utterly gratified. He reared back, gripped her hips with both hands and lifted her into him. He took her with a fierce, unforgiving rhythm, simply seized her and wrung from her shattering body every last thing he wanted. And when he came it was with a roar that Addy felt in every one of her quivering cells. Delight poured through her that had nothing to do with the satisfaction still ripping through her body.

She'd done this to him. Wanting her had undone him.

There had probably been finer moments in her life, but at the moment she couldn't come up with a single one.

Chapter 25

WIND KNIFED BRUTALLY down the dark alley behind Main Street where Matty crouched but he didn't care. He welcomed it. Rage still pulsed in his head, hatred gnawed at his ribs, failure twisted in his gut. Sweat slid icily down his back, the slimy left-overs of his furious bike ride down the hill — *get away, get away, get away* — but his fingers were numb as he tried once again to flick to life the lighter in his hand. It had been his dad's once, this lighter. Or so they told him, like that was supposed to mean something to him. Why would it, though? It wasn't like Matty had ever met the guy.

And since you couldn't miss what you'd never had, Joe's absence hadn't ever really bothered Matty. Not until lately, anyway. Because if his dad were still alive, maybe his mom wouldn't be such a head case. If she hadn't lost both her son *and* her husband, maybe she wouldn't be so damn obsessed with shoving Matty into Diego's art-legend shoes.

The wind backed off for a minute and the scent of turpentine and oil paints rose to his nose. He wore the smell like some sick perfume these days — eau de disappointment — and his stomach roiled. He tried again with the lighter. The papers in his other hand — a tight roll of thick-ass, expensive drawing paper — shook and he clenched his teeth until his jaw ached. Worked that stupid little wheel until he thought his thumb would bleed.

"Come on, you bastard, *light*." How was he supposed to burn this shit — this sub-standard, mother-crushing *shit* that was all he seemed capable of drawing — if he couldn't even work a goddamn lighter?

Pain bloomed, bright and shocking, on his scalp and he was suddenly jerked to his feet. The lighter clattered to the pavement and his papers scattered as he scrabbled at the fist in his hair that had yanked him away from the wall and into the watery moonlight. Recognition and relief crashed over him in equal parts when he realized it was only Peter. The guy didn't look a thing like the smooth-talking, shaved-headed business man who'd pretended to eat Bianca's art project with them earlier that night, though, and his relief faded warily.

"Hey, Matty," Peter said, his tone as easy as always. But his face was hard in the thin light. Dangerous. "What's a nice kid like you doing in my back alley so late?"

Matty swallowed. The Wooden Spoon shared a wall and an alley with the Devil's Tap Room, which was just one of the local businesses Peter owned. He hadn't thought of it. Definitely hadn't imagined he'd run into Peter here. He just knew there was a Dumpster back here, and that what he needed to burn this time was too big for his own trashcan.

"The carriage house wasn't enough for you?" Peter said evenly, as if he could read Matty's mind. "You're after lighting up my Dumpster this time?"

Matty glanced toward the mouth of the alley, wondered if he was fast enough to make a break for it. Peter smiled coldly and renewed his grip on Matty's hair. Gave him a light shake.

"Matty, Matty, Matty. What would mommy say?"

"Screw you." Matty ducked and twisted underneath Peter's arm, freeing himself. He lost a few hairs but the pain was nothing compared to the nuclear flash of rage inside his head. "Screw her, too." He bent to snatch up the lighter at his feet, to claw together the scattered papers. Peter bent, too, snagged one of the sheets and angled it toward the moonlight. Lifted a brow. "You came all the way down to my Dumpster to burn superheroes?"

"Yeah, sure." Matty lifted his chin, gave him that *whatever, dude* look that drove his mother bonkers. "Everybody needs a hobby, right?"

Peter gave that the moment of skeptical silence it deserved, then stuffed the paper in his pocket. He turned toward the back entrance of his bar, jerked his head at Matty. "Step into my office, son."

Matty backed up a step and Peter bared his teeth in a kid-eating grin. "You don't want to run, buddy. I used to put guys twice your size on the turf every day." He had, actually. Matty had seen the framed newspaper articles — along with the entire trophy case dedicated to Peter — at the high school.

"Go, Demons," Matty sneered and Peter actually smiled.

"I haven't put the hurt on anybody in years but I'd do it tonight. With pleasure." He swung the door wide. "Now quit being such a little dick and get inside."

"Fine." He shoved his numb hands into his pockets and slouched inside.

He followed Peter into the stingy back hall of the tap room. The men's and ladies' rooms were to the right, Peter's office was to the left, and the bar itself was on the other side of a dogleg. It smelled like beer and pee back here, and

Matty wished with everything in him that he'd never left the house.

Peter shouldered open the office door, nodded Matty to the chair in front of the desk. When Matty took it, Peter hitched a hip onto the desk and folded his arms. A long moment of sweaty silence strung out between them. Matty stared at his boots until they slid out of focus.

"So, Matty," Peter said finally. "I'm disappointed in you."

"Yeah? Maybe you and my mom can form, like, a club or something."

"You mean Bianca? Or your actual mom?"

Matty blinked, uncomprehending. Peter laughed.

"Come on, Matty. Connect the dots with me, huh? Think about it. A woman with Bianca's build delivering a full-term surprise-a-baby? The odds on that are somewhere between slim and I-don't-think-so." He shook his head, amused. "You're not Bianca's kid. No way on earth. She claimed you, but you're not hers. And you know it."

Confusion, hope and a blank white terror tangled inside him. He wasn't Bianca's son? More importantly, he wasn't Diego's brother? "Then whose am I?" he asked, his lips numb and strange.

Peter tipped his head, a small smile playing around his mouth. "Does it really matter when you're wearing that face?" He shrugged. "Then again, if you don't live up to those bones of yours — and it sounds like you haven't been — do you really think Bianca's going to keep you around? Especially now that you've developed a taste for arson?"

"For the last time, the carriage house was an accident." Matty said the words automatically, his brain in a nauseating spiral. "But if she wants to disown me? Fine. Let her."

That small smile went indulgent. "You might want to think that one through, son."

"Like I care about being a Davis," Matty sneered, even as the world tipped sickly around him. The family name had been his own personal prison for months now. He'd prayed for deliverance, and what do you know? He'd actually gotten it. And now he understood why people said to be careful what you wished for. Because it only just now occurred to him that being somebody — even a shitty somebody — was probably better than being nobody.

Than being nobody's.

"Of course you care about being a Davis." Peter chuckled, as if he really could read Matty's mind. "Life's expensive, kid. Team Money wants you? Sign the contract. It's always better to be rich than to be poor, and believe me, I know."

"I do believe you." Matty gave a jagged laugh. "Unfortunately, Team Davis is broke."

Peter stared at him, blank and astonished.

"Good thing you don't really need that dowry, huh?"

Jax's pants rang. Or the phone inside them did and Addy jumped in Jax's arms, her skull cracking smartly into his chin.

"Ow," he murmured. She leapt off the bed like she'd been tased so Jax sat up and gave his jaw an experimental wiggle. "Remind me not to sneak up on you," he told her. "You're more dangerous than you look."

"Good lord." She danced foot to foot and patted her chest. She was as naked as the day she was born, which he appreciated. "My heart."

"I don't *think* my jaw is broken," he told her. "But you're sweet to be so concerned."

She closed her eyes and breathed. Evidently it required some concentration. "Answer your phone, Jackson."

He shrugged and found his khakis, fished the phone out of his pocket and inspected the caller info. His mom? At this hour? He punched the answer icon.

"Hey, Mom—" he started, then broke off as his mother unleashed a high-speed, panicky tirade. He sorted through the sound and the fury to pick out a few key words — *fire*, *Matty*, and *missing* — then cut her off. "Five minutes," he said. "Stay put."

He ended the call, tossed the phone onto the bed and snatched up his boxers.

"What?" Addy said, her eyes huge. "*What?*"

"Matty's missing," he said.

"Oh no," she breathed. "I have to—"

"Get up to Hill Top House," Jax told her and jumped into a pair of trousers. "Mom will need you." He dragged a t-shirt and a sweater over his head. "I have to get to the fire."

"The *what?*"

"According to Mom, somebody blew up the Dumpster behind the Wooden Spoon. I'm off duty, or I'd have gotten the call."

She dropped to her knees and swept up a jumble of socks and shoes and undergarments. She dumped it all on the bed and began sorting. "He wouldn't," she said firmly. "Matty wouldn't do anything like that, Jax."

But her hand shook as she handed him a boot. He took it and watched her shimmy into her underwear and jeans. "I hope to hell that's true." He found his other boot, handed her that pretty purple sweater he'd enjoying taking off her so much. "I'm about to find out."

She dragged it over her head, shot an arm through the sleeve and grabbed his elbow. "Not without me, you're not."

"Addy, I've got to go." But the armpit of his sweater suddenly felt bunchy and weird, so he dug into it and came up with her bra. He handed it over and watched with some fascination as she wriggled into it without showing more than an inch or two of skin at her waist. How did women *do* that?

"Fine. I'm ready." She patted at the crazy bird's nest of her hair. "Let's go."

His phone screamed again, the old-fashioned fire engine wail he'd programmed for the station's number.

"You're off duty," she said, her eyes huge as he answered, listened grimly. "Why are they calling you in?"

He hung up. "There's a second fire."

"Where?"

"The Hideaway."

"Peter's Hideaway? The one he wanted to give Georgie for an engagement present?"

"That's the one. Girl's got all the luck. If she'd just accepted the resort instead of trying to bargain for better, her wedding present could be burning down right now."

She sighed. "I don't know if I'd call anything about tonight lucky. Not if Matty's—" She broke off, unable or unwilling to voice the thought.

"—there?" He met her eyes in the darkened room. "If he's at the resort, watching it burn?"

"He's not." Her pretty mouth went stubborn.

"How do you know?"

"He's angry but he's not an idiot, Jax."

"Debatable."

She folded her arms and glared.

"Arsonists like to hang around," he pointed out flatly. He didn't like it any more than she did, but facts were facts. "They come back, Addison. They like to see their work."

"He's not an arsonist," she said sharply. "He's a mixed up kid, laboring under the crushing weight of his grieving mother's expectations."

He snatched up the keys to the mini-pumper. "I guess we're about to find out, aren't we?"

Chapter 26

IT WAS LATE. So late as to be technically early. The fire at the Hideaway was out but it had done a lot more damage than it should've. Protecting the businesses on Main Street had been a first priority, so Jax had opted to leave most of his volunteers on the Dumpster fire. He'd relied on the Hornby Harbor crew until his own crew could join him at the resort.

If Peter could salvage anything from this place, Jax would be shocked.

He headed back to the mini-pumper, which he'd moved down the beach a ways when the larger Hornby rig had finally turned up. He was mildly surprised to find Addy still leaning against it right where he'd left her, her arms folded, her hair in the kind of crazy spikes that suggested she'd just rolled out of bed. Out from underneath the man *in* her bed, maybe.

Which she had. Yeah, that had been him.

A completely inappropriate grin threatened to split his face and he dumped an armload of wet hoses on the ground next to the truck.

"He wasn't here," she said. "Matty."

"No, I know." That was part of the stupid grinning, too. Sheer relief. He doubted the kid was blameless but at least

255

Jax hadn't seen his baby brother driven off in the back of a squad car tonight. He dropped to his haunches and started coiling the hoses into neat piles. "I looked, too."

"He didn't start the Dumpster fire, either."

"How do we know that?"

"I talked to your mom."

"How does she know that?" He looked up. Couldn't be more than forty degrees out and he was down to a wife-beater but heat still pumped off him. He pushed a wrist over his sweaty forehead — his hands were filthy — and studied her. She looked unhappy but not panicked. So not awful news. But not good, either.

"Peter brought him home," she said.

"Peter?"

"According to Bianca, Peter was heading to his office at the Devil's Tap Room to take care of some business and saw Matty in town. He was concerned, of course, it being so late, and brought him inside. He was planning to drive him home but thought maybe a man-to-man was in order. They were talking in his office when the Dumpster blew." She shrugged. "Peter was understandably distracted for a while but eventually got Bianca on the phone and let her know that Matty was fine. He dropped him home an hour or so ago."

Jax absorbed that in thoughtful silence.

Graham Graves appeared next to the pumper, his round, cheerful face shining like the full moon. "Hey, you want a hand with those hoses?"

"Nah," Jax said. "I got this. You get on home. You're on duty in a couple hours."

"So are you." The guy eyed Addy the way a dieter eyes a plate of nachos. "I've got time."

She smiled at him. "Hey, Graham."

"Hey, Addy." He grinned back. "Looking good, girl. What are you doing here? You thinking about volunteering for the squad?" He paused, biceps flexed for maximum exposure. He dropped his voice to what he presumably thought passed for a sexy growl. "I could show you the ropes, if you know what I mean."

Addy bit her lip, clearly fighting a startled giggle. "Oh, goodness, no. Fire's not my thing. I'm here for—" She stopped short. Jax sat back on his heels and watched her, curious. She was here for…what? For Matty? For Jax? Which secret was she planning to spill?

"I'm waiting for Jax," she finally said. She gave Graham a dazzling smile, all dimples and sunshine. "As soon as he's done here, he's taking me back to bed."

"Yeah?" Graham grinned back automatically, predictably blinded by that smile of hers. "That sounds like—" He broke off. "Wait, what?"

"Well, we were in bed when he got called away to deal with all this." Addy swept a reasonable hand toward the smoking ruins of the Hideaway. "I'm hoping to take him back there once it's done."

"Almost done now," Jax said easily, his heart bursting into song inside him.

"Oh, good." Addy turned that blinding smile his way. "I'm cold."

"Not for long."

Graham's gaze bounced back and forth between them for a long, searching moment. The kid was sweet as pie, and strong as two mules, but he didn't process quickly. Finally he said, "You two are…together? Like, Facebook official and all that?"

Jax finished coiling the hoses and stood. Stretched the

kinks out of his back. "Looks that way."

Addy gave him a cheerfully apologetic shrug. "Surprised me, too, honestly."

Graham nodded slowly. "I'd heard Bianca was on the war path about something, and I mean really on the war path, you know? Diego's Angel jumping in the sack with anybody would be bad enough, but Jax is like the total opposite of Diego, isn't he?" He folded his arms and chuckled, considering it. "Yeah, that would definitely put Bianca's panties in a bundle." He leaned in, lifted a leering brow. "Is she really going to put naked pictures of you on Main Street for Devil Days, though? Is she that mad?"

Jax stepped forward and put one stern finger into Graham's inflated pectoral. "You interested in seeing Addy naked?"

"Sure." The kid continued to leer at Addy with his usual bovine good humor. "She's a girl, isn't she?"

"My girl." Jax put enough bite behind that finger to break through the hormones clouding Graham's better judgment.

"Hmm?" The kid finally looked up, and Jax showed him his teeth. "Oh! Well, good deal, then." He took a hasty step back. "You're sure you don't need a hand with the hoses?"

"I'm sure," Jax said and the kid turned and galloped away, his boots smacking the sand with big wet flaps. "Hey, Graham?" he called.

Graham froze and turned with some reluctance.

"Did you put in that call to the Fire Marshall?"

Relief washed across his open face. "Sure did. She said somebody would be up to do an on-site assessment at two on Monday. Fastest she could work you in."

"Okay. Thanks. Go on home now. And Graham?"

"Yeah?"

"Don't believe everything you hear." Jax smiled at him again, made a warning of it. "Don't repeat everything you hear, either."

"No, sir." He sent Addy an apologetic glance. "I'm real sorry about the naked picture thing, Addy. I didn't mean—"

"I know." Addy smiled at him, pure sweetness and sunshine, and Graham all but bloomed under the beam of it. "It's okay, Graham. Go get some sleep."

"Right, okay." Graham shook himself free from the dazzle of Addy's smile, turned and galumphed into the night. The state trooper who'd responded had already taken off, so now it was just Jax, Addy, and a ruined lodge, sullenly smoking and cordoned off with crime scene tape.

"The Fire Marshall?" she asked. "You're classifying this as arson?"

"Yep." Jax began winding the hoses into the truck. He'd unload them at the station for cleaning and drying later. He cut her a look over his shoulder. "Resorts don't blow up by themselves, Addy."

"Construction sites do. They come equipped with all kinds of flammable liquids — gas, oil, whatever." She kicked at the ground and came up with a cigarette butt. "Smokers."

"They'd have to ash directly into the heating oil tank to cause what we saw here tonight."

"You have a more likely scenario in mind?"

"Yeah. Arson."

"You really think Matty's capable of something like that?"

He looked away. "He blew up the carriage house, didn't he?"

"That was an *accident*."

"I know it was. Just like I know that, for some folks, a taste is all it takes to get hooked." She stared at him, and the stricken shock in her face made him feel like he'd slapped her. "The kid is so angry, Addison. And if the carriage house was his taste…" She stepped away from him, rejecting what? The words? The idea? Him? He dragged a filthy hand down his face and blew out a breath. "Listen, you think I like this? You think I *want* Matty to be tangled up in this? Of course I don't! He's my brother! I'll do everything I can to protect him, but I won't conceal evidence."

"Good heavens, Jax, I wasn't suggesting you should!"

"Well, good, because it's out of my hands. The Fire Marshall's been alerted, and there's nothing we can do until she processes the scene."

"Yes, there is." She turned and jerked open the door to the mini-pumper, climbed into the cab. "Let's go."

"Addy. It's three o'clock in the morning." He put a hand on her door, stopped her from yanking it shut. "Go where?"

"Hill Top House." She stared straight out the windshield, her pretty mouth tight and grim. "We're going to deal with this right now."

In the end, Addy arrived at Hill Top House alone, and about eight hours later than she'd hoped as Jax had flatly refused to drive her up the hill at three a.m. He had a literal mountain of paperwork to deal with the morning after two separate fires, and with the Fire Inspector due in less than 48 hours, he couldn't break away. So Addy showed up all by herself, unless you counted the half-dozen doughnuts and the carry-out tray of coffee in her hands. Sugar and caffeine weren't a solution, she knew, but they never hurt, either. She found Bianca in the breakfast nook that looked out over the bird feeders, a cup of tea in front of her going cold.

She lifted her eyes, dark and worried, to Addy's. "Oh, Addison. You're here."

"Of course I am." Addy dropped a kiss on her mother-in-law's ruler-straight part, pried a paper cup from the holder and placed it on the table. "Skim latte, full caffeine. Drink up."

"Bless you, child." Bianca pried off the lid, wrapped her hands around the paper cup and inhaled deeply. "Bless you."

Addy slid into a curvy little cafe chair, and pulled out her own to-go cup full of the coffee that Walt down at the Sugar Rush had pressed on her, loaded with so much cream and sugar she was almost happy to see it. "Where's Georgie?"

"Sleeping." Bianca took a delicate sip of her latte. "It was a late night and Georgie's not exactly a morning person."

Addy had to smile at that. Georgie wasn't an afternoon or an evening person, either. "Matty?"

"In his room." Bianca's lips twisted. "I check every half hour to make sure he's still there."

Addy's heart squeezed and she laid a hand on Bianca's arm. "So...what happened?"

Bianca barked out a humorless laugh. "You'll have to ask Matisse about that one. He's currently not speaking to me."

"Best guess?"

She pressed her fingers to the line that had taken up permanent residence between her brows. "You saw most of it — the perfectly lovely dinner with Peter and Georgie, then Matty stomping off in a fit of adolescent angst." She dropped her hand, studied it where it lay on the table. "Evidently he decided at some point to amuse himself by burning things in

261

the studio's trash can." Her lips twisted. "With the help of some paint thinner."

Addy's stomach dropped. "Oh, no."

"Oh, yes. Of course he set off the fire alarms. I nearly had a heart attack. Thank God for the fire extinguishers Jax has hung all over this place." A smile ghosted over her lips. "They're incredibly ugly hanging there in plain sight but I was never so happy in my life to have one handy."

"He'll be glad to hear it."

"Tell him and I'll disown you. For real this time."

Addy swallowed involuntarily, her mouth suddenly Sahara dry. "It wasn't real last time?"

Bianca flicked the thought away. "Of course not. I was angry. You know you can't trust a thing I say when I'm angry."

"But you weren't angry later," Addy said carefully, the pain still a sullen ache inside her. "All the next week, you let me think—"

"Oh, darling." Bianca reached across the table, took her hand. "It wasn't you I was letting think. It was everybody else."

"Everybody else?"

"Nan, Gerte, Matty." She waved that expansive hand. "The whole town."

"What were you letting them think?"

"That we were in chaos up here." She smiled enigmatically. "That those paintings you rescued from the carriage house fire were game changers. That they had us at each others' throats."

"They are." She stared. "They do."

"Ah, but nobody knows why, do they? We could be showing Diego's early nudes. We could be debuting Matty's

work. We could be showing Diego's post-*Angel* works of
you. Possibly of you *and* him, if you take my meaning. You
know how people's minds work." Addy's stomach twisted
She did know, in fact. Bianca's smile hardened dangerously.
"Or we could be showing those paintings of Julia Gates."

Her heart rocketed painfully into her throat. "Julia—"

"That self-serving, hatchet-faced, girl-reporter harpy."
Bianca's dark eyes burned. "You think I didn't recognize
her? You think I didn't know what she did to you? To my
boy?" She shook her head. "Diego was…he had his
weaknesses. You were good for him, Addison. You brought
out what was good *in* him. I really thought, or maybe I only
hoped…" She shrugged. "It doesn't matter what I'd hoped.
Julia destroyed my hopes. She destroyed my son. She
encouraged the sex, the drugs, the dirty. Everything that
made him hate himself, she magnified. She gloried in it. She
was the photo negative of you, and she sank her hooks into
him in a way that nobody could undo. She drove him to
madness, then into his grave."

"But why?" Addy's throat tried to close. Shock rang in
her ears and she couldn't feel her fingers. "Why would she
do that?"

"Because she couldn't have him. She couldn't have my
boy, so she decided that nobody could." She smiled bitterly.
"Certainly not some farm-fresh twenty-one-year-old virgin.
So she found the cracks in his soul and wormed her way into
each one. She indulged his taste for the dirty, the dark. She
fed him drugs, taught him her kinks, catered to his. God only
knows what else they got up to. But by the time she was
done with him, he was addicted. Damaged beyond repair."
Tears gathered in her dark eyes. "You can see it in every
brush stroke of those paintings you hid all those years. He's

unravelling, going mad with self-hatred, with agony. He simply can't bear what he's becoming. What he'd become. But he was powerless to stop himself, and she only urged him on. And that last painting, *Broken*?" She shook her head. "That's not you. Well, it is, obviously. I don't mean to mitigate your pain, darling." She covered Addy's hand with her own again. Addy hardly felt it. "But it's a self-portrait, too. He was finally broken, and it was breaking you that forced him to see it."

Chapter 27

"WHY DIDN'T YOU tell me?" Addy's throat was on fire, her head spinning. "Why didn't you tell me you knew?"

"There's no place within a marriage for a mother-in-law." Bianca sat back, flicked the question away with impatient fingers. "Believe me, I know."

"But if I'd known you knew—"

"What?" Bianca's eyes burned into hers. "What would you have done differently? Would you have brought me those paintings? Would you have been ready to show them? Would you have asked me for help, for counsel? Would you have asked me to side with you against my son? Would you have asked me to protect you from him when I couldn't even protect him from himself?"

"No." Addy twisted her fingers together on the table and stared at them. Willed her heart to stop bleeding. "No, I'd never have asked that."

"Then what? What would you have had me do?"

Just be with me, she thought. *Hold me. Keep me. Promise me. I was so alone. So afraid.*

But the Davises weren't her family. Or, if they were, they were Diego's family first. They'd had to hold, keep, promise him first. Oh, they loved her. She didn't doubt that. But she could never come before blood.

"Nothing," she said finally. "There was nothing you could do for me."

Bianca covered Addy's twisted fingers with her cool palm again. "I can do something for you now. Something for all of us."

"What?"

"I can destroy Julia Gates." A smile flickered at the corner of Bianca's mouth, like a flame licking at the curtains. It was a house fire waiting to happen, that smile. "Let me show those paintings, Addy. Let me expose her for the poison she's always been. Let me make sure she'll never do to anybody else what she's done to us. To Diego."

"And if I do?" Addy lifted her eyes to Bianca's, forced herself not to recoil from the agony burning in the older woman's face. "Will you tell Matty he's free? That he never needs to paint so much as an apple again, and you'll love him just the same?"

"No."

She stared, startled. "Why not?"

"First, because the boy has a gift, and I refuse to let him waste it."

"He's not wasting it. He's just finding his own way to it."

"Maybe. Maybe not." Bianca rolled a shoulder. "But do we really want to take that chance? Do we really want to leave a teenager in charge of a gift of this magnitude?" She folded her hands with an air of finality. "He needs guidance. He doesn't want it, no. But he needs it and I'm going to give it to him. I'm not making the same mistake with him that I made with Diego."

"Which was?"

"Letting him find his own way to his gift." Her smile was wry. "But I'll agree to tell Matty I have no intention of showing his work alongside Diego's for Devil Days."

"Thank God." Addy exhaled for the first time in what felt like minutes.

"Just not yet."

She should've known better. "Why not?"

"Because he's a terrible liar and we both know it. If I want Nan to believe I'm showing his work — alongside whatever else the tiny minds in this town want to think — *he* needs to believe I'm showing his work."

"Nan? What's Nan got to do—"

"She's the closest thing Devil's Kettle has to actual press." Bianca wrinkled her nose, a little moue of distaste. "You heard her in the gallery yesterday — Julia Gates is all over her, desperate to know what we pulled out of the carriage house."

Her stomach went sour. "Julia knows exactly what we pulled out of the carriage house."

"Oh, but she doesn't." Bianca pointed at her. "And she's very aware of that fact. Why do you think she's all over Nan? She's evil, not stupid. She's hardly going to release the memoir unless she knows for sure that we're releasing her nudes."

Addy drew back, startled. "Memoir?"

"Of course." Bianca's mouth tightened. "She'll cast herself as Diego's *true* muse, I'm sure, the angel of sex and mercy to a man trapped by his honor in a loveless marriage, separated from his gift by his up-tight little bride's provincial morals. You'll be the villain, the woman who demanded a good husband for herself and didn't care that she cost the world a great artist. Julia will be the forbidden fruit who brought him back to life but in the end simply wasn't enough to undo your damage."

Nausea roiled in Addy's stomach. "She *wants* us to show those paintings?"

"Oh, she needs us to." Bianca leaned in. "How else is the world to know that she was Diego's true angel? That *she* was his final, blazing masterpiece, not you?"

"But she wasn't." Addy's mouth felt stiff, odd. She had no idea how she was forming words. "He painted *Broken*."

"I know that." Bianca's lips curved but Addy would never call it a smile. "And you know that. But does Julia know that?"

"I…" She broke off, her head spinning. "I don't know."

"Neither do I. But I intend to find out. Which is exactly why Matty can't know he won't be making his triumphant debut over Devil Days. If he believes I'm showing him, then Nan believes I'm showing him. Which means—"

"Which means Julia believes you might be showing him—"

"—instead of Diego's nudes of her, yes. She'd rather we went with the nudes, of course, but if she thinks there's a chance — any chance at all — that Matty is as good as Diego was? That he's better? She'd never let somebody else get that story first." Bianca spread innocent hands. "Or maybe I *am* showing those nudes, and this is simply a clever smoke screen. In the end, there's only one way for her to be certain."

Addy closed her eyes, overwhelmed with horror and yet utterly unsurprised. "You want her to come here."

"I want to destroy her." Bianca flattened both palms on the table and leaned in. "She was never anything but a drug to Diego, just one more sordid weakness he was ashamed of. *Broken* can reveal that in one astonishing instant. It can show the world exactly what she was. But not if she sees it coming. Not if she knows it exists. Which is why I need to see her, face to face. So that *I* can know."

"And Matty is the bait you'll use to get her here, is that it?"

Bianca made an impatient noise. "I know you disagree. I know you'd rather I told him, spared him this pain. But what about my pain, Addy? I still *bleed* for Diego, every single day. The wound just won't close and lord knows I've tried to let it. But if I can do this? If I can make Julia Gates pay for what she did? I think maybe it can finally start."

Addy considered her for a long moment, then slowly nodded. "Okay," she said. "I understand. I won't tell him, not until you give me permission. But I'm still going to talk to him."

"You should. Matty needs somebody on his side right now, and he's not going to believe it's me. So until I can be his mother again — just his mother and nothing else — please impress upon him that we'd rather he didn't burn the house down."

"Or anything else."

"Excuse me?" Bianca's eyes were sharp, fierce.

"Did you ask him?" Addy held that gaze, didn't allow herself to even blink, let alone flinch. "Did you ask him if he had anything to do with the other two fires in town last night?"

"Of course I didn't. I didn't need to." Bianca lifted her chin. "He was with Peter when both fires started, first of all. Secondly, I wouldn't insult him with the question. He's not Diego. You may think I don't know the difference, but I do. Matty would never do such a thing. That sort of destruction simply isn't in him."

"But it was in Diego?"

Bianca didn't look away. "You know the answer to that as well as I do."

Addy mounted the curved stairs toward Matty's bedroom, a hot chocolate in one hand, the doughnut box in the other. It wouldn't make the conversation any easier, but it certainly wouldn't hurt her cause. She hit the top of the stairs and hung a left, her shoes soundless on the thick carpet runner. She stopped in front of Matty's closed door, and lifted a hand to knock.

"Matty?"

"Go away." His voice was flat and thin through the door.

"It's Addy."

Pause. "Go away please?"

"I've got doughnuts."

"Oh, fine. Come in."

She opened the door and found Matty lying on the bed fully dressed, hands stacked under his head, regarding his ceiling as if the answers to the universe had been written there in invisible ink. Every other square inch of the room was covered with comic book covers and movie posters — *The Avengers*, *The X-Men*, *Spiderman*, that flaming guy on the motorcycle, and some Addy didn't recognize. But a few patches of bare wall stood out like missing teeth, and Addy's heart cracked.

"Oh, Matty. Is that what you were burning?"

"It was time to move on." His eyes stayed fixed on the ceiling. "Mom said so."

"But, Matty, they were *yours*. You loved—"

"It doesn't matter. They're gone." And the dead finality

in his tone cut through her protest. So she set the cocoa and the pastry box on the nightstand and drifted from wall to wall, touching the blank spaces while fury and sorrow churned inside her. While she struggled to contain them both.

From the time he could operate a thumb tack Matty had covered his walls with heroes. Movie posters, pages from his favorite comic books, shelves of outrageously muscled action figures. And he'd put himself among them as soon as he could hold a pencil. He'd spent hours pulling lantern-jawed crime fighters from his imagination, giving them life on paper. And he'd tacked his creations shoulder-by-cape with Spiderman, Wolverine, Iron Man. But now that place — Matty's place — was empty. He'd taken down his work and burned it.

She resisted the urge to fling her arms around him and pour all her affection and acceptance into his wounds. She doubted he'd even allow it, much less thank her for it. So she scooped up the to-go cup she'd left on the nightstand, and poked at Matty's man-sized boots. He sighed but sat up and she perched on the edge of his bed.

"Doughnut?" She slid the box off the nightstand and onto the bed between them, flipped open the lid with a little flourish. "I stopped by the Sugar Rush on my way up the hill. Some of them are still warm."

Fat and sugar fumes wafted into the air between them and Matty leaned over for a look. He selected a chocolate-frosted custard bomb and polished it off in two listless bites. She nudged the box a little closer and he went the powdered sugar route this time. It sprinkled down the front of his *Last Gunslinger* t-shirt and gave him an endearing white mustache as he chewed. Addy wanted to wrap him up in her arms and rock him but contented herself watching him eat.

"Matty—" she began when he'd polished off a third doughnut.

"I'm not going to talk about last night," he said, but there was no heat in his words, no fire. Just a cold, implacable finality. He'd arrived at some decision. Settled something within himself. Apprehension gripped the back of her neck with icy fingers.

"Okay," she said carefully. "You don't need to."

He shot her a suspicious look and she held up her hands in surrender.

"Seriously," she said. "You don't want to talk about last night, fine. I'm not your mom. You don't answer to me. I'm here because I'm your sister, Matty. I'm here because I love you and I don't know who you are lately."

He gave a crack of laughter so abrupt it startled her. "Yeah, there's been some speculation on that point, hasn't there?"

"As to who you are?"

"Yeah."

"Who are you, then, Matty? Tell me, and I promise I'll love whoever that is."

He stared at her for a long time. For a solid two minutes she wondered if he was going to say anything.

"You don't know?" he asked finally. "Really?"

"How would I?" She smiled. "You haven't said it yet. So who are you, Matty?"

"I'm not who I've always thought I was, that's for sure." He gave a soft, sad laugh. "Definitely not who Mom wishes I were."

"None of us are who our parents wish we were." Lord knew she wasn't.

"Yeah, but Mom's taken it farther than most." He took a deep breath and met her eyes. "She's been lying to me."

Addy stared. He *knew*? He knew Bianca wasn't planning to show his work at Devil Days? She swallowed, then said carefully, "About what?"

"About who I am."

"What does that mean?"

"It means I finally caught a clue, Addison." He turned away from her. "I finally get the situation, okay? I'll be a good boy from now on. I can't make myself talented but I can at least be cooperative."

"You don't need to be talented *or* cooperative, Matty." Fear uncurled inside her. Something was wrong here. Did he know somehow what Bianca needed from him? What she was planning? "You just have to be *you*."

"Sure, Addy. Tell Mom it was an accident, okay?"

Fear leapt into dread. "What was an accident, Matisse?"

He waved a hand at the blank spaces standing out on his walls. "Mom said drawing what I like was selfish, and it was time to burn that bridge. So I did." He jerked a shrug. "I didn't mean to set off the fire alarms, though."

A surge of pity closed Addy's throat. The kid was thirteen. He had a right to be selfish. No, he had a *responsibility* to be selfish. To go through his mental dress-up trunk, try everything on, accept and reject until he'd patched together the man he was supposed to be. The man he *wanted* to be. Unfortunately, Matty's rights had been trampled by grown-up concerns and machinations that had nothing to do with him. His needs had been superseded by his mother's desperate attempt to put her grief behind her once and for all. And if taking down Julia Gates was what Bianca needed to finally let go of one son so she could be

273

present for another, well, Addy had to help her. She only hoped that Matty would still be open to his mother's love once it was finally his again.

She pushed to her feet, put a hand on Matty's shoulder. "Listen, leave your mom to me. Don't worry about her, or about painting, or any of that, okay? Just leave it to me."

"What are you going to do?" Matty barked out a laugh. "You don't even live here anymore."

"I know. Just…trust me. There's more going on than I can tell you right now. But you have to believe that I would never let anything bad happen to you."

"I don't think you're in charge of that kind of thing." The bleak knowledge in his eyes sliced her heart wide open. "But thanks."

Chapter 28

THE NEXT DAY — Monday, midmorning, right on schedule — Addy pulled open the Wooden Spoon's heavy glass door and pushed Matty inside. He'd been silent for the four block ride from the middle school where she'd picked him up, so the jingle and hum of Monday Brunch in full swing was a balm to Addy's nerves. She didn't care for Silent Matty; he worried her. She'd rather have Angry Matty back.

At least it was a pretty day finally. The calendar had just rolled over to June, and the North Shore was celebrating. The sky was brilliantly blue, and a golden sun flooded the street with warmth and welcome. Even so, Addy pulled the door carefully shut behind her, always mindful of the unpredictable nature of lake-shore weather.

"Packed today," Addy said cheerfully to Matty's back, then grunted as somebody's massive purse caught her in the midsection.

"Gosh." Matty flicked her an ironic eyebrow. "Wonder why."

"Well, everybody loves Monday Brunch."

"They're not here for brunch." He stretched his lips in a ghastly smile. "They're here for the show."

"What show?" She bounced to her toes to scan the

packed room, and just caught a glimpse of Jax's messy chestnut head in the back corner booth. Without warning, her brain provided an instant replay of all that unruly hair between her fingers, that hot mouth on hers. Her heart bumped predictably and she dropped back to her heels. He loved her, she thought dizzily. He'd said so. She still hadn't quite wrapped her mind around that — what he meant by it, what she believed about it, where they went from there. They hadn't had much time to discuss it.

They would, she told herself firmly. Just as soon as everything settled down a little, they'd talk. They'd figure things out. Except that when they did, he'd likely want to know how *she* felt about *him*. Was she in love with him, too?

She didn't know. How could she? Once upon a time, she'd thought she was in love with Diego. If she'd thought that was love, but also thought this was love, she obviously had no idea what the word even meant. Which was why she wanted to know exactly what Jax thought it meant before she decided what to call the desperate hunger, the sweet peace, and the uncertain longing he inspired in her.

They'd figure it out, she assured herself again. Just as soon as they had enough time to concentrate on it.

"They're here for the Davis show," Matty told her. "The one where an arsonist tries to burn the town down over the weekend, then he and his family show up for Monday Brunch like nothing happened."

"Don't be ridiculous," she said. "Nobody thinks you lit those fires." She snagged a handful of his Captain America t-shirt and began excusing her way toward the back booth, towing him behind her. She smiled at Josh Martin, who was back to busing tables although on one of those walking cast/boot things. Huh. Eli must've made enough cash to resupply and move on. She wondered vaguely if Gerte had ever pried his life story out of him. "Everybody knows you were with Peter. He said so."

"I know he did," Matty murmured. "But do we believe him?"

"Of course we believe him. Why would he lie about something like that?" She paused, distracted by the glass bakery case at her elbow. "Oh, man," she said. "Look at that, would you?" She pointed her chin at a small army of Gerte's mile-high pies. "Okay, forget looking. *Smell* that." She pulled in a lungful of warm, butter-scented air and grinned. "Let's have pie for brunch. Want to? I think we—"

She was going to say *deserve it* except that she was suddenly talking too loudly. Either that or the room had gone quiet.

She broke off and glanced around. Coffee cups were frozen beneath avid eyes, loaded forks teetered halfway to open mouths. It was like they were in a movie and somebody had hit the pause button. Addy followed the stares to Matty — now conveniently center stage — who scowled at his boots.

"Are you sure, Addy?" he mumbled. "Are you *sure* we're all just taking Peter's word for it?"

Addy smiled brightly at their audience and released her strangle hold on Captain America to slip a more companionable arm through Matty's stiff one. Somebody hit the play button again and the hum of brunch in progress came back online, though slightly muted, slightly watchful. "Yes," she said through her teeth. "We are absolutely all taking Peter's word on this."

He only hunched deeper into his t-shirt and fell silent until they arrived at the Davis booth. Jax came to his feet.

"There you are," he said. "I was starting to think you weren't coming."

Matty slid into the booth next to Georgie and smiled acidly. "What? And miss the chance to show off my scarlet letter?"

Addy slid into the booth beside Bianca and Jax sat down next to her.

"Oh, please," Jax said. "You're no Hester Prynne."

"Of course he is," Georgie said. "Did you hear the crickets when people spotted him? I thought for a minute there he was going to have to make a speech or fight a duel or something."

"Oh, let them talk." Bianca tucked the menus out of the way and leaned forward to pat Matty's knotted hands. "Small minds, small conclusions."

"I don't know, Mom." Georgie toyed idly with a spoon. "Jax hasn't been this busy since Walter tried to install his own deep fat fryer at the Sugar Rush. Three fires in two weeks is kind of a record around here. And Matty's right next to all of them?" She threw him a sharp grin. "Anything you want to tell us, little brother?"

"Besides screw off?"

Bianca sighed. "Georgie, leave your brother alone."

Gerte arrived at the table, a loaded tray riding her forearm. Addy smiled at her, braced for the coffee she didn't order and would force herself to drink. But Gerte didn't deal out the coffee. She didn't slide Matty an extravagant hot chocolate loaded up with those bittersweet chocolate curls Addy would envy all day. She met Addy's smile with cold fury and said, "You're not welcome here."

"Excuse me?" Bianca slid her bright blue cheaters to the top of her head, and regarded Gerte with haughty disbelief.

"You heard me. You're not welcome here," Gerte said, her voice taut and trembling. "None of you."

"Is that so?" Bianca tipped her head and gave the other woman a cool study. Color flashed into Gerte's soft cheeks and she drew herself up with rigid dignity.

"We can't stop you from putting porn in your gallery window, Bianca," she said tightly. "If you don't care what it'll do to the rest of us, there's no reasoning with you, and I guess that's your business. But this?" She threw her free hand out to the side, took in the cozy little shoe-box of a diner, the sugar-laden air, the companionable clink of flatware and coffee cups. "This is *my* business. The Wooden Spoon has been in my family for three generations. We've been here nearly as long as you have, and we might not be rich but we've put everything we had into building something here. Something your privileged little monster—" She shot an ugly glare toward Matty. "—might have burned to the ground in a fit of temper. So do whatever you please, Bianca, but get out of my restaurant."

Lainey appeared at her mother's elbow, all flour-coated hands and pink cheeks, as if she'd sprinted there from the kitchen. "Mom, stop." She turned a stricken face to the table. Addy stared back, stunned. "I'm sorry, she's distraught. It was a terrible weekend, we haven't slept. She doesn't mean—"

"Don't tell me what I mean," Gerte bit out coldly, her eyes never leaving Bianca's. "I know just what I mean, and I mean what I say. Get out."

Lainey put a miserable hand on Gerte's shoulder but dropped her eyes and stayed silent.

"As I said," Bianca announced in a clear, carrying voice. "Small minds, small conclusions. Come along, children.

Let's go."

Matty scrambled out of the booth, followed much more leisurely by Georgie. Jax, Addy and Bianca all rose from the other side. Jax touched Lainey's elbow and she sent him a grateful glance. Bianca only put her nose in the air and sailed toward the door. Matty stalked after her. Georgie shook back that silvery sheet of hair and began to follow, but stopped in front of Gerte.

"Matty was with Peter," she said softly.

"So he says," Gerte sneered.

"You think he'd lie like that?" Georgie smiled pleasantly, as if amused by the whole situation. "To the police? For me?"

Gerte met her gaze with hard eyes. "Why wouldn't he lie for you? About you? We've been doing it for years, this whole town, and none of us is even trying to marry your money."

Georgie's beautiful face went momentarily blank, then she tossed back her head and laughed, a merry chime of silvery bells. "I'll give you credit for saying that to my face, Gerte. You're the only person in this town who ever has. Good for you." She patted the woman's plump arm. Gerte drew back like Georgie was contagious. "That said? Mom's totally right about you." She shook her head, hooked an elbow through Addy's numb arm and drew her toward the door. "Small minds, small conclusions."

Jax fell in behind them and Addy let Georgie tow her through the crowd. She was grateful for the guiding hand, really. Considering that she couldn't feel her feet, she doubted she could have gotten there on her own.

It was all falling apart, she realized dumbly. The town she cherished, the family she adored, the social structure she'd built her life around? It was all crumbling. Her eyes flew frantically over the crowd, over all the familiar faces watching their departure with eyes that skated away from hers every time she tried to connect.

Only one set of eyes caught and held, and they were a cool, knowing hazel. The same color as Jax's, down to the last fleck.

Addy held Nan's gaze as Jax opened the door and let Georgie sail through. Addy faltered, struck suddenly by the question — the offer? — burning in that stare. She didn't have to accept Bianca's reign, she realized slowly. She had another option. She could stay here, throw in her lot with the rest of the town. Rally against porn on Main Street, betray Bianca's plan, tell Matty he wouldn't have to paint his mother a masterpiece. Keep Diego's ugly new paintings in a dark garage for the rest of her natural life.

She lifted her chin high and sailed onto the sidewalk after Georgie. It wasn't even a choice. Family was family, and the Davises were hers, for better or for worse.

She caught the tiny disappointed shake of Nan's head just before the door whispered shut behind Jax. They stood on the sidewalk for three suspended moments, then the Wooden Spoon erupted in applause behind them. Raucous, spontaneous, hooting applause.

They were cheering, Addy realized, for their hero.

For the woman with enough courage to say what everybody else had been thinking. For the David who'd finally slung that killing stone at Goliath.

They were cheering for Gerte.

—◉—

"Well, that was different," Jax said.

"Understatement," Georgie muttered.

"Please." His mother fluttered a dismissive hand. "Gerte's been waiting years to throw a scene like that. It'll blow over."

Jax wasn't so sure about that but he trailed his mother in silence as she turned and strolled toward the gallery. She fitted a key in the lock and twisted.

"Jax," she said, "do you mind getting Matty back to school? If you hurry, he can still catch lunch in the cafeteria."

"I can walk," Matty said dully.

"I'll take you," Addy said but he'd already turned on one big boot and stalked off in the direction of the middle school. Jax squinted after him.

"I'm going to call the school in half an hour," he announced to nobody in particular and followed his mother into the gallery. "If he's not in class—"

"He will be," Addy said with a resigned certainty that only added to the worry brewing in Jax's gut.

"How do you know?"

"He's done making trouble." She drifted to a stop in the center of the gallery, right next to *Diego's Angel*. She gazed up at the idealized version of herself with unutterable weariness. "He told me so yesterday. If he can't be talented, he can at least be cooperative."

"He said that?" Jax stared in disbelief while worry tried to morph into fear.

"I think he meant it, too." Addy said, and brought her eyes to Jax's. "What teenaged boy talks like that, Jax?"

"They don't."

"I know. Something's wrong with him." She shifted that

look to Bianca who met it with unusual inscrutability. "He wouldn't tell me what it was when I talked to him yesterday, but something's not right. He's not telling us something."

"Don't be dramatic," she said lightly. "Leave that to Matty. He's thirteen; he's allowed." She tucked her purse in the desk drawer and fluttered her hands at them. "Oh, don't look at me like that. I said it will blow over, and it will. It always does. Now go away, you two. You need to get back to work, and so do Georgie and I." She offered him a cheeky smile and headed for the long white table dividing the back half of the gallery into two promenades. She gazed lovingly down at the unframed canvases spread across the table. The masterworks, he saw, his stomach souring. Addy's secret paintings. Every bruise Diego had put on her soul, captured in oil and blood. Bianca sighed happily. "We have a lot of porn to frame."

Incredulous fury shot down his spine, and his hands clenched into automatic fists. "No."

Bianca frowned at him. "I'm sorry, what?"

His fists were throbbing at his sides so he shoved them into his pockets where they'd be safe. He hoped. He turned to Addy, who gazed back at him, her face smooth as milk, her eyes remote as Jupiter. "You're okay with this?" he asked. "You're going to let her frame up the train wreck of your marriage and lob it at the town like a grenade?"

"Of course she is." Bianca made a disapproving noise and went back to fawning over those damn paintings. "This is astonishing work. It represents Diego's potential in glorious flower and she's not going to allow pedestrian concerns about the content — yours or anybody else's — to prevent the world from—"

"That's not your decision to make, Mom."

Susan Sey

Bianca paused. "Excuse me?"

"Those paintings aren't yours to show." Jax didn't take his eyes away from Addison. Couldn't. "They're Addy's. And I can't believe she'd want to show them." He gazed down into her wide, unblinking eyes. "You don't want to show them, Addy." He sounded...desperate. Angry. Half insane. "Do you?"

She hesitated. "They're masterworks," she said finally, and Jax knew with a sick pang that she was thinking bank accounts. Not hers, though. His family's. "I hid them because I didn't want you all to know the truth about what my marriage had become. But now that you do know—" She shrugged. "I don't care what anybody else thinks of them, or of me. You're the only ones who matter to me. You're my family."

"And we will be whether you show them or not." Fear bit into the edges of his anger, along with a bleak realization. His love, no matter how strong, might not be enough to break the spell Diego and his family had cast on her vulnerable heart all those years ago. She was still convinced that their love was more than she deserved, that her place in their family was conditional. That every day of her life as a Davis was a campaign for re-election and she had to win it. "At least I will be. I can't speak for her—" He hooked a thumb toward his mother. "—but I love you, Addison. I'm *in* love with you, and it's not because you're Diego's Angel. And it's not because you could make the family a pile of money selling tickets to the implosion of your marriage." She flinched but he barreled on, desperate to get through to her. To make her see. "It's because you're *Addison*."

"Jax, be reasonable." She stretched out a hand to him, and he seized it. Her diamond bit into his palm. Diego's ring,

284

he thought dully. She'd never taken it off. Pain-laced fear twisted inside him. What if she never did? What if she simply couldn't? "They're just paintings."

"Like hell they are. They're your history, Addison. They're the worst chapter of your life. They're *private*. And every time I look at them — because they're a goddamn train wreck and I can't *not* look — I feel ashamed. Like I'm seeing something I shouldn't. Something I wish I hadn't seen. Something I looked away from for years because it was *your* private pain. And now I'm watching like it's television. We all are." He heaved in a breath, and it felt hot in his lungs. Thin. "And you want to invite the world? Don't do it, Addy." Jax knew he was begging. He didn't care. "Please just don't."

She only gazed at him, her eyes shiny with tears and full of apology. Acid backed up his throat, and it tasted bitter. Like defeat. Like failure.

"Okay, then. That's your decision, I guess." He lifted the hand he still held, let that giant diamond shatter the light. "I do love you, Addy. I probably always will." He dropped her hand, his heart screaming inside him. "But I don't think I can love you enough for both of us."

Chapter 29

ADDY WATCHED IN disbelief as Jax turned away from her and walked stiffly out the door. Agony lapped gently at her, from her knees to her hair. She barely felt Georgie's hand steering her to the nearest chair, or Bianca's little nudge that folded her into it.

"Now wait a darn minute," Addy said to nobody in particular. She couldn't seem to think past the shock of Jax walking away from her. *Leaving* her. Which was exactly what everybody else who'd ever professed to love her had done. So why Jax doing it surprised her, she couldn't really say. On some level, she thought slowly, she must've believed Jax was different. She must've believed that Jax defined love the way her heart did. That when he said he loved her, he meant he'd be her family. That he'd stay when everybody else left, no matter how hard it was, no matter how tempting she made it to go. Because he was in love with her. He was supposed to stay. And yet… "He left."

"No, he stomped off," Georgie said in wondering tones, staring at the door through which he'd disappeared. "In a *huff*." She shook her head and grinned. "If I hadn't seen that with my own eyes, I wouldn't have believed it." She turned that grin on Addy. "Well *done*, Addison."

"What, did I set a new record?" She pushed out the

words. Normal didn't seem to exist at the moment but keeping up appearances was a hard habit to break. "True love to bitter acrimony in under two weeks?"

"True love, is it?" Bianca's eyes were sharp on her, but Addy couldn't make herself care. Jax had walked away from her.

"I must've thought so." Addy shrugged. "Then again, I've been wrong before."

"Not this time." Georgie hugged her arms and performed a minor jig. Addy would've been astonished at the display of energy if she hadn't been too busy trying to drag together the severed halves of her heart. "You pushed *Jax* into a huffy walk off! He completely lost it! If that's not true love, what is it?"

The chimes at the door jingled again and a breeze tugged at Addy's curls. It smelled like sun-warmed stones. She couldn't dredge up any interest.

Then Bianca said in frozen tones, "Well my goodness. Willa Zinc. To what do we owe the pleasure?"

Surprise filtered dully through the pain. Addy turned without curiosity and found Willa standing just inside the gallery door, ball cap pulled low, fingers tucked in the pockets of her dirty jeans like she was reminding herself not to touch anything. Or like the place might be contagious. Something about the way she stood there, so straight and tense, made Addy wonder if she was holding her breath.

"Hey, Addison," Willa said. "You still want to get those turkeys out from under your porch?"

"*My* porch," Bianca said, smiling tightly.

Willa ignored that. Addy just blinked at her, unable to comprehend. How could turkeys possibly matter at a time like this? She'd just been forced to choose between the town and her family. She'd made her choice and hadn't cried about it. But then Jax had insisted she choose between the family and him. She'd chosen wrong. She might just cry about that. As soon as she could remember how.

"Addison?" Willa prompted. "The turkeys?"

"Right." Addy pushed to her feet, mildly surprised to find she could. *Act normal*, she reminded herself. That's how a new normal always started. You pretended it existed. Then one day, it did. Then you moved again and started over but thinking about that was no way to survive today. "The turkeys. Thanks for getting back to me."

"It would've been easier if you ever answered your phone."

"Yeah." Addy headed for the door. "That's been a problem lately." A semi-hysterical laugh bubbled up her throat. Her phone didn't come close to the top of her list of problems these days. "Do you have time right now?"

Willa didn't look away, her eyes dark and penetrating. "That's why I'm here."

"Let's go."

"I'll drive," Willa said and pointed toward her truck parked at the curb outside the bait and tackle. Addy followed her. Soren and the usual assortment of fisherfolk and liars were leaning on the counter inside the bait and tackle. Nan was there, too, probably getting quotes for the article she was undoubtedly writing. (*Porn on Main Street! Shock and Scandal!*) Addy knew she should smile at them, give them a little finger wave, something. Because that would be normal, and how she acted now would set the tone for the new normal, whatever it turned out to be.

She couldn't quite manage it, though. Not with her heart still aching like an abscessed tooth. The best she could manage was a glance on her way by. Cold stares greeted her. Nobody lifted so much as a coffee cup her way. An ominous weight settled on the back of her neck.

"Thanks for tracking me down, Willa." She stood in the shadow of Soren's enormous plaster fish and tried to smile while Willa unlocked her truck. "My phone's been on the fritz."

"Lucky you." Willa slid into the cab and reached across the bench seat to unlock Addy's door. Before she could get in, the scent of black coffee and cigarettes enveloped her, which could only mean one thing. She closed her eyes briefly then turned to find Jax's grandmother standing on the curb, gazing at her with his eyes. She didn't flinch, but it was a near thing.

"Addison," Nan said. "Do you have a minute?"

"Sure, Nan." She pasted on a smile. "What can I do for you?"

"You can tell me what the hell's going on in that twisty little head of my daughter-in-law's."

Willa sighed and got back out of the truck. Leaned her elbows on the hood and settled in to wait. To listen, evidently. Addy produced a quizzical smile for Nan and a helpless shrug.

"She doesn't exactly confide in me, Nan. You know her as well as I do. What do you think she's up to?"

"If I knew, why would I be asking you?"

"You've got me there."

Nan rummaged in her bag, never taking her eyes off Addy's. She found her cigarettes, plucked one out, and tapped it thoughtfully on her little paw of a hand. "I don't believe you."

Addy gave her innocent eyes. "Don't believe me about what?"

"That you have no idea what Bianca's up to." She flicked a fat silver lighter, leaned into the flame and puffed until her cigarette glowed dangerously. "You know exactly what she's doing."

"I do?"

"You can't lie for shit, Addy. I've always liked that about you. Don't start now."

Addy felt herself trying to smile, automatically trying to distract and deflect. She let the smile die before it was born and lifted her shoulders instead. "I don't know what you want me to say, Nan."

"How about the truth?" Nan exhaled a lungful of tar and nicotine, and squinted at Addy through the smoke. "Are you planning to put your and Diego's sex life on display for Devil Days?"

"Is that what people think?" A brutal pulse of hatred seized Addy by the throat. Damn Diego. Hadn't he cost her enough already? Him and those stupid paintings? "That Diego painted the two of us having sex?"

"Some do." She shrugged. "But that's hardly the point. It doesn't matter *who* he painted. It's the *what* that's concerning people." She aimed her cigarette toward Addy's chest. "We're talking about you putting sexual content on Main Street during the biggest tourist event of the year. A traditionally *family-friendly* tourist event, mind you. The gallery is on the same block as the doughnut shop, for Christ's sake. The bait and tackle is across the street. Any father and son wandering in to charter a boat, any mother and daughter looking to rent a couple fishing poles, and any grandpa looking to buy his grandbaby a doughnut? They'd have to walk right by your big ass window display full of, well, ass."

Nan paused significantly, her penciled-on brows lifted in a silent *well*? Addy just stared back, anger pulsing dangerously at the base of her skull. She knew Nan had a point. She knew Jax had one, too. Bianca had a point of her own, come to that. But Addison was too raw right now to think about what everybody else wanted from her. Too raw to deal with their needs, their demands or their reactions to Addy's own pain. But everybody had an opinion, didn't they? They always did.

To Bianca, those paintings were art, and showing them would avenge her lost boy's death. To Jax, they were pain and *not* showing them was the only way Addy could prove herself worthy of his love. To Nan and the rest of the town they were smut, the sort of thing decent people kept private. The intimate details of her marriage had been keeping the town in the black for years, of course, but those were only the pretty bits. The ugly, mean, humiliating bits? Evidently, she was meant to keep those to herself. To deal with her pain all alone.

Which was, she realized suddenly, exactly the point she'd been missing. This was *her* pain. *Her* humiliation. *Her* history. Jax had said it himself. This whole mess belonged to her. She'd earned it with blood and tears, and it was hers to do with as she pleased. Nobody else's opinion mattered unless she wanted it to.

Gerte emerged unexpectedly from the bait and tackle, and Addy realized that she was about to be treated to another big swallow of public opinion, whether she wanted it or not.

Soren trudged onto the sidewalk behind Gerte, coffee mug in hand, followed by a half-dozen of his friends. Old guys. Fishermen. Retirees. They would've been in there since the scene in the Wooden Spoon, gossiping like middle schoolers. Matty the arsonist. Porn on Main Street. Bianca the bitch queen. Whipping themselves into a frenzy of outrage over Addy's role in all of it until they'd convinced themselves that somebody needed a lynching.

And here was Addy, right on the sidewalk waiting. How convenient.

"May we have a word?" Gerte asked. Her tone was all civility, but Addy wasn't fooled. She knew a mob when she saw one. Fury and fear twined together in her stomach but she folded her arms and smiled.

"Sure."

"I'm glad I spotted you out here," Gerte said with grave concern but her eyes were full of avid anticipation. "You should know the city council has called an emergency meeting for this evening."

Bianca had been right, Addy realized abruptly. Gerte was enjoying this. She was *loving* it. And suddenly the agony inside her erupted into rage. It just exploded in a single, cleansing nuclear blast, filling her brain with a stark field of spotless white.

"Is that so?" she said softly, fury dancing inside her. "What seems to be the problem?"

"What's the problem?" Gerte widened her eyes. "You have the gall to display porn on Main Street, then you want to know what the problem is?"

Addy's jaw clenched. "You have an awfully strong opinion about paintings you've never seen, Gerte."

"Like I need to see them." Gerte flicked this away. "I

don't know what kind of nastiness Diego painted the two of you getting up to. Lord knows I'd rather not."

Well, that makes two of us, Addy thought.

"What I do know is that anybody who'd call it art and sell tickets to the show is nothing but a common tramp." Her round cheeks pinked with a hectic excitement and her chest inflated importantly. "And I, for one, would rather go bankrupt than sell a single slice of pie to the kind of people who'd come see it. And I'm quite certain I speak for us all when I say that."

Addy opened her mouth to, well, she didn't actually know what. Breathe fire like a dragon and reduce Gerte to a pile of smoking ashes? It seemed possible. Likely, even, given the way anger was banging in her head.

But Willa said, "Hey, at least she's doing something."

"What?" Gerte drew back, a quick frown pinching her fine brows.

"We need tourists, and Addy's delivering them," Willa said reasonably. "Which is more than I can say for anybody else around here."

Addy blinked at Willa, shocked that she — that anybody — would wade in to defend her on this.

"I don't see how hanging filth in the shop windows does anything worthwhile for this town," Gerte said. She turned that cold gaze back to Addy. "But you can't be expected to understand that. You're a Davis, after all. Arson is just boys being boys to you, and to hell with anybody who even tries to object." Her eyes narrowed. "The sheriff's been invited to the council meeting tonight, by the way. You can bet she'll be asked to have a good look at your precious Matty's whereabouts on Saturday night."

"I see." Addy folded her arms and met Gerte's gaze. Held

it. Forced herself to recognize what she saw there. The vicious thrill of cutting loose with some real venom. The relief of finally having an excuse, however flimsy, to say every nasty thing civil society normally forbade. The pleasure of being perfectly, cruelly, horribly honest.

Her anger shifted abruptly from hot to cold and she bared her teeth in a fierce smile. Gerte wanted honest? She could do that.

"I see," she said again. "And I'm sorry. Very sorry."

"You should be," Gerte murmured, flushed with triumph.

"See there," Soren said to Gerte. He shambled forward, laid a hand on Gerte's plump shoulder. "I told you to calm down. Addy's good people. I knew she'd see reason."

"Oh, I'm not apologizing. Not about the paintings, and not about Matty. I make it a habit not to say I'm sorry unless I am," Addy said sweetly. "But I am sorry that I won't make that emergency council meeting tonight. Gosh, it sounds like fun. Unfortunately I have a tremendous lot of slutting around to do today, and it's just so hard to fit everything in. Rest assured, however, that I've heard your concerns. I've heard them and I want to thank you all — but you, especially, Gerte — for your honesty. In return, I'm going to be just as honest with you as you've been with me."

She paused to relish the growing alarm in their unfriendly faces. "I'm showing Diego's paintings." An ugly smile spread over her face and she didn't try to stop it. She just aimed it straight at Gerte, who grimaced like Addy had slid a plateful of burning garbage under her nose. "Oh, yeah, the showing is *on*. Every last allegedly pornographic brush stroke will be in a frame and on the wall for Devil Days." Her smile was all teeth now, nearly a snarl. It felt fantastic. "And there's not a damn thing you can do about it."

Gerte simply stared, open-mouthed and flushed. Soren heaved a deep sigh. The fisherfolk grumbled ominously, and Willa might've chuckled. Nan, however, narrowed her eyes and aimed that cigarette at Addy once more.

"Don't do anything you're going to regret, Addison."

Addy yanked open the door of Willa's truck. "I regret a lot of things," she told Nan, her teeth bared in a vicious smile. "What's one more?"

Chapter 30

SEVERAL HOURS LATER, Jax warily considered the steps of Davis Place's front porch and prayed like hell that Willa had gotten the turkey situation under control. Not that he didn't deserve to be humiliated by a pack of rogue turkeys. He deserved worse. He'd been a fool earlier, walking out of the gallery that way. Walking out on Addison.

Shame pooled in his gut, black and oily, and he dragged a hand down his face. It had taken nearly six hours of punishing physical activity — his hoses had never been cleaner and he'd out-lifted even Graham Graves in the station's weight room — but he'd finally achieved the kind of bone-deep exhaustion that occupied every inch of his body and soul. The kind that left no room for emotion. The kind that allowed him to finally see with brutal clarity what he'd done.

He'd sworn that his love was unconditional, then he'd put a big old condition on it. And when Addison hadn't immediately met it, he'd walked out on her.

He'd been hard in the grip of love-induced insanity, yes, but it was no excuse. Abandonment was her nuclear button and he'd punched it. He'd jumped on it with both stupid feet. He was truly his mother's son, wasn't he? Hurting his wayward beloved as much and as efficiently as possible. Unlike Bianca, he hadn't done it on purpose. There was that grim bit of comfort but it would hardly matter from Addy's point of view, now would it?

He'd raced home, praying the entire way that it wasn't as bad as he thought it was. That it was fixable. That there was something he could do or say, some penance he could perform that could erase the hurt he'd caused, undo the damage he'd done. But Addison wasn't at home. Neither were her things. Every last trace of her — from her shampoo to her suitcase — had vanished.

She'd left him.

It was a stunning slap, the pain dizzying and savage even as he understood how well he'd earned it. Holy Christ, she'd left their *home*.

Denial rose up like a towering wave inside him and he thought, *Fuck that*. He'd just bring her back.

Then again, he'd have to find her first.

It had taken a while but he'd finally tracked her here to Davis Place. To the safety net she was building his family out of her own dreams and bank account. He didn't deserve this woman. Fear gripped his nape with cold fingers as that realization sank in. That kind of heart? That kind of straight-up loyalty, no-holds-barred generosity? He was unworthy. Which was as stupid and old-fashioned a conviction as it was unquestionably true.

Unfortunately, he couldn't live without her, so what the hell. Time to throw all the cards on the table.

He sucked in a breath and marched up Davis Place's precarious front steps. He knocked on that massive door and stood back, uncomfortably aware of his pulse thudding in his ears.

He'd knocked twice more before the door finally rattled, then there she was, beautifully rumpled, disconcertingly pale. She studied him with green, suspicious eyes. Jax's heart tumbled like a puppy inside his rib cage and he leaned into the door frame.

"Hey, Addy." He gave her what he hoped was a charming smile.

She didn't smile back. "Jax. What are you doing here?"

"Oh, I was in the neighborhood, feeling like a jackass. Thought I'd stop by to see if you thought the same and wanted to discuss it."

She blinked, clearly startled by his decision to go with flat-out honesty. "I don't know," she said slowly. Evidently, she was going with honesty as well. Relief warred with worry inside him. At least she hadn't slammed the door in his face.

"You don't know if I'm a jackass, or you don't know if you want to discuss it?"

"Oh, I know you're a jackass." She tipped her head, considering him. "I just don't know that I'm interested in discussing it."

He made a show of stuffing his hands into his pockets and hunching against the wind. The temperature had definitely dropped back into the wintery range since sunset but Jax wasn't cold. He rarely was. In fact, he was feeling markedly sweaty at the moment and not in a good way. But Addy didn't know that. "Can I come in while you think about it?" he asked, all innocence. "It's chilly."

"Oh. Sure." She stepped back from the door as he'd known she would, bless her innately hospitable soul. She gestured him into what had once been the foyer, the parlor and the dining room but was now a single generous space.

She closed the door behind him and Jax whistled. "Wow. You didn't waste any time getting Graham up here."

"He had a few free hours over the weekend." She turned and walked to the enormous fireplace that had previously been stuffed into a tiny slice of the main floor and now anchored a burgeoning great room. She ran a loving finger over the elaborate granite surround. "He gave them to me."

Jax studied that fireplace. He'd seen it right there all his life but had clearly never *seen* it. Not the way Addy had. If he had, he'd have known that those walls were only hemming it in. He'd have understood that a fireplace like this was supposed to be the living, beating heart of the whole damn house, an irresistible invitation to gathering and warmth.

Or maybe he wouldn't have. Maybe that was the kind of thing only Addy saw. Or maybe the invitation and the warmth came from her. He couldn't be sure but that was exactly why he needed her. To show him what he missed. To be the invitation and the warmth and the heart.

But all he said — all he allowed himself to say — was, "He does nice work. This is really coming along."

A corner of her mouth lifted, and he wanted to kiss it with every ounce of his soul. "You should see the kitchen."

"Frank and Mason had a few hours, too?"

"They did." That smile died. "I don't imagine it'll be quite so easy to get on their calendars from now on, though. I had quite an afternoon."

"Did you?"

"Might've burned a few bridges."

"Yeah?"

She leaned back against the granite fireplace, folded her arms. "I'm showing those paintings, Jax."

His stomach twisted and he bit back an instinctive protest. "Where are they?"

"Upstairs. Bianca decided to hold off on framing them in case the framer leaked photos or something." She tipped her head slowly. "Why?"

"I'd like to see them again," he said. "If you'll let me."

She studied him carefully. He didn't know what she was looking for, nor what she found. But she blew out a breath and nodded. "Yeah, okay. Come on up."

The hall light beamed into the bedroom where Addy had dumped her meager pile of stuff. It shot across the dirty floor like a spotlight and hit the folio propped up against the wall.

Addy stopped just inside the door, nerves jittering, and hit the switch. The naked bulb above glared to life and she stepped aside to let Jax into the room. She wanted to reach for him so she tucked her fingertips into her pockets instead and pointed her chin at the folio.

"There you go," she said.

Jax didn't move. He gave the folio a long look, and Addy's nerves stretched until she thought they'd twang like banjo strings.

"What are you waiting for?" she asked. "There they are. Go ahead. Open them up. Look all you want."

He turned away from the folio. Turned toward her. And what she saw in his face twisted her nerves beyond tight and into snap-any-minute.

"You know what? I don't want to see them." He stepped toward her. She stepped back. Found her butt against the wall. "I've spent years trying *not* to see them but they're carved on my damn heart. It doesn't matter if you show them or not. They're yours, Addy. Do whatever you want with them. Just don't leave."

"Don't leave?" Her heart thudded inside her ribs, shock stealing her breath and hope giving it back. "Jax, *you* left *me*. I just batted cleanup." But a thought fragment scratched at her subconscious, just below the surface, and part of her brain split off and bore down, trying to catch it.

"I know I did." He stepped in closer, and the heat of him reached out to claim her. "I'm a jackass."

"Yeah, you are." She spread her hands on the cool plaster wall behind her and tried to think. She had to *think*. Because the memory dangled like a thread, just out of reach. She didn't know what it was, but understood somehow that it was important. What had he said? *I've spent years trying* not *to see them…*

"But I came back."

"You did."

"I'm here now."

"I know." She swallowed down a mortifying tightness in her throat, and it took all her concentration to keep her voice steady. She wouldn't cry in front of him. She refused. "But you scared me." It was bitter and humiliating, but it was the truth. She wouldn't lie any more than she'd cry. It was all weakness, and she was done with that. "I thought—"

He took that last step, fitted his body deliberately into hers. She hissed like water tossed into a hot frying pan and arched into him. He felt so good. His mouth found the curve of her jaw and he murmured, "You thought what? You thought I could walk away? You thought you could do anything, say anything, be anything I wouldn't want?"

"I—" His lips moved to her throat and the words fizzled

out, thought disappeared. That broken bit of a memory still nudged at the fuzzy edges of her mind though, tried to filter through the heat of his body and the strength of her yearning. It had been there before, too, she realized. At the gallery this afternoon. It was like finding a puzzle piece months after you'd already given up on the puzzle — you should obviously keep it but where were you supposed to put it?

"Addison." He turned his face into her hair and breathed her in like she was oxygen itself. "For God's sake, I *love* you. I have since the moment Diego brought you home with this hideous old honker on your finger and all that terror behind your beautiful smile." He twined his fingers through hers, lifted her diamond ring until even the ordinary light of the bare bulb above them shattered into rainbows. "I fell ass over teakettle for you right then and I haven't breathed right since. I've waited years for you to wake up, to see me, to choose me. I thought you finally had."

"I did." Tears swam into her eyes. "I do."

"But he's still there, isn't he? Diego. He still has a hold on you." He tipped her ring this way and that, catching and splitting the light. "He can still hurt you, and those paintings prove it." He gazed thoughtfully at that stone-cold diamond. "I'd erase him if I could, you know. My own brother. I would. I'd scrub him right out of your memory, out of your heart. I hate what he did to you. I'd undo it if I could." He huffed out a half-laugh. "Oh, I know I can't. I'm not delusional. I could burn those paintings to ashes but you'd still have the scars, wouldn't you? So do whatever you want to with them. Burn them, hang them, use them for tea towels. I don't care. Just stay. Let me love you the way he should have. The way you deserve. I can make you happy, Addison. Give me a chance."

"Jax." Hope shimmered and glowed inside her, tried to overshadow that nudging awareness, that lost puzzle piece. *I've been trying* not *to see them for years.* She stopped, struck. "Wait, what did you say about the paintings?"

"They're yours." He gripped her arms, held her eyes. "It'll kill me to let you put them on display but end of the day? They're yours — your property, your history. You should do whatever you want with them. Not—" He dropped his chin and eyed her. "—whatever my mother wants you to do, mind you. Whatever *you* want to do."

"No, before that." She brought her forearms up, wedged them between their bodies and levered him back a few inches. "You said you'd been trying not to see them for years."

He scowled. "I have been."

"For years, Jax?" She seized the word with both hands. Relief filled her, the reflexive satisfaction of having solved a thorny riddle. But pain roared in after it, ate up her relief like a bonfire. Because up until a week ago, nobody outside of Addy, Diego and Julia Gates had known those paintings even existed.

Or so she'd believed.

"How many years?"

He froze but she saw it in his eyes, the guilt and the anguish. She didn't need him to answer. She knew. But she wanted to hear him say it.

"Addy, listen—"

"You knew?" She spoke over him, betrayal knifing through her like the winter wind over the frozen lake. "You *knew* about the paintings?"

"No!" He backed away, though. Dropped his hands to his sides. "I had no idea Diego was still painting."

"But you knew *what* he was painting," she said dully. Pain pounded inside her head, filled up her heart. "You knew what my marriage was. You let me smile and pretend and make a fool of myself for years. And the whole time you *knew*?"

"Yes." He dipped his head to catch her gaze and those hazel eyes were wary, guarded. "I knew."

"How?"

"I just did." He smiled bitterly. "That's how it goes when you're in love with your brother's wife, Addison. You notice everything, whether you want to or not. And believe me, I didn't want to. But nobody would stop talking about you — the starry-eyed child bride, too young but so in love! And lord, hadn't she just bewitched Diego? Look at the two of them!" He shook his head. "So I did. I looked. And you know what I saw?"

"What?"

"Disaster, looming large. Diego was crazy into his sweet, fresh-faced little angel but that was the thing about my brother. He loved all his toys, right up until he broke them. And, Addy, he broke them all. He was going to break you, and I knew it."

She forced herself to swallow, and her throat was so dry it hurt. "Why didn't you say anything?"

"What was I supposed to say?" He folded his arms and glared at his boots. "Talking wasn't going to fix anything. Either you knew what he was and were okay with it, or you didn't know and were happy that way." He looked up, and his eyes were full of furious sorrow. Her heart — poor damaged thing that it was — managed to ache for him. Poor Jax. Hard-wired to serve and protect, doomed to stand helplessly by while Diego broke his funny little bride. The bride Jax himself had some inexplicable itch for. It must have nearly killed him.

"It wasn't your fault, Addy." He leaned in urgently. "You have to know that. Diego was one huge appetite. Whiskey, women, and song, you know? He never met a party he didn't like, and fidelity wasn't really in his skill set."

"No," Addy murmured. "It wasn't."

"I know you could have used a friend," he said. "Hell, you *needed* a friend and, Jesus, I wanted to be there for you. But I couldn't do it, Addy. Not when I knew it meant I'd have to stand by and let him…" His hands fisted at his sides and he pressed his mouth flat. "I just couldn't *do* that, okay?"

"No, of course not." She spread her lips into an understanding smile even as she twisted her cold, shaking fingers into a tight knot at her waist. Because, oh merciful heavens, she was connecting the dots. That final puzzle piece had changed the whole picture, and not for the better. The shame in her chest annexed most of her stomach in one slow dip. "Heaven's sakes, Jax, don't be ridiculous. Whatever my marriage was or wasn't, it was hardly your business to—"

"Bullshit." His head snapped up, his face thunderous, and she wanted to die. Just expire right there. Because Jax didn't love her. Not really. He felt *sorry* for her. He felt *responsible* for her. Diego had damaged her and rejected her. He'd been careless with the gift of her heart and that offended Jax down to his very marrow. Shamed him. And he simply wasn't designed to tolerate shame. Take one mile-wide streak of chivalry, add an oddball spark of sexual chemistry and let it stew for four long years, and what did you get? A do-over. A guy bound and determined to fix his feckless brother's poor widow. To kiss her hurts all better.

He'd gone considerably farther than a kiss.

She shook her head silently, too sick to speak.

Jax seized both her hands. "It damn well *was* my business, Addison. No matter what else you are, you're my family, and I failed you. I had a responsibility to—"

She whirled savagely away, jerking her hands from his. "No." Furious tears seized her by the throat and she had to pause. Swallow. She turned back. "No, you didn't. You had — you *have* — no responsibility for me. For my happiness. Because I'm *fine*. Better than fine, in fact. I have a life I love and a family I adore. A family that adores me back." He opened his mouth and she threw up a hand to stop him. "Including you, I know. Not that I'm feeling particularly grateful right now, you jerk." He shut his mouth on a frown and she leaned in. "So I have all those things, Jax. An abundance of blessings. Which means I do *not* require help, fixing, or — God help us both — another pity bang from my misguided brother-in-law."

"A *pity bang*?" His mouth fell open. "I'm in love with you, Addy."

"No," she said, almost gently. Pain wept inside her like drizzle, the ugly kind that could go on without ceasing for days. Weeks. Seasons. "You aren't. You're in love with Diego's Angel, just like everybody else. And seeing me like that—" She waved a shaking hand at the folio propped against the wall. "—all bloody and human? It offends you. You want to fix it. Heal it. Diego broke me and you want to put me back together." She put a hand on his arm, and it was rigid under her hand, unyielding. "But Jax, I'm exactly who and how I'm supposed to be. The painting is called *Broken*, but I'm not. I survived."

She dropped her hand and stepped back. "I don't doubt

your heart, Jax. If you say you're in love, you are. But not with a real live woman. You're in love with a ghost."

"You're wrong, Addison." But a thin thread of doubt uncurled in his voice.

"I wish I were." Agony throbbed through her veins but her head was light and clear, as if she were operating on pure oxygen. She watched her own hand reach out, steady as a rock, and pull the door invitingly open for him. "You should go home."

Chapter 31

TWO WEEKS LATER, the gallery door jingled open, and the unmistakable clomp of heavy boots filled the air. Addy's heart took flight like a startled bird.

Jax.

Then her brain joined the party and she noticed the lighter tread, the less confident bang of boot heel on wood. Not Jax. Matty. Her heart — stupid, stubborn thing — dipped with disappointment. Which was ridiculous, because Addy had gently but very firmly refused every attempt Jax had made at private conversation for the past two weeks. Of course he wasn't going to keep pressing her. He wasn't a stalker, for heaven's sake. So why on earth was she disappointed that he'd finally accepted her decision?

Because it had been such a lovely dream, probably. She could admit that much, at least to herself. She'd gotten attached to it, that make-believe future where she and Jax had lived happily ever after in his cozy house in town, swinging on that jewel-box front porch of his while curly-headed babies played in the yard. Even now her heart yearned toward that pretty vision but she wrenched it back. It was a dream, she told herself firmly. Because Jax didn't love *her*. He loved what he saw when he looked at her, and Addy had been Diego's Angel long enough to know the difference.

She refused to make the same mistake twice.

Not that she had a choice. Refusing Jax was agony but letting herself love him would be worse. She knew exactly how it would unfold, after all. Reality would grind away at his vision of her like the Devil River ate at its own stream bed, and eventually there would be nothing left of his love but a big black kettle of contempt. She'd survived it with Diego but her love for him had been barely a shadow of what she felt for Jax. She wouldn't survive failing Jax that way. No chance.

She hated that she was hurting him, though. Hated it with a burning, visceral ferocity that only multiplied her own pain. But she loved him too much, too truly, to cave on this. She had to stay strong, to do the right thing for both of them. He'd thank her eventually. She only hoped she lived that long. Some days it felt like a long shot.

Matty arrived at the edge of her desk. The smell of dirt and sunscreen filled the air, evidence of his summer job as Jax's man-of-all-work. He leaned silently against a pine pillar instead of greeting her, his usual habit these days.

"Hey, Matty," she said. "I thought you were going to be with Jax all day."

"Mom called. She wants me home."

"What for?"

He moved those skinny shoulders, his face an utter blank. "Jax had to drive down to the Twin Cities anyway. Meeting with the Fire Marshall or something. Said to see if you could take me up the hill."

"Sure. I'm heading up to Davis Place here in a minute anyway." She put her attention casually back on her laptop screen but worry nibbled at her stomach. She didn't like this new taciturn Matty, this silent kid who shrugged more than he spoke. He'd always been a yeller and a banger, expressing everything in his heart at top volume and with no hesitation. But he'd gone dark lately, ever since...

She frowned, and her hands stalled over the keyboard. Since the fires, she realized. Since the night the Dumpster and the Hideaway had gone up in flames. Since Gerte had accused him — loudly and in public — of having set them. Peter had cleared him, but still. It was enough to turn any kid dark, she supposed.

"Just let me finish up this email," she said, and forced herself to start typing again. She skimmed quickly and hit send. "That Devil Days app was as buggy as August in the Boundary Waters." She manufactured a smile and sent it his way. "Just gave the programmer a piece of my mind."

"Fun."

"You know me." She scooped her bag out of the bottom drawer of the desk and rose. "I love a good negotiation."

Matty shrugged and came off the pillar, followed her out the door and onto Main Street like a tall, sullen shadow. Addy locked up the gallery.

"Come on. I'm parked over there." She pointed toward Soren Buck's giant fish. He shrugged and fell in beside her.

"Excuse me! Addison Davis?"

She turned to find a breathless young woman sidling from foot to foot on the sidewalk behind them, a gauzy skirt twisting around her ankles, a long, romantic braid snaking over one shoulder. A low-grade anxiety rolled up inside her, tightening her throat and dampening her palms. Oh lord, a Diego fan. Just what she needed today. She shored up her smile and nudged Matty discreetly into the shadow of the fish.

"Yes?"

"Oh my God, it *is* you." The woman pulled in a jerky breath. "I just want to tell you how much your husband's work means to me." She twined pale fingers together at her waist. "I so admire your strength. I mean, you were his *muse*. He painted *Diego's Angel* and then *stopped painting*." She gave a little laugh. "To be loved like that? By Diego Davis? And then to *lose* him?" She blinked rapidly and gave a watery laugh. "Oh. I'm getting emotional."

"Don't worry about it," Addy murmured through clamped teeth and a twitch of relief. Weepers were generally too focused on their own grief to get overly hung up on that whole *painted you then stopped painting* business. Slappers, on the other hand, focused on nothing else. She reached for patience and said, "Listen, I'm sorry for your loss. But I'm in sort of a hurry just now so—"

The woman's gaze flicked past Addy's shoulder, and her mouth fell open. She stared, white with shock. Addy turned, alarmed, and found only Matty behind her. Oh, no.

"Diego," the woman breathed, her shock melting into radiant joy. "Oh my God. *Diego*?" She stepped forward, reached a trembling hand toward Matty's jaw.

"What? No." He reared back until he bumped into the flower boxes under the bait and tackle's picture window. "Diego's dead, lady. Get a grip."

"You could paint me," she whispered as if she hadn't heard him. She stepped closer yet, eyes wide. Matty leaned away from her until his hair brushed the glass. "I would do anything for you. Anything. If you'd just—"

"Hey, you know what?" Addy leapt forward and took the girl by the shoulders. "The gallery's right there." She turned her gently down the sidewalk. "It's closed for lunch right now but you can window shop. Why don't you go spend some time with the real Diego? I bet you'll feel better. I know I always do."

"Yes." She blinked bravely. Focused. "Diego. All right."

"Off you go, then, sweetie." And she gave her an encouraging nudge that sent her drifting down the sidewalk.

"Crap," Matty said, squinting after her. "That was fun."

"Right?" But her stomach clutched at the white-lipped disgust on his face. She tried a weak smile. "You get used to it."

"Whatever." He jerked a shrug, but his hands were fisted in his pockets. "It doesn't matter. Let's just go before Mom blows a gasket, all right?"

Chapter 32

ADDY PARKED IN the turnaround in front of the carriage house and killed the engine. Matty lifted a brow. "You're coming in?"

"Yeah. I'm going to grab Georgie."

"Why?"

"Willa's coming by Davis Place to talk turkeys in a little while, and Georgie's my partner." She gave him an innocent smile. "She should be part of the conversation."

Matty shook his head. "What did Willa ever do to you?"

"Willa's tough. She'll survive but Georgie needs to learn to talk to contractors."

He leaned in with comically pleading eyes. "Take me with you. I want to watch. Come on, Addy. I deserve a treat, don't I? I've been so good."

She laughed. "You have been good, actually. Really good." Her laughter faded. "Too good." She leaned in, too. "What's wrong, honey?"

He sat back, shifted his gaze to the trees outside the windshield. "Nothing's wrong, Addy."

"Are you sure? Because if there is, you can talk to me. You know that, right? Maybe I could do something to help."

"There's nothing you can do—"

"About *what*?"

"—because nothing's wrong."

He was lying to her. He was a terrible liar. She loved him for that but it killed her that he couldn't — or wouldn't — tell her whatever had him so twisted up.

"But if something was?" She touched his arm, found it stiff, wary. "You'd tell me?"

"Why?" He laughed unpleasantly. "So you could kiss my boo boo? I'm not a baby, Addy. I didn't break a toy, and nobody knocked down my sand castle, okay?" He shoved open his door. "Besides, what's the point? You couldn't fix it anyway."

He stepped out and slammed the door.

"Fix *what*?" she wailed to the empty car. She shoved open her own door and jogged after him. "Matty, wait!" But he was already up the porch steps and into the house.

She followed him inside, but paused when she found him stalled uncertainly in the archway to the great room. His mother had risen from the white suede couch beyond, her smile fierce and glittering. "Come in, darling," she said to him. "I have somebody I want you to meet."

Addy's eyes shot to the sharply tailored woman beside her mother-in-law, and she froze. A smooth, dark bob swung to the woman's shoulders, framing angular cheekbones and fashionably bright glasses. She'd cut her hair but her face was as smooth and unlined as ever, and her eyes were the same shrewd blue Addy remembered.

Bianca said, "Matty, this is Julia Gates of the *New York Art Report*. And Julia, this—" She came to Matty then, looped a hand through his elbow and tugged him forward. "—is my Matisse."

"Hello, Matisse," Julia murmured politely but her eyes brightened, filled with a darker, more dangerous strain of the

314

desire Addy had last seen a few minutes ago in the eyes of a misguided young woman in town. "I've heard a lot about you."

"Oh boy," Matty murmured as he shook her outstretched hand.

"It's a real pleasure to finally meet you," Julia purred and Addy's stomach soured. Matty had said it didn't matter, the way people reacted to that face of his, but it did. Of course it did. Work like Diego's wrenched staggering emotions from even the most well-adjusted people. But what it did to people like Julia Gates, people for whom sex and ambition were all tangled up, people who couldn't tell desire from love, people for whom rational limits didn't exactly exist? It was downright dangerous.

And Addy ought to know. She'd been dealing with Diego's fans for years. She'd taken them on willingly, though. Keeping Diego alive for his devoted followers brought desperately needed tourist dollars into town, first of all, but it also eased Bianca's pain. It was a gift Addy gave her every day.

Matty hadn't asked for any of this, though. He hadn't signed up to keep his brother's legend alive. He was just a kid with an unlucky face and a desperately grieving mother who hurt too badly to protect him.

Nausea uncurled inside her belly as a future unfolded in her mind's eye. A future in which Diego's devotees weren't just her burden. A future in which Bianca pushed Matty into the public eye to assuage her endless grief. In which pathetic, unbalanced people like Julia Gates smeared their dark need all over him until he, too, suffered minor panic attacks every time a stranger addressed him on the street. Or possibly until he became callous enough to take advantage of what was so baldly offered, because how long could a vulnerable kid stay pure and strong under that kind of warped worship? Certainly Diego hadn't managed to.

She embraced the surge of horrified adrenaline and stepped forward. She slipped her hand through Matty's other elbow and said, "Hello, Julia. It's been a while."

"You know her?" Matty asked, startled.

"Oh sure," Addy told him. "Julia was Diego's pet reporter."

"Addison!" Bianca gave a startled laugh but Julia shifted that sharp smile Addy's way.

"That was me," she said hitting exactly the right note of self-deprecating charm. "I was — *am* — a huge believer in Diego's talent. Which is why I'm here now." She leaned in to inspect Matty a little more closely. "It's uncanny, the resemblance," she said softly. Those eyes flicked up to catch Matty's. He swallowed audibly. "I'll bet you hear that all the time."

"Uh." He stared, mesmerized. "Yeah."

Snake charmer, Addy thought, and firmed up her grip on Matty's arm. "You're here to write a story on Matty's resemblance to Diego?"

Julia reached out and actually tapped Matty's chin with a teasing finger. "If this face is any indication of your talent," she said to him, "I'll be writing about you for sure, sugar. But that's only one reason for my little visit." She turned back to Addy while Matty blinked like a startled owl. Her eyes drifted down, fixed briefly on Addy's wedding ring, then skated back up. Her lips curved in a slick smile. "I hear you have something to show me."

Addy lifted innocent brows. "I do?"

Julia's smile curdled. "Good lord, are you still doing

that? The wide-eye ingenue routine? You're getting a little old for it, aren't you?"

"You recognize age barriers now?" Addy smiled, too. "How refreshing."

"Aw. The kitten has claws. Adorable." Julia narrowed her eyes. "Listen, Addison. Everybody knows Diego didn't stop painting after the angel. A gift like his? Please. *Diego's Angel* is pretty enough but it's plain vanilla. And Diego was decidedly…" She pursed her lips in a knowing little moue. "…not. There isn't a person on this planet — not an adult anyway — who truly believes he considered *Angel* his greatest achievement and put away his brushes. No, we know there was more." She paused significantly, her smile spreading like evil. "Some of us better than others." Addy endured that in silence, her face utterly impassive. Julia shrugged lightly and continued. "So you can keep telling yourself that you're protecting him, protecting his legacy by keeping those paintings from the world, but that's a lie and we all know it. Worse, so do you."

"Julia, my goodness." Bianca blinked wide eyes and stepped forward, all startled graciousness. "I'm so sorry, but you've misunderstood. My press release was deliberately vague but I never intended to imply—"

Julia spoke over her, her eyes hard on Addy's. "I know exactly what you intended, Bianca. Why do you think I'm here? No, the only question I still have is whether or not our sweet Addison is finally ready to show those paintings. To let the world see Diego for the mature master he became *after* her. In spite of her. If she's finally ready to quit protecting her angelic image and do the right thing for somebody else for a change."

Ten minutes later, Addy let herself into Davis Place with shaking hands, nausea churning in her stomach. The way Julia had looked at Matty played over and over in her brain — those hard blue eyes hot with both professional interest and twisted desire. A fresh wave of horror swept over her, and she had to lean against the doorjamb until it receded. She stood there for a long moment, staring blankly at the door knob still in one trembling hand, at Diego's diamond still glittering on her ring finger.

Addy had been resigned to showing those paintings before Julia had ever hit town. Even knowing it would cost her Jax — or at least the dream of Jax — she'd been prepared to go ahead with the showing. It would have freed her from the prison Diego's Angel had become, it would've bought Matty a couple years of breathing room from Bianca's expectations, and it would've allowed Bianca to ruin Julia Gates. Or at least allowed her to try. Most importantly, though, it would've forced the world to acknowledge what fairy tales cost. It might've tarnished Diego's legend to the point where Matty could have chosen to live it down rather than measure up. Showing the whole series, from *Angel* through *Broken* would've gathered all the loose ends Diego's sudden death had left dangling and tied them up in one neat — if bloody — bow.

Or so Addy had thought.

She'd forgotten the sick lust that had bloomed in Julia's eyes, though, hadn't she? The showing would drag into town every last fame whore and art tart Diego had ever slept with, each one praying that *she* had been special. That Diego had painted *her* one last fix of fame. And when they found they hadn't been special and he hadn't painted them as such, they would immediately transfer all those wretched hopes and dark needs to the thirteen-year-old boy wearing Diego's face and — according to his mother — wielding his magic.

And Addy *wasn't* resigned to that. Not by a long shot.

She dragged her keys from the lock, pushed the door shut, and leaned back against it. She closed her eyes, breathed in the scent of sawdust and progress. She'd figure something out, she told herself. She'd find some way to take off the halo and protect Matty at the same time. She had no idea how but she would.

She crossed the half-sanded hardwood floor of her would-be great room, pushed through a swinging door beside the fireplace and stepped into the greatest accomplishment of her life so far: an absolutely finished and totally functional commercial kitchen.

A parquet tile floor gleamed black and white under her feet, ringed by yards of poured concrete counters studded with sea glass hand-harvested from Lake Superior. A massive farm house sink sat under the window on the far wall, the buttery yellow curtains above it caught back with jaunty bows. A generous island stood in the center of the room, a loaded pot rack suspended above its professional-grade range. An espresso machine the size of a Mini Cooper sat on the island as well. It had cost nearly what the stove had but Addy didn't regret a penny. Maybe she didn't love coffee herself but she was in the hospitality business now. Nobody understood better than she what a steaming cup of welcome could mean to a stranger.

Plus, if the internet could be believed, this machine could churn out a cup of cocoa that would make Gerte weep with envy. Addy was looking forward to finding out.

"Aren't you pretty?" she murmured to it now. She ran a reverent finger over the gleaming steel nozzles, along a row of cunning buttons and switches. "Aren't you just gorgeous?"

"Who are you talking to?"

Addy whirled to find Willa Zinc just inside the swinging door, her fingers tucked into the pockets of filthy jeans, a dark, thick ponytail snaking down her back. She was wearing what Addy had come to think of as her uniform — a gray t-shirt that read *Zinc Pest Control*, scarred work boots and that Saint Paul Saints cap pulled practically to her chin.

"Good lord!" Addy clapped a hand to her thumping heart. "Willa! When did you get here?"

"On time." Willa consulted her watch. "You ready? I don't have all day."

"Oh no." Addy closed her eyes and sighed. "I forgot Georgie."

"Lucky you."

"No, I was supposed to pick her up when I dropped Matty off at Hill Top House but I—" *Ran away.* "—got distracted." She rummaged in her satchel, came up with her phone and a pleading smile. "Do you mind if I call her just super quick? She's an official partner in the project now, and I promised to involve her."

"Up to you." Willa moved into the room to eye the espresso machine more closely. "I work by the hour, though."

The kitchen's swinging door flapped open again and Georgie breezed in on a pair of platform espadrilles, her rich plum wrap dress swishing expensively. She pushed enormous sunglasses to the top of her head.

"Hey, Addy. Matty told me you wanted me up here so

I—" She paused just long enough to be rude. "Oh. Hello, Willa. I thought I smelled something."

"Oh, look," Willa murmured and sank to her haunches to inspect the espresso machine's undercarriage. "It's Trust Fund Barbie."

"For heaven's sake, Georgie." Addy glared at her sister-in-law. "Be nice."

"No."

"Seriously?" Addy stared, taken aback. "Just no?"

Georgie smiled. Willa pushed a complicated series of buttons. The espresso machine let out a massive whine and a blast of steam. A jet of thick, black liquid shot into a waiting porcelain cup. Willa grunted with satisfaction, picked up the tiny cup and took a cautious sip.

"Not bad." She set the cup on the counter, and retrieved her clipboard. "That's a quality piece of equipment you've got there."

Georgie frowned. "It's an espresso machine?" She minced cautiously forward on her platforms. "Good God. It's the size of a lawnmower."

Willa sent her a sideways glance. "Your lawn mower is a guy named Jeff. And just FYI, he overcharges. Because he hates you." She wiped down the machine with a dishtowel, powered it off, and leaned around to unplug it. "You always want to unplug appliances," she said to Addy. "The timing mechanism fails just once on stuff like this — toasters, coffee makers — and it's hello, house fire."

"Thank you, Jax." Georgie rolled her eyes.

Willa ignored her. "So. Addison. You ready to see what I've rigged up for the turkeys?"

"And that's my cue." Georgie turned on one heel. "I'm out."

Addy leapt forward, looped her arm through Georgie's and plastered on a determined smile. "*We* are definitely ready to talk turkeys."

Willa eyed Georgie's platform sandals for a long moment, then cut loose with that slow, surprising smile of hers. "We'll start underneath the porch."

Georgie said, "I hate you, Willa Zinc."

Chapter 33

"WELL, HERE WE are." Georgie opened the door to Hill Top House a few hours later with a little flourish and gestured Addy inside. "Home sweet home."

Addy didn't move. She loved Hill Top House but it wasn't home anymore. Home was Davis Place. Her treacherous heart whispered about leather couches and goose-down duvets that smelled just faintly of smoke but she refused to listen. Davis Place was *home*, she told herself firmly. And she wanted — she *needed* — to stay there. To retreat. To lick her wounds until they scabbed over enough for her to think. To figure out what on earth she was going to do about those paintings. About what *not* showing them might mean.

Her heart whispered Jax's name this time and she had to breathe through a ridiculous bolt of hope. She set her bag down on the porch.

"Tell me again why I have to sleep here?"

Georgie cocked an expertly plucked brow. "Because Davis Place is a turkey-infested health hazard?"

"Oh come on. It's not that bad. I have electricity—"

"A bare light bulb in your bedroom?"

"—running water—"

"In the kitchen only."

"—and I don't need heat because summer finally got here! So, really, I don't see why you're all worked up about my staying there. It's *fine*."

Georgie gazed at her for a long moment, a stone wall of skepticism. Finally she said, "I called Jax in the car on the way here and told him you were sleeping in a fire hazard."

Addy stared. "You did not."

"I absolutely did. He was not best pleased. He was all set to drive straight here from the Cities to drag you off to his cave by your curly little head but I told him that we were having ourselves a sleepover, no boys allowed." She smiled evilly. "You're welcome." She pointed at Addy's bag. "Now bring that inside."

Defeated, Addy hefted her bag and trudged into the house. "I can't believe you tattled on me to Jax."

"That's what you get for ambushing me with Willa Zinc." Georgie drifted through the foyer and up the staircase at the back of the great room. "Plus you're going to have to talk to him eventually, Addison. You know that, don't you?"

"I talk to him." Addy stomped up the stairs behind Georgie. "I spoke to him just yesterday about scheduling his guys for the Devil Days slip and slide."

Georgie sent her a look of silent approbation over her shoulder and Addy scowled.

"He thinks he's in love with me, Georgie," she muttered.

"He is," Georgie said serenely and floated down the hall toward Addy's old room.

"No, he's not." Addy marched after her. "He feels sorry for me."

"Of course he does. Diego was a dick and put you through hell. I feel sorry for you, too." She smiled. "That doesn't mean I don't love you."

"That's different. You're not Jax."

Georgie shuddered delicately. "Thanks be for that." She pushed open the door to Addy's room and waved her magnanimously inside. "But let's give Jackson this — he knows exactly who he is and doesn't give one good rip what anybody else thinks of that. He follows his own lights, marches to his own stars, drums his own whatever." She drifted into the room behind Addy and sank to the bed, beautifully exhausted by goodness only knew what since she'd flatly refused to crawl under the porch with Addy and Willa. "All of which is to say, Addison, that my brother doesn't lie."

"I didn't say that." Addy dropped her bag by the door, suddenly weary beyond description. Everything was exactly where she'd left it a month ago. There was her quilt on the bed, her knickknacks on the dresser, her art on the walls. Being separated from these things had brought her to near-hysteria a few short weeks ago. Now they looked like a stranger's things. Her heart didn't even recognize them. "Jax isn't a liar. He's just wrong."

"About what's in his own heart?" Georgie smoothed her pretty plum dress with satisfied hands and speared Addy with surprisingly sharp eyes. "No."

"No?" Addy stood there, her hands empty, her heart aching. "What does that mean, no?"

"Jax is *careful*, Addison. It's who he is. It's probably the most important thing about him. He wouldn't throw the l-word around any more than he'd play with matches. And if you don't know that by now, maybe *you're* the one who doesn't love *him*."

Addy closed her eyes against her second hard shock of the day.

Georgie came off the bed; Addy heard the whisper of fabric, the squeak of the frame. Then she was in Georgie's arms, those cool hands smoothing her hair, that expensive dress of hers absorbing Addy's helpless tears.

"Oh, honey." Georgie rocked her slowly. "I'm sorry. That was unnecessarily harsh. I really do hate Willa Zinc. She put me straight into the bitch zone."

"No, it's fine. You're right." Addy pulled in a shuddering breath but the tears just kept coming, sliding down her cheeks like a river, an endless current of pain. "It's just...Georgie, I'm so afraid. I thought Diego loved me, too. How on earth am I supposed to know?"

"Know what?"

"If it's real this time. I was so wrong before but if I let myself believe—" She broke off, unable to even say the words. "If I believed him but I was wrong? If he didn't love me, or stopped loving me, or if I screwed up and ruined it..." She curled her arms around her stomach, around the ache and the fear pulsing there. "I wouldn't survive it, Georgie. I wouldn't."

"Of course you would." Georgie rested her cheek on Addy's curls and ran a comforting hand up and down her trembling back. "You'd never die when somebody needed you, and I do, so there you go. Problem solved." She drew back to inspect Addy's face. "For heaven's sake, Addison. How are you not a mess of mascara?"

"I'm not wearing any."

Georgie blinked, sincerely shocked. "I don't want you to take this the wrong way but how did you manage to make *both* of my brothers fall in love with you?"

"I have no idea."

"You can tell me all about it at the slumber party." She

turned and headed for the door.

"Wait, we're actually doing that?"

"Of course. I don't lie to my brother." Georgie stopped in the doorjamb, sent a smile over her shoulder. "We'll have wine and I'll introduce you to the wonders of modern cosmetics. By the time I'm done with you, Jax will be on his knees, begging to apologize for everything *you've* done wrong."

"I don't think even mascara is that powerful."

Georgie only laughed. "Oh, Addy. You're adorable."

Addy jerked awake when her phone chirped. She lunged for it, missed the nightstand completely and crashed to the floor. What on earth? She rubbed her throbbing elbow, shoved a handful of ringlets out of her face and squinted around in the darkness for her phone. Where was it? Wait, where was *she*?

Georgie's room. Right. Memory trickled back in. A bottle and a half of wine, an ill-advised amount of Mackinac Island Fudge ice cream, then dozing off on her half-acre of Georgie's king-sized bed. Which would explain both her missing nightstand and the gentle snoring from the bed beside her.

The phone chirped again and Addy groped along the floor boards until she came up with her discarded fleece jacket, which she pawed until she found the pocket and her phone. Which chirped again.

"For pity's sake," Georgie moaned, "will you answer the damn phone?"

"It's not ringing. It's a text." Addy squinted at the display and had to blink several times before she could make sense of what she saw there. "It's Willa," she said, surprise melting into concern.

"Willa Zinc?" Georgie cracked an eye.

"Do you know any other Willas?"

"Thank Christ, no."

Addy peered at the screen.

Addison. Willa. You need to get up here.

She typed back, *Where?*

Davis Place.

Why?

Now.

Addy frowned down at the phone in her hands.

"I have to go to Davis Place," she said. She leapt up and hit the lights.

"Argh." Georgie flung an arm over her face.

"Sorry." Addy was still wearing the sweats and t-shirt she'd fallen asleep in, so she shoved her feet into her sandals and snatched up her fleece jacket. The temperature dropped cruelly after sunset this close to the lake, no matter what the daytime high had been. She turned to sprint out the door and nearly barreled into Bianca.

Her mother-in-law stood in the doorway, tying a silky robe around her long, slim body. She arched a pale brow. "Going somewhere, Addison?"

"If there's a God in heaven, she is," Georgie said from under her quilt. "And turning out the lights, too."

"Willa texted," Addy said. "Something's going on at Davis Place, and I have to—"

"Willa Zinc?"

"Yes." Addy frowned. "Why does everybody ask that?"

Bianca's nose wrinkled delicately, like she smelled

something bad but was too polite to mention it. "Why does that girl even have your number?"

"She's pied-pipering the turkeys out of Davis Place." Georgie's voice floated out of the bed. "Can we please turn out the lights now?"

"And the two of you have become chummy, is that it?" Bianca kept her eyes on Addy, her second brow lifting to join the first. "Trading cell phone numbers and midnight texts?"

"It's 1:36, actually." Georgie said with injured precision. "A. M."

"She's never texted before," Addy said. Urgency beat in her veins and she shifted foot to foot.

"I should hope not." Bianca tightened her belt with a satisfied tug that Addy didn't like for some reason.

"Not that I'd mind. I like Willa—"

"You like your purse, too." Georgie gave a massive yawn. "Shows what you know."

"—which is neither here nor there," Addy finished, all but bouncing on her toes with the urge to run. "Something's wrong and I have to *go now*." She stepped right into Bianca's space. "Do you mind?"

"You're not going anywhere," Bianca said sharply.

"I'm not?" Addy fell back a startled step.

"Not alone, anyway."

"For heaven's sake, Willa Zinc is not dangerous! She's dependable, no-nonsense and really, really good at what she does." And she was. Willa had spent the afternoon turning Addy's porch and most of the side yard into a para-military anti-turkey zone. It had been fascinating. "I trust her, Bianca. If she says I need to get up there, I need to get up there." She stepped back into the hot zone, prepared to do battle. "Now."

329

Bianca studied her for a long tense moment, then tossed up her hands. "Good lord. You and Jackson deserve each other." She shook her head and stepped into the room, backing Addy up along the way. "Fine, you can go. But take Georgie."

"I knew it." Georgie's words floated mournfully into the air. "I knew I wasn't going back to sleep. I *hate* Willa Zinc."

"Don't we all?" Bianca poked her daughter. "Go."

"All right, all *right*. God."

Ten minutes later, Addy pulled Georgie's Range Rover into the drive at Davis Place, Georgie snoring lightly in the passenger seat. Georgie had refused to either drive or fold herself into Addy's little Honda, citing a deep need to continue sleeping. Not surprisingly, she'd strapped herself in and immediately nodded off. The girl truly could sleep anywhere. Addy threw the truck into park.

"Wake up, Sleeping Beauty."

Georgie blinked herself awake and peered out the windshield at Willa standing on the back porch. Her lip did the exact same curl of disgust Bianca's had.

"Okay, what?" Addy said. "Is there some kind of Davis/Zinc feud I don't know about? Why do we hate Willa?"

"Heavens, Addy." Georgie clicked open her seatbelt and stretched gracefully. "We don't *really* hate Willa." She stepped out of the truck and leaned back in to smile. "We wouldn't bother." She shut the door on Addy's frown.

Addy shouldered open her own door, stepped out and slammed it shut. She shot Georgie a narrow look over the hood and said, "You're going to explain that later."

Willa came down the steps in her big boots and ball cap, ponytail swinging. "This way."

She strode off into the darkness, the rising half-moon picking up the reflective piping on her fleece vest. Addy jogged after her and Georgie fell in behind with a long-suffering sigh.

Willa hiked through the narrow side yard, and Addy stayed tight behind her. She had no desire to run afoul of Willa's anti-turkey campaign. Georgie teetered along behind Addy, cursing anything that offended her sandals.

Just when it looked like Willa was leading them straight over the rock wall protecting the casual viewer from plunging into the lake, she made an abrupt left turn toward the Kettle and disappeared into the bramble.

"Oh, now we're going off road?" Georgie made an aggrieved noise. "I *hate* that girl."

"I thought you wouldn't bother." Addy shoved at the branches and scrambled after Willa. "Seriously, what do you and your mom have against—"

Then she stopped abruptly. It was either that or run Willa over. She'd stopped just inside the trees, her mouth a grim line, her eyes shadowed beneath the brim of her ball cap.

"There you go," she said and nudged a pile at her feet. She turned as if to go and Addy grabbed her sleeve.

"What is it?" Addy peered into the incomprehensible jumble of undergrowth.

Willa produced a flashlight, snapped it on and hit the ground with a brilliant white beam of light.

Matty lay at their feet, tangled in what looked like an oversized net. A bright smear of blood trailed from his nose down his chin and matted his t-shirt. Addy dropped to her knees beside him, patting frantically for some way to untangle him.

"Matty? What on earth?"

He was trussed up like a Christmas roast, his arms pinned at his sides, his knees bound tight. His yellow work boots — incongruously big — poked helplessly out the bottom. About all he could move was his head, and his eyes were brilliantly silver in the beam of Willa's flashlight.

"Nice," Georgie said on a breath of disgust only a sister could muster. "Mom's going to *love* this, Matisse."

"Matty, are you all right?" Addy's heart hammered as she dragged at the coarse netting. "What happened?"

He gazed at her, his eyes defiant and angry. Then he deliberately turned his head away from her, his mouth a thin, silent line.

"He must've tripped the compressed-air net," Willa said.

"You got caught in a turkey net." Georgie shook her head and laughed. "You *are* an idiot."

"What were you even doing up here?" Addy asked. She tore a nail on the rough rope and swallowed a curse. Sat back on her heels and stuck her finger in her mouth. "Crap." Her throat went hot and tight as tears of fear and frustration crept in. "For heaven's sake, Matty, why won't you talk to me?" Nothing. "Okay, fine." She stood and slapped the dirty leaves off her knees. "You want to stay here a while? Fine by me. You can just sit here until—"

She broke off, sniffed. Her heart clenched. "Is something burning?"

Chapter 34

JAX TOOK A corner on two wheels, then put his foot to the floor and sent the mini-pumper roaring up the hill toward Davis Place. Peter rode shotgun, his face grim, his knuckles white on the oh-shit handle.

"When did your mom notice Matty missing?" Peter asked.

"Maybe 1:30, 1:45. After Addy and Georgie left." Jax glared at the darkened street like the blame lay out there instead of in here with him. "God damn it, I knew he was lighting those fires. I just didn't want to believe it."

"But you do believe it? You're sure?" Peter shot him a swift look across the cab. "I'm sorry, I know you went over it earlier but I have to admit I wasn't completely awake."

"Yeah, sorry about that. I figured you could wait until morning to find out who torched your Dumpster and the resort, but then Addy and Georgie zip off to some emergency at Davis Place — without their cell phones, naturally — and suddenly Mom discovers Matty missing?" Fear locked his molars together but he flexed his fingers and breathed. "I didn't like it," he said quietly. "I gave you the wake up call because I figured you wouldn't either."

"Damn right I don't." Peter pulled his free hand down his face and blinked wearily. "I'm just having a hard time wrapping my mind around this. Davis Place is supposed to be *empty*. I talked to Georgie myself a few hours ago. She and Addison are supposed to be painting each others' goddamn *toenails*, Jackson."

"I know. But they aren't." He gripped the steering wheel with clammy hands. "And Matty's supposed to be in bed like a good little boy. But he isn't, either."

"What a goat rope." Peter leaned his head back and spoke to the ceiling. "Tell me again about Matty. I think I'm awake enough to connect the dots this time if you go slowly and use small words."

"I had a meeting with the Fire Marshall this afternoon down in the Cities. Turns out the Dumpster fire and the Hideaway fire were both started with the same type of ignition device," Jax said, accelerating out of a curve.

"Ignition device? What does that mean?"

"It means both fires started the same way. Evidently Matty's a fan of the molotov cocktail." His lips twisted bitterly. "Rolled up a few sheets of paper, stuffed them into a fuel source — a soda bottle of gasoline in this case — and lit them up. We recovered some of the paper."

"The *paper?* How is that even possible?"

"You'd be surprised at what doesn't burn in a fire." He shook his head. "God knows arsonists usually are."

"And the Fire Marshall tied the paper to *Matty?*"

"No, I did that." Jax's jaw was starting to ache. "It turned out to be a particularly high grade drawing paper. The same paper Mom's kept Matty up to his eyeballs in since birth."

Peter frowned. "Okay, that's not good news but it's not exactly proof either, is it?" He rubbed his free hand over his scalp and said, "I mean, Matty can't be the only kid in the county to draw on nice paper."

"No, I know. I thought about that. But they pulled a pretty sizable chunk out of the resort fire." He stopped. This was the part that particularly pained him. "Big enough for me to recognize what was on it."

"Which was?"

"A superhero. One of Matty's. He's been drawing them since he could hold a pencil. And since Mom got on his case about painting — I mean seriously on his case? —he's been burning them."

Peter stared. "Fuck. Me."

"I know, right?" Jax skidded to a halt behind Davis Place. He threw off his seatbelt, opened his door and dropped to the gravel. Peter did the same. He frowned at the pickup beside the Rover.

"Willa's here?"

"Yeah," Jax said. "Mom says she was the one who called Addy. Texted her. Whatever. Addy's phone is hosed."

"Yeah, I heard."

Jax squinted into the darkness of the side yard. "I swear, Peter, the second I make sure everybody's okay? I'm going to kill them all."

"I'll do Georgie for you." Peter rubbed a palm over his heart. "Because she told me she was *staying home*. And keeping Addy with her."

Jax stopped abruptly. "What's that smell?"

Peter stopped. Sniffed. "Something burning?"

"No shit." Jax lifted his nose to the night like a bloodhound. He knew what burning leaves smelled like. Knew what a forest fire smelled like. Could tell the difference between an electrical fire and a chemical fire at a dozen paces, and this smelled electrical to him. "But what?"

He didn't wonder long.

He backed up to scan the house and found it. A pale tongue of fire licking slyly at the kitchen window overlooking the back porch. It played peek-a-boo with the sill for a moment, then leaped up to taste the curtains. Addy's cheerful yellow curtains. Horror grabbed Jax by the throat

"Fuck *me*," he breathed. He watched with helpless paralysis as a flame punched out the window and laid greedily into the siding. The roar was a physical tremor that rocked the air and slapped Jax into motion.

For the first time in his life, he didn't think. He didn't consider the consequences. He didn't assess the situation, weigh options, invoke protocol.

Addy was in there.

Jax ran.

"Jax!" Peter watched in horrified dismay as his future brother-in-law, the most level-headed man he'd ever personally met, charged toward a burning building like a tackle with his eye on the quarterback. Fear clutched at his gut but he snatched with shaking hands at the latches and panels on the side of Jax's mini-pumper.

This wasn't supposed to be happening. The words ran through his head in a desperate chant as he groped for whatever the hell Jax usually ran into a fire with. A jacket, an extinguisher, an axe? Fuck, all of it. *This wasn't supposed to be happening.* Nobody was supposed to be here, not even Matty. The kid was supposed to just fray the cord on a random kitchen appliance, plug it in and go *home* so they could all collect their insurance payouts in safety.

As business plans went, insurance fraud wasn't ideal. Peter understood that. But the Devil's Tap Room — by far the most profitable business in his fast-crumbling empire — had barely survived the recession. His rental properties were barely covering their own mortgages at this point, let alone generating the income stream he'd assured the bank they did when he'd used them to secure a monstrous loan to renovate the Hideaway last summer. One more tourist season, and he'd have been fine. One more healthy infusion of vacation dollars from all those city-weary tourists who flocked to Devil's Kettle to paint Lake Superior or stare at *Diego's Angel*, and he'd have made it. What had he gotten instead? A national economic collapse and the winter that wouldn't end.

But Peter had been too poor for too long and too hungry too often to be without a backup plan. Risk tolerance was one thing; stupidity was something else. No, he had an escape hatch. A golden ticket. A Plan B.

He had Georgie Davis.

Or so he'd thought. Turned out, he'd *been had* by Georgie Davis. Because her family was just as deep in the red as he was. And thank you, Matty, for cluing him in. And for being so cooperatively fucked-up.

Because Peter wasn't a monster. He wouldn't have made an arsonist out of an innocent kid. But Matty had been burning shit down long before Peter had gotten involved. All Peter had done was suggest — strongly, and with some incentive — that Matty include a few of Peter's well-insured money pits on his list of potential targets.

It wasn't Peter's first choice, no. It was, however, his last resort. And if everybody had just cooperated, they'd have been *fine*. Everything would've been fine.

But it was obviously far too late for fine, so he threw the

extinguisher and the jacket under his arm, shouldered the axe and sprinted for the front porch after Jax. Jesus, this stuff was heavier than it looked.

Jax had already rounded the house and was tearing open the front door with a lack of caution even Peter knew was foolhardy. "Addison!" Jax shouted. "Addy?" Then he disappeared into the gaping maw of the house.

As far as Peter could see, the great room was dark — as it should be if Matty had started a kitchen fire as per *instructions.* Assuming he had — a big fucking assumption — and assuming Peter remembered the layout of the house correctly, there was still only a single wall separating the flaming kitchen from the great room. Not much to protect a guy who was acting like he was made of Teflon.

Fucking cowboy. A welcome wash of anger flooded his chest and Peter encouraged it. It was a hell of a lot better than the horror and guilty fear it covered up.

"Damn it, Jax, stop!" he snarled and leapt up the porch steps. "You're not going to help anybody if you're—"

Dead. He was going to say *dead* but he got sidetracked when, bogged down by forty or so pounds of fire fighting gear, his leap fell somewhat short of the porch. He cracked his shin on the top step, his chin on the fire extinguisher in his arms, then his skull on the solid pine pillar holding up the roof. Stars exploded inside his head and he rolled like an armadillo until he met up with the siding. He kept his eyes closed while pain did its little happy dance around his nervous system.

"Peter?"

He opened his eyes. Addy. Where had she come from?

She dropped to her knees beside him, her sweet, soft face tight with something approaching panic. "Oh my goodness,

Peter, what happened? Are you—" Her eyes flew to the open door. "Jax?"

"He went in." Peter heaved himself to a sitting position and the world did that weird sideways slosh he remembered from his football days. Concussion. Nice.

"Why?" she wailed.

"Looking for you." He squinted into the darkness at her. "But you're out here."

"No shit."

But, wait, that wasn't Addy. She hadn't said anything, plus she didn't swear. She never swore. No, Addy was still gazing at the open door in wide-eyed concern. Maybe outright panic. He looked past Addy's shoulder and found his sister Willa there, her arms folded over her skinny body, gazing down at him with that self-possession he'd always hated. He'd been such an unruly kid, all want and ambition and wild desire. He'd endured their mutual childhood without anything approaching the quiet grace Willa seemed to wear like a mink coat. He hated her for that.

Had hated her for that, he told himself quickly. He didn't hate her now. Of course not. That would be immature.

"Hey, Willa," he said and spread his lips in a smile that was offensive even to him in its patent insincerity.

Addy leapt to her feet and eyed the door. Before Peter could even analyze that look and give it a name — intent — Willa had Addy by the elbow.

"Don't you dare," she snapped. "Jax is a professional firefighter. He's trained, prepared and equipped to go into burning buildings. You're not. And while I'd wait a decent interval after your fiery death before bringing him a hot dish, you should know I'd totally work that action. But all things being equal I'd rather you survived and spared me the polite rejection. So sit your ass down or I'll put it down for you."

Addy glared at Willa, and Peter wondered why his sister didn't just spontaneously combust. Or at least pony up some sweaty girl-on-girl action because, damn. That glare with the dimples? Guys would stand in line for the evil eye Addy was giving Willa.

"You're so pretty, Addy," his concussion said suddenly. A dim slice of his consciousness groaned in dismay but his mouth seemed to have developed independent steering. "Like a mean little Betty Crocker. Why didn't I pick you? You'd have been so much easier than Georgie."

"No, she wouldn't," Willa said, glaring back at Addy. "She'd have been worse because she isn't an idiot."

"Neither is Georgie," Addy snapped. "Now let go of my arm."

"Why? So you can go burn yourself to ashes trying to save a guy who doesn't need your help?"

Peter shifted. Man, something was just crunching his nuts. He frowned down at his crotch and realized he was still snuggling a lapful of fire fighting equipment. "Hey, Addy. If you do go inside, will you take these to Jax? He ran in without them."

"*What?*"

He wasn't sure which woman said that. Maybe both. Probably just one, though. His vision was doubling. No reason his hearing shouldn't double, too.

"Don't go into the kitchen, though. I had Matty start the fire in there so it's all…on fire and stuff. The rest of the house is probably okay." He blinked owlishly into their staring faces. "For now."

Addy executed a perfect elbow-lift-and-drop that broke Willa's grip on her arm. She snatched the jacket and the extinguisher from his lap and raced into the house. Peter watched her go with a mournful sigh.

"Shit!" Willa snatched up her cell phone and stabbed at the screen. "Shit, shit, shit!" She grabbed her ponytail, twisted it hard around her free hand and listened. "Yeah, I need to report a house fire." She stalked off the porch to pace the front lawn while giving the details to the 911 dispatcher or whoever she was talking to.

Peter said, "I love Betty Crocker."

Then he closed his eyes and passed out.

Addison shoved her arms into the jacket as she ran into her budding great room. The heat made the air into a solid thing, a thick press of smoke and scorch. The jacket was way too big but she was grateful for it. Her throat stung and her eyes watered as she croaked, "Jax! Damn it, Jax, where are you?"

She spun in a tight circle in the middle of the space. Where would he go? Where would he think she'd gone? She dropped to her knees, where the air was noticeably cooler and clearer, to suck in a deep breath and get her bearings.

The kitchen door was there to her left — she could see the dancing, pulsing lick of fire under the door — which meant the new picture window was at about three o'clock and the stairs were at about ten. She crawled toward them, pushing the fire extinguisher in front of her across the semi-sanded floor that had had so much potential.

She shoved the thought out of her mind. Ripped that small ache right out of her heart. The floor was nothing. She could build a new house, have a new floor, dream a new dream. What she couldn't replace, what she couldn't live without, ever?

Jax.

And he was in here, someplace, looking for her.

She pulled her head inside the huge jacket. It was somewhat cooler in there, though not much. She started crawling up the steps, dragging the heavy extinguisher up behind her. Because she knew her Jackson. Knew how he thought. And regardless of how ridiculously, dangerously thoughtless he'd been racing into a burning building without gear, she knew that orderly brain of his wouldn't desert him entirely. He'd think to himself, *now what was Addy after the last time she ran into a burning building? Maybe I'll save us all some time and trouble and start there.*

Which meant he'd be in her room, going after that stupid folio. Terror clutched in her chest.

"Jax!" she shouted but ended with a coughing spasm that would have done Nan proud. "Jackson!"

Then suddenly he was there, his boots anyway, right in front of her face. She shoved them aside before he could put one through her jaw and he exploded into a flurry of motion that ended with the folio bouncing off her back and him beside her on the steps, his hands latched onto her shoulders, his grimy face inches from hers.

"Addy, oh thank God!" He dragged her into his arms and Addy felt something click into place inside her. It was as if something afraid and needy cracked off and that soft, vulnerable bit of her heart she'd been saving, keeping for herself alone, just fell into him. He'd gone into a burning building after her, and when he'd failed to find her, he'd dragged out the one thing he thought she'd want to have: the folio where she kept all the damage his brother had done her.

The tangible proof of Diego's claim on her. The past she'd held onto even while refusing the future Jax offered her.

The one thing any other man would have cheerfully let burn.

She whipped off her jacket, spread it over them both. Jax snatched up the folio and Addy snatched it away from him. He didn't fight her for it, just grabbed the fire extinguisher — he was Jax, after all — and nearly carried her down the stairs.

When Jax would have hauled her straight to the front door, Addy veered away. She flung off the protection of the jacket and bolted for the swinging kitchen door and the flames licking all around it.

"Addison!" Jax shouted but Addy lifted her foot and booted open the door. It swung into the flames with a blast of heat that reached out and sucker punched her, stripping the air from her lungs. It was a hell-scape that met her eyes, her beautiful kitchen made over into a flaming tribute to eternal damnation.

With a broken cry, she heaved the folio into the gaping maw. Jax's arm came around her waist, dragged her back. She wrestled free and lunged toward the fire again.

"Addy, goddamn it, stop fighting!" He seized her arm. "We have to get out of here."

"No," she panted as she jerked away from his hold. She twisted frantically at her wedding ring. "Not yet. I need to—"

With a final, knuckle-peeling yank, Diego's ring popped off her finger. She held it up between them and Jax froze, wary, as the diamond glittered and danced like something possessed.

"Addy, what are you—"

She turned away and threw it into the hell beyond the door. Jax's jaw dropped.

"Holy shit, Addison, you just—"

She turned back and seized him by the shirt front, boosted herself up on her toes and fused her lips to his. She put it all into that kiss — the pain of her past, the promise of their future, the bloody necessity of letting go of one to reach for the other. It was hope and hurt, joy and loss, risk and reward. It was love.

"I choose you," she yelled over the roar of the flames. "*You.* You got that?"

"You—" He stopped. "You just threw, like, ten thousand dollars worth of diamonds into a burning kitchen."

"*You.*" She narrowed her eyes and gave him a little shake. "Do I need to repeat myself?"

He blinked. Focused. Then a smile dawned, slowly, transforming his dear, familiar face into something of breathtaking beauty. "Would you? Repeat yourself? I wouldn't mind hearing that again."

An answering smile started in her heart and moved toward the surface. "Maybe later. When we're not about to die."

"It's a date."

He opened the jacket again and she ducked under his arm. Then they ran.

Chapter 35

WILLA GRABBED PETER by the ankles and pulled. He was no light-weight but Willa had heaved around bigger sacks of shit. His head thudded down each of the three porch steps as she tugged, and the hollow-melon noise of it gave her a thrill of fierce satisfaction. Bastard. When she'd dragged him as far as the rock wall, she dropped his Italian loafer-ed feet and headed for the woods where she'd left Georgie guarding her zip-lipped little brother.

Whom she now, she had to admit, felt a little sorry for.

Okay, a *lot* sorry for. The Davises were one fucked up family, and between Bianca and — for reasons she couldn't begin to imagine — *Peter* ganging up on him, the kid didn't stand a chance.

She hadn't even cleared the side yard when she heard the shouting.

"God, Georgie, will you just admit it?"

"Admit what?" Georgie yelled back.

Willa stopped. Georgia Davis didn't yell. She didn't need to. Willa eased into the brambly forest, careful not to crack so much as a branch, her heart banging wildly inside her chest.

Matty was still tangled in the net, but curled on his side like he was nursing an appendix situation. Tears were thick in his voice, and still he shouted. It was a broken, hoarse sound, jagged with pain and resignation. "For God's sake, Georgie, I know she's not my mother!"

Willa's heart just went ahead and stopped. He knew. He knew Bianca wasn't his mother. He knew he wasn't Bianca's son. But he also looked in the mirror every day and saw Diego's face, which meant he wasn't entirely in the wrong nest. He'd followed that train of thought right to Georgie, the only other Davis in Italy at the time of his miraculous birth.

Georgie sighed. "I hate this goddamn town. I hate this town and every last idiot in it. Don't you believe a word those bastards say."

"I found my birth certificate, Georgie." His voice dropped to something so tired, so devoid of hope that Willa's heart came back to life just so it could bleed some more. "I was adopted. It's hard to tell but I knew what to look for. Thank you, Google." He laughed but Willa's heart only squeezed out a few more drops of blood. "It lists my real birthday but wasn't registered anywhere close to that date. I should have an Italian birth certificate, too, but I don't. Because they get rid of that and everything else when you're officially adopted and they issue an updated birth certificate to your new parents."

Georgie's silence was damning.

"You lied to me, Georgie. You, Mom, everybody. You lied to me my whole life, made me believe I was somebody I wasn't just on the off chance that I might grow up to be another Diego."

"Matty, don't—"

"Turns out, I can't paint for shit. And now I'm an arsonist." He let out a long, shuddering breath. "Think

Mom'll keep me now?"

"Oh, Matty," Georgie murmured, and her face was a perfect porcelain tribute to misery. "God, Matty."

"It doesn't matter. I've ruined everything anyway. I'm going to juvie for sure. Before I go, though, just tell me one thing, will you?"

"What?"

"The truth. It's the only thing I've ever wanted that Mom wouldn't give me." The bitter acknowledgement of his charmed life and Bianca's stubborn claim lodged in Willa's soul like a sharp-edged stone. "So, please, Georgie. The truth. Am I your son?"

"Oh, Matty," she whispered again, her eyes shining with tears. "Oh, Matty. No. You're not."

"Then whose am I?" Matty's anguished cry flayed Willa's heart. "Please, Georgie, I need to know."

The silence that followed hummed with raw pain and Willa stopped breathing.

Finally Georgie said, "Not mine. That's all I can tell you."

Willa crept back out to the yard, counted her heartbeats until they dropped out of panicked hummingbird territory, then headed back into the woods. This time she made sure they heard her coming.

"Okay," she said, and knelt to cut Matty free of her net. "Party's over. Time to face the music, kid." She kept a cautious hand on his shoulder as she marched him through the side yard to put him in the cab of her truck for safe keeping. Georgie fell in behind them, for once absolutely silent.

Fire, Addy knew, was a community event in a town as small as Devil's Kettle. If whatever was burning wasn't yours, it likely belonged to somebody you knew. It was only neighborly to come out to show your support.

So people came while Davis Place burned. Of course they did. But they didn't come to show support. They came to watch. To bear witness. To condemn.

But only one came to ask a question.

"I assume the paintings were in there," Julia Gates said. She'd appeared a few minutes ago, planted herself at the caution tape next to Addy's shoulder and watched the firefighters in grim silence. "Diego's post-*Angel* works?"

"Yeah," Addy said softly. It seemed like the least complicated answer. "They were."

"Quite a move. I'll admit, I didn't see it coming. I didn't think you had that kind of ruthlessness in you, frankly." She sent Addy an assessing sideways glance. "Well played, Addison."

Addy turned, met those shrewd blue eyes. "You think this is a game?"

"Of course it is." Julia's lips curled into a dangerous smile. "You probably think you won it, too, but you didn't." She gave Addy's shoulder a friendly pat that had cold dread balling in her stomach. "Well, I'm off," she said lightly. "I'm sure we'll be seeing each other again, though. Soon."

She turned and the crowd swallowed her up. Addy watched her disappear, too baffled and tired to even try to figure out what on earth had just happened. She turned back to the smoking bones of her dream. "Mercy." She linked her fingers on top of her head and blinked tears away from her gritty eyes. "Look at this."

"What did you expect, Addison?" Gerte broke from the crowd this time, put herself in the hostile vacuum Julia had left at Addy's side. "Devil Days is this town's bread and butter, and showing those dirty paintings of yours could bankrupt people. I gave you the chance to tell your side of the story and you refused." She nodded toward the smoking remains of Addy's dream. "Folks won't be disrespected that way."

Addy absorbed her implication with dull resignation. "Skipping a council meeting didn't used to be a torching offense," she pointed out.

"I'm not saying it is now," Gerte said, eyes wide and innocent. "Goodness, the idea. But to my way of thinking, you're either dealing with a vigilante or a —" She paused delicately and slid those eyes toward Matty in the cab of Willa's truck. "—a family situation. I'd prefer the vigilante, wouldn't you?"

Addy stared at her, disgusted by the vindictive glee hiding behind all that grave concern. Matty was in this up to his ears, of course, but he was a child. He was a confused, heart-broken, miserable child laboring under impossible expectations. And nobody was taking care of him. They were all using him — to ease their grief, to further their ambitions, to vent their fury.

"Since the minute I got here," Addy said to Gerte, "I've loved you." Her voice trembled and she paused to steady it. To lift it. "I've loved all of you. Loved this place. Loved my place in it. And I tried — lord, I tried so hard — to earn that place. To be a good friend and neighbor. To be one of you. I've volunteered for your committees, served on your boards and smiled for your tourists. I've sent business to each and every one of you—"

"And you think we owe you something for that," Gerte said calmly, coldly. "Well, we don't. We didn't ask for your favors and we don't want them. All we want is for you to keep your filth—" She shot a malevolent look at Matty. "—to yourself."

"Mom!" Lainey shot from the crowd and latched onto Gerte's elbow. "Mom, stop it!"

"No," Gerte snapped. "I've had enough of pretending the Davises are royalty. They behave like trash and I refuse to—"

"Matty didn't blow up our Dumpster, for heaven's sake!" Lainey's lips were white, tight. "That was my fault, so stop torturing the poor child."

"Your fault?" Gerte stared, her soft mouth dropping open in shock.

"Oh, don't look like that. I said it was my fault, not that I blew it up myself," Lainey said irritably. "But I think I know who did." She straightened her shoulders and lifted her chin. "I think it was Eli Walker."

"Eli?" Addy asked. "Your bus boy?"

"Yes." She sent a swift look Addy's way. "The night of the Dumpster fire, Eli and I had…words."

"You fought?" Gerte asked faintly. "But I never saw the two of you even speak much."

Lainey's mouth curved bitterly. "No, I know. I was lucky if I got three words out of him over the course of an entire shift. I wanted more, and I made it clear that night. Very, very clear."

Gerte stared. "You propositioned him?"

Lainey rolled her eyes. "He was the only man in town between eighteen and forty that I didn't go to kindergarten with, Mom. Of course I propositioned him."

Gerte's hand crept to her throat. "I see."

"He wasn't interested but I refused to take no for an answer and things got...ugly. *I* got ugly, shamefully so." She pressed her mouth flat and looked away. "He was gone by morning, and God help me, I was relieved." She shook her head with a jagged laugh. "I'd take the Dumpster fire over sexual harassment charges any day. As for Peter's old resort, well, Eli had been camping out there—"

"He had? How on earth do you know that?"

"Because I followed him all over town like the pathetic spinster stalker I am, that's how." Lainey brought her eyes back to her mother's. "As for why he burned the resort down, too, I'm just going to assume he decided to flip the whole town the bird and go out in a blaze of glory."

Gerte only stared wordlessly at her daughter.

"I'm not saying Matty's an angel but if Peter says he didn't do anything to us, then he didn't do anything to us." Lainey's chin came up, her mouth went firm. "So don't go connecting dots that don't exist. If you want to blame somebody for our fire, then blame Eli. Blame me for refusing to take no for an answer. Blame yourself for hiring a vagrant firebug. But quit torturing some poor kid because you're angry at his family. And stop pretending you know anything about what happened here, because you don't." She turned blazing eyes on the crowd. "None of you do."

An uncomfortable murmur rose from the crowd, like a collective shuffling of feet. Nobody, Addy noticed, could look at her. Gerte stared at her daughter, eyes round and hurt. Lainey turned away from her, faced Addy again.

"I'm sorry, Addison," Lainey said. "I'm sorry for my mom, for myself. For the way we've all treated you." Her voice broke but she shored it up. "I'm sorry for all of it. For everything. You've been nothing but good to us, and we've been horrible to you."

"It's okay, Lainey." Addy stepped forward and rubbed Lainey's tight shoulder. She smiled, took a breath and let it go. Let all of it go — the betrayal, the hurt, the disappointment and shock. "It's not your fault." She ran a weary eye over the townsfolk. "It's not anybody's fault."

"But the paintings?" Gerte had recovered herself somewhat, had drawn herself stiffly up. "Do you still plan to show them?"

Addy took a long look at the blackened house smoking on the cliff's edge. "They burned."

Gerte blinked, shocked, but Lainey touched Addy's arm. "I'm sorry for your loss," the younger woman said. "If it means anything."

Addy smiled. "Thanks."

Lainey slipped a hand through her mother's arm and drew her back into the crowd.

By the time dawn brightened the smoky sky, they'd all come. One by one, they'd all come to her. Soren and Graham, Mason and Frank. Shopkeepers, innkeepers, farmers and teachers. They all touched her arm, her shoulder, her cheek. Some spoke, some didn't, but they all came. And when they were done, that aching void inside her where her roots used to live was less empty. It wasn't repaired, not by any means, but it wasn't empty. And that was something.

Suddenly Willa was there beside her. "You okay?" she asked.

"Yep." And she thought she really was. Addy nodded toward the smoking house. "Place bones, doesn't it?"

"It does," Willa agreed. "You going to rebuild?"

"I don't know." Addy frowned. "Everything's so..." She

waved a hand to fill in the blank. "I don't know."

"Tell me about it." Willa tucked her fingers into her pockets, shook her head and turned to go.

"Willa, wait."

She stopped, cocked a brow.

"Would you really have worked the hot dish action?"

Willa sucked her teeth. "I don't actually cook." She pushed her hands deeper into her pockets and rocked back on the heels of her boots to consider it. "Might've brought him a pizza and a six pack, though."

A laugh burbled up out of Addy's chest, surprising them both. "I'd claw your eyes out."

"No doubt. That's why I'd have waited till after your fiery death." What might have been a smile flickered at the corner of her mouth, though with the brim of her cap pulled so low it was hard to tell. "See you around."

"See you," Addy said, unaccountably cheerful.

"Willa Zinc!"

Addy turned to find Bianca hustling toward them.

Willa stiffened at the imperious command in Bianca's tone.

Bianca stopped next to Addy. She folded her hands at her waist, as composed as if she were about to belt out an aria. "A moment, if you please."

Willa turned warily, an eyebrow lifted in question. "Can I help you, Ms. Davis?"

"You already have," Bianca said, and tipped her head delicately toward Matty. He'd been retrieved from Willa's truck and was now sitting on the ground in front of Georgie's bumper, his arms wrapped around his knees, his head bowed. "Thank you."

Addy expected to see her own open-mouthed stupor

reflected in Willa's face, but all she saw there was a flat, white calm. Willa shrugged. "Not my story to tell."

Bianca peered at her in the smoky dawn for a long, tense moment during which Addy had absolutely no idea what passed between them. But something evidently did because Bianca said, "Exactly so," in a satisfied tone. "People in this town talk too much."

"Amen." Willa touched the brim of her cap, then turned and headed for her truck. Addy watched her go.

"What was that about?" she asked. Bianca's eyes followed Willa's tail lights until they disappeared around the bend in the road.

"That's a story for another day." Bianca patted her shoulder. "Come now." She turned and headed back to their family standing in a tight cluster around Matty's bowed head. "We have our hands full with today."

Chapter 36

SEVERAL HOURS LATER, a freshly showered Jax sat on his mother's couch and listened to her spout some of the most ridiculous bullshit he'd ever heard.

"I'm not suggesting we pretend nothing's *happened*," Bianca said, holding out those long, elegant hands. "But let's be reasonable. There's a great deal at stake and we can't afford to be emotional."

"You're right." Jax nodded firmly. "This is a legal matter. We need to get the cops involved." He shifted, dug in his pocket for his phone. "Peter's got lawyers — damn good ones — but I have friends and they owe me favors. I can't guarantee justice, but I can make damn sure he spends a couple nights in jail while we figure out how to sue him into the next galaxy."

Beside him on the couch, Georgie made a noise — damp and vicious — that sent Jax's rage dancing even higher. He touched her knee, a comfort and a promise. Because blackmailing Matty into arson was Peter's biggest offense, but Jax wasn't about to overlook the way the bastard had disrespected his sister. He wouldn't call in any favors to deal with that, though. No, he'd take care of that one personally. And enjoy it.

Bianca said, "Put the phone away, Jackson."

Jax stared, shocked. "You're protecting him? After what he did to us — to Georgie, to Matty — you'd protect him?"

"I'm not protecting him." Bianca lifted her chin, cold anger spilling off her. "I'm protecting Matty."

"Bullshit," Jax snapped. "You're too focused on Diego to think about anybody else. But Matty's not him, Mom. He's a kid. He's *your* kid, just as much as Diego was, and he damn well deserves—"

"But I'm not, am I?" Matty asked dully. "I'm not her kid."

Jax froze, then turned slowly to Matty. The boy hadn't spoken a word since Willa had delivered him to Bianca outside a flaming Davis Place. Peter had done all the talking — concussions evidently made him chatty — but Matty had sat silently on the gravel, arms around his shins, forehead on his knees, while Peter had given them the whole ugly story.

"I don't know why you're all pissed at Peter." Matty gave a broken laugh. "He was the only one with the guts to tell me the truth. You're the ones who lied to me. All of you, but especially you." He turned flat eyes on Bianca. "You were never pregnant with me," he said, his voice achingly empty. "I didn't surprise you in Italy. You're not my mother."

Bianca came slowly to her feet. She crossed the room with deliberate grace, planted herself in front of Matty's knees and waited until he brought those fog-gray eyes to hers. The pain in them was like a punch to Jax's throat, and he leaned into the steady warmth of Addy beside him on the couch. Her hand crept up his back, spread strong and sure over his spine.

"Not in the way you mean, no," Bianca said softly. "I'm not."

The air left his lungs on a hiss of shock and Jax closed his eyes. He'd never believed the rumors. Heard them of course, but hadn't believed them. What was the point? Matty was his brother. He just was.

Bianca went on. "But you are mine nonetheless."

Matty let out a breath, half relief, half agony, and tried to turn away but Bianca caught his chin. She lifted it, tipped his face to the light. "You're so much like him in some ways."

"Diego," Matty whispered and closed his eyes. Jax didn't blame him. It was always Diego with their mom, wasn't it? "My...father?"

She only sighed. "All this anger and impulse. The need to put your emotions where nobody can ignore them. I can't say he ever burned down a house — not to mention an entire resort — but he certainly got into his share of trouble." She smiled, small and crooked. "And when he did, I protected him. Sheltered him. Not because he could paint, and not for the Davis name but because he was my blood. *Our* blood. I may not have given birth to you, Matisse, but that's our blood in your veins. Look there." She caught up his hands, lifted them. "These are Joe's hands, and you use them with Georgie's grace. You have Jax's stubborn spirit, Diego's shocking beauty. And you have my heart." She folded her hands around his and bent to stare hard into his face. "You are my child. Mine. And nothing you do, say, burn, paint — or don't paint — will ever change that. I will never let you go; I will never let you down. And whatever I did to bring you here, to make you ours? It was absolutely necessary. And that is all I'm ever going to say on this matter. Are we clear here?"

Matty returned her gaze for an endless heartbeat. Then tears flooded into his silvery eyes and he dropped his head. Nodded as his shoulders shuddered under the weight of emotion. Bianca slid to her knees and threw her arms around her boy, rocked him like the baby he'd once been. Addy wiped her eyes on Jax's t-shirt sleeve and Jax found his own throat slightly tighter than was comfortable.

"Excellent." Bianca seated herself on the couch beside Matty, threaded her fingers through his and turned to Addy and Jax with a serene purpose that had the hair standing up on the back of Jax's neck. "Addison," she said. "Darling. You have the power to fix this whole thing."

Beside him, Addy blinked cautiously. "I do?"

"Of course. We're all victims here but going public with the truth of that will only inflict further punishment on people this night has already damaged. I see no need to follow the letter of the law."

Jax tensed. He didn't like the sound of this. "What does that mean?"

Bianca kept her eyes on Addy as she continued. "Our insurance policy certainly won't honor a claim on Davis Place, not once Peter's and Matty's involvement comes out, as I assume it eventually will."

"Oh, it will," Jax assured her. "It definitely will. I won't lie about something like this. Peter and Matty both need to face the consequences of what they've done and—"

"Agreed. But there needn't be any *legal* consequences," Bianca said. "That's all I'm trying to say. The only people affected by these fires are Peter, Georgie, Addy and me. And if we don't press charges or file an insurance claim, there are no legal ramifications of this whole ugly episode."

"That's true." Addy leaned forward, her face intent.

"If Addy's willing to simply write off whatever personal monies she had invested in Davis Place," Bianca said with a small smile, "we can proceed as if nothing ever happened.

One big family, building on and loving this land where our roots have been sunk so deep." She leaned in urgently, her face glowing with fervor. "Diego may not have been a perfect husband, or even a good one, Addy, but he left you with the resources to protect the family you love from harm. Will you do it? Will you show those paintings?"

He shot Addy a sideways glance — *how the hell do we play this one?* — then froze, startled. Because he knew that look. Addy was running numbers in that tidy brain of hers. His family needed money and she was thinking up some way to give it to them.

What the hell? He'd *seen* those paintings burn. Hadn't he?

Addison leaned in and kissed the sudden doubt right off Jax's face. Then she turned to his mother.

"I have an alternative proposal."

Bianca lifted her brows. "I'm all ears, Addison."

"I want the house."

"What house?"

"Davis Place. I want it."

"But it's already ours."

"No, I want to buy it," Addy clarified. "I want to buy it from you."

"There's no need, Addison. We *own* it already."

"You don't understand." Addy leaned forward. "I want the house deeded to me alone, free and clear. No partners, not even you. And in exchange I'll deed over to you all of Diego's remaining works."

Bianca narrowed her eyes. "Remaining works?"

Addy smiled. "I burned a few tonight."

Bianca closed her eyes, pained. "The new canvases?"

"Most of them."

"Most?" Jax asked warily.

"*Broken* is in my car." She took his hand. "I wanted to see how it looked, framed up and side by side with the *Angel*. I wondered if it could be the end to Diego's story all by itself."

"And Julia Gates can just go without her fame fix?"

"That was going to be a bonus." She grinned sheepishly. "But if we look at it, and it makes you unhappy, we can negotiate."

His hand was warm and strong on hers. "Deal."

Bianca simply put a hand to her chest, evidently beyond words.

"I'm also planning to sell some of the smaller oils," Addy went on.

Bianca's eyes flicked open. "How many?"

"Enough to fund a complete rehab on Davis Place as it currently stands plus a full year of operations once we open for business."

Bianca winced but didn't argue. "Fine," she said. "I didn't relish the idea of going into the hospitality business anyway."

"Oh, no. I want you, too." Addy smiled. "Twenty hours a week."

"What?"

"Somebody's got to teach the art classes, and lord knows it can't be me. You'll be paid on a profit-sharing basis. Davis Place makes money, so do you. You slack off? Well, there's always that teaching position at UMD."

Bianca stared at her in silence and Addy lifted her

shoulders. "Hey, you wanted to live on the Davis family name, here's your chance. It's a fair deal. And—" She squeezed Jax's hand. "—it's all I have to offer."

"What about you, dear?" Bianca asked Addy, her eyes dark and shrewd. "What do you get out of this deal beside dish-pan hands and continuous overnight guests?"

She sank into Jax's side and grinned up at him. "I get the house, the family and True Love." She tipped her head onto his shoulder, breathed in the soap-and-smoke and everything inside her slid into place.

Home.

"I get everything I ever wanted."

Epilogue

TWO WEEKS LATER, even the locals were willing to admit that maybe summer really had come to the North Shore to stay. Addy curled her legs onto the porch swing underneath her and leaned into Jax, utterly and completely content. He kept them at a lazy tick-tock with one boot, his arm around her shoulders while the moon painted silvery light all over the floor. She closed her eyes, breathed in the warm night air and listened to the lake swirl in the distance. The smoke-and-soap scent of him wrapped itself around her heart and she closed her eyes.

"I think we should get married," he said, his lips in her hair.

She sat up, startled. "We should?"

He smiled easily. "I think so, yeah. Don't you?"

"Well, of course. Eventually." She touched her naked ring finger. "I just finally took Diego's ring off, though."

"I know." He scowled at her hand. "Which is exactly why you should put mine on. Men are bastards. I don't want anybody getting ideas."

She rolled her eyes and settled back into his side. "They won't."

"Yeah? Why not?"

"Because I love you."

She felt his chest rise and fall under her cheek as he let out a long slow breath. "I never get tired of hearing that. You should say it again."

She smiled and took his wide warm hand between both of hers. "I love you, Jackson," she said solemnly. "I love you like kids love puppies. Like flowers love sunshine."

"Yeah?" He lifted his free hand to her cheek, traced the curve of her jaw to her throat. Hit the neckline of her tank top and slid lower. Dangerously lower. Interestingly lower. Her belly quivered with anticipation "That much?"

She leaned helpfully into his touch. "Like Matty loves comic books," she managed. She only sounded a little desperate, too. Good for her.

"Graphic novels," he corrected easily. She hardly heard him, not with that finger of his dipping inside her scoop neck to toy with the lacy edge of her bra.

"You get my point."

He shrugged. "You could be more convincing."

"I could?" He abandoned her neckline, traced the side seam of her tank down to the bottom hem. His hand slid warm and sneaky up the ladder of her ribs to the swell of her breast.

"Tell me again," he suggested and tugged delicately at the sensitive bud of her nipple. A minor light show went off in her head and she gasped.

"Tell you what again?"

"How much you love me, then why you don't want to get married."

She could hardly think let alone speak, not when those wicked fingers were tracing and flicking and generally laying waste to her higher order thinking. "You don't play fair, do you?"

"Hell, no. I don't plan to, either. I'm offering you a once-in-a-lifetime, eternal-love, soul-mate kind of thing here, Addison. Messy-headed, dimply babies who can't draw and won't, by God, be bastards. You think I'm going to be satisfied with puppies, sunshine and comic books?"

"Graphic novels," she breathed while visions of talent-free babies with Jax's hair and her dimples competed with his devastating fingers and the mad thudding of her heart.

"I'm waiting," he said.

Laughter threatened even as need clawed and howled. She set her lips to the hollow of his throat, and he sucked in a rewarding breath. "I love you," she said solemnly, "like I love pie."

"You'd marry pie in a heartbeat," he pointed out.

She thought about it. "That's true, actually."

His grin was a flash of lightning. "There's the answer I was looking for."

He scooped her into his arms and came to his feet.

"Jax!" The laugh burbled up out of her. "What are you doing?"

"Taking my fiancée to bed, that's what." He booted open the front door and hit the stairs. He paused just outside the bedroom, though, gazed down at her with an aching vulnerability that squeezed her heart and filled her soul. "You will, won't you?" He searched her eyes. "You'll wear my ring, have my kids, be my wife?"

She hesitated. "Your mom will kill me."

He made a dismissive noise. "You're not afraid of Bianca. Not anymore."

Addy blinked. He was right. She wasn't. She wasn't afraid of anybody anymore. All the fear she'd lived with all those years? It had vacated the building. Maybe that was what had shifted aside to make room for love. For Jax. "You know what?" She felt the smile start deep inside her, and bloom until it took over her heart, her soul, her face. "You're absolutely right."

"Sweet," he said, and took her to their bed. Forever.

ABOUT THE AUTHOR

Once upon a time Susan Sey was a software trainer with nice clothes and free time, but now she has kids. She lives with them and her incredibly patient husband in St. Paul, MN, where she produces smart, sexy contemporary romances on an annual basis. She loves ice cream, her family and happy endings, though not necessarily in that order. She does not enjoy laundry, failure or mowing the lawn, but rises to the occasion as necessary.

You can find her on the web at www.susansey.com, on Facebook or Twitter. Or drop her a line at susan@susansey.com. She dearly loves a good letter.